The Little House Omnibus

LAURA INGALLS WILDER

THE
LITTLE HOUSE
OMNIBUS

Little House in the Big Woods
Little House on the Prairie
On the Banks of Plum Creek

Illustrated by Garth Williams

METHUEN CHILDREN'S BOOKS
LONDON

This edition first published in Great Britain 1978
by Methuen Children's Books Ltd
11 New Fetter Lane, London EC4P 4EE
Reprinted 1981
Little House in the Big Woods first published in April 5, 1956
by Methuen & Co Ltd
Little House on the Prairie first published October 3, 1957
by Methuen & Co Ltd
On the Banks of Plum Creek first published October 30, 1958
by Methuen & Co Ltd

Printed and bound in Great Britain by
Lowe & Brydone Printers Limited, Leeds, Yorkshire

ISBN 0 416 86800 2

Little House in the Big Woods

Contents

Little House in the Big Woods

ONCE upon a time, sixty years ago, a little girl lived in the Big Woods of Wisconsin, in a little grey house made of logs.

The great, dark trees of the Big Woods stood all around the house, and beyond them were other trees and beyond them were more trees. As far as a man could go to the north in a day, or a week, or a whole month, there was nothing but woods. There were no houses. There were no roads. There were no people. There were only trees and the wild animals who had their homes among them.

Wolves lived in the Big Woods, and bears, and huge wild cats. Muskrats and mink and otter lived by the streams. Foxes had dens in the hills and deer roamed everywhere.

To the east of the little log house, and to the west,

there were miles upon miles of trees, and only a few little log houses scattered far apart in the edge of the Big Woods.

So far as the little girl could see, there was only the one little house where she lived with her Father and Mother, her sister Mary and baby sister Carrie. A wagon track ran before the house, turning and twisting out of sight in the woods where the animals lived, but the little girl did not know where it went, nor what might be at the end of it.

The little girl was named Laura and she called her father, Pa, and her mother, Ma. In those days and in that place, children did not say Father and Mother, nor Mamma and Papa, as they do now.

At night, when Laura lay awake in the trundle bed, she listened and could not hear anything at all but the sound of the trees whispering together. Sometimes, far away in the night, a wolf howled. Then he came nearer, and howled again.

It was a scary sound. Laura knew that wolves would eat little girls. But she was safe inside the solid log walls. Her father's gun hung over the door and good old Jack, the brindle bulldog, lay on guard before it. Her father would say,

'Go to sleep, Laura. Jack won't let the wolves in.' So Laura snuggled under the covers of the trundle bed, close beside Mary, and went to sleep.

One night her father picked her up out of bed and carried her to the window so that she might see the wolves. There were two of them sitting in front of the house. They looked like shaggy dogs. They pointed their noses at the big, bright moon, and howled.

Jack paced up and down before the door, growling. The hair stood up along his back and he showed his sharp, fierce teeth to the wolves. They howled, but they could not get in.

The house was a comfortable house. Upstairs there was a large attic, pleasant to play in when the rain drummed on the roof. Downstairs was the small bedroom, and the big room. The bedroom had a window that closed with a wooden shutter. The big room had two windows with glass in the panes, and it had two doors, a front door and a back door.

All around the house was a crooked rail fence, to keep the bears and the deer away.

In the yard in front of the house were two beautiful big oak trees. Every morning as soon as she was awake Laura ran to look out of the window, and one morning she saw in each of the big trees a dead deer hanging from a branch.

Pa had shot the deer the day before and Laura had been asleep when he brought them home at night and hung them high in the trees so the wolves could not get the meat.

That day Pa and Ma and Laura and Mary had fresh venison for dinner. It was so good that Laura wished they could eat it all. But most of the meat must be salted and smoked and packed away to be eaten in the winter.

For winter was coming. The days were shorter, and frost crawled up the window panes at night. Soon the snow would come. Then the log house would be almost buried in snowdrifts, and the lake and the streams would freeze. In the bitter cold weather Pa could not be sure of finding any wild game to shoot for meat.

The bears would be hidden away in their dens where they slept soundly all winter long. The squirrels would be curled in their nests in hollow trees, with their furry

tails wrapped snugly around their noses. The deer and
the rabbits would be shy and swift. Even if Pa could get
a deer, it would be poor and thin, not fat and plump as
deer are in the fall.

Pa might hunt alone all day in the bitter cold, in the
Big Woods covered with snow, and come home at night
with nothing for Ma and Mary and Laura to eat.

So as much food as possible must be stored away in the
little house before winter came.

Pa skinned the deer carefully and salted and stretched
the hides, for he would make soft leather of them. Then
he cut up the meat, and sprinkled salt over the pieces as
he laid them on a board.

Standing on end in the yard was a tall length cut from
the trunk of a big hollow tree. Pa had driven nails inside
as far as he could reach from each end. Then he stood it
up, put a little roof over the top, and cut a little door on
one side near the bottom. On the piece that he cut out
he fastened leather hinges; then he fitted it into place,
and that was the little door, with the bark still on it.

After the deer meat had been salted several days, Pa
cut a hole near the end of each piece and put a string
through it. Laura watched him do this, and then she
watched him hang the meat on the nails in the hollow
log.

He reached up through the little door and hung meat
on the nails, as far up as he could reach. Then he put a
ladder against the log, climbed up to the top, moved the
roof to one side, and reached down inside to hang meat
on those nails.

Then Pa put the roof back again, climbed down the
ladder, and said to Laura:

'Run over to the chopping block and fetch me some of
those green hickory chips—new, clean, white ones.'

So Laura ran to the block where Pa chopped wood, and filled her apron with the fresh, sweet-smelling chips.

Just inside the little door in the hollow log Pa built a

fire of tiny bits of bark and moss, and he laid some of the chips on it very carefully.

Instead of burning quickly, the green chips smouldered and filled the hollow log with thick, choking smoke. Pa shut the door, and a little smoke squeezed through the crack around it, and a little smoke came out through the roof, but most of it was shut in with the meat.

'There's nothing better than good hickory smoke,' Pa said. 'That will make good venison that will keep anywhere, in any weather.'

Then he took his gun, and slinging his axe on his shoulder he went away to the clearing to cut down some more trees.

Laura and Ma watched the fire for several days. When smoke stopped coming through the cracks, Laura would bring more hickory chips and Ma would put them on the fire under the meat. All the time there was a little smell of smoke in the yard, and when the door was opened a thick, smoky, meaty smell came out.

At last Pa said the venison had smoked long enough. Then they let the fire go out, and Pa took all the strips and pieces of meat out of the hollow tree. Ma wrapped each piece neatly in paper and hung them in the attic where they would keep safe and dry.

One morning Pa went away before daylight with the horses and wagon, and that night he came home with a wagonload of fish. The big wagon box was piled full, and some of the fish were as big as Laura. Pa had gone to Lake Pepin and caught them all with a net.

Ma cut large slices of flaky white fish, without one bone, for Laura and Mary. They all feasted on the good, fresh fish. All they did not eat fresh was salted down in barrels for the winter.

Pa owned a pig. It ran wild in the Big Woods, living on acorns and nuts and roots. Now he caught it and put it in a pen made of logs, to fatten. He would butcher it as soon as the weather was cold enough to keep the pork frozen.

Once in the middle of the night Laura woke up and

heard the pig squealing. Pa jumped out of bed, snatched his gun from the wall, and ran outdoors. Then Laura heard the gun go off, once, twice.

When Pa came back, he told what had happened. He had seen a big black bear standing beside the pigpen. The bear was reaching into the pen to grab the pig, and the pig was running and squealing. Pa saw this in the starlight and he fired quickly. But the light was dim and in his haste he missed the bear. The bear ran away into the woods, not hurt at all.

Laura was sorry Pa did not get the bear. She liked bear meat so much. Pa was sorry, too, but he said:

'Anyway, I saved the bacon.'

The garden behind the little house had been growing all summer. It was so near the house that the deer did not jump the fence and eat the vegetables in the daytime, and at night Jack kept them away. Sometimes in the morning there were little hoof-prints among the carrots and the cabbages. But Jack's tracks were there, too, and the deer had jumped right out again.

Now the potatoes and carrots, the beets and turnips and cabbages were gathered and stored in the cellar, for freezing nights had come.

Onions were made into long ropes, braided together by their tops, and then were hung in the attic beside wreaths of red peppers strung on threads. The pumpkins and the squashes were piled in orange and yellow and green heaps in the attic's corners.

The barrels of salted fish were in the pantry, and yellow cheeses were stacked on the pantry shelves.

Then one day Uncle Henry came riding out of the Big Woods. He had come to help Pa butcher. Ma's big butcher knife was already sharpened, and Uncle Henry had brought Aunt Polly's butcher knife.

Near the pigpen Pa and Uncle Henry built a bonfire, and heated a great kettle of water over it. When the water was boiling they went to kill the hog. Then Laura ran and hid her head on the bed and stopped her ears with her fingers so she could not hear the hog squeal.

'It doesn't hurt him, Laura,' Pa said. 'We do it so quickly.' But she did not want to hear him squeal.

In a minute she took one finger cautiously out of an ear, and listened. The hog had stopped squealing. After that, Butchering Time was great fun.

It was such a busy day, with so much to see and do. Uncle Henry and Pa were jolly, and there would be spare-ribs for dinner, and Pa had promised Laura and Mary the bladder and the pig's tail.

As soon as the hog was dead Pa and Uncle Henry lifted it up and down in the boiling water till it was well scalded. Then they laid it on a board and scraped it with their knives, and all the bristles came off. After that they hung the hog in a tree, took out the insides, and left it hanging to cool.

When it was cool they took it down and cut it up. There were hams and shoulders, side meat and spare-ribs and belly. There was the heart and the liver and the tongue, and the head to be made into headcheese, and the dish-pan full of bits to be made into sausage.

The meat was laid on a board in the back-door shed, and every piece was sprinkled with salt. The hams and the shoulders were put to pickle in brine, for they would be smoked, like the venison, in the hollow log.

'You can't beat hickory-cured ham,' Pa said.

He was blowing up the bladder. It made a little white balloon, and he tied the end tight with a string and gave it to Mary and Laura to play with. They could throw it into the air and pat it back and forth with their hands.

Or it would bounce along the ground and they could kick it. But even better fun than a balloon was the pig's tail.

Pa skinned it for them carefully, and into the large end he thrust a sharpened stick. Ma opened the front of the cookstove and raked hot coals out into the iron hearth. Then Laura and Mary took turns holding the pig's tail over the coals.

It sizzled and fried, and drops of fat dripped off it and blazed on the coals. Ma sprinkled it with salt. Their hands and their faces got very hot, and Laura burned her finger, but she was so excited she did not care. Roasting the pig's tail was such fun that it was hard to play fair, taking turns.

At last it was done. It was nicely browned all over, and how good it smelled! They carried it into the yard to cool it, and even before it was cool enough they began tasting it and burned their tongues.

They ate every little bit of meat off the bones, and then they gave the bones to Jack. And that was the end of the pig's tail. There would not be another one till next year.

Uncle Henry went home after dinner, and Pa went away to his work in the Big Woods. But for Laura and Mary and Ma, Butchering Time had only begun. There was a great deal for Ma to do, and Laura and Mary helped her.

All that day and the next, Ma was trying out the lard in big iron pots on the cookstove. Laura and Mary carried wood and watched the fire. It must be hot, but not too hot, or the lard would burn. The big pots simmered and boiled, but they must not smoke. From time to time Ma skimmed out the brown cracklings. She put them in a cloth and squeezed out every bit of the lard, and then she put the cracklings away. She would use them to flavour johnny-cake later.

Cracklings were very good to eat, but Laura and Mary could only have a taste. They were too rich for little girls, Ma said.

Ma scraped and cleaned the head carefully, and then she boiled it till all the meat fell off the bones. She chopped the meat fine with her chopping knife in the wooden bowl, she seasoned it with pepper and salt and spices. Then she mixed the pot-liquor with it, and set it away in a pan to cool. When it was cool it would cut in slices, and that was headcheese.

The little pieces of meat, lean and fat, that had been cut off the large pieces, Ma chopped and chopped until it was all chopped fine. She seasoned it with salt and pepper and with dried sage leaves from the garden. Then with her hands she tossed and turned it until it was well mixed, and she moulded it into balls. She put the balls in a pan out in the shed, where they would freeze and be good to eat all winter. That was the sausage.

When Butchering Time was over, there were the sausages and the headcheese, the big jars of lard and the keg of white salt-pork out in the shed, and in the attic hung the smoked hams and shoulders.

The little house was fairly bursting with good food stored away for the long winter. The pantry and the shed and the cellar were full, and so was the attic.

Laura and Mary must play in the house now, for it was cold outdoors and the brown leaves were all falling from the trees. The fire in the cookstove never went out. At night Pa banked it with ashes to keep the coals alive till morning.

The attic was a lovely place to play. The large, round, coloured pumpkins made beautiful chairs and tables. The red peppers and the onions dangled overhead. The hams and the venison hung in their paper wrappings, and all the bunches of dried herbs, the spicy herbs for cooking and the bitter herbs for medicine, gave the place a dusty-spicy smell.

Often the wind howled outside with a cold and lonesome sound. But in the attic Laura and Mary played house with the squashes and the pumpkins, and everything was snug and cosy.

Mary was bigger than Laura, and she had a rag doll named Nettie. Laura had only a corncob wrapped in a handkerchief, but it was a good doll. It was named Susan. It wasn't Susan's fault that she was only a corncob. Sometimes Mary let Laura hold Nettie, but she did it only when Susan couldn't see.

The best times of all were at night. After supper Pa brought his traps in from the shed to grease them by the fire. He rubbed them bright and greased the hinges of the jaws and the springs of the pans with a feather dipped in bear's grease.

There were small traps and middle-sized traps and great bear traps with teeth in their jaws that Pa said would break a man's leg if they shut on to it.

While he greased the traps, Pa told Laura and Mary little jokes and stories, and afterward he would play his fiddle.

The doors and windows were tightly shut, and the cracks of the window frames stuffed with cloth, to keep out the cold. But Black Susan, the cat, came and went as she pleased, day and night, through the swinging door of the cat-hole in the bottom of the front door. She always went very quickly, so the door would not catch her tail when it fell shut behind her.

One night when Pa was greasing the traps he watched Black Susan come in, and he said:

'There was once a man who had two cats, a big cat and a little cat.'

Laura and Mary ran to lean on his knees and hear the rest.

'He had two cats,' Pa repeated, 'a big cat and a little cat. So he made a big cat-hole in his door for the big cat. And then he made a little cat-hole for the little cat.'

There Pa stopped.

'But why couldn't the little cat——' Mary began.

'Because the big cat wouldn't let it,' Laura interrupted.

'Laura, that is very rude. You must never interrupt,' said Pa.

'But I see,' he said, 'that either one of you has more sense than the man who cut the two cat-holes in his door.'

Then he laid away the traps, and he took his fiddle out of its box and began to play. That was the best time of all.

2

Winter Days and Winter Nights

THE first snow came, and the bitter cold. Every morning Pa took his gun and his traps and was gone all day in the Big Woods, setting the small traps for muskrats and mink along the creeks, the middle-sized traps for foxes and wolves in the woods. He set out the big bear traps hoping to get a fat bear before they all went into their dens for the winter.

One morning he came back, took the horses and sled, and hurried away again. He had shot a bear. Laura and Mary jumped up and down and clapped their hands, they were so glad. Mary shouted:

'I want the drumstick! I want the drumstick!'

Mary did not know how big a bear's drumstick is.

When Pa came back he had both a bear and a pig in the wagon. He had been going through the woods, with a big bear trap in his hands and the gun on his shoulder, when he walked around a big pine tree covered with snow, and the bear was behind the tree.

The bear had just killed the pig and was picking it up to eat it. Pa said the bear was standing up on its hind legs, holding the pig in its paws just as though they were hands.

Pa shot the bear, and there was no way of knowing where the pig came from nor whose pig it was.

'So I just brought home the bacon,' Pa said.

There was plenty of fresh meat to last for a long time.

The days and the nights were so cold that the pork in a box and the bear meat hanging in the little shed outside the back door were solidly frozen and did not thaw.

When Ma wanted fresh meat for dinner Pa took the axe and cut off a chunk of frozen bear meat or pork. But the sausage balls, or the salt pork, or the smoked hams and the venison, Ma could get for herself from the shed or the attic.

The snow kept coming till it was drifted and banked against the house. In the mornings the window panes were covered with frost in beautiful pictures of trees and flowers and fairies.

Ma said that Jack Frost came in the night and made the pictures, while everyone was asleep. Laura thought that Jack Frost was a little man all in snowy white, wearing a glittering white pointed cap and soft white knee-boots made of deer-skin. His coat was white and his mittens were white, and he did not carry a gun on his back, but in his hands he had shining sharp tools with which he carved the pictures.

Laura and Mary were allowed to take Ma's thimble and made pretty patterns of circles in the frost on the

glass. But they never spoiled the pictures that Jack Frost had made in the night.

When they put their mouths close to the pane and blew their breath on it, the white frost melted and ran in drops down the glass. Then they could see the drifts of snow outdoors and the great trees standing bare and black, making thin blue shadows on the white snow.

Laura and Mary helped Ma with the work. Every morning there were the dishes to wipe. Mary wiped more of them than Laura because she was bigger, but Laura always wiped carefully her own little cup and plate.

By the time the dishes were all wiped and set away, the trundle bed was aired. Then, standing one on each side, Laura and Mary straightened the covers, tucked them in well at the foot and the sides, plumped up the pillows and put them in place. Then Ma pushed the trundle bed into its place under the big bed.

After this was done, Ma began the work that belonged to that day. Each day had its own proper work. Ma used to say:

> "Wash on Monday,
> Iron on Tuesday,
> Mend on Wednesday,
> Churn on Thursday,
> Clean on Friday,
> Bake on Saturday,
> Rest on Sunday."

Laura liked the churning and the baking days best of all the week.

In winter the cream was not yellow as it was in summer, and butter churned from it was white and not so pretty. Ma liked everything on her table to be pretty, so in the wintertime she coloured the butter.

After she had put the cream in the tall crockery churn and set it near the stove to warm, she washed and scraped a long orange-coloured carrot. Then she grated it on the bottom of the old, leaky tin pan that Pa had punched full of nail-holes for her. Ma rubbed the carrot across the roughness until she had rubbed it all through the holes, and when she lifted up the pan, there was a soft, juicy mound of grated carrot.

She put this in a little pan of milk on the stove and when the milk was hot she poured milk and carrot into a cloth bag. Then she squeezed the bright yellow milk into the churn, where it coloured all the cream. Now the butter would be yellow.

Laura and Mary were allowed to eat the carrot after the milk had been squeezed out. Mary thought she ought to have the larger share because she was older, and Laura said she should have it because she was littler. But Ma said they must divide it evenly. It was very good.

When the cream was ready, Ma scalded the long wooden churn-dash, put it in the churn, and dropped the wooden churn-cover over it. The churn-cover had a little round hole in the middle, and Ma moved the dash up and down, up and down, through the hole.

She churned for a long time. Mary could sometimes churn while Ma rested, but the dash was too heavy for Laura.

At first the splashes of cream showed thick and smooth around the little hole. After a long time, they began to look grainy. Then Ma churned more slowly, and on the dash there began to appear tiny grains of yellow butter.

When Ma took off the churn-cover, there was the butter in a golden lump, drowning in the buttermilk. Then Ma took out the lump with a wooden paddle, into a wooden bowl, and she washed it many times in cold water, turning it over and over and working it with the paddle until the water ran clear. After that she salted it.

Now came the best part of the churning. Ma moulded the butter. On the loose bottom of the wooden butter-mould was the carved picture of a strawberry with two strawberry leaves.

With the paddle Ma packed butter tightly into the mould until it was full. Then she turned it upside-down over a plate, and pushed on the handle of the loose bottom. The little, firm pat of golden butter came out, with the strawberry and its leaves moulded on the top.

Laura and Mary watched, breathless, one on each side of Ma, while the golden little butter-pats, each with its strawberry on the top, dropped on to the plate as Ma put all the butter through the mould. Then Ma gave them each a drink of good, fresh buttermilk.

On Saturdays, when Ma made the bread, they each had a little piece of dough to make into a little loaf. They might have a bit of cookie dough, too, to make little cookies, and once Laura even made a pie in her patty-pan.

After the day's work was done, Ma sometimes cut paper dolls for them. She cut the dolls out of stiff white paper, and drew the faces with a pencil. Then from bits of coloured paper she cut dresses and hats, ribbons and laces, so that Laura and Mary could dress their dolls beautifully.

But the best time of all was at night, when Pa came home.

He would come in from his tramping through the snowy woods with tiny icicles hanging on the end of his moustaches. He would hang his gun on the wall over the

door, throw off his fur cap and coat and mittens, and call:
'Where's my little half-pint of sweet cider half drunk up?'

That was Laura, because she was so small.

Laura and Mary would run to climb on his knees and

sit there while he warmed himself by the fire. Then he
would put on his coat and cap and mittens again and go
out to do the chores and bring in plenty of wood for the fire

Sometimes, when Pa had walked his trap-lines quickly
because the traps were empty, or when he had got some
game sooner than usual, he would come home early. Then
he would have time to play with Laura and Mary.

One game they loved was called mad dog. Pa would run his fingers through his thick, brown hair, standing it all up on end. Then he dropped on all fours and, growling, he chased Laura and Mary all around the room, trying to get them cornered where they couldn't get away.

They were quick at dodging and running, but once he caught them against the woodbox, behind the stove. They couldn't get past Pa, and there was no other way out.

Then Pa growled so terribly, his hair was so wild and his eyes so fierce that it all seemed real. Mary was so frightened that she could not move. But as Pa came nearer Laura screamed, and with a wild leap and a scramble she went over the wood-box, dragging Mary with her.

And at once there was no mad dog at all. There was only Pa standing there with his blue eyes shining, looking at Laura.

'Well!' he said to her. 'You're only a little half-pint of cider half drunk up, but by Jinks! you're as strong as a little French horse!'

'You shouldn't frighten the children so, Charles,' Ma said. 'Look how big their eyes are.'

Pa looked, and then he took down his fiddle. He began to play and sing.

> "Yankee Doodle went to town,
>   He wore his striped trousies,
>   He swore he couldn't see the town,
>   There was so many houses."

Laura and Mary forgot all about the mad dog.

> "And there he saw some great big guns,
>   Big as a log of maple,
>   And every time they turned 'em round,
>   It took two yoke of cattle.

"And every time they fired 'em off,
  It took a horn of powder,
  It made a noise like father's gun,
  Only a nation louder."

Pa was keeping time with his foot, and Laura clapped
her hands to the music when he sang,

"And I'll sing Yankee Doodle-de-do,
  And I'll sing Yankee Doodle,
  And I'll sing Yankee-Doodle-de-do,
  And I'll sing Yankee Doodle!"

All alone in the wild Big Woods, and the snow, and
the cold, the little log house was warm and snug and cosy.
Pa and Ma and Mary and Laura and Baby Carrie were
comfortable and happy there, especially at night.

Then the fire was shining on the hearth, the cold and
the dark and the wild beasts were all shut out, and Jack
the brindle bulldog and Black Susan the cat lay blinking
at the flames in the fireplace.

Ma sat in her rocking chair, sewing by the light of the
lamp on the table. The lamp was bright and shiny. There
was salt in the bottom of its glass bowl with the kerosene,
to keep the kerosene from exploding, and there were bits of
red flannel among the salt to make it pretty. It was pretty.

Laura loved to look at the lamp, with its glass chimney
so clean and sparkling, its yellow flame burning so steadily,
and its bowl of clear kerosene coloured red by the bits of
flannel.   She loved to look at the fire in the fireplace,
flickering and changing all the time, burning yellow and
red and sometimes green above the logs, and hovering
blue over the golden and ruby coals.

And then, Pa told stories.

When Laura and Mary begged him for a story, he
would take them on his knees and tickle their faces with

his long whiskers until they laughed aloud. His eyes were blue and merry.

One night Pa looked at Black Susan, stretching herself before the fire and running her claws out and in, and he said:

'Do you know that a panther is a cat? a great, big, wild cat?'

'No,' said Laura.

'Well, it is,' said Pa. 'Just imagine Black Susan bigger than Jack, and fiercer than Jack when he growls. Then she would be just like a panther.'

He settled Laura and Mary more comfortably on his knees and he said, 'I'll tell you about Grandpa and the panther.'

'Your Grandpa?' Laura asked.

'No, Laura, your Grandpa. My father.'

'Oh,' Laura said, and she wriggled closer against Pa's arm. She knew her Grandpa. He lived far away in the Big Woods, in a big log house. Pa began:

The Story of Grandpa and the Panther

'Your Grandpa went to town one day and was late starting home. It was dark when he came riding his horse through the Big Woods, so dark that he could hardly see the road, and when he heard a panther scream he was frightened, for he had no gun.'

'How does a panther scream?' Laura asked.

'Like a woman,' said Pa. 'Like this.' Then he screamed so that Laura and Mary shivered with terror.

Ma jumped in her chair, and said, 'Mercy, Charles!'

But Laura and Mary loved to be scared like that.

'The horse, with Grandpa on him, ran fast, for it was frightened, too. But it could not get away from the panther. The panther followed through the dark woods. It was a hungry panther, and it came as fast as the horse could run. It screamed now on this side of the road, now on the other side, and it was always close behind.

'Grandpa leaned forward in the saddle and urged the horse to run faster. The horse was running as fast as it could possibly run, and still the panther screamed close behind.

'Then Grandpa caught a glimpse of it, as it leaped from treetop to treetop, almost overhead.

'It was a huge, black panther, leaping through the air like Black Susan leaping on a mouse. It was many, many times bigger than Black Susan. It was so big that if it leaped on Grandpa it could kill him with its enormous, slashing claws and its long sharp teeth.

'Grandpa, on his horse, was running away from it just as a mouse runs from a cat.

'The panther did not scream any more. Grandpa did not see it any more. But he knew that it was coming, leaping after him in the dark woods behind him. The horse ran with all its might.

'At last the horse ran up to Grandpa's house. Grandpa saw the panther springing. Grandpa jumped off the horse, against the door. He burst through the door and slammed it behind him. The panther landed on the horse's back, just where Grandpa had been.

'The horse screamed terribly, and ran. He was running away into the Big Woods, with the panther riding on his back and ripping his back with its claws. But Grandpa grabbed his gun from the wall and got to the window, just in time to shoot the panther dead.

'Grandpa said he would never again go into the Big Woods without his gun.'

When Pa told this story, Laura and Mary shivered and snuggled closer to him. They were safe and snug on his knees, with his strong arms around them.

They liked to be there, before the warm fire, with Black Susan purring on the hearth and good dog Jack stretched out beside her. When they heard a wolf howl, Jack's head lifted and the hairs rose stiff along his back. But Laura and Mary listened to that lonely sound in the dark and the cold of the Big Woods, and they were not afraid.

They were cosy and comfortable in their little house made of logs, with the snow drifted around it and the wind crying because it could not get in by the fire.

3

The Long Rifle

EVERY evening before he began to tell stories, Pa made the bullets for his next day's hunting.

Laura and Mary helped him. They brought the big, long-handled spoon, and the box full of bits of lead, and the bullet-mould. Then while he squatted on the hearth and made the bullets, they sat one on each side of him, and watched.

First he melted the bits of lead in the big spoon held in the coals. When the lead was melted, he poured it carefully from the spoon into the little hole in the bullet-mould. He waited a minute, then he opened the mould, and out dropped a bright new bullet on to the hearth.

The bullet was too hot to touch, but it shone so temptingly that sometimes Laura or Mary could not help touching it. Then they burned their fingers. But they did not say anything, because Pa had told them never to touch a new bullet. If they burned their fingers, that was their own fault; they should have minded him. So they put their fingers in their mouths to cool them, and watched Pa make more bullets.

There would be a shining pile of them on the hearth before Pa stopped. He let them cool, then with his jack-knife he trimmed off the little lumps left by the hole in the mould. He gathered up the tiny shavings of lead and saved them carefully, to melt again the next time he made bullets.

The finished bullets he put into his bullet pouch. This was a little bag which Ma had made beautifully of buckskin, from a buck Pa had shot.

After the bullets were made, Pa would take his gun down from the wall and clean it. Out in the snowy woods all day, it might have gathered a little dampness, and the inside of the barrel was sure to be dirty from powder smoke.

So Pa would take the ramrod from its place under the gun barrel, and fasten a piece of clean cloth on its end. He stood the butt of the gun in a pan on the hearth and poured boiling water from the tea kettle into the gun barrel. Then quickly he dropped the ramrod in and rubbed it up and down, up and down, while the hot water blackened with powder smoke spurted out through the little hole on which the cap was placed when the gun was loaded.

Pa kept pouring in more water and washing the gun barrel with the cloth on the ramrod until the water ran out clear. Then the gun was clean. The water must always be boiling, so that the heated steel would dry instantly.

Then Pa put a clean, greased rag on the ramrod, and while the gun barrel was still hot he greased it well on the inside. With another clean, greased cloth he rubbed it all over, outside, until every bit of it was oiled and sleek. After that he rubbed and polished the gunstock until the wood of it was bright and shining, too.

Now he was ready to load the gun again, and Laura and Mary must help him. Standing straight and tall, holding the long gun upright on its butt, while Laura and Mary stood on either side of him, Pa said:

'You watch me, now, and tell me if I make a mistake.'

So they watched very carefully, but he never made a mistake.

Laura handed him the smooth, polished cow-horn full

of gunpowder. The top of the horn was a little metal cap.
Pa filled this cap full of the gunpowder and poured the
powder down the barrel of the gun. Then he shook the
gun a little, and tapped the barrel, to be sure that all the
powder was together in the bottom.

'Where's my patch box?' he asked then, and Mary
gave him the little tin box full of little pieces of greased
cloth. Pa laid one of these bits of greasy cloth over the
muzzle of the gun, put one of the shiny new bullets on it,
and with the ramrod he pushed the bullet and the cloth
down the gun barrel.

Then he pounded them tightly against the powder.
When he hit them with the ramrod, the ramrod bounced
up in the gun barrel, and Pa caught it and thrust it down
again. He did this for a long time.

Next he put the ramrod back in its place against the
gun barrel. Then taking a box of caps from his pocket, he
raised the hammer of the gun and slipped one of the little
bright caps over the hollow pin that was under the
hammer.

He let the hammer down, slowly and carefully. If it
came down quickly—bang!—the gun would go off.

Now the gun was loaded, and Pa laid it on its hooks
over the door.

When Pa was at home the gun always lay across those
two wooden hooks above the door. Pa had whittled the
hooks out of a green stick with his knife, and had driven
their straight ends deep into holes in the log. The hooked
ends curved upward and held the gun securely.

The gun was always loaded, and always above the door
so that Pa could get it quickly and easily, any time he
needed a gun.

When Pa went into the Big Woods, he always made
sure that the bullet pouch was full of bullets, and that the

tin patch box and the box of caps were with it in his pockets. The powder horn and a small sharp hatchet hung at his belt and he carried the gun ready loaded on his shoulder.

He always reloaded the gun as soon as he had fired it, for, he said, he did not want to meet trouble with an empty gun.

Whenever he shot at a wild animal, he had to stop and load the gun—measure the powder, put it in and shake it down, put in the patch and the bullet and pound them down, and then put a fresh cap under the hammer— before he could shoot again. When he shot at a bear or a panther, he must kill it with the first shot. A wounded bear or panther could kill a man before he had time to load his gun again.

But Laura and Mary were never afraid when Pa went alone into the Big Woods. They knew he could always kill bears and panthers with the first shot.

After the bullets were made and the gun was loaded, came story-telling time.

'Tell us about the Voice in the Woods,' Laura would beg him.

Pa crinkled up his eyes at her. 'Oh, no!' he said. 'You don't want to hear about the time I was a naughty little boy.'

'Oh, yes, we do! We do!' Laura and Mary said. So Pa began.

The Story of Pa and the Voice in the Woods

'WHEN I was a little boy, not much bigger than Mary, I had to go every afternoon to find the cows in the woods and drive them home. My father told me never to play by the way, but to hurry and bring the cows home before dark, because there were bears and wolves and panthers in the woods.

'One day I started earlier than usual, so I thought I did not need to hurry. There were so many things to see in the woods that I forgot that dark was coming. There were red squirrels in the trees, chipmunks scurrying through the leaves, and little rabbits playing games together in the open places. Little rabbits, you know, always have games together before they go to bed.

'I began to play I was a mighty hunter, stalking the wild animals and the Indians. I played I was fighting the Indians, until the woods seemed full of wild men, and then all at once I heard the birds twittering "good night". It was dusky in the path, and dark in the woods.

'I knew that I must get the cows home quickly, or it would be black night before they were safe in the barn. And I couldn't find the cows!

'I listened, but I could not hear their bells. I called, but the cows didn't come.

'I was afraid of the dark and the wild beasts, but I dared not go home to my father without the cows. So I ran through the woods, hunting and calling. All the time the shadows were getting thicker and darker, and the woods seemed larger, and the trees and the bushes looked strange.

'I could not find the cows anywhere. I climbed up hills, looking for them and calling, and I went down into dark ravines, calling and looking. I stopped and listened for the cowbells and there was not a sound but the rustling of leaves.

'Then I heard loud breathing and thought a panther was there, in the dark behind me. But it was only my own breathing.

'My bare legs were scratched by the briars, and when I ran through the bushes their branches struck me. But I kept on, looking and calling, "Sukey! Sukey!"

' "Sukey!   Sukey!" I shouted with all my might. "Sukey!"

'Right over my head something asked, "Who?"

'My hair stood straight on end.

' "Who? Who?" the Voice said again. And then *how* I did run!

'I forgot all about the cows. All I wanted was to get out of the dark woods, to get home.

'That thing in the dark came after me and called again, "Who-oo?"'

'I ran with all my might. I ran till I couldn't breathe and still I kept on running. Something grabbed my foot, and down I went. Up I jumped, and then I *ran*. Not even a wolf could have caught me.

'At last I came out of the dark woods, by the barn. There stood all the cows, waiting to be let through the bars. I let them in, and then ran to the house.

'My father looked up and said, "Young man, what makes you so late? Been playing by the way?"

'I looked down at my feet, and then I saw that one big-toe nail had been torn clean off. I had been so scared that I had not felt it hurt till that minute.'

Pa always stopped telling the story here, and waited until Laura said:

'Go on, Pa! Please go on.'

'Well,' Pa said, 'then your Grandpa went out into the yard and cut a stout switch. And he came back into the house and gave me a good thrashing, so that I would remember to mind him after that.

' "A big boy nine years old is old enough to remember to mind," he said. "There's a good reason for what I tell you to do," he said, "and if you'll do as you're told, no harm will come to you." '

'Yes, yes, Pa!' Laura would say, bouncing up and down on Pa's knee. 'And then what did he say?'

'He said, "If you'd obeyed me, as you should, you wouldn't have been out in the Big Woods after dark, and you wouldn't have been scared by a screech-owl." '

4

Christmas

CHRISTMAS was coming.
The little log house was almost buried in snow.
Great drifts were banked against the walls and windows,
and in the morning when Pa opened the door, there was
a wall of snow as high as Laura's head. Pa took the shovel
and shovelled it away, and then he shovelled a path to
the barn, where the horses and cows were snug and warm
in their stalls.

The days were clear and bright. Laura and Mary
stood on chairs by the window and looked out across the
glittering snow at the glittering trees. Snow was piled all
along their bare, dark branches, and it sparkled in the
sunshine. Icicles hung from the eaves of the house to the
snow-banks, great icicles as large at the top as Laura's
arm. They were like glass and full of sharp lights.

Pa's breath hung in the air like smoke, when he came
along the path from the barn. He breathed it out in

clouds and it froze in white frost on his moustache and beard.

When he came in, stamping the snow from his boots, and caught Laura up in a bear's hug against his cold, big coat, his moustache was beaded with little drops of melting frost.

Every night he was busy, working on a large piece of board and two small pieces. He whittled them with his knife, he rubbed them with sandpaper and with the palm of his hand, until when Laura touched them they felt soft and smooth as silk.

Then with his sharp jack-knife he worked at them, cutting the edges of the large one into little peaks and towers, with a large star curved on the very tallest point. He cut little holes through the wood. He cut the holes in shapes of windows, and little stars, and crescent moons, and circles. All around them he carved tiny leaves, and flowers, and birds.

One of the little boards he shaped in a lovely curve, and around its edges he carved leaves and flowers and stars, and through it he cut crescent moons and curlicues.

Around the edges of the smallest board he carved a tiny flowering vine.

He made the tiniest shavings, cutting very slowly and carefully, making whatever he thought would be pretty.

At last he had the pieces finished and one night he fitted them together. When this was done, the large piece was a beautifully carved back for a smooth little shelf across its middle. The large star was at the very top of it. The curved piece supported the shelf underneath, and it was carved beautifully, too. And the little vine ran around the edge of the shelf.

Pa had made this bracket for a Christmas present for Ma. He hung it carefully against the log wall between the windows, and Ma stood her little china woman on the shelf.

The little china woman had a china bonnet on her head, and china curls hung against her china neck. Her china dress was laced across in front, and she wore a pale pink china apron and little gilt china shoes. She was beautiful, standing on the shelf with flowers and leaves

and birds and moons carved all around her, and the large star at the very top.

Ma was busy all day long, cooking good things for Christmas. She baked salt-rising bread and rye'n'Injun bread, and Swedish crackers, and a huge pan of baked beans, with salt pork and molasses. She baked vinegar pies and dried-apple pies, and filled a big jar with cookies, and she let Laura and Mary lick the cake spoon.

One morning she boiled molasses and sugar together until they made a thick syrup, and Pa brought in two

pans of clean, white snow from outdoors. Laura and
Mary each had a pan, and Pa and Ma showed them
how to pour the dark syrup in little streams on to the
snow.

They made circles, and curlicues, and squiggledy
things, and these hardened at once and were candy.
Laura and Mary might eat one piece each, but the rest
was saved for Christmas Day.

All this was done because Aunt Eliza and Uncle Peter
and the cousins, Peter and Alice and Ella, were coming
to spend Christmas.

The day before Christmas they came. Laura and Mary
heard the gay ringing of sleigh bells, growing louder every
moment, and then the big bobsled came out of the woods
and drove up to the gate. Aunt Eliza and Uncle Peter
and the cousins were in it, all covered up, under blankets
and robes and buffalo skins.

They were wrapped up in so many coats and mufflers
and veils and shawls that they looked like big, shapeless
bundles.

When they all came in, the little house was full and
running over. Black Susan ran out and hid in the barn,
but Jack leaped in circles through the snow, barking as
though he would never stop. Now there were cousins to
play with!

As soon as Aunt Eliza had unwrapped them, Peter and
Alice and Ella and Laura and Mary began to run and
shout. At last Aunt Eliza told them to be quiet. Then
Alice said:

'I'll tell you what let's do. Let's make pictures.'

Alice said they must go outdoors to do it, and Ma
thought it was too cold for Laura to play outdoors. But
when she saw how disappointed Laura was, she said she
might go, after all, for a little while. She put on Laura's

coat and mittens and the warm cape with the hood, and wrapped a muffler around her neck, and let her go.

Laura had never had so much fun. All morning she played outdoors in the snow with Alice and Ella and Peter

and Mary, making pictures. The way they did it was this:

Each one by herself climbed up on a stump, and then all at once, holding their arms out wide, they fell off the stumps into the soft, deep snow. They fell flat on their

faces. Then they tried to get up without spoiling the
marks they made when they fell. If they did it well, there
in the snow were five holes, shaped almost exactly like
four little girls and a boy, arms and legs and all. They
called these their pictures.

They played so hard all day that when night came they
were too excited to sleep. But they must sleep, or Santa
Claus would not come. So they hung their stockings by
the fireplace, and said their prayers, and went to bed—
Alice and Ella and Mary and Laura all in one big bed
on the floor.

Peter had the trundle bed. Aunt Eliza and Uncle Peter
were going to sleep in the big bed, and another bed was
made on the attic floor for Pa and Ma. The buffalo robes
and all the blankets had been brought in from Uncle
Peter's sled, so there were enough covers for everybody.

Pa and Ma and Aunt Eliza and Uncle Peter sat by the
fire, talking. And just as Laura was drifting off to sleep,
she heard Uncle Peter say:

'Eliza had a narrow squeak the other day, when I was
away at Lake City. You know Prince, ᵗhat big dog of
mine?'

Laura was wide awake at once. She always liked to
hear about dogs. She lay still as a mouse, and looked at
the fire-light flickering on the log walls, and listened to
Uncle Peter.

'Well,' Uncle Peter said, 'early in the morning Eliza
started to the spring to get a pail of water, and Prince
was following her. She got to the edge of the ravine,
where the path goes down to the spring, and all of a
sudden Prince set his teeth in the back of her skirt and
pulled.

'You know what a big dog he is. Eliza scolded him,
but he wouldn't let go, and he's so big and strong she

couldn't get away from him. He kept backing and pulling, till he tore a piece out of her skirt.'

'It was my blue print,' Aunt Eliza said to Ma.

'Dear me!' Ma said.

'He tore a big piece right out of the back of it,' Aunt Eliza said. 'I was so mad I could have whipped him for it. But he growled at me.'

'Prince growled at you?' Pa said.

'Yes,' said Aunt Eliza.

'So then she started on again toward the spring,' Uncle Peter went on. 'But Prince jumped into the path ahead of her and snarled at her. He paid no attention to her talking and scolding. He just kept on showing his teeth and snarling, and when she tried to get past him he kept in front of her and snapped at her. That scared her.'

'I should think it would!' Ma said.

'He was so savage, I thought he was going to bite me,' said Aunt Eliza. 'I believe he would have.'

'I never heard of such a thing!' said Ma. 'What on earth did you do?'

'I turned right around and ran into the house where the children were, and slammed the door,' Aunt Eliza answered.

'Of course Prince was savage with strangers,' said Uncle Peter. 'But he was always so kind to Eliza and the children I felt perfectly safe to leave them with him. Eliza couldn't understand it at all.

'After she got into the house he kept pacing around and growling. Every time she started to open the door he jumped at her and snarled.'

'Had he gone mad?' said Ma.

'That's what I thought,' Aunt Eliza said. 'I didn't know what to do. There I was, shut up in the house with the children, and not daring to go out. And we didn't have any water. I couldn't even get any snow to melt. Every time I opened the door so much as a crack, Prince acted like he would tear me to pieces.'

'How long did this go on?' Pa asked.

'All day, till late in the afternoon,' Aunt Eliza said. 'Peter had taken the gun, or I would have shot him.'

'Along late in the afternoon,' Uncle Peter said, 'he got quiet, and lay down in front of the door. Eliza thought he was asleep, and she made up her mind to try to slip past him and get to the spring for some water.

'So she opened the door very quietly, but of course he woke up right away. When he saw she had the water pail in her hand, he got up and walked ahead of her to the spring, just the same as usual. And there, all around the spring in the snow, were the fresh tracks of a panther.'

'The tracks were as big as my hand,' said Aunt Eliza.

'Yes,' Uncle Peter said, 'he was a big fellow. His tracks were the biggest I ever saw. He would have got Eliza sure, if Prince had let her go to the spring in the morning. I saw the tracks. He had been lying up in that big oak over the spring, waiting for some animal to come there for water. Undoubtedly he would have dropped down on her.

'Night was coming on, when she saw the tracks, and she didn't waste any time getting back to the house with her pail of water. Prince followed close behind her, looking back into the ravine now and then.'

'I took him into the house with me,' Aunt Eliza said, 'and we all stayed inside, till Peter came home.'

'Did you get him?' Pa asked Uncle Peter.

'No,' Uncle Peter said. 'I took my gun and hunted all round the place, but I couldn't find him. I saw some more of his tracks. He'd gone on north, farther into the Big Woods.'

Alice and Ella and Mary were all wide awake now,

and Laura put her head under the covers and whispered to Alice, 'My! weren't you scared?'

Alice whispered back that she was scared, but Ella was scareder. And Ella whispered that she wasn't, either, any such thing.

'Well, anyway, you made more fuss about being thirsty,' Alice whispered.

They lay there whispering about it till Ma said: 'Charles, those children never will get to sleep unless you play for them.' So Pa got his fiddle.

The room was still and warm and full of firelight. Ma's shadow, and Aunt Eliza's and Uncle Peter's were big and quivering on the walls in the flickering firelight, and Pa's fiddle sang merrily to itself.

It sang 'Money Musk', and 'The Red Heifer', 'The Devil's Dream', and 'Arkansas Traveller'. And Laura went to sleep while Pa and the fiddle were both softly singing:

"My darling Nelly Gray, they have taken you away,
    And I'll never see my darling any more. . . ."

In the morning they all woke up almost at the same moment. They looked at their stockings, and something was in them. Santa Claus had been there. Alice and Ella and Laura in their red flannel night-gowns and Peter in his red flannel nightshirt, all ran shouting to see what he had brought.

In each stocking there was a pair of bright red mittens and there was a long flat stick of red-and-white-striped, peppermint candy, all beautifully notched along each side.

They were all so happy they could hardly speak at first. They just looked with shining eyes at those lovely Christmas presents. But Laura was happiest of all. Laura had a rag doll.

She was a beautiful doll. She had a face of white cloth with black button eyes. A black pencil had made her eyebrows, and her cheeks and her mouth were red with the ink made from pokeberries. Her hair was black yarn that had been knit and ravelled, so that it was curly.

She had little red flannel stockings and little black cloth gaiters for shoes, and her dress was pretty pink and blue calico.

She was so beautiful that Laura could not say a word. She just held her tight and forgot everything else. She did not know that everyone was looking at her, till Aunt Eliza said:

'Did you ever see such big eyes!'

The other girls were not jealous because Laura had mittens, and candy, *and* a doll, because Laura was the littlest girl, except Baby Carrie and Aunt Eliza's little baby, Dolly Varden. The babies were too small for dolls. They were so small they did not even know about Santa Claus. They just put their fingers in their mouths and wriggled because of all the excitement.

Laura sat down on the edge of the bed and held her doll. She loved her red mittens and she loved the candy, but she loved her doll best of all. She named her Charlotte.

Then they all looked at each other's mittens, and tried on their own, and Peter bit a large piece out of his stick of candy, but Alice and Ella and Mary and Laura licked theirs, to make it last longer.

'Well, well!' Uncle Peter said. 'Isn't there even one stocking with nothing but a switch in it? My, my, have you all been such good children?'

But they didn't believe that Santa Claus could, really, have given any of them nothing but a switch. That happened to some children, but it couldn't happen to them. It was so hard to be good all the time, every day, for a whole year.

'You mustn't tease the children, Peter,' Aunt Eliza said.

Ma said, 'Laura, aren't you going to let the other girls hold your doll?' She meant, 'Little girls must not be so selfish.'

So Laura let Mary take the beautiful doll, and then Alice held her a minute, and then Ella. They smoothed the pretty dress and admired the red flannel stockings and the gaiters, and the curly woollen hair. But Laura was glad when at last Charlotte was safe in her arms again.

Pa and Uncle Peter had each a pair of new, warm mittens, knit in little squares of red and white. Ma and Aunt Eliza had made them.

Aunt Eliza had brought Ma a large red apple stuck full of cloves. How good it smelled! And it would not spoil, for so many cloves would keep it sound and sweet.

Ma gave Aunt Eliza a little needle-book she had made, with bits of silk for covers and soft white flannel leaves into which to stick the needles. The flannel would keep the needles from rusting.

They all admired Ma's beautiful bracket, and Aunt Eliza said that Uncle Peter had made one for her—of course, with different carving.

Santa Claus had not given them anything at all. Santa Claus did not give grown people presents, but that was not because they had not been good. Pa and Ma were good. It was because they were grown up, and grown people must give each other presents.

Then all the presents must be laid away for a little while. Peter went out with Pa and Uncle Peter to do the chores, and Alice and Ella helped Aunt Eliza make the beds, and Laura and Mary set the table, while Ma got breakfast.

For breakfast there were pancakes, and Ma made a pancake man for each one of the children. Ma called each one in turn to bring her plate, and each could stand by the stove and watch, while with the spoonful of batter Ma put on the arms and the legs and the head. It was exciting to watch her turn the whole little man over, quickly and carefully, on a hot griddle. When it was done, she put it smoking hot on the plate.

Peter ate the head off his man, right away. But Alice and Ella and Mary and Laura ate theirs slowly in little bits, first the arms and legs and then the middle, saving the head for the last.

To-day the weather was so cold that they could not play outdoors, but there were the new mittens to admire, and the candy to lick. And they all sat on the floor together and looked at the pictures in the Bible, and the pictures of all kinds of animals and birds in Pa's big green book. Laura kept Charlotte in her arms the whole time.

Then there was the Christmas dinner. Alice and Ella and Peter and Mary and Laura did not say a word at table, for they knew that children should be seen and not heard. But they did not need to ask for second helpings. Ma and Aunt Eliza kept their plates full and let them eat all the good things they could hold.

'Christmas comes but once a year,' said Aunt Eliza.

Dinner was early, because Aunt Eliza, Uncle Peter and the cousins had such a long way to go.

'Best the horses can do,' Uncle Peter said, 'we'll hardly make it home before dark.'

So as soon as they had eaten dinner, Uncle Peter and Pa went to put the horses to the sled, while Ma and Aunt Eliza wrapped up the cousins.

They pulled heavy woollen stockings over the woollen stockings and the shoes they were already wearing. They put on mittens and coats and warm hoods and shawls, and wrapped mufflers around their necks and thick woollen veils over their faces. Ma slipped piping hot baked potatoes into their pockets to keep their fingers warm, and Aunt Eliza's flat-irons were hot on the stove, ready to put at their feet in the sled. The blankets and the quilts and the buffalo robes were warmed, too.

So they all got into the big bobsled, cosy and warm, and Pa tucked the last robe well in around them.

'Good-bye! Good-bye!' they called, and off they went, the horses trotting gaily and the sleigh bells ringing.

In just a little while the merry sound of the bells was gone, and Christmas was over. But what a happy Christmas it had been!

5

Sundays

Now the winter seemed long. Laura and Mary began to be tired of staying always in the house. Especially on Sundays, the time went so slowly.

Every Sunday Mary and Laura were dressed from the skin out in their best clothes, with fresh ribbons in their hair. They were very clean, because they had their baths on Saturday night.

In the summer they were bathed in water from the spring. But in the wintertime Pa filled and heaped the washtub with clean snow, and on the cookstove it melted to water. Then close by the warm stove, behind a screen made of a blanket over two chairs, Ma bathed Laura, and then she bathed Mary.

Laura was bathed first, because she was littler than Mary. She had to go to bed early on Saturday nights, with Charlotte, because after she was bathed and put into her clean nightgown, Pa must empty the washtub and fill it with snow again for Mary's bath. Then after Mary came to bed, Ma had her bath behind the blanket, and then Pa had his. And they were all clean, for Sunday.

On Sundays Mary and Laura must not run or shout or be noisy in their play. Mary could not sew on her nine-patch quilt, and Laura could not knit on the tiny mittens she was making for Baby Carrie. They might look quietly at their paper dolls, but they must not make anything new for them. They were not allowed to sew on doll clothes, not even with pins.

They must sit quietly and listen while Ma read Bible stories to them, or stories about lions and tigers and white bears from Pa's big green book, *The Wonders of the Animal World*. They might look at pictures, and they might hold their rag dolls nicely and talk to them. But there was nothing else they could do.

Laura liked best to look at the pictures in the big Bible, with its paper covers. Best of all was the picture of Adam naming the animals.

Adam sat on a rock, and all the animals and birds, big and little, were gathered around him anxiously waiting to be told what kind of animals they were. Adam looked so comfortable. He did not have to be careful to keep his clothes clean, because he had no clothes on. He wore only a skin around his middle.

'Did Adam have good clothes to wear on Sundays?' Laura asked Ma.

'No,' Ma said. 'Poor Adam, all he had to wear was skins.'

Laura did not pity Adam. She wished she had nothing to wear but skins.

One Sunday after supper she could not bear it any longer. She began to play with Jack, and in a few minutes she was running and shouting. Pa told her to sit in her chair and be quiet, but when Laura sat down she began to cry and kick the chair with her heels.

'I hate Sunday!' she said.

Pa put down his book. 'Laura,' he said sternly, 'come here.'

Her feet dragged as she went, because she knew she deserved a spanking. But when she reached Pa, he looked at her sorrowfully for a moment, and then took her on his knee and cuddled her against him. He held out his other arm to Mary, and said:

'I'm going to tell you a story about when Grandpa was a boy.'

The Story of Grandpa's Sled and the Pig

'WHEN your grandpa was a boy, Laura, Sunday did not begin on Sunday morning, as it does now. It began at sundown on Saturday night. Then everyone stopped every kind of work or play.

'Supper was solemn. After supper, Grandpa's father read aloud a chapter of the Bible, while everyone sat straight and still in his chair. Then they all knelt down, and their father said a long prayer. When he said "Amen" they got up from their knees and each took a candle and went to bed. They must go straight to bed, with no playing, laughing, or even talking.

'Sunday morning they ate a cold breakfast, because nothing could be cooked on Sunday. Then they all dressed in their best clothes and walked to church. They walked, because hitching up the horses was work, and no work could be done on Sunday.

'They must walk slowly and solemnly, looking straight ahead. They must not joke or laugh, or even smile. Grandpa and his two brothers walked ahead, and their father and mother walked behind them.

'In church, Grandpa and his brothers must sit perfectly still for two long hours and listen to the sermon. They dared not fidget on the hard bench. They dared not swing their feet. They dared not turn their heads to look at the windows or the walls or the ceiling of the church. They must sit perfectly motionless, and never for one instant take their eyes from the preacher.

'When church was over, they walked slowly home. They might talk on the way, but they must not talk loudly and they must never laugh or smile. At home they ate a cold dinner which had been cooked the day before. Then all the long afternoon they must sit in a row on a bench and study their catechism, until at last the sun went down and Sunday was over.

'Now Grandpa's home was about half-way down the side of a steep hill. The road went from the top of the hill to the bottom, right past the front door, and in winter it was the best place for sliding downhill that you can possibly imagine.

'One week Grandpa and his two brothers, James and George, were making a new sled. They worked at it every minute of their playtime. It was the best sled they had ever made, and it was so long that all three of them could sit on it, one behind the other. They planned to finish it in time to slide downhill Saturday afternoon. For every Saturday afternoon they had two or three hours to play.

'But that week their father was cutting down trees in

the Big Woods. He was working hard and he kept the
boys working with him. They did all the morning chores
by lantern-light and were hard at work in the woods
when the sun came up. They worked till dark, and then
there were the chores to do, and after supper they had
to go to bed so they could get up early in the morning.

'They had no time to work on the sled until Saturday
afternoon. Then they worked at it just as fast as they
could, but they didn't get it finished till just as the sun
went down, Saturday night.

'After the sun went down, they could not slide down-

hill, not even once. That would be breaking the Sabbath.
So they put the sled in the shed behind the house, to wait
until Sunday was over.

'All the two long hours in church next day, while they
kept their feet still and their eyes on the preacher, they
were thinking about the sled. At home while they ate
dinner they couldn't think of anything else. After dinner
their father sat down to read the Bible, and Grandpa and
James and George sat as still as mice on their bench with
their catechism. But they were thinking about the sled.

'The sun shone brightly and the snow was smooth and
glittering on the road; they could see it through the
window. It was a perfect day for sliding downhill. They

looked at their catechism and they thought about the new sled, and it seemed that Sunday would never end.

'After a long time they heard a snore. They looked at their father, and they saw that his head had fallen against the back of his chair and he was fast asleep.

'Then James looked at George, and James got up from the bench and tiptoed out of the room through the back door. George looked at Grandpa, and George tiptoed after James. And Grandpa looked fearfully at their father, but on tiptoe he followed George and left their father snoring.

'They took their new sled and went quietly up to the top of the hill. They meant to slide down, just once. Then they would put the sled away, and slip back to their bench and the catechism before their father woke up.

'James sat in front on the sled, then George, and then Grandpa, because he was the littlest. The sled started, at first slowly, then faster and faster. It was running, flying, down the long steep hill, but the boys dared not shout. They must slide silently past the house, without waking their father.

'There was no sound except the little whirr of the runners on the snow, and the wind rushing past.

'Then just as the sled was swooping toward the house, a big black pig stepped out of the woods. He walked into the middle of the road and stood there.

'The sled was going so fast it couldn't be stopped. There wasn't time to turn it. The sled went right under the hog and picked him up. With a squeal he sat down on James, and he kept on squealing, long and loud and shrill, "Squee-ee-ee-ee-ee! Squee-ee-ee-ee-ee-ee!"

'They flashed by the house, the pig sitting in front, then James, then George, then Grandpa, and they saw their father standing in the doorway looking at them. They couldn't stop, they couldn't hide, there was no time to say anything. Down the hill they went, the hog sitting on James and squealing all the way.

'At the bottom of the hill they stopped. The hog jumped off James and ran away into the woods, still squealing.

'The boys walked slowly and solemnly up the hill. They

put the sled away. They sneaked into the house and slipped quietly to their places on the bench. Their father was reading his Bible. He looked up at them without saying a word.

'Then he went on reading, and they studied their catechism.

'But when the sun went down and the Sabbath day was over, their father took them out to the woodshed and tanned their jackets, first James, then George, then Grandpa.

'So you see, Laura and Mary,' Pa said, 'you may find it hard to be good, but you should be glad that it isn't as hard to be good now as it was when Grandpa was a boy.'

'Did little girls have to be as good as that?' Laura asked, and Ma said:

'It was harder for little girls. Because they had to behave like little ladies all the time, not only on Sundays. Little girls could never slide downhill, like boys. Little girls had to sit in the house and stitch on samplers.'

'Now run along and let Ma put you to bed,' said Pa, and he took his fiddle out of its box.

Laura and Mary lay in their trundle bed and listened to the Sunday hymns, for even the fiddle must not sing the week-day songs on Sundays.

'Rock of Ages, cleft for me,' Pa sang, with the fiddle. Then he sang:

> "Shall I be carried to the skies,
>   On flowery beds of ease,
>   While others fought to win the prize,
>   And sailed through bloody seas?"

Laura began to float away on the music, and then she heard a clattering noise, and there was Ma by the stove, getting breakfast. It was Monday morning, and Sunday would not come again for a whole week.

That morning when Pa came in to breakfast he caught Laura and said he must give her a spanking.

First he explained that to-day was her birthday, and

she would not grow properly next year unless she had a spanking. And then he spanked so gently and carefully that it did not hurt a bit.

'One—two—three—four—five—six,' he counted and spanked, slowly. One spank for each year, and at the last one big spank to grow on.

Then Pa gave her a little wooden man he had whittled out of a stick, to be company for Charlotte. Ma gave her five little cakes, one for each year that Laura had lived with her and Pa. And Mary gave her a new dress for Charlotte. Mary had made the dress herself, when Laura thought she was sewing on her patchwork quilt.

And that night, for a special birthday treat, Pa played 'Pop Goes the Weasel' for her.

He sat with Laura and Mary close against his knees while he played. 'Now watch,' he said. 'Watch, and maybe you can see the weasel pop out this time.' Then he sang:

> "A penny for a spool of thread,
> Another for a needle,
> That's the way the money goes——"

Laura and Mary bent close, watching, for they knew now was the time.

> "Pop! (said Pa's finger on the string)
>   Goes the weasel!" (sang the fiddle, plain as plain.)

But Laura and Mary hadn't seen Pa's finger make the string pop.

'Oh, please, please, do it again!' they begged him. Pa's blue eyes laughed, and the fiddle went on while he sang:

> "All around the cobbler's bench,
>   The monkey chased the weasel,
>   The preacher kissed the cobbler's wife—
>   Pop! goes the weasel!"

They hadn't seen Pa's finger that time, either. He was so quick they could never catch him.

So they went laughing to bed and lay listening to Pa and the fiddle singing:

> "There was an old darkey
>   And his name was Uncle Ned,
>   And he died long, long ago.
>   There was no wool on the top of his head,
>   In the place where the wool ought to grow.

> "His fingers were as long
>   As the cane in the brake,
>   His eyes they could hardly see,
>   And he had no teeth for to eat the hoe-cake,
>   So he had to let the hoe-cake be.

> So hand up the shovel and the hoe,
>   Lay down the fiddle and the bow,
>   There's no more work for old Uncle Ned,
>   For he's gone where the good darkeys go."

6

Two Big Bears

THEN one day Pa said that spring was coming.

In the Big Woods the snow was beginning to thaw. Bits of it dropped from the branches of the trees and made little holes in the softening snow-banks below. At noon all the big icicles along the eaves of the little house quivered and sparkled in the sunshine, and drops of water hung trembling at their tips.

Pa said he must go to town to trade the furs of the wild animals he had been trapping all winter. So one evening he made a big bundle of them. There were so many furs that when they were packed tightly and tied together they made a bundle almost as big as Pa.

Very early one morning Pa strapped the bundle of furs on his shoulders, and started to walk to town. There were so many furs to carry that he could not take his gun.

Ma was worried, but Pa said that by starting before sun-up and walking very fast all day he could get home again before dark.

The nearest town was far away. Laura and Mary had never seen a town. They had never seen a store. They had never seen even two houses standing together. But they knew that in a town there were many houses, and a store full of candy and calico and other wonderful things —powder, and shot, and salt, and store sugar.

They knew that Pa would trade his furs to the store-keeper for beautiful things from town, and all day they were expecting the presents he would bring them. When the sun sank low above the treetops and no more drops fell from the tips of the icicles they began to watch eagerly for Pa.

The sun sank out of sight, the woods grew dark, and he did not come. Ma started supper and set the table, but he did not come. It was time to do the chores, and still he had not come.

Ma said that Laura might come with her while she milked the cow. Laura could carry the lantern.

So Laura put on her coat and Ma buttoned it up. And Laura put her hands into her red mittens that hung by a red yarn string around her neck, while Ma lighted the candle in the lantern.

Laura was proud to be helping Ma with the milking, and she carried the lantern very carefully. Its sides were of tin, with places cut in them for the candle-light to shine through.

When Laura walked behind Ma on the path to the barn, the little bits of candle-light from the lantern leaped all around her on the snow. The night was not yet quite dark. The woods were dark, but there was a grey light on the snowy path, and in the sky there were a few faint stars. The stars did not look as warm and bright as the little lights that came from the lantern.

Laura was surprised to see the dark shape of Sukey,

the brown cow, standing at the barnyard gate. Ma was surprised, too.

It was too early in the spring for Sukey to be let out in the Big Woods to eat grass. She lived in the barn. But sometimes on warm days Pa left the door of her stall open

so she could come into the barnyard. Now Ma and Laura saw her behind the bars, waiting for them.

Ma went up to the gate, and pushed against it to open it. But it did not open very far, because there was Sukey, standing against it. Ma said,

'Sukey, get over!' She reached across the gate and slapped Sukey's shoulder.

Just then one of the dancing bits of light from the lantern jumped between the bars of the gate, and Laura saw long, shaggy, black fur, and two little, glittering eyes. Sukey had thin, short, brown fur. Sukey had large, gentle eyes.

Ma said, 'Laura, walk back to the house.'

So Laura turned around and began to walk toward the house. Ma came behind her. When they had gone part way, Ma snatched her up, lantern and all, and ran. Ma ran with her into the house, and slammed the door.

Then Laura said, 'Ma, was it a bear?'

'Yes, Laura,' Ma said. 'It was a bear.'

Laura began to cry. She hung on to Ma and sobbed, 'Oh, will he eat Sukey?'

'No,' Ma said, hugging her. 'Sukey is safe in the barn. Think, Laura—all those big, heavy logs in the barn walls. And the door is heavy and solid, made to keep bears out. No, the bear cannot get in and eat Sukey.'

Laura felt better then. 'But he could have hurt us, couldn't he?' she asked.

'He didn't hurt us,' Ma said. 'You were a good girl, Laura, to do exactly as I told you, and to do it quickly, without asking why.'

Ma was trembling, and she began to laugh a little. 'To think,' she said, 'I've slapped a bear!'

Then she put supper on the table for Laura and Mary. Pa had not come yet. He didn't come. Laura and Mary were undressed, and they said their prayers and snuggled into the trundle bed.

Ma sat by the lamp, mending one of Pa's shirts. The house seemed cold and still and strange, without Pa.

Laura listened to the wind in the Big Woods. All around the house the wind went crying as though it were lost in the dark and the cold. The wind sounded frightened.

Ma finished mending the shirt. Laura saw her fold it slowly and carefully. She smoothed it with her hand. Then she did a thing she had never done before. She went to the door and pulled the leather latch-string through its hole in the door, so that nobody could get in from outside unless she lifted the latch. She came and took Carrie, all limp and sleeping, out of the big bed.

She saw that Laura and Mary were still awake, and she said to them: 'Go to sleep, girls. Everything is all right. Pa will be here in the morning.'

Then she went back to her rocking chair and sat there rocking gently and holding Baby Carrie in her arms.

She was sitting up late, waiting for Pa, and Laura and Mary meant to stay awake, too, till he came. But at last they went to sleep.

In the morning Pa was there. He had brought candy for Laura and Mary, and two pieces of pretty calico to make them each a dress. Mary's was a china-blue pattern on a white ground, and Laura's was dark red with little golden-brown dots on it. Ma had calico for a dress, too; it was brown, with a big, feathery white pattern all over it.

They were all happy because Pa had got such good prices for his furs that he could afford to get them such beautiful presents.

The tracks of the big bear were all around the barn, and there were marks of his claws on the walls. But Sukey and the horses were safe inside.

All that day the sun shone, the snow melted, and little streams of water ran from the icicles, which all the time grew thinner. Before the sun set that night, the bear tracks were only shapeless marks in the wet, soft snow.

After supper Pa took Laura and Mary on his knees and said he had a new story to tell them.

The Story of Pa and the Bear in the Way

'WHEN I went to town yesterday with the furs I found it hard walking in the soft snow. It took me a long time to get to town, and other men with furs had come in earlier to do their trading. The storekeeper was busy, and I had to wait until he could look at my furs.

'Then we had to bargain about the price of each one, and then I had to pick out the things I wanted to take in trade.

'So it was nearly sundown before I could start home.

'I tried to hurry, but the walking was hard and I was tired, so I had not gone far before night came. And I was alone in the Big Woods without my gun.

'There were still six miles to walk, and I came along as fast as I could. The night grew darker and darker, and I wished for my gun, because I knew that some of the bears had come out of their winter dens. I had seen their tracks when I went to town in the morning.

'Bears are hungry and cross at this time of year; you know they have been sleeping in their dens all winter long with nothing to eat, and that makes them thin and angry when they wake up. I did not want to meet one.

'I hurried along as quick as I could in the dark. By and by the stars gave a little light. It was still black as pitch where the woods were thick, but in the open places I could see, dimly. I could see the snowy road ahead a little way, and I could see the dark woods standing all around me. I was glad when I came into an open place where the stars gave me this faint light.

'All the time I was watching, as well as I could, for bears. I was listening for the sounds they make when they go carelessly through the bushes.

'Then I came again into an open place, and there, right in the middle of my road, I saw a big black bear.

'He was standing up on his hind legs, looking at me. I could see his eyes shine. I could see his pig-snout. I could even see one of his claws, in the starlight.

'My scalp prickled, and my hair stood straight up. I stopped in my tracks, and stood still. The bear did not move. There he stood, looking at me.

'I knew it would do no good to try to go around him. He would follow me into the dark woods, where he could see better than I could. I did not want to fight a winter-starved bear in the dark. Oh, how I wished for my gun!

'I had to pass that bear, to get home. I thought that if I could scare him, he might get out of the road and let me go by. So I took a deep breath, and suddenly I shouted with all my might and ran at him, waving my arms.

'He didn't move.

'I did not run very far toward him, I tell you! I stopped and looked at him, and he stood looking at me. Then I shouted again. There he stood. I kept on shouting and waving my arms, but he did not budge.

'Well, it would do me no good to run away. There were other bears in the woods. I might meet one any time. I might as well deal with this one as with another. Besides, I was coming home to Ma and you girls. I would never get here, if I ran away from everything in the woods that scared me.

'So at last I looked around, and I got a good big club, a solid, heavy branch that had been broken from a tree by the weight of snow in the winter.

'I lifted it up in my hands, and I ran straight at that bear. I swung my club as hard as I could and brought it down, bang! on his head.

'And there he still stood, for he was nothing but a big, black, burned stump!

'I had passed it on my way to town that morning. It wasn't a bear at all. I only thought it was a bear, because I had been thinking all the time about bears and being afraid I'd meet one.'

'It really wasn't a bear at all?' Mary asked.

'No, Mary, it wasn't a bear at all. There I had been

yelling and dancing, and waving my arms, all by myself in the Big Woods, trying to scare a stump!'

Laura said: 'Ours was really a bear. But we were not scared, because we thought it was Sukey.'

Pa did not say anything, but he hugged her tighter.

'Oo-oo! That bear might have eaten Ma and me all up?' Laura said, snuggling closer to him. 'But Ma walked right up to him and slapped him, and he didn't do anything at all. Why didn't he do anything?'

'I guess he was too surprised to do anything, Laura,'
Pa said. 'I guess he was afraid, when the lantern shone
in his eyes. And when Ma walked up to him and slapped
him, he knew *she* wasn't afraid.'

'Well, you were brave, too,' Laura said. 'Even if it was
only a stump, you thought it was a bear. You'd have hit
him on the head with a club, if he *had* been a bear,
wouldn't you, Pa?'

'Yes,' said Pa, 'I would. You see, I had to.'

Then Ma said it was bedtime. She helped Laura and
Mary undress and button up their red flannel nightgowns.
They knelt down by the trundle bed and said their
prayers.

> "Now I lay me down to sleep,
> I pray the Lord my soul to keep.
> If I should die before I wake,
> I pray the Lord my soul to take."

Ma kissed them both, and tucked the covers in around
them. They lay there awhile, looking at Ma's smooth,
parted hair and her hands busy with sewing in the lamplight. Her needle made little clicking sounds against her
thimble and then the thread went softly, swish! through
the pretty calico that Pa had traded furs for.

Laura looked at Pa, who was greasing his boots. His
moustaches and his hair and his long brown beard were
silky in the lamplight, and the colours of his plaid jacket
were gay. He whistled cheerfully while he worked, and
then he sang:

> "The birds were singing in the morning,
> And the myrtle and the ivy were in bloom,
> And the sun o'er the hills was a-dawning,
> 'Twas then that I laid her in the tomb."

It was a warm night. The fire had gone to coals on the hearth, and Pa did not build it up. All around the little house, in the Big Woods, there were little sounds of falling snow, and from the eaves there was the drip, drip of the melting icicles.

In just a little while the trees would be putting out their baby leaves, all rosy and yellow and pale green, and there would be wild flowers and birds in the woods.

Then there would be no more stories by the fire at night, but all day long Laura and Mary would run and play among the trees, for it would be spring.

7

The Sugar Snow

For days the sun shone and the weather was warm. There was no frost on the windows in the mornings. All day the icicles fell one by one from the eaves with soft smashing and crackling sounds in the snow-banks beneath. The trees shook their wet, black branches, and chunks of snow fell down.

When Mary and Laura pressed their noses against the cold window pane they could see the drip of water from the eaves and the bare branches of the trees. The snow did not glitter; it looked soft and tired. Under the trees it was pitted where the chunks of snow had fallen, and the banks beside the path were shrinking and settling.

Then one day Laura saw a patch of bare ground in the

yard. All day it grew bigger, and before night the whole yard was bare mud. Only the icy path was left, and the snow-banks along the path and the fence and beside the woodpile.

'Can't I go out to play, Ma?' Laura asked, and Ma said:

' "May", Laura.'

'May I go out to play?' she asked.

'You may to-morrow,' Ma promised.

That night Laura woke up, shivering. The bed-covers felt thin, and her nose was icy cold. Ma was tucking another quilt over her.

'Snuggle close to Mary,' Ma said, 'and you'll get warm.'

In the morning the house was warm from the stove, but when Laura looked out of the window she saw that the ground was covered with soft, thick snow. All along the branches of the trees the snow was piled like feathers, and it lay in mounds along the top of the rail fence, and stood up in great, white balls on top of the gate-posts.

Pa came in, shaking the soft snow from his shoulders and stamping it from his boots.

'It's a sugar snow,' he said.

Laura put her tongue quickly to a little bit of the white snow that lay in a fold of his sleeve. It was nothing but wet on her tongue, like any snow. She was glad that nobody had seen her taste it.

'Why is it a sugar snow, Pa?' she asked him, but he said he didn't have time to explain now. He must hurry away, he was going to Grandpa's.

Grandpa lived far away in the Big Woods, where the trees were closer together and larger.

Laura stood at the window and watched Pa, big and swift and strong, walking away over the snow. His gun was on his shoulder, his hatchet and powder horn hung at his side, and his tall boots made great tracks in the soft snow. Laura watched him till he was out of sight in the woods.

It was late before he came home that night. Ma had already lighted the lamp when he came in. Under one arm he carried a large package, and in the other hand was a big, covered, wooden bucket.

'Here, Caroline,' he said, handing the package and the bucket to Ma, and then he put the gun on its hooks over the door.

'If I'd met a bear,' he said, 'I couldn't have shot him without dropping my load.' Then he laughed. 'And if I'd dropped that bucket and bundle, I wouldn't have had to shoot him. I could have stood and watched him eat what's in them and lick his chops.'

Ma unwrapped the package and there were two hard, brown cakes, each as large as a milk pan. She uncovered the bucket, and it was full of dark brown syrup.

'Here, Laura and Mary,' Pa said, and he gave them each a little round package out of his pocket.

They took off the paper wrappings, and each had a little, hard, brown cake, with beautifully crinkled edges.

'Bite it,' said Pa, and his blue eyes twinkled.

Each bit off one little crinkle, and it was sweet. It crumbled in their mouths. It was better even than their Christmas candy.

'Maple sugar,' said Pa.

Supper was ready, and Laura and Mary laid the little maple sugar cakes beside their plates, while they ate the maple syrup on their bread.

After supper, Pa took them on his knees as he sat before the fire, and told them about his day at Grandpa's, and the sugar snow.

'All winter,' Pa said, 'Grandpa has been making wooden buckets and little troughs. He made them of cedar and white ash, for those woods won't give a bad taste to the maple syrup.

'To make the troughs, he split out little sticks as long as my hand and as big as my two fingers. Near one end, Grandpa cut the stick half through, and split one half off. This left him a flat stick, with a square piece at one end. Then with a bit he bored a hole lengthwise through the square part, and with his knife he whittled the wood till it was only a thin shell around the round hole. The flat

part of the stick he hollowed out with his knife till it was a little trough.

'He made dozens of them, and he made ten new wooden buckets. He had them all ready when the first warm weather came and the sap began to move in the trees.

'Then he went into the maple woods and with the bit he bored a hole in each maple tree, and he hammered the round end of the little trough into the hole, and he set a cedar bucket on the ground under the flat end.

'The sap, you know, is the blood of a tree. It comes up from the roots, when warm weather begins in the spring, and it goes to the very tip of each branch and twig, to make the green leaves grow.

'Well, when the maple sap came to the hole in the tree, it ran out of the tree, down the little trough and into the bucket.'

'Oh, didn't it hurt the poor tree?' Laura asked.

'No more than it hurts you when you prick your finger and it bleeds,' said Pa.

'Every day Grandpa puts on his boots and his warm coat and his fur cap and he goes out into the snowy woods and gathers the sap. With a barrel on a sled, he drives from tree to tree and empties the sap from the buckets into the barrel. Then he hauls it to a big iron kettle, that hangs by a chain from a cross-timber between two trees.

'He empties the sap into the iron kettle. There is a big

bonfire under the kettle, and the sap boils, and Grandpa watches it carefully. The fire must be hot enough to keep the sap boiling, but not hot enough to make it boil over.

'Every few minutes the sap must be skimmed. Grandpa skims it with a big, long-handled, wooden ladle that he made of basswood. When the sap gets too hot, Grandpa

lifts ladlefuls of it high in the air and pours it back slowly. This cools the sap a little and keeps it from boiling too fast.

'When the sap has boiled down just enough, he fills the buckets with the syrup. After that, he boils the sap until it grains when he cools it in a saucer.

'The instant the sap is graining, Grandpa jumps to the fire and rakes it all out from beneath the kettle. Then as fast as he can, he ladles the thick syrup into the milk pans that are standing ready. In the pans the syrup turns to cakes of hard, brown, maple sugar.'

'So that's why it's a sugar snow, because Grandpa is making sugar?' Laura asked.

'No,' Pa said. 'It's called a sugar snow, because a snow this time of year means that men can make more sugar. You see, this little cold spell and the snow will hold back the leafing of the trees, and that makes a longer run of sap.

'When there's a long run of sap, it means that Grandpa can make enough maple sugar to last all the year, for common every day. When he takes his furs to town, he will not need to trade for much store sugar. He will get only a little store sugar, to have on the table when company comes.'

'Grandpa must be glad there's a sugar snow,' Laura said.

'Yes,' Pa said, 'he's very glad. He's going to sugar off again next Monday, and he says we must all come.'

Pa's blue eyes twinkled; he had been saving the best for the last, and he said to Ma:

'Hey, Caroline! There'll be a dance!'

Ma smiled. She looked very happy, and she laid down her mending for a minute. 'Oh, Charles!' she said.

Then she went on with her mending, but she kept on smiling. She said, 'I'll wear my delaine.'

Ma's delaine dress was beautiful. It was a dark green, with a little pattern all over it that looked like ripe strawberries. A dressmaker had made it, in the East, in the place where Ma came from when she married Pa and moved out west to the Big Woods in Wisconsin. Ma had been very fashionable, before she married Pa, and a dress-maker had made her clothes.

The delaine was kept wrapped in paper and laid away. Laura and Mary had never seen Ma wear it, but she had shown it to them once. She had let them touch the beautiful dark red buttons that buttoned the basque up the front, and she had shown them how neatly the whale-bones were put in the seams, inside, with hundreds of little criss-cross stitches.

It showed how important a dance was, if Ma was going to wear the beautiful delaine dress. Laura and Mary were excited. They bounced up and down on Pa's knees, and asked questions about the dance until at last he said:

'Now you girls run along to bed! You'll know all about the dance when you see it. I have to put a new string on my fiddle.'

There were sticky fingers and sweet mouths to be washed. Then there were prayers to be said. By the time Laura and Mary were snug in their trundle bed, Pa and the fiddle were both singing, while he kept time with his foot on the floor:

> "I'm Captain Jinks of the Horse Marines,
>   I feed my horse on corn and beans,
>   And I often go beyond my means,
>   For I'm Captain Jinks of the Horse Marines,
>   I'm captain in the army!"

8

Dance at Grandpa's

MONDAY morning everybody got up early, in a hurry to get started to Grandpa's. Pa wanted to be there to help with the work of gathering and boiling the sap. Ma would help Grandma and the aunts make good things to eat for all the people who were coming to the dance.

Breakfast was eaten and the dishes washed and the beds made by lamplight. Pa packed his fiddle carefully in its box and put it in the big sled that was already waiting at the gate.

The air was cold and frosty and the light was grey, when Laura and Mary and Ma with Baby Carrie were tucked in snug and warm under the robes on the straw in the bottom of the sled.

The horses shook their heads and pranced, making the sleigh bells ring merrily, and away they went on the road through the Big Woods to Grandpa's.

The snow was damp and smooth in the road, so the sled slipped quickly over it, and the big trees seemed to be hurrying by on either side.

After a while there was sunshine in the woods and the air sparkled. The long streaks of yellow light lay between the shadows of the tree trunks, and the snow was coloured faintly pink. All the shadows were thin and blue, and every little curve of snowdrifts and every little track in the snow had a shadow.

Pa showed Laura the tracks of the wild creatures in the

snow at the sides of the road. The small, leaping tracks of cottontail rabbits, the tiny tracks of field mice, and the feather-stitching tracks of snow-birds. There were larger tracks, like dogs' tracks, where foxes had run, and there were the tracks of a deer that had bounded away into the woods.

The air was growing warmer already and Pa said that the snow wouldn't last long.

It did not seem long until they were sweeping into the clearing at Grandpa's house, all the sleigh bells jingling. Grandma came to the door and stood there smiling, calling to them to come in.

She said that Grandpa and Uncle George were already at work out in the maple woods. So Pa went to help them, while Laura and Mary and Ma, with Baby Carrie in her arms, went into Grandma's house and took off their wraps.

Laura loved Grandma's house. It was much larger than their house at home. There was one great big room, and then there was a little room that belonged to Uncle George, and there was another room for the aunts, Aunt Docia and Aunt Ruby. And then there was the kitchen, with a big cookstove.

It was fun to run the whole length of the big room from the large fireplace at one end all the way to Grandma's bed, under the window in the other end. The floor was made of wide, thick slabs that Grandpa had hewed from the logs with his axe. The floor was smoothed all over, and scrubbed clean and white, and the big bed under the window was soft with feathers.

The day seemed very short while Laura and Mary played in the big room and Ma helped Grandma and the aunts in the kitchen. The men had taken their dinners to the maple woods, so for dinner they did not set the table, but ate cold venison sandwiches and drank milk. But for supper Grandma made hasty pudding.

She stood by the stove, sifting the yellow corn meal from her fingers into a kettle of boiling, salted water. She stirred the water all the time with a big wooden spoon, and sifted in the meal until the kettle was full of a thick, yellow, bubbling mass. Then she set it on the back of the stove where it would cook slowly.

It smelled good. The whole house smelled good, with the sweet and spicy smells from the kitchen, and the smell of the hickory logs burning with clear, bright flames in the fireplace, and the smell of a clove-apple beside Grandma's mending basket on the table. The sunshine came in through the sparkling window panes, and everything was large and spacious and clean.

At supper time Pa and Grandpa came from the woods. Each had on his shoulders a wooden yoke that Grandpa

had made. It was cut to fit around their necks in the back, and hollowed out to fit over their shoulders. From each end hung a chain with a hook, and on each hook hung a big wooden bucket full of hot maple syrup.

Pa and Grandpa had brought the syrup from the big kettle in the woods. They steadied the buckets with their hands, but the weight hung from the yokes on their shoulders.

Grandma made room for a huge brass kettle on the stove. Pa and Grandpa poured the syrup into the brass kettle, and it was so large that it held all the syrup from the four big buckets.

Then Uncle George came with a smaller bucket of syrup, and everybody ate the hot hasty pudding with maple syrup for supper.

Uncle George was home from the army. He wore his blue army coat with the brass buttons, and he had bold, merry blue eyes. He was big and broad and he walked with a swagger.

Laura looked at him all the time she was eating her hasty pudding, because she had heard Pa say to Ma that he was wild.

'George is wild, since he came back from the war,' Pa had said, shaking his head as if he were sorry, but it couldn't be helped. Uncle George had run away to be a drummer boy in the army, when he was fourteen years old.

Laura had never seen a wild man before. She did not know whether she was afraid of Uncle George or not.

When supper was over, Uncle George went outside the door and blew his army bugle, long and loud. It made a lovely, ringing sound, far away through the Big Woods. The woods were dark and silent and the trees stood still as though they were listening. Then from very far away the sound came back, thin and clear and small, like a little bugle answering the big one.

'Listen,' Uncle George said, 'isn't that pretty?' Laura looked at him but she did not say anything, and when Uncle George stopped blowing the bugle she ran into the house.

Ma and Grandma cleared away the dishes and washed them, and swept the hearth, while Aunt Docia and Aunt Ruby made themselves pretty in their room.

Laura sat on their bed and watched them comb out their long hair and part it carefully. They parted it from their foreheads to the napes of their necks and then they parted it across from ear to ear. They braided their back hair in long braids and then they did the braids up carefully in big knots.

They had washed their hands and faces and scrubbed them well with soap, at the wash-basin on the bench in the kitchen. They had used store soap, not the slimy, soft, dark brown soap that Grandma made and kept in a big jar to use for common every day.

They fussed for a long time with their front hair, holding up the lamp and looking at their hair in the little looking-glass that hung on the log wall. They brushed it so smooth on each side of the straight white part that it shone like silk in the lamplight. The little puff on each side shone, too, and the ends were coiled and twisted neatly under the big knot in the back.

They they pulled on their beautiful white stockings, that they had knit of fine cotton thread in lacy, openwork patterns, and they buttoned up their best shoes. They helped each other with their corsets. Aunt Docia pulled as hard as she could on Aunt Ruby's corset strings, and then Aunt Docia hung on to the foot of the bed while Aunt Ruby pulled on hers.

'Pull, Ruby, pull!' Aunt Docia said, breathless. 'Pull harder.' So Aunt Ruby braced her feet and pulled harder. Aunt Docia kept measuring her waist with her hands, and at last she gasped, 'I guess that's the best you can do.'

She said, 'Caroline says Charles could span her waist with his hands, when they were married.'

Caroline was Laura's Ma, and when she heard this Laura felt proud.

Then Aunt Ruby and Aunt Docia put on their flannel

petticoats and their plain petticoats and their stiff, starched white petticoats with knitted lace all around the flounces. And they put on their beautiful dresses.

Aunt Docia's dress was a sprigged print, dark blue, with sprigs of red flowers and green leaves thick upon it. The basque was buttoned down the front with black buttons which looked so exactly like juicy big blackberries that Laura wanted to taste them.

Aunt Ruby's dress was wine-coloured calico, covered all over with a feathery pattern in lighter wine colour. It buttoned with gold-coloured buttons, and every button had a little castle and a tree carved on it.

Aunt Docia's pretty white collar was fastened in front with a large round cameo pin, which had a lady's head on it. But Aunt Ruby pinned her collar with a red rose made of sealing-wax. She had made it herself, on the head of a darning needle which had a broken eye, so it couldn't be used as a needle any more.

They looked lovely, sailing over the floor so smoothly with their large, round skirts. Their little waists rose up tight and slender in the middle, and their cheeks were red and their eyes bright, under the wings of shining, sleek hair.

Ma was beautiful, too, in her dark green delaine, with the little leaves that looked like strawberries scattered over it. The skirt was ruffled and flounced and draped and trimmed with knots of dark green ribbon, and nestling at her throat was a gold pin. The pin was flat, as long and as wide as Laura's two biggest fingers, and it was carved all over, and scalloped on the edges. Ma looked so rich and fine that Laura was afraid to touch her.

People had begun to come. They were coming on foot through the snowy woods, with their lanterns, and they were driving up to the door in sleds and in wagons. Sleigh bells were jingling all the time.

The big room filled with tall boots and swishing skirts, and ever so many babies were lying in rows on Grandma's bed. Uncle James and Aunt Libby had come with their

little girl, whose name was Laura Ingalls, too. The two Lauras leaned on the bed and looked at the babies, and the other Laura said her baby was prettier than Baby Carrie.

'She is not, either!' Laura said. 'Carrie's the prettiest baby in the whole world.'

'No, she isn't,' the other Laura said.

'Yes, she is!'

'No, she isn't!'

Ma came sailing over in her fine delaine, and said severely:

'Laura!'

So neither Laura said anything more.

Uncle George was blowing his bugle. It made a loud, ringing sound in the big room, and Uncle George joked and laughed and danced, blowing the bugle. Then Pa took his fiddle out of its box and began to play, and all the couples stood in squares on the floor and began to dance when Pa called the figures.

'Grand right and left!' Pa called out, and all the skirts began to swirl and all the boots began to stamp. The circles went round and round, all the skirts going one way and all the boots going the other way, and hands clasping and parting high up in the air.

'Swing your partners!' Pa called, and 'Each gent bow to the lady on the left!'

They all did as Pa said. Laura watched Ma's skirt swaying and her little waist bending and her dark head bowing, and she thought Ma was the loveliest dancer in the world. The fiddle was singing:

> "Oh, you Buffalo gals,
>   Aren't you coming out to-night,
>   Aren't you coming out to-night,
>   Aren't you coming out to-night,
>   Oh, you Buffalo gals,
>   Aren't you coming out to-night,
>   To dance by the light of the moon?"

The little circles and the big circles went round and round, and the skirts swirled and the boots stamped, and partners bowed and separated and met and bowed again.

In the kitchen Grandma was all by herself, stirring the boiling syrup in the big brass kettle. She stirred in time to the music. By the back door was a pail of clean snow, and sometimes Grandma took a spoonful of syrup from the kettle and poured it on some of the snow in a saucer.

Laura watched the dancers again. Pa was playing 'The Irish Washerwoman' now. He called:

"Doe see, ladies, doe see doe,
  Come down heavy on your heel and toe!"

Laura could not keep her feet still. Uncle George looked at her and laughed. Then he caught her by the hand and did a little dance with her, in the corner. She liked Uncle George.

Everybody was laughing, over by the kitchen door. They were dragging Grandma in from the kitchen. Grandma's dress was beautiful, too; a dark blue calico with autumn-coloured leaves scattered over it. Her cheeks were pink from laughing, and she was shaking her head. The wooden spoon was in her hand.

'I can't leave the syrup,' she said.

But Pa began to play 'The Arkansas Traveller', and everybody began to clap in time to the music. So Grandma bowed to them all and did a few steps by herself. She could dance as prettily as any of them. The clapping almost drowned the music of Pa's fiddle.

Suddenly Uncle George did a pigeon wing, and bowing low before Grandma he began to jig. Grandma tossed her spoon to somebody. She put her hands on her hips and faced Uncle George, and everybody shouted. Grandma was jigging.

Laura clapped her hands in time to the music, with all the other clapping hands. The fiddle sang as it had never sung before. Grandma's eyes were snapping and her cheeks were red, and underneath her skirts her heels were clicking as fast as the thumping of Uncle George's boots.

Everybody was excited. Uncle George kept on jigging and Grandma kept on facing him, jigging too. The fiddle did not stop. Uncle George began to breathe loudly, and he wiped sweat off his forehead. Grandma's eyes twinkled.

'You can't beat her, George!' somebody shouted.

Uncle George jigged faster. He jigged twice as fast as he had been jigging. So did Grandma. Everybody cheered again. All the women were laughing and clapping their hands, and all the men were teasing George. George did not care, but he did not have breath enough to laugh. He was jigging.

Pa's blue eyes were snapping and sparkling. He was standing up, watching George and Grandma, and the bow danced over the fiddle strings, Laura jumped up and down and squealed and clapped her hands.

Grandma kept on jigging. Her hands were on her hips and her chin was up and she was smiling. George kept on jigging, but his boots did not thump as loudly as they had thumped at first. Grandma's heels kept on clickety-clacking gaily. A drop of sweat dripped off George's fore-head and shone on his cheek.

All at once he threw up both arms and gasped, 'I'm beat!' He stopped jigging.

Everybody made a terrific noise, shouting and yelling and stamping, cheering Grandma. Grandma jigged just a little minute more, then she stopped. She laughed in gasps. Her eyes sparkled just like Pa's when he laughed. George was laughing, too, and wiping his forehead on his sleeve.

Suddenly Grandma stopped laughing. She turned and ran as fast as she could into the kitchen. The fiddle had stopped playing. All the women were talking at once and all the men teasing George, but everybody was still for a minute, when Grandma looked like that.

Then she came to the door between the kitchen and the big room, and said:

'The syrup is waxing. Come and help yourselves.'

Then everybody began to talk and laugh again. They all hurried to the kitchen for plates, and outdoors to fill the plates with snow. The kitchen door was open and the cold air came in.

Outdoors the stars were frosty in the sky and the air nipped Laura's cheeks and nose. Her breath was like smoke.

She and the other Laura, and all the other children, scooped up clean snow with their plates. Then they went back into the crowded kitchen.

Grandma stood by the brass kettle and with the big wooden spoon she poured hot syrup on each plate of snow. It cooled into soft candy, and as fast as it cooled they ate it.

They could eat all they wanted, for maple sugar never hurt anybody. There was plenty of syrup in the kettle, and plenty of snow outdoors. As soon as they ate one plateful, they filled their plates with snow again, and Grandma poured more syrup on it.

When they had eaten the soft maple candy until they could eat no more of it, then they helped themselves from the long table loaded with pumpkin pies and dried berry pies and cookies and cakes. There was salt-rising bread, too, and cold boiled pork, and pickles. Oo, how sour the pickles were!

They all ate till they could hold no more, and then they

began to dance again. But Grandma watched the syrup in the kettle. Many times she took a little of it out into a saucer, and stirred it round and round. Then she shook her head and poured the syrup back into the kettle.

The other room was loud and merry with the music of the fiddle and the noise of the dancing.

At last, as Grandma stirred, the syrup in the saucer turned into little grains like sand, and Grandma called:

'Quick, girls! It's graining!'

Aunt Ruby and Aunt Docia and Ma left the dance and came running. They set out pans, big pans and little pans, and as fast as Grandma filled them with the syrup they set out more. They set the filled ones away, to cool into maple sugar.

Then Grandma said:

'Now bring the patty-pans for the children.'

There was a patty-pan, or at least a broken cup or a saucer, for every little girl and boy. They all watched anxiously while Grandma ladled out the syrup. Perhaps there would not be enough. Then somebody would have to be unselfish and polite.

There was just enough syrup to go round. The last scrapings of the brass kettle exactly filled the very last patty-pan. Nobody was left out.

The fiddling and the dancing went on and on. Laura and the other Laura stood around and watched the dancers. Then they sat down on the floor in a corner, and watched. The dancing was so pretty and the music so gay that Laura knew she could never get tired of it.

All the beautiful skirts went swirling by, and the boots went stamping, and the fiddle kept on singing gaily.

Then Laura woke up, and she was lying across the foot of Grandma's bed. It was morning. Ma and Grandma and Baby Carrie were in the bed. Pa and Grandpa were sleeping rolled up in blankets on the floor by the fireplace. Mary was nowhere in sight; she was sleeping with Aunt Docia and Aunt Ruby in their bed.

Soon everybody was getting up. There were pancakes and maple syrup for breakfast, and then Pa brought the horses and sled to the door.

He helped Ma and Carrie in, while Grandpa picked up Mary and Uncle George picked up Laura and they tossed them over the edge of the sled into the straw. Pa tucked in the robes around them, and Grandpa and Grandma and Uncle George stood calling, 'Good-bye! Good-bye!' as they rode away into the Big Woods, going home.

The sun was warm, and the trotting horses threw up bits of muddy snow with their hoofs. Behind the sled Laura could see their footprints, and every footprint had gone through the thin snow into the mud.

'Before night,' Pa said, 'we'll see the last of the sugar snow.'

9

Going to Town

AFTER the sugar snow had gone, spring came. Birds sang in the leafing hazel bushes along the crooked rail fence. The grass grew green again and the woods were full of wild flowers. Buttercups and violets, thimble flowers and tiny starry grassflowers were everywhere.

As soon as the days were warm, Laura and Mary begged to be allowed to run barefoot. At first they might only run out around the woodpile and back, in their bare feet. Next day they could run farther, and soon their shoes were oiled and put away and they ran barefoot all day long.

Every night they had to wash their feet before they went to bed. Under the hems of their skirts their ankles and feet were as brown as their faces.

They had playhouses under the two big oak trees in front of the house. Mary's playhouse was under Mary's tree, and Laura's playhouse was under Laura's tree. The soft grass made a green carpet for them. The green leaves were the roofs, and through them they could see bits of the blue sky.

Pa made a swing of tough bark and hung it to a large, low branch of Laura's tree. It was her swing because it was her tree, but she had to be unselfish and let Mary swing in it whenever she wanted to.

Mary had a cracked saucer to play with, and Laura had a beautiful cup with only one big piece broken out of it. Charlotte and Nettie, and the two little wooden men Pa had made, lived in the playhouse with them. Every day they made fresh leaf hats for Charlotte and Nettie, and they made little leaf cups and saucers to set on their table. The table was a nice, smooth rock.

Sukey and Rosie, the cows, were turned loose in the woods now, to eat the wild grass and the juicy new leaves. There were two little calves in the barnyard, and seven little pigs with the mother hog in the pigpen.

In the clearing he had made last year, Pa was ploughing around the stumps and putting in his crops. One night he came in from work and said to Laura:

'What do you think I saw to-day?'

She couldn't guess.

'Well,' Pa said, 'when I was working in the clearing this morning, I looked up, and there at the edge of the woods stood a deer. She was a doe, a mother deer, and you'll never guess what was with her!'

'A baby deer!' Laura and Mary guessed together, clasping their hands.

'Yes,' Pa said, 'her fawn was with her. It was a pretty little thing, the softest fawn colour, with big dark eyes. It had the tiniest feet, not much bigger than my thumb, and it had slender little legs, and the softest muzzle.

'It stood there and looked at me with its large, soft eyes, wondering what I was. It was not afraid at all.'

'You wouldn't shoot a little baby deer, would you, Pa?' Laura said.

'No, never!' he answered. 'Nor its Ma, nor its Pa. No more hunting, now, till all the little wild animals have grown up. We'll just have to do without fresh meat till fall.'

Pa said that as soon as he had the crops in, they would all go to town. Laura and Mary could go, too. They were old enough now.

They were very much excited, and next day they tried to play going to town. They could not do it very well, because they were not quite sure what a town was like. They knew there was a store in town, but they had never seen a store.

Nearly every day after that, Charlotte and Nettie would ask if they could go to town. But Laura and Mary always said: 'No, dear, you can't go this year. Perhaps next year, if you are good, then you can go.'

Then one night Pa said, 'We'll go to town to-morrow.'

That night, though it was the middle of the week, Ma bathed Laura and Mary all over, and she put up their hair. She divided their long hair into wisps, combed each wisp with a wet comb and wound it tightly on a bit of rag. There were knobby little bumps all over their heads, whichever way they turned on their pillows. In the morning their hair would be curly.

They were so excited that they did not go to sleep at once. Ma was not sitting with her mending basket as usual. She was busy getting everything ready for a quick breakfast and laying out the best stockings and petticoats and dresses, and Pa's good shirt, and her own dark brown calico with the little purple flowers on it.

The days were longer now. In the morning Ma blew

out the lamp before they finished breakfast. It was a beautiful, clear spring morning.

Ma hurried Laura and Mary with their breakfast and she washed the dishes quickly. They put on their stockings and shoes while she made the beds. Then she helped them put on their best dresses—Mary's china-blue calico and Laura's dark red calico. Mary buttoned Laura up the back, and then Ma buttoned Mary.

Ma took the rags off their hair and combed it into long, round curls that hung down over their shoulders. She combed so fast that the snarls hurt dreadfully. Mary's hair was beautifully golden, but Laura's was only a dirt-coloured brown.

When their curls were done, Ma tied their sun-bonnets under their chins. She fastened her collar with the gold pin, and she was putting on her hat when Pa drove up to the gate.

He had curried the horses till they shone. He had swept the wagon box clean and laid a clean blanket on the wagon seat. Ma, with Baby Carrie in her arms, sat up on the wagon seat with Pa, and Laura and Mary sat on a board fastened across the wagon box behind the seat.

They were happy as they drove through the spring-time woods. Carrie laughed and bounced, Ma was smiling, and Pa whistled while he drove the horses. The sun was bright and warm on the road. Sweet, cool smells came out of the leafy woods.

Rabbits stood up in the road ahead, their little front paws dangling down and their noses sniffing, and the sun shone through their tall, twitching ears. Then they bounded away, with a flash of little white tail. Twice Laura and Mary saw deer looking at them with their large, dark eyes, from the shadows among the trees.

It was seven miles to town. The town was named Pepin, and it was on the shore of Lake Pepin.

After a long time Laura began to see glimpses of blue water between the trees. The hard road turned to soft sand. The wagon wheels went deep down in it and the horses pulled and sweated. Often Pa stopped them to rest for a few minutes.

Then all at once the road came out of the woods and Laura saw the lake. It was as blue as the sky, and it went to the edge of the world. As far as she could see, there was nothing but flat, blue water. Very far away, the sky and the water met, and there was a darker blue line.

The sky was large overhead. Laura had never known that the sky was so big. There was so much empty space

all around her that she felt small and frightened, and
glad that Pa and Ma were there.

Suddenly the sunshine was hot. The sun was almost
overhead in the large, empty sky, and the cool woods
stood back from the edge of the lake. Even the Big Woods
seemed smaller under so much sky.

Pa stopped the horses, and turned around on the wagon
seat. He pointed ahead with his whip.

'There you are, Laura and Mary!' he said. 'There's
the town of Pepin.'

Laura stood up on the board and Pa held her safe by
the arm, so she could see the town. When she saw it, she
could hardly breathe. She knew how Yankee Doodle felt,
when he could not see the town because there were so
many houses.

Right on the edge of the lake, there was one great big
building. That was the store, Pa told her. It was not
made of logs. It was made of wide, grey boards, running
up and down. The sand spread all around it.

Behind the store there was a clearing, larger than Pa's
clearing in the woods at home. Standing among the
stumps, there were more houses than Laura could count.
They were not made of logs, either; they were made of
boards, like the store.

Laura had never imagined so many houses, and they
were so close together. Of course, they were much smaller
than the store. One of them was made of new boards
that had not had time to get grey; it was the yellow colour
of newly-cut wood.

People were living in all these houses. Smoke rose up
from their chimneys. Though it was not Monday, some
woman had spread out a washing on the bushes and
stumps by her house.

Several girls and boys were playing in the sunshine, in

the open space between the store and the houses. They were jumping from one stump to the next stump and shouting.

'Well, that's Pepin,' Pa said.

Laura just nodded her head. She looked and looked, and could not say a word. After a while she sat down again, and the horses went on.

They left the wagon on the shore of the lake. Pa un-hitched the horses and tied one to each side of the wagon box. Then he took Laura and Mary by the hand, and Ma came beside them carrying Baby Carrie. They walked through the deep sand to the store. The warm sand came in over the tops of Laura's shoes.

There was a wide platform in front of the store, and at one end of it steps went up to it out of the sand. Laura's heart was beating so fast that she could hardly climb the steps. She was trembling all over.

This was the store to which Pa came to trade his furs. When they went in, the storekeeper knew him. The storekeeper came out from behind the counter and spoke to him and to Ma, and then Laura and Mary had to show their manners.

Mary said, 'How do you do?' but Laura could not say anything.

The storekeeper said to Pa and Ma, 'That's a pretty little girl you've got there,' and he admired Mary's golden curls. But he did not say anything about Laura, or about her curls. They were ugly and brown.

The store was full of things to look at. All along one side of it were shelves full of coloured prints and calicoes. There were beautiful pinks and blues and reds and browns and purples. On the floor along the sides of the plank counters there were kegs of nails, and kegs of round, grey shot, and there were big wooden pails full of candy. There were sacks of salt, and sacks of store sugar.

In the middle of the store was a plough made of shiny wood, with a glittering bright ploughshare, and there were steel axe heads, and hammer heads, and saws, and all kinds of knives—hunting knives and skinning knives and butcher knives and jack-knives. There were big boots and little boots, big shoes and little shoes.

Laura could have looked for weeks and not seen all the things that were in that store. She had not known there were so many things in the world.

Pa and Ma traded for a long time. The storekeeper took down bolts and bolts of beautiful calicoes and spread them out for Ma to finger and look at and price. Laura and Mary looked, but must not touch. Every new colour and pattern was prettier than the last, and there were so many of them! Laura did not know how Ma could ever choose.

Ma chose two patterns of calico to make shirts for Pa, and a piece of brown denim to make him a jumper. Then she got some white cloth to make sheets and underwear.

Pa got enough calico to make Ma a new apron. Ma said:

'Oh, no, Charles, I don't really need it.'

But Pa laughed and said she must pick it out, or he would get her the turkey red piece with the big yellow pattern. Ma smiled and flushed pink, and she picked out a pattern of rosebuds and leaves on a soft, fawn-coloured ground.

Then Pa got for himself a pair of galluses and some tobacco to smoke in his pipe. And Ma got a pound of tea, and a little paper package of store sugar to have in the house when company came. It was a pale brown sugar, not dark brown like the maple sugar Ma used for every day.

When all the trading was done, the storekeeper gave

Mary and Laura each a piece of candy. They were so astonished and so pleased that they just stood looking at their candies. Then Mary remembered and said, 'Thank you.'

Laura could not speak. Everybody was waiting, and she could not make a sound. Ma had to ask her:

'What do you say, Laura?'

Then Laura opened her mouth and gulped and whispered, 'Thank you.'

After that they went out of the store. Both pieces of candy were white, and flat and thin and heart-shaped.

There was printing on them, in red letters. Ma read it for them. Mary's said:

> "Roses are red,
> Violets are blue,
> Sugar is sweet,
> And so are you."

Laura's said only:

> "Sweets to the sweet."

The pieces of candy were exactly the same size. Laura's printing was larger than Mary's.

They all went back through the sand to the wagon on the lake shore. Pa fed the horses, on the bottom of the wagon box, some oats he had brought for their dinner. Ma opened the picnic box.

They all sat on the warm sand near the wagon and ate bread and butter and cheese, hard-boiled eggs and cookies. The waves of Lake Pepin curled up on the shore at their feet and slid back with the smallest hissing sound.

After dinner, Pa went back to the store to talk awhile with other men. Ma sat holding Carrie quietly until she went to sleep. But Laura and Mary ran along the lake shore, picking up pretty pebbles that had been rolled back and forth by the waves until they were polished smooth.

There were no pebbles like that in the Big Woods.

When she found a pretty one, Laura put it in her pocket, and there were so many, each prettier than the last, that she filled her pocket full. Then Pa called, and they ran back to the wagon, for the horses were hitched up and it was time to go home.

Laura was so happy, when she ran through the sand to

Pa, with all those beautiful pebbles in her pocket. But when Pa picked her up and tossed her into the wagon, a dreadful thing happened.

The heavy pebbles tore her pocket right out of her dress. The pocket fell, and the pebbles rolled all over the bottom of the wagon box.

Laura cried because she had torn her best dress.

Ma gave Carrie to Pa and came quickly to look at the torn place. Then she said it was all right.

'Stop crying, Laura,' she said. 'I can fix it.' She showed Laura that the dress was not torn at all, nor the pocket. The pocket was a little bag, sewed into the seam of the dress skirt, and hanging under it. Only the seams had ripped. Ma could sew the pocket in again, as good as new.

'Pick up the pretty pebbles, Laura,' Ma said. 'And another time, don't be so greedy.'

So Laura gathered up the pebbles, put them in the pocket, and carried the pocket in her lap. She did not mind very much when Pa laughed at her for being such a greedy little girl that she took more than she could carry away.

Nothing like that ever happened to Mary. Mary was a good little girl who always kept her dress clean and neat and minded her manners. Mary had lovely golden curls, and her candy heart had a poem on it.

Mary looked very good and sweet, unrumpled and clean, sitting on the board beside Laura. Laura did not think it was fair.

But it had been a wonderful day, the most wonderful day in her whole life. She thought about the beautiful lake, and the town she had seen, and the big store full of so many things. She held the pebbles carefully in her lap, and her candy heart wrapped carefully in her handkerchief until she got home and could put it away to keep always. It was too pretty to eat.

The wagon jolted along on the homeward road through the Big Woods. The sun set, and the woods grew darker, but before the last of the twilight was gone the moon rose. And they were safe, because Pa had his gun.

The soft moonlight came down through the treetops and made patches of light and shade on the road ahead. The horses' hoofs made a cheerful clippety-clop.

Laura and Mary did not say anything because they were very tired, and Ma sat silently holding Baby Carrie, sleeping in her arms. But Pa sang softly:

> " 'Mid pleasures and palaces, though we may roam,
> Be it ever so humble, there's no place like home."

10

Summertime

Now it was summertime, and people went visiting. Sometimes Uncle Henry, or Uncle George, or Grandpa, came riding out of the Big Woods to see Pa. Ma would come to the door and ask how all the folks were, and she would say:

'Charles is in the clearing.'

Then she would cook more dinner than usual, and dinner time would be longer. Pa and Ma and the visitor would sit talking a little while before they went back to work.

Sometimes Ma let Laura and Mary go across the road and down the hill, to see Mrs Peterson. The Petersons had just moved in. Their house was new, and always very neat, because Mrs Peterson had no little girls to mess it up. She was a Swede, and she let Laura and Mary look at the pretty things she had brought from Sweden—laces, and coloured embroideries, and china.

Mrs Peterson talked Swedish to them, and they talked English to her, and they understood each other perfectly. She always gave them each a cookie when they left, and they nibbled the cookies very slowly while they walked home.

Laura nibbled away exactly half of hers, and Mary nibbled exactly half of hers, and the other halves they saved for Baby Carrie. Then when they got home, Carrie had two half-cookies, and that was a whole cookie.

This wasn't right. All they wanted to do was to divide

the cookies fairly with Carrie. Still, if Mary saved half her cookie, while Laura ate the whole of hers, or if Laura saved half, and Mary ate her whole cookie, that wouldn't be fair, either.

They didn't know what to do. So each saved half, and gave it to Baby Carrie. But they always felt that some-how that wasn't quite fair.

Sometimes a neighbour sent word that the family was coming to spend the day. Then Ma did extra cleaning and cooking, and opened the package of store sugar. And on the day set, a wagon would come driving up to the gate in the morning and there would be strange children to play with.

When Mr and Mrs Huleatt came, they brought Eva and Clarence with them. Eva was a pretty girl, with dark eyes and black curls. She played carefully and kept

her dress clean and smooth. Mary liked that, but Laura liked better to play with Clarence.

Clarence was red-headed and freckled, and always laughing. His clothes were pretty, too. He wore a blue suit buttoned all the way up the front with bright gilt buttons, and trimmed with braid, and he had copper-toed shoes.

The strips of copper across the toes were so glittering bright that Laura wished she were a boy. Little girls didn't wear copper-toes.

Laura and Clarence ran and shouted and climbed trees, while Mary and Eva walked nicely together and talked. Ma and Mrs Huleatt visited and looked at a *Godey's Lady's Book* which Mrs Huleatt had brought, and Pa and Mr Huleatt looked at the horses and the crops and smoked their pipes.

Once Aunt Lotty came to spend the day. That morning Laura had to stand still a long time while Ma unwound her hair from the cloth strings and combed it into long curls. Mary was all ready, sitting primly on a chair, with her golden curls shining and her china-blue dress fresh and crisp.

Laura liked her own red dress. But Ma pulled her hair dreadfully, and it was brown instead of golden, so that no one noticed it. Everyone noticed and admired Mary's.

'There!' Ma said at last. 'Your hair is curled beautifully, and Lotty is coming. Run meet her, both of you, and ask her which she likes best, brown curls or golden curls.'

Laura and Mary ran out of the door and down the path, for Aunt Lotty was already at the gate. Aunt Lotty was a big girl, much taller than Mary. Her dress was a beautiful pink and she was swinging a pink sun-bonnet by one string.

'Which do you like best, Aunt Lotty,' Mary asked, 'brown curls, or golden curls?' Ma had told them to ask that, and Mary was a very good little girl who always did exactly as she was told.

Laura waited to hear what Aunt Lotty would say, and she felt miserable.

'I like both kinds best,' Aunt Lotty said, smiling. She took Laura and Mary by the hand, one on either side, and they danced along to the door where Ma stood.

The sunshine came streaming through the windows into the house, and everything was so neat and pretty. The table was covered with a red cloth, and the cookstove was polished shining black. Through the bedroom door Laura could see the trundle bed in its place under the big bed. The pantry door stood wide open, giving the sight and smell of goodies on the shelves, and Black Susan came purring down the stairs from the attic, where she had been taking a nap.

It was all so pleasant, and Laura felt so gay and good that no one would ever have thought she could be as naughty as she was that evening.

Aunt Lotty had gone, and Laura and Mary were tired and cross. They were at the woodpile, gathering a pan of chips to kindle the fire in the morning. They always hated to pick up chips, but every day they had to do it. To-night they hated it more than ever.

Laura grabbed the biggest chip, and Mary said:

'I don't care. Aunt Lotty likes my hair best, anyway. Golden hair is lots prettier than brown.'

Laura's throat swelled tight, and she could not speak. She knew golden hair was prettier than brown. She couldn't speak, so she reached out quickly and slapped Mary's face.

Then she heard Pa say, 'Come here, Laura.'

She went slowly, dragging her feet. Pa was sitting just inside the door. He had seen her slap Mary.

'You remember,' Pa said, 'I told you girls you must never strike each other.'

Laura began, 'But Mary said——'

'That makes no difference,' said Pa. 'It is what I say that you must mind.'

Then he took down a strap from the wall, and he whipped Laura with the strap.

Laura sat on a chair in the corner and sobbed. When she stopped sobbing, she sulked. The only thing in the world to be glad about was that Mary had to fill the chip pan all by herself.

At last, when it was getting dark, Pa said again, 'Come here, Laura.' His voice was kind, and when Laura came he took her on his knee and hugged her close. She sat in the crook of his arm, her head against his shoulder and his long brown whiskers partly covering her eyes, and everything was all right again.

She told Pa all about it, and she asked him, 'You don't like golden hair better than brown, do you?'

Pa's blue eyes shone down at her, and he said, 'Well, Laura, my hair is brown.'

She had not thought of that. Pa's hair was brown, and his whiskers were brown, and she thought brown was a lovely colour. But she was glad that Mary had had to gather all the chips.

In the summer evenings Pa did not tell stories or play the fiddle. Summer days were long, and he was tired after he had worked hard all day in the fields.

Ma was busy, too. Laura and Mary helped her weed the garden, and they helped her feed the calves and the hens. They gathered the eggs, and they helped make cheese.

When the grass was tall and thick in the woods and the cows were giving plenty of milk, that was the time to make cheese.

Somebody must kill a calf, for cheese could not be made without rennet, and rennet is the lining of a young calf's stomach. The calf must be very young, so that it had never eaten anything but milk.

Laura was afraid that Pa must kill one of the little calves in the barn. They were so sweet. One was fawn-coloured and one was red, and their hair was so soft and their large eyes so wondering. Laura's heart beat fast when Ma talked to Pa about making cheese.

Pa would not kill either of his calves, because they were

heifers and would grow into cows. He went to Grandpa's and to Uncle Henry's, to talk about the cheese-making, and Uncle Henry said he would kill one of his calves. There would be enough rennet for Aunt Polly and Grandma and Ma.

So Pa went again to Uncle Henry's, and came back with a piece of the little calf's stomach. It was like a piece of soft, greyish-white leather, all ridged and rough on one side.

When the cows were milked at night, Ma set the milk away in pans. In the morning she skimmed off the cream to make into butter later. Then when the morning's milk had cooled, she mixed it with the skimmed milk and set it all on the stove to heat.

A bit of the rennet, tied in a cloth, was soaking in warm water.

When the milk was heated enough, Ma squeezed every drop of water from the rennet in the cloth, and she poured the water into the milk. She stirred it well and left it in a warm place by the stove. In a little while it thickened into a smooth, quivery mass.

With a long knife Ma cut this mass into little squares, and let it stand while the curd separated from the whey. Then she poured it all into a cloth and let the thin, yellowish whey drain out.

When no more whey dripped from the cloth, Ma emptied the curd into a big pan and salted it, turning and mixing it well.

Laura and Mary were always there, helping all they could. They loved to eat bits of the curd when Ma was salting it. It squeaked in their teeth.

Under the cherry tree outside the back door Pa had put up the board to press the cheese on. He had cut two grooves the length of the board, and laid the board on blocks, one end a little higher than the other. Under the lower end stood an empty pail.

Ma put her wooden cheese hoop on the board, spread a clean, wet cloth all over the inside of it, and filled it heaping full of the chunks of salted curd. She covered this with another clean, wet cloth, and laid on top of it a round board, cut small enough to go inside the cheese

hoop. Then she lifted a heavy rock on top of the board.

All day long the round board settled slowly under the weight of the rock, and whey pressed out and ran down the grooves of the board into the pail.

Next morning, Ma would take out the round, pale yellow cheese, as large as a milk pan. Then she made more curd, and filled the cheese hoop again.

Every morning she took the new cheese out of the press, and trimmed it smooth. She sewed a cloth tightly around it, and rubbed the cloth all over with fresh butter. Then she put the cheese on a shelf in the pantry.

Every day she wiped every cheese carefully with a wet cloth, then rubbed it all over with fresh butter once more, and laid it down on its other side. After a great many days, the cheese was ripe, and there was a hard rind all over it.

Then Ma wrapped each cheese in paper and laid it away on the high shelf. There was nothing more to do with it but eat it.

Laura and Mary liked cheese-making. They liked to eat the curd that squeaked in their teeth and they liked to eat the edges Ma pared off the big, round, yellow cheeses to make them smooth, before she sewed them up in cloth.

Ma laughed at them for eating green cheese.

'The moon is made of green cheese, some people say,' she told them.

The new cheese did look like the round moon when it came up behind the trees. But it was not green; it was yellow, like the moon.

'It's green,' Ma said, 'because it isn't ripened yet. When it's cured and ripened, it won't be a green cheese.'

'Is the moon really made of green cheese?' Laura asked, and Ma laughed.

'I think people say that, because it looks like a green cheese,' she said. 'But appearances are deceiving.' Then while she wiped all the green cheeses and rubbed them with butter, she told them about the dead, cold moon that is like a little world on which nothing grows.

The first day Ma made cheese, Laura tasted the whey.

She tasted it without saying anything to Ma, and when Ma turned around and saw her face, Ma laughed. That night while she was washing the supper dishes and Mary and Laura were wiping them, Ma told Pa that Laura had tasted the whey and didn't like it.

'You wouldn't starve to death on Ma's whey, like Old Grimes did on his wife's,' Pa said.

Laura begged him to tell her about Old Grimes. So, though Pa was tired, he took his fiddle out of its box and played and sang for Laura:

> "Old Grimes is dead, that good old man,
> We ne'er shall see him more,
> He used to wear an old grey coat,
> All buttoned down before.

> "Old Grimes's wife made skim-milk cheese,
> Old Grimes, he drank the whey,
> There came an east wind from the west,
> And blew Old Grimes away."

'There you have it!' said Pa. 'She was a mean, tight-fisted woman. If she hadn't skimmed all the milk, a little cream would have run off in the whey, and Old Grimes might have staggered along.

'But she skimmed off every bit of cream, and poor Old Grimes got so thin the wind blew him away. Plumb starved to death.'

Then Pa looked at Ma and said, 'Nobody'd starve to death when you were around, Caroline.'

'Well, no,' Ma said. 'No, Charles, not if you were there to provide for us.'

Pa was pleased. It was all so pleasant, the doors and windows wide open to the summer evening, the dishes making little cheerful sounds together as Ma washed them and Mary and Laura wiped, and Pa putting away the fiddle and smiling and whistling softly to himself.

After a while he said, 'I'm going over to Henry's to-morrow morning, Caroline, to borrow his grubbing hoe. Those sprouts are getting waist-high around the stumps in the wheat-field. A man just has to keep everlasting at it, or the woods'll take back the place.'

Early next morning he started to walk to Uncle Henry's. But before long he came hurrying back, hitched the horses to the wagon, threw in his axe, the two wash-tubs, the washboiler and all the pails and wooden buckets there were.

'I don't know if I'll need 'em all, Caroline,' he said, 'but I'd hate to want 'em and not have 'em.'

'Oh, what is it? What is it?' Laura asked, jumping up and down with excitement.

'Pa's found a bee tree,' Ma said. 'Maybe he'll bring us some honey.'

It was noon before Pa came driving home. Laura had been watching for him, and she ran out to the wagon as soon as it stopped by the barnyard. But she could not see into it.

Pa called, 'Caroline, if you'll come take this pail of honey, I'll go unhitch.'

Ma came out to the wagon, disappointed. She said:

'Well, Charles, even a pail of honey is something.' Then she looked into the wagon and threw up her hands. Pa laughed.

All the pails and buckets were heaping full of dripping, golden honeycomb. Both tubs were piled full, and so was the wash-boiler.

Pa and Ma went back and forth, carrying the two loaded tubs and the wash-boiler and all the buckets and pails into the house. Ma heaped a plate high with the golden pieces, and covered all the rest neatly with cloths.

For dinner they all had as much of the delicious honey as they could eat, and Pa told them how he found the bee tree.

'I didn't take my gun,' he said, 'because I wasn't hunting, and now it's summer there wasn't much danger of meeting trouble. Panthers and bears are so fat, this time of year, that they're lazy and good-natured.

'Well, I took a short cut through the woods, and I nearly ran into a big bear. I came around a clump of underbrush, and there he was, not as far from me as across this room.

'He looked around at me, and I guess he saw I didn't have a gun. Anyway, he didn't pay any more attention to me.

'He was standing at the foot of a big tree, and bees were buzzing all around him. They couldn't sting through his thick fur, and he kept brushing them away from his head with one paw.

'I stood watching him, and he put the other paw into a hole in the tree and drew it out all dripping with honey. He licked the honey off his paw and reached in for more. But by that time I had found me a club. I wanted that honey myself.

'So I made a great racket, banging the club against a tree and yelling. The bear was so fat and so full of honey that he just dropped on all fours and waddled off among the trees. I chased him some distance and got him going fast, away from the bee tree, and then I came back for the wagon.'

Laura asked him how he got the honey away from the bees.

'That was easy,' Pa said. 'I left the horses back in the

woods, where they wouldn't get stung, and then I chopped the tree down and split it open.'

'Didn't the bees sting you?'

'No,' said Pa. 'Bees never sting me.

'The whole tree was hollow, and filled from top to bottom with honey. The bees must have been storing

honey there for years. Some of it was old and dark, but I guess I got enough good, clean honey to last us a long time.'

Laura was sorry for the poor bees. She said:

'They worked so hard, and now they won't have any honey.'

But Pa said there was lots of honey left for the bees, and there was another large, hollow tree near by, into which they could move. He said it was time they had a clean, new home.

They would take the old honey he had left in the old tree, make it into fresh, new honey, and store it in their new house. They would save every drop of the spilled honey and put it away, and they would have plenty of honey again, long before winter came.

11

Harvest

Pa and Uncle Henry traded work. When the grain got ripe in the fields, Uncle Henry came to work with Pa, and Aunt Polly and all the cousins came to spend the day. Then Pa went to help Uncle Henry cut his grain, and Ma took Laura and Mary and Carrie to spend the day with Aunt Polly.

Ma and Aunt Polly worked in the house and all the cousins played together in the yard till dinner time. Aunt Polly's yard was a fine place to play, because the stumps were so thick. The cousins played jumping from stump to stump without ever touching the ground.

Even Laura, who was littlest, could do this easily in the places where the smallest trees had grown close together. Cousin Charley was a big boy, going on eleven years old, and he could jump from stump to stump all over the yard. The smaller stumps he could jump two at a time, and he could walk on the top rail of the fence without being afraid.

Pa and Uncle Henry were out in the field, cutting the oats with cradles. A cradle was a sharp steel blade fastened to a framework of wooden slats that caught and held the stalks of grain when the blade cut them. Pa and Uncle Henry carried the cradles by their long, curved handles, and swung the blades into the standing oats. When they had cut enough to make a pile, they slid the cut stalks off the slats, into neat heaps on the ground.

It was hard work, walking around and around the field in the hot sun, and with both hands swinging the heavy cradles into the grain and cutting it, then sliding it into the piles.

After the grain was cut, they must go over the field again. This time they would stoop over each pile, and

taking up a handful of the stalks in each hand they would knot them together to make a longer strand. Then gathering up the pile of grain in their arms they would bind it tightly around with the band they had made, and tie the band, and tuck in its ends.

After they made seven such bundles, then the bundles

must be shocked. To make a shock, they stood five bundles upright, snugly together with the oat-heads up. Then over these they put two more bundles, spreading out the stalks to make a little roof and shelter the five bundles from dew and rain.

Every stalk of the cut grain must always be safely in the shock before dark, for lying on the dewy ground all night would spoil it.

Pa and Uncle Henry were working very hard, because the air was so heavy and hot and still that they expected rain. The oats were ripe, and if they were not cut and in the shock before rain came, the crop would be lost. Then Uncle Henry's horses would be hungry all winter.

At noon Pa and Uncle Henry came to the house in a great hurry, and swallowed their dinner as quickly as they could. Uncle Henry said that Charley must help them that afternoon.

Laura looked at Pa, when Uncle Henry said that. At home, Pa had said to Ma that Uncle Henry and Aunt Polly spoiled Charley. When Pa was eleven years old, he had done a good day's work every day in the fields, driving a team. But Charley did hardly any work at all.

Now Uncle Henry said that Charley must come to the field. He could save them a great deal of time. He could go to the spring for water, and he could fetch them the water-jug when they needed a drink. He could fetch the whetstone when the blades needed sharpening.

All the children looked at Charley. Charley did not want to go to the field. He wanted to stay in the yard and play. But, of course, he did not say so.

Pa and Uncle Henry did not rest at all. They ate in a hurry and went right back to work, and Charley went with them.

Now Mary was oldest, and she wanted to play a quiet, ladylike play. So in the afternoon the cousins made a playhouse in the yard. The stumps were chairs and tables and stoves, and leaves were dishes, and sticks were the children.

On the way home that night, Laura and Mary heard Pa tell Ma what happened in the field.

Instead of helping Pa and Uncle Henry, Charley was making all the trouble he could. He got in their way so they couldn't swing the cradles. He hid the whetstone, so they had to hunt for it when the blades needed sharpening. He didn't bring the water-jug till Uncle Henry shouted at him three or four times, and then he was sullen.

After that he followed them around, talking and asking questions. They were working too hard to pay any attention to him, so they told him to go away and not bother them.

But they dropped their cradles and ran to him across the field when they heard him scream. The woods were all around the field, and there were snakes in the oats.

When they got to Charley, there was nothing wrong, and he laughed at them. He said:

'I fooled you that time!'

Pa said if he had been Uncle Henry, he would have tanned that boy's hide for him, right then and there. But Uncle Henry did not do it.

So they took a drink of water and went back to work.

Three times Charley screamed, and they ran to him as fast as they could, and he laughed at them. He thought it was a good joke. And still, Uncle Henry did not tan his hide.

Then a fourth time he screamed, louder than ever. Pa and Uncle Henry looked at him, and he was jumping up and down, screaming. They saw nothing wrong with him and they had been fooled so many times that they went on with their work.

Charley kept on screaming, louder and shriller. Pa did not say anything, but Uncle Henry said, 'Let him scream.' So they went on working and let him scream.

He kept on jumping up and down, screaming. He did not stop. At last Uncle Henry said:

'Maybe something really is wrong.' They laid down their cradles and went across the field to him.

And all that time Charley had been jumping up and down on a yellow jackets' nest!

The yellow jackets lived in a nest in the ground and Charley stepped on it by mistake. Then all the little bees in their bright yellow jackets came swarming out with their red-hot stings, and they hurt Charley so that he couldn't get away.

He was jumping up and down and hundreds of bees were stinging him all over. They were stinging his face and his hands and his neck and his nose, they were crawling up his pants' legs and stinging and crawling down the back of his neck and stinging. The more he jumped and screamed the harder they stung.

Pa and Uncle Henry took him by the arms and ran him away from the yellow jackets' nest. They undressed him, and his clothes were full of yellow jackets and their stings were swelling up all over him. They killed the bees that were stinging him and they shook the bees out of his clothes and then they dressed him again and sent him to the house.

Laura and Mary and the cousins were playing quietly in the yard, when they heard a loud, blubbering cry. Charley came bawling into the yard and his face was so swollen that the tears could hardly squeeze out of his eyes.

His hands were puffed up, and his neck was puffed out, and his cheeks were big, hard puffs. His fingers stood out stiff and swollen. There were little hard, white dents all over his puffed-out face and neck.

Laura and Mary and the cousins stood and looked at him.

Ma and Aunt Polly came running out of the house and

asked him what was the matter. Charley blubbered and bawled. Ma said it was yellow jackets. She ran to the garden and got a big pan of earth, while Aunt Polly took Charley into the house and undressed him.

They made a big panful of mud, and plastered him all over with it. They rolled him up in an old sheet and put him to bed. His eyes were swollen shut and his nose was a funny shape. Ma and Aunt Polly covered his whole face with mud and tied the mud on with cloths. Only the end of his nose and his mouth showed.

Aunt Polly steeped some herbs, to give him for his fever. Laura and Mary and the cousins stood around for some time, looking at him.

It was dark that night when Pa and Uncle Henry came from the field. All the oats were in the shock, and now the rain could come and it would not do any harm.

Pa could not stay to supper; he had to get home and do the milking. The cows were already waiting, at home, and when cows are not milked on time they do not give so much milk. He hitched up quickly and they all got into the wagon.

Pa was very tired and his hands ached so that he could not drive very well, but the horses knew the way home. Ma sat beside him with Baby Carrie, and Laura and Mary sat on the board behind them. Then they heard Pa tell about what Charley had done.

Laura and Mary were horrified. They were often naughty, themselves, but they had never imagined that anyone could be as naughty as Charley had been. He hadn't worked to help save the oats. He hadn't minded his father quickly when his father spoke to him. He had bothered Pa and Uncle Henry when they were hard at work.

Then Pa told about the yellow jackets' nest, and he said:

'It served the little liar right.'

After she was in the trundle bed that night, Laura lay and listened to the rain drumming on the roof and streaming from the eaves, and she thought about what Pa had said.

She thought about what the yellow jackets had done

to Charley. She thought it served Charley right, too. It served him right because he had been so monstrously naughty. And the bees had a right to sting him, when he jumped on their home.

But she didn't understand why Pa had called him a little liar. She didn't understand how Charley could be a liar, when he had not said a word.

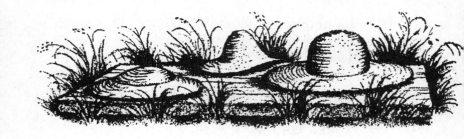

12

The Wonderful Machine

NEXT day Pa cut the heads from several bundles of the oats, and brought the clean, bright, yellow straws to Ma. She put them in a tub of water, to soften them and keep them soft. Then she sat in the chair by the side of the tub, and braided the straws.

She took up several of them, knotted their ends together, and began to braid. The straws were different lengths, and when she came near the end of one straw, she put a new, long one from the tub in its place and went on braiding.

She let the end of the braid fall back into the water and kept on braiding till she had many yards of braid. All her spare time for days, she was braiding straws.

She made a fine, narrow, smooth braid, using seven of the smallest straws. She used nine larger straws for a wider braid, and made it notched all along the edges. And from the very largest straws she made the widest braid of all.

When all the straws were braided, she threaded a needle with strong white thread, and beginning at the end of a braid she sewed it round and round, holding the braid so it would lie flat after it was sewed. This made a little mat, and Ma said it was the top of the crown of a hat.

Then she held the braid tighter on one edge, and kept on sewing it around and around. The braid drew in and made the sides of the crown. When the crown was high enough, Ma held the braid loosely again as she kept on sewing around, and the braid lay flat and was the hat brim.

When the brim was wide enough, Ma cut the braid and sewed the end fast so that it could not unbraid itself.

Ma sewed hats for Mary and Laura of the finest, narrowest braid. For Pa and for herself she made hats of the wider, notched braid. That was Pa's Sunday hat. Then she made him two everyday hats of the coarser, widest braid.

When she finished a hat, Ma set it on a board to dry, shaping it nicely as she did so, and when it dried it stayed in the shape she gave it.

Ma could make beautiful hats. Laura liked to watch her, and she learned how to braid the straw and made a little hat for Charlotte.

The days were growing shorter and the nights were cooler. One night Jack Frost passed by, and in the morning there were bright colours here and there among the green leaves of the Big Woods. Then all the leaves stopped being green. They were yellow and scarlet and crimson and golden and brown.

Along the rail fence the sumac held up its dark red cones of berries above bright flame-coloured leaves. Acorns were falling from the oaks, and Laura and Mary made little acorn cups and saucers for the playhouses. Walnuts and hickory nuts were dropping to the ground in the Big Woods, and squirrels were scampering busily everywhere, gathering their winter's store of nuts and hiding them away in hollow trees.

Laura and Mary went with Ma to gather walnuts and hickory nuts and hazelnuts. They spread them in the sun to dry, then they beat off the dried outer hulls and stored the nuts in the attic for winter.

It was fun to gather the large round walnuts and the smaller hickory nuts, and the little hazelnuts that grew in bunches on the bushes. The soft outer hulls of the walnuts were full of a brown juice that stained their hands, but the hazelnut hulls smelled good and tasted good, too, when Laura used her teeth to pry a nut loose.

Everyone was busy now, for all the garden vegetables must be stored away. Laura and Mary helped, picking up the dusty potatoes after Pa had dug them from the ground, and pulling the long yellow carrots and the round, purple-topped turnips, and they helped Ma cook the pumpkin for pumpkin pies.

With the butcher knife Ma cut the big, orange-coloured pumpkins into halves. She cleaned the seeds out of the centre and cut the pumpkin into long slices, from which she pared the rind. Laura helped her cut the slices into cubes.

Ma put the cubes into the big iron pot on the stove, poured in some water, and then watched while the pumpkin slowly boiled down, all day long. All the water and the juice must be boiled away, and the pumpkin must never burn.

The pumpkin was a thick, dark, good-smelling mass in the kettle. It did not boil like water, but bubbles came up in it and suddenly exploded, leaving holes that closed quickly. Every time a bubble exploded, the rich, hot, pumpkin smell came out.

Laura stood on a chair and watched the pumpkin for

Ma, and stirred it with a wooden paddle. She held the paddle in both hands and stirred carefully, because if the pumpkin burned there wouldn't be any pumpkin pies.

For dinner they ate the stewed pumpkin with their bread. They made it into pretty shapes on their plates. It was a beautiful colour, and smoothed and moulded so prettily with their knives. Ma never allowed them to play with their food at table; they must always eat nicely everything that was set before them, leaving nothing on their plates. But she did let them make the rich, brown, stewed pumpkin into pretty shapes before they ate it.

At other times they had baked Hubbard squash for dinner. The rind was so hard that Ma had to take Pa's axe to cut the squash into pieces. When the pieces were baked in the oven, Laura loved to spread the soft insides with butter and then scoop the yellow flesh from the rind and eat it.

For supper, now, they often had hulled corn and milk. That was good, too. It was so good that Laura could hardly wait for the corn to be ready, after Ma started to hull it. It took two or three days to make hulled corn.

The first day, Ma cleaned and brushed all the ashes out of the cookstove. Then she burned some clean, bright hardwood, and saved its ashes. She put the hardwood ashes in a little cloth bag.

That night Pa brought in some ears of corn with large plump kernels. He nubbed the ears—shelling off the small, chaffy kernels at their tips. Then he shelled the rest into a large pan, until the pan was full.

Early next day Ma put the shelled corn and the bag of ashes into the big iron kettle. She filled the kettle with water, and kept it boiling a long time. At last the kernels of corn began to swell, and they swelled and swelled until their skins split open and began to peel off.

When every skin was loose and peeling, Ma lugged the heavy kettle outdoors. She filled a clean washtub with cold water from the spring, and she dipped the corn out of the kettle into the tub.

Then she rolled the sleeves of her flowered calico dress above her elbows, and she knelt by the tub. With her hands she rubbed and scrubbed the corn until the hulls came off and floated on top of the water.

Often she poured the water off, and filled the tub again with buckets of water from the spring. She kept on rub-

bing and scrubbing the corn between her hands, and changing the water, until every hull came off and was washed away.

Ma looked pretty, with her bare arms plump and white, her cheeks so red and her dark hair smooth and shining, while she scrubbed and rubbed the corn in the clear water.

She never splashed one drop of water on her pretty dress. When at last the corn was done, Ma put all the soft, white kernels in a big jar in the pantry. Then at last, they had hulled corn and milk for supper.

Sometimes they had hulled corn for breakfast, with maple syrup, and sometimes Ma fried the soft kernels in pork drippings. But Laura liked them best with milk.

Autumn was great fun. There was so much work to do, so many good things to eat, so many new things to see. Laura was scampering and chattering like the squirrels, from morning to night.

One frosty morning, a machine came up the road. Four horses were pulling it, and two men were on it. The horses hauled it up into the field where Pa and Uncle Henry and Grandpa and Mr Peterson had stacked their wheat.

Two more men drove after it another, smaller machine.

Pa called to Ma that the threshers had come; then he hurried out to the field with his team. Laura and Mary asked Ma, and then they ran out to the field after him. They might watch, if they were careful not to get in the way.

Uncle Henry came riding up and tied his horse to a tree. Then he and Pa hitched all the other horses, eight of them, to the smaller machine. They hitched each team to the end of a long stick that came out from the centre of the machine. A long iron rod lay along the ground, from this machine to the big machine.

Afterward Laura and Mary asked questions, and Pa told them that the big machine was called the separator, and the rod was called the tumbling rod, and the little machine was called the horse-power. Eight horses were hitched to it and made it go, so this was an eight-horse-power machine.

A man sat on top of the horse-power, and when everything was ready he clucked to the horses, and they began to go. They walked around him in a circle, each team pulling on the long stick to which it was hitched, and following the team ahead. As they went around, they stepped carefully over the tumbling rod, which was tumbling over and over on the ground.

Their pulling made the tumbling rod keep rolling over, and the rod moved the machinery of the separator, which stood beside the stack of wheat.

All this machinery made an enormous racket, rackety-banging and clanging. Laura and Mary held tight to each other's hand, at the edge of the field, and watched with all their eyes. They had never seen a machine before. They had never heard such a racket.

Pa and Uncle Henry, on top of the wheat stack, were pitching bundles down on to a board. A man stood at the board and cut the bands on the bundles and crowded the bundles one at a time into a hole at the end of the separator.

The hole looked like the separator's mouth, and it had long, iron teeth. The teeth were chewing. They chewed the bundles and the separator swallowed them. Straw blew out at the separator's other end, and wheat poured out of its side.

Two men were working fast, trampling the straw and building it into a stack. One man was working fast,

sacking the pouring grain. The grains of wheat poured out of the separator into a half-bushel measure, and as fast as the measure filled, the man slipped an empty one into its place and emptied the full one into a sack. He had just time to empty it and slip it back under the spout before the other measure ran over.

All the men were working as fast as they possibly could, but the machine kept right up with them. Laura and Mary were so excited they could hardly breathe. They held hands tightly and stared.

The horses walked around and around. The man who was driving them cracked his whip and shouted, 'Giddap there, John! No use trying to shirk!' Crack! went the whip. 'Careful there, Billy! Easy, boy! You can't go but so fast nohow.'

The separator swallowed the bundles, the golden straw blew out in a golden cloud, the wheat streamed golden-brown out of the spout, while the men hurried. Pa and Uncle Henry pitched bundles down as fast as they could. And chaff and dust blew over everything.

Laura and Mary watched as long as they could. Then

they ran back to the house to help Ma get dinner for all those men.

A big kettle of cabbage and meat was boiling on the stove; a big pan of beans and a johnny-cake were baking in the oven. Laura and Mary set the table for the threshers. They put on salt-rising bread and butter, bowls of stewed pumpkin, pumpkin pies and dried berry pies and cookies, cheese and honey and pitchers of milk.

Then Ma put on the boiled potatoes and cabbage and meat, the baked beans, the hot johnny-cake and the baked Hubbard squash, and she poured the tea.

Laura always wondered why bread made of corn meal was called johnny-cake. It wasn't cake. Ma didn't know, unless the Northern soldiers called it johnny-cake because the people in the South, where they fought, ate so much of it. They called the Southern soldiers Johnny Rebs. Maybe, they called the Southern bread, cake, just for fun.

Ma had heard some say it should be called journey-cake. She didn't know. It wouldn't be very good bread to take on a journey.

At noon the threshers came in to the table loaded with food. But there was none too much, for threshers work hard and get very hungry.

By the middle of the afternoon the machines had finished all the threshing, and the men who owned them drove them away into the Big Woods, taking with them the sacks of wheat that were their pay. They were going to the next place where neighbours had stacked their wheat and wanted the machines to thresh it.

Pa was very tired that night, but he was happy. He said to Ma:

'It would have taken Henry and Peterson and Grandpa and me a couple of weeks apiece to thresh as much grain with flails as that machine threshed to-day. We wouldn't have got as much wheat, either, and it wouldn't have been as clean.

'That machine's a great invention!' he said. 'Other folks can stick to old-fashioned ways if they want to, but I'm all for progress. It's a great age we're living in. As long as I raise wheat, I'm going to have a machine come and thresh it, if there's one anywhere in the neighbourhood.'

He was too tired that night to talk to Laura, but Laura was proud of him. It was Pa who had got the other men to stack their wheat together and send for the threshing machine, and it was a wonderful machine. Everybody was glad it had come.

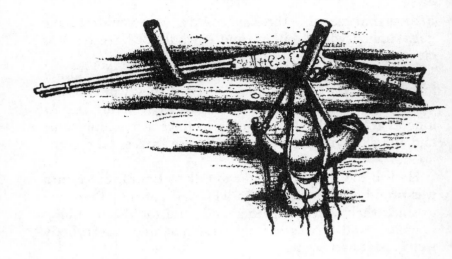

13

The Deer in the Wood

THE grass was dry and withered, and the cows must be taken out of the woods and kept in the barn to be fed. All the bright-coloured leaves became dull brown when the cold fall rains began.

There was no more playing under the trees. But Pa was in the house when it rained, and he began again to play the fiddle after supper.

Then the rains stopped. The weather grew colder. In the early mornings everything sparkled with frost. The days were growing short and a little fire burned all day in the cookstove to keep the house warm. Winter was not far away.

The attic and the cellar were full of good things once more, and Laura and Mary had started to make patchwork quilts. Everything was beginning to be snug and cosy again.

One night when he came in from doing the chores Pa said that after supper he would go to his deer-lick and watch for a deer. There had been no fresh meat in the little house since spring, but now the fawns were grown up, and Pa would go hunting again.

Pa had made a deer-lick, in an open place in the woods, with trees near by in which he could sit to watch it. A deer-lick was a place where the deer came to get salt. When they found a salty place in the ground they came there to lick it, and that was called a deer-lick. Pa had made one by sprinkling salt over the ground.

After supper Pa took his gun and went into the woods, and Laura and Mary went to sleep without any stories or music.

As soon as they woke in the morning they ran to the window, but there was no deer hanging in the trees. Pa had never before gone out to get a deer and come home without one. Laura and Mary did not know what to think.

All day Pa was busy, banking the little house and the barn with dead leaves and straw, held down by stones, to keep out the cold. The weather grew colder all day, and that night there was once more a fire on the hearth and the windows were shut tight and chinked for the winter.

After supper Pa took Laura on his knee, while Mary sat close in her little chair. And Pa said:

'Now I'll tell you why you had no fresh meat to eat to-day.

'When I went out to the deer-lick, I climbed up into a big oak tree. I found a place on a branch where I was comfortable and could watch the deer-lick. I was near

enough to shoot any animal that came to it, and my gun
was loaded and ready on my knee.

'There I sat and waited for the moon to rise and light
the clearing.

'I was a little tired from chopping wood all day yesterday, and I must have fallen asleep, for I found myself
opening my eyes.

'The big, round moon was just rising. I could see it
between the bare branches of the trees, low in the sky.

And right against it I saw a deer standing. His head was
up and he was listening. His great, branching horns stood
out above his head. He was dark against the moon.

'It was a perfect shot. But he was so beautiful, he looked
so strong and free and wild, that I couldn't kill him. I sat
there and looked at him, until he bounded away into the
dark woods.

'Then I remembered that Ma and my little girls were
waiting for me to bring home some good fresh venison.
I made up my mind that next time I would shoot.

'After a while a big bear came lumbering out into the open. He was so fat from feasting on berries and roots and grubs all summer that he was nearly as large as two bears. His head swayed from side to side as he went on all fours across the clear space in the moonlight, until he came to a rotten log. He smelled it, and listened. Then he pawed it apart and sniffed among the broken pieces, eating up the fat white grubs.

'Then he stood up on his hind legs, perfectly still, looking all around him. He seemed to be suspicious that something was wrong. He was trying to see or smell what it was.

'He was a perfect mark to shoot at, but I was so much interested in watching him, and the woods were so peaceful in the moonlight, that I forgot all about my gun. I did not even think of shooting him, until he was waddling away into the woods.

' "This will never do," I thought. "I'll never get any meat this way."

'I settled myself in the tree and waited again. This time I was determined to shoot the next game I saw.

'The moon had risen higher and the moonlight was bright in the little open place. All around it the shadows were dark among the trees.

'After a long while, a doe and her yearling fawn came stepping daintily out of the shadows. They were not afraid at all. They walked over to the place where I had sprinkled the salt, and they both licked up a little of it.

'Then they raised their heads and looked at each other. The fawn stepped over and stood beside the doe. They stood there together, looking at the woods and the moonlight. Their large eyes were shining and soft.

'I just sat there looking at them, until they walked

away among the shadows. Then I climbed down out of the tree and came home.'

Laura whispered in his ear, 'I'm *glad* you didn't shoot them!'

Mary said, 'We can eat bread and butter.'

Pa lifted Mary up out of her chair and hugged them both together.

'You're my good girls,' he said. 'And now it's bedtime. Run along, while I get my fiddle.'

When Laura and Mary had said their prayers and were tucked snugly under the trundle bed's covers, Pa was sitting in the firelight with the fiddle. Ma had blown out the lamp because she did not need its light. On the other side of the hearth she was swaying gently in her rocking chair and her knitting needles flashed in and out above the sock she was knitting.

The long winter evenings of firelight and music had come again.

Pa's fiddle wailed while Pa was singing:

> "Oh, Susi—an—na, don't you cry for me,
> I'm going to Cal—i—for—ni—a,
> The gold dust for to see."

Then Pa began to play again the song about Old Grimes. But he did not sing the words he had sung when Ma was making cheese. These words were different. Pa's strong, sweet voice was softly singing:

> "Shall auld acquaintance be forgot,
> And never brought to mind?
> Shall auld acquaintance be forgot,
> And the days of auld lang syne?
> And the days of auld lang syne, my friend,
> And the days of auld lang syne,

Shall auld acquaintance be forgot,
And the days of auld lang syne?"

When the fiddle had stopped singing Laura called out softly, 'What are days of auld lang syne, Pa?'

'They are the days of a long time ago, Laura,' Pa said. 'Go to sleep, now.'

But Laura lay awake a little while, listening to Pa's fiddle softly playing and to the lonely sound of the wind in the Big Woods. She looked at Pa sitting on the bench by the hearth, the firelight gleaming on his brown hair and beard and glistening on the honey-brown fiddle. She looked at Ma, gently rocking and knitting.

She thought to herself, 'This is now.'

She was glad that the cosy house, and Pa and Ma and the firelight and the music, were now. They could not be forgotten, she thought, because now is now. It can never be a long time ago.

Little House on the Prairie

Contents

Going West

A LONG TIME AGO, when all the grandfathers and grandmothers of today were little boys and little girls or very small babies, or perhaps not even born, Pa and Ma and Mary and Laura and Baby Carrie left their little house in the Big Woods of Wisconsin. They drove away and left it lonely and empty in the clearing among the big trees, and they never saw that little house again.

They were going to the Indian country.

Pa said there were too many people in the Big Woods now. Quite often Laura heard the ringing thud of an axe which was not Pa's axe, or the echo of a shot that did not come from his gun. The path that went by the little house had become a road. Almost every day Laura and Mary stopped their playing and stared in surprise at a wagon slowly creaking by on that road.

Wild animals would not stay in a country where there were so many people. Pa did not like to stay, either. He liked a country where the wild animals lived without being afraid. He liked to see the little fawns and their mothers looking at him from the shadowy woods, and the fat, lazy bears eating berries in the wild-berry patches.

In the long winter evenings he talked to Ma about the Western country. In the West the land was level, and there were no trees. The grass grew thick and high. There the wild animals wandered and fed as though they were in a pasture that stretched much farther than a man could see, and there were no settlers. Only Indians lived there.

One day in the very last of the winter Pa said to Ma, 'Seeing you don't object, I've decided to go see the West. I've had an offer for this place, and we can sell it now for as much as we're ever likely to get, enough to give us a start in a new country.'

'Oh, Charles, must we go now?' Ma said. The weather was so cold and the snug house was so comfortable.

'If we are going this year, we must go now,' said Pa. 'We can't get across the Mississippi after the ice breaks.'

So Pa sold the little house. He sold the cow and calf. He made hickory bows and fastened them upright to the wagon box. Ma helped him stretch white canvas over them.

In the thin dark morning Ma gently shook Mary and Laura till they got up. In firelight and candlelight she washed and combed them and dressed them warmly. Over their long red flannel underwear she put wool petticoats and wool dresses and long wool stockings. She put their coats on them, and their rabbit-skin hoods and their red yarn mittens.

Everything from the little house was in the wagon, except the beds and tables and chairs. They did not need to take these, because Pa could always make new ones.

There was thin snow on the ground. The air was still

and cold and dark. The bare trees stood up against the frosty stars. But in the east the sky was pale and through the grey woods came lanterns with wagons and horses, bringing Grandpa and Grandma and aunts and uncles and cousins.

Mary and Laura clung tight to their rag dolls and did not say anything. The cousins stood around and looked at them. Grandma and all the aunts hugged and kissed them and hugged and kissed them again, saying good-bye.

Pa hung his gun to the wagon bows inside the canvas top, where he could reach it quickly from the seat. He hung his bullet-pouch and powder-horn beneath it. He laid the fiddle-box carefully between pillows, where jolting would not hurt the fiddle.

The uncles helped him hitch the horses to the wagon. All the cousins were told to kiss Mary and Laura, so they did. Pa picked up Mary and then Laura, and set them on the bed in the back of the wagon. He helped Ma climb up to the wagon seat, and Grandma reached up and gave her Baby Carrie. Pa swung up and sat beside Ma, and Jack, the brindle bulldog, went under the wagon.

So they all went away from the little log house. The shutters were over the windows, so the little house could not see them go. It stayed there inside the log fence, behind the two big oak trees that in the summertime had made green roofs for Mary and Laura to play under. And that was the last of the little house.

Pa promised that when they came to the West, Laura should see a papoose.

'What is a papoose?' she asked him, and he said, 'A papoose is a little, brown, Indian baby.'

They drove a long way through the snowy woods, till they came to the town of Pepin. Mary and Laura had seen it once before, but it looked different now. The door of the store and the doors of all the houses were shut, the stumps were covered with snow, and no little children were playing outdoors. Big cords of wood stood among the stumps. Only two or three men in boots and fur caps and bright plaid coats were to be seen.

Ma and Laura and Mary ate bread and molasses in the wagon, and the horses ate corn from nosebags, while inside the store Pa traded his furs for things they would need on the journey. They could not stay long in the town, because they must cross the lake that day.

The enormous lake stretched flat and smooth and white all the way to the edge of the grey sky. Wagon tracks went away across it, so far that you could not see where they went; they ended in nothing at all.

Pa drove the wagon out on to the ice, following those wagon tracks. The horses' hoofs clop-clopped with a dull sound, the wagon wheels went crunching. The town grew smaller and smaller behind, till even the tall store was only a dot. All around the wagon there was nothing but empty and silent space. Laura didn't like it. But Pa was on the wagon seat and Jack was under the wagon; she knew that nothing could hurt her while Pa and Jack were there.

At last the wagon was pulling up a slope of earth again, and again there were trees. There was a little log house, too, among the trees. So Laura felt better.

Nobody lived in the little house; it was a place to camp in. It was a tiny house, and strange, with a big fireplace and rough bunks against all the walls. But it was warm when Pa had built a fire in the fireplace. That night Mary and Laura and Baby Carrie slept with Ma in a bed made on the floor before the fire, while Pa slept outside in the wagon, to guard it and the horses.

In the night a strange noise wakened Laura. It sounded

like a shot, but it was sharper and longer than a shot. Again and again she heard it. Mary and Carrie were asleep, but Laura couldn't sleep until Ma's voice came softly through the dark. 'Go to sleep, Laura,' Ma said. 'It's only the ice cracking.'

Next morning Pa said, 'It's lucky we crossed yesterday, Caroline. Wouldn't wonder if the ice broke up today. We made a late crossing, and we're lucky it didn't start breaking up while we were out in the middle of it.'

'I thought about that yesterday, Charles,' Ma replied, gently.

Laura hadn't thought about it before, but now she thought what would have happened if the ice had cracked under the wagon wheels and they had all gone down into the cold water in the middle of that vast lake.

'You're frightening somebody, Charles,' Ma said, and Pa caught Laura up in his safe, big hug.

'We're across the Mississippi!' he said, hugging her joyously. 'How do you like that, little half-pint of sweet cider half drunk up? Do you like going out west where Indians live?'

Laura said she liked it, and she asked if they were in the Indian country now. But they were not; they were in Minnesota.

It was a long, long way to Indian territory. Almost every day the horses travelled as far as they could; almost every night Pa and Ma made camp in a new place. Sometimes they had to stay several days in one camp because a creek was in flood and they couldn't cross it till the water went down. They crossed too many creeks to count. They saw strange woods and hills, and stranger country with no trees. They drove across rivers on long wooden bridges, and they came to one wide yellow river that had no bridge.

That was the Missouri River. Pa drove on to a raft, and

they all sat still in the wagon while the raft went swaying away from the safe land and slowly crossed all that rolling muddy-yellow water.

After more days they came to hills again. In a valley the wagon stuck fast in deep black mud. Rain poured down and thunder crashed and lightning flared. There was no place to make camp and build a fire. Everything was damp and cold and miserable in the wagon, but they had to stay in it and eat cold bits of food.

Next day Pa found a place on a hillside where they could camp. The rain had stopped, but they had to wait a week before the creek went down and the mud dried so that Pa could dig the wagon wheels out of it and go on.

One day, while they were waiting, a tall, lean man came out of the woods, riding a black pony. He and Pa talked awhile, then they went off into the woods together, and

when they came back, both of them were riding black ponies. Pa had traded the tired brown horses for those ponies.

They were beautiful little horses, and Pa said they were not really ponies; they were western mustangs. 'They're strong as mules and gentle as kittens,' Pa said. They had large, soft, gentle eyes, and long manes and tails, and slender legs and feet much smaller and quicker than the feet of horses in the Big Woods.

When Laura asked what their names were, Pa said that she and Mary could name them. So Mary named one, Pet, and Laura named the other, Patty. When the creek's roar was not so loud and the road was drier, Pa dug the wagon out of the mud. He hitched Pet and Patty to it, and they all went on together.

They had come in the covered wagon all the long way from the Big Woods of Wisconsin, across Minnesota and Iowa and Missouri. All that long way, Jack had trotted under the wagon. Now they set out to go across Kansas.

Kansas was an endless flat land covered with tall grass blowing in the wind. Day after day they travelled in

Kansas, and saw nothing but the rippling grass and the enormous sky. In a perfect circle the sky curved down to the level land, and the wagon was in the circle's exact middle.

All day long Pet and Patty went forward, trotting and walking and trotting again, but they couldn't get out of the middle of that circle. When the sun went down, the circle was still around them and the edge of the sky was pink. Then slowly the land became black. The wind made a lonely sound in the grass. The camp fire was small and lost in so much space. But large stars hung from the sky, glittering so near that Laura felt she could almost touch them.

Next day the land was the same, the sky was the same, the circle did not change. Laura and Mary were tired of them all. There was nothing new to do and nothing new to look at. The bed was made in the back of the wagon and neatly covered with a grey blanket; Laura and Mary sat on it. The canvas sides of the wagon-top were rolled up and tied, so the prairie wind blew in. It whipped Laura's straight brown hair and Mary's golden curls every-which-way, and the strong light screwed up their eyelids.

Sometimes a big jack rabbit bounded in big bounds away over the blowing grass. Jack paid no attention. Poor Jack was tired, too, and his paws were sore from travelling so far. The wagon kept on jolting, the canvas top snapped in the wind. Two faint wheel tracks kept going away behind the wagon, always the same.

Pa's back was hunched. The reins were loose in his hands, the wind blew his long brown beard. Ma sat straight and quiet, her hands folded in her lap. Baby Carrie slept in a nest among the soft bundles.

'Ah-wow!' Mary yawned, and Laura said: 'Ma, can't

we get out and run behind the wagon? My legs are so tired.'

'No, Laura,' Ma said.

'Aren't we going to camp pretty soon?' Laura asked. It seemed such a long time since noon, when they had eaten their lunch sitting on the clean grass in the shade of the wagon.

Pa answered: 'Not yet. It's too early to camp now.'

'I want to camp, now! I'm so tired,' Laura said.

Then Ma said, 'Laura.' That was all, but it meant that Laura must not complain. So she did not complain any more out loud, but she was still naughty, inside. She sat and thought complaints to herself.

Her legs ached and the wind wouldn't stop blowing her hair. The grass waved and the wagon jolted and nothing else happened for a long time.

'We're coming to a creek or a river,' Pa said. 'Girls, can you see those trees ahead?'

Laura stood up and held to one of the wagon bows. Far ahead she saw a low dark smudge. 'That's trees,' Pa said. 'You can tell by the shape of the shadows. In this country, trees mean water. That's where we'll camp tonight.'

2

Crossing the Creek

PET AND PATTY began to trot briskly, as if they were
glad, too. Laura held tight to the wagon bow and
stood up in the jolting wagon. Beyond Pa's shoulder
and far across the waves of green grass she could see the
trees, and they were not like any trees she had seen before.
They were no taller than bushes.

'Whoa!' said Pa, suddenly. 'Now which way?' he muttered to himself.

The road divided here, and you could not tell which
was the more-travelled way. Both of them were faint wheel
tracks in the grass. One went towards the west, the other
sloped downward a little, towards the south. Both soon
vanished in the tall, blowing grass.

'Better go downhill, I guess,' Pa decided. 'The creek's
down in the bottoms. Must be this is the way to the ford.'
He turned Pet and Patty towards the south.

The road went down and up and down and up again,
over gently curving land. The trees were nearer now, but
they were no taller. Then Laura gasped and clutched the
wagon bow, for almost under Pet's and Patty's noses there
was no more blowing grass, there was no land at all. She
looked beyond the edge of the land and across the tops of
trees.

The road turned there. For a little way it went along the
cliff's top, then it went sharply downward. Pa put on the
brakes; Pet and Patty braced themselves backward and
almost sat down. The wagon wheels slid onward, little by
little lowering the wagon farther down the steep slope into
the ground. Jagged cliffs of bare red earth rose up on
both sides of the wagon. Grass waved along their tops, but
nothing grew on their seamed, straight-up-and-down sides.
They were hot, and heat came from them against Laura's
face. The wind was still blowing overhead, but it did not
blow down into this deep crack in the ground. The stillness
seemed strange and empty.

Then once more the wagon was level. The narrow
crack down which it had come opened into the bottom
lands. Here grew the tall trees whose tops Laura had seen
from the prairie above. Shady groves were scattered on the
rolling meadows, and in the groves deer were lying down,

hardly to be seen among the shadows. The deer turned their heads towards the wagon, and curious fawns stood up to see it more clearly.

Laura was surprised because she did not see the creek. But the bottom lands were wide. Down here, below the prairie, there were gentle hills and open sunny places. The air was still and hot. Under the wagon wheels the ground was soft. In the sunny open spaces the grass grew thin, and deer had cropped it short.

For a while the high, bare cliffs of red earth stood up behind the wagon. But they were almost hidden behind hills and trees when Pet and Patty stopped to drink from the creek.

The rushing sound of the water filled the still air. All along the creek banks the trees hung over it and made it dark with shadows. In the middle it ran swiftly, sparkling silver and blue.

'This creek's pretty high,' Pa said. 'But I guess we can make it all right. You can see this is a ford, by the old wheel ruts. What do you say, Caroline?'

'Whatever you say, Charles,' Ma answered.

Pet and Patty lifted their wet noses. They pricked their ears forward, looking at the creek; then they pricked them backward to hear what Pa would say. They sighed and laid their soft noses together to whisper to each other. A little way upstream, Jack was lapping the water with his red tongue.

'I'll tie down the wagon-cover,' Pa said. He climbed down from the seat, unrolled the canvas sides and tied them firmly to the wagon box. Then he pulled the rope at the back, so that the canvas puckered together in the middle, leaving only a tiny round hole, too small to see through.

Mary huddled down on the bed. She did not like fords;

she was afraid of the rushing water. But Laura was excited; she liked the splashing. Pa climbed to the seat, saying, 'They may have to swim, out there in the middle. But we'll make it all right, Caroline.'

Laura thought of Jack and said, 'I wish Jack could ride in the wagon, Pa.'

Pa did not answer. He gathered the reins tightly in his hands. Ma said, 'Jack can swim, Laura. He will be all right.'

The wagon went forward softly in mud. Water began to splash against the wheels. The splashing grew louder. The wagon shook as the noisy water struck at it. Then all at once the wagon lifted and balanced and swayed. It was a lovely feeling.

The noise stopped, and Ma said, sharply, 'Lie down, girls!'

Quick as a flash, Mary and Laura dropped flat on the bed. When Ma spoke like that, they did as they were told. Ma's arm pulled a smothering blanket over them, heads and all.

'Be still, just as you are. Don't move!' she said.

Mary did not move; she was trembling and still. But Laura could not help wriggling a little bit. She did so want to see what was happening. She could feel the wagon swaying and turning; the splashing was noisy again, and again it died away. Then Pa's voice frightened Laura. It said, 'Take them, Caroline!'

The wagon lurched; there was a sudden heavy splash beside it. Laura sat straight up and clawed the blanket from her head.

Pa was gone. Ma sat alone, holding tight to the reins with both hands. Mary hid her face in the blanket again, but Laura rose up farther. She couldn't see the creek bank. She couldn't see anything in front of the wagon but water

rushing at it. And in the water, three heads; Pet's head
and Patty's head and Pa's small, wet head. Pa's fist in the
water was holding tight to Pet's bridle.

Laura could faintly hear Pa's voice through the rushing
of the water. It sounded calm and cheerful, but she
couldn't hear what he said. He was talking to the horses.
Ma's face was white and scared.

'Lie down, Laura,' Ma said.

Laura lay down. She felt cold and sick. Her eyes were
shut tight, but she could still see the terrible water and
Pa's brown beard drowning in it.

For a long, long time the wagon swayed and swung,
and Mary cried without making a sound, and Laura's
stomach felt sicker and sicker. Then the front wheels struck
and grated, and Pa shouted. The whole wagon jerked and

jolted and tipped backward, but the wheels were turning on the ground. Laura was up again, holding to the seat; she saw Pet's and Patty's scrambling wet backs climbing a steep bank, and Pa running beside them, shouting, 'Hi, Patty! Hi, Pet! Get up! Get up! Whoopsy-daisy! Good girls!'

At the top of the bank they stood still, panting and dripping. And the wagon stood still, safely out of that creek.

Pa stood panting and dripping, too, and Ma said, 'Oh, Charles!'

'There, there, Caroline,' said Pa. 'We're all safe, thanks to a good tight wagon-box well fastened to the running-gear. I never saw a creek rise so fast in my life. Pet and Patty are good swimmers, but I guess they wouldn't have made it if I hadn't helped them.'

If Pa had not known what to do, or if Ma had been too frightened to drive, or if Laura and Mary had been naughty and bothered her, then they would all have been lost. The river would have rolled them over and over and carried them away and drowned them, and nobody would ever have known what became of them. For weeks, perhaps, no other person would come along that road.

'Well,' said Pa, 'all's well that ends well,' and Ma said, 'Charles, you're wet to the skin.'

Before Pa could answer, Laura cried, 'Oh, where's Jack?'

They had forgotten Jack. They had left him on the other side of that dreadful water and now they could not see him anywhere. He must have tried to swim after them, but they could not see him struggling in the water now.

Laura swallowed hard, to keep from crying. She knew it was shameful to cry, but there was crying inside her. All the long way from Wisconsin poor Jack had followed them so patiently and faithfully, and now they had left him to drown. He was so tired, and they might have taken him into the wagon. He had stood on the bank and seen the wagon going away from him, as if they didn't care for him at all. And he would never know how much they wanted him.

Pa said he wouldn't have done such a thing to Jack, not for a million dollars. If he'd known how that creek would rise when they were in midstream, he would never have let Jack try to swim it. 'But that can't be helped now,' he said.

He went far up and down the creek bank, looking for Jack, calling him and whistling for him.

It was no use. Jack was gone.

At last there was nothing to do but to go on. Pet and Patty were rested. Pa's clothes had dried on him while he searched for Jack. He took the reins again, and drove uphill, out of the river bottoms.

Laura looked back all the way. She knew she wouldn't see Jack again, but she wanted to. She didn't see anything but low curves of land coming between the wagon and the creek, and beyond the creek those strange cliffs of red earth rose up again.

Then other bluffs just like them stood up in front of the wagon. Faint wheel tracks went into a crack between those earthen walls. Pet and Patty climbed till the crack became a small grassy valley. And the valley widened out to the High Prairie once more.

No road, not even the faintest trace of wheels or of a rider's passing, could be seen anywhere. That prairie looked as if no human eye had ever seen it before. Only the tall wild grass covered the endless empty land and a great empty sky arched over it. Far away the sun's edge touched the rim of the earth. The sun was enormous and it was throbbing and pulsing with light. All around the sky's edge ran a pale pink glow, and above the pink was yellow, and above that blue. Above the blue the sky was no colour at all. Purple shadows were gathering over the land, and the wind was mourning.

Pa stopped the mustangs. He and Ma got out of the wagon to make camp, and Mary and Laura climbed down to the ground, too.

'Oh, Ma,' Laura begged, 'Jack has gone to heaven, hasn't he? He was such a good dog, can't he go to heaven?'

Ma did not know what to answer, but Pa said: 'Yes, Laura, he can. God that doesn't forget the sparrows won't leave a good dog like Jack out in the cold.'

Laura felt only a little better. She was not happy. Pa did not whistle about his work as usual, and after a while he said, 'And what we'll do in a wild country without a good watchdog I don't know.'

3

Camp on the High Prairie

PA MADE CAMP as usual. First, he unhitched and unharnessed Pet and Patty, and he put them on their picket-lines. Picket-lines were long ropes fastened to iron pegs driven into the ground. The pegs were called picket-pins. When horses were on picket-lines they could eat all the grass that the long ropes would let them reach. But when Pet and Patty were put on them, the first thing they did was to lie down and roll back and forth and over. They rolled till the feeling of the harness was all gone from their backs.

While Pet and Patty were rolling, Pa pulled all the grass from a large, round space of ground. There was old, dead grass at the roots of the green grass, and Pa would take no chance of setting the prairie on fire. If fire once started in that dry under-grass, it would sweep the whole country bare and black. Pa said, 'Best be on the safe side, it saves trouble in the end.'

When the space was clear of grass, Pa laid a handful of

dry grass in its centre. From the creek bottoms he brought an armful of twigs and dead wood. He laid small twigs and larger twigs and then the wood on the handful of dry grass, and he lighted the grass. The fire crackled merrily inside the ring of bare ground that it couldn't get out of.

Then Pa brought water from the creek, while Mary and Laura helped Ma get supper. Ma measured coffee beans into the coffee-mill and Mary ground them. Laura filled the coffee-pot with the water Pa brought, and Ma set the pot in the coals. She set the iron bake-oven in the coals, too.

While it heated, she mixed cornmeal and salt with water and patted it into little cakes. She greased the bake-oven with a pork-rind, laid the cornmeal cakes in it, and put on its iron cover. Then Pa raked more coals over the cover, while Ma sliced fat salt pork. She fried the slices in the iron spider. The spider had short legs to stand on in the coals, and that was why it was called a spider. If it had had no legs, it would have been only a frying pan.

The coffee boiled, the cakes baked, the meat fried, and they all smelled so good that Laura grew hungrier and hungrier.

Pa set the wagon-seat near the fire. He and Ma sat on it. Mary and Laura sat on the wagon tongue. Each of them had a tin plate, and a steel knife and a steel fork with white bone handles. Ma had a tin cup and Pa had a tin cup, and Baby Carrie had a little one all her own, but Mary and Laura had to share their tin cup. They drank water. They could not drink coffee until they grew up.

While they were eating supper the purple shadows closed around the camp fire. The vast prairie was dark and still. Only the wind moved stealthily through the grass, and the large, low stars hung glittering from the great sky.

The camp fire was cosy in the big, chill darkness. The slices of pork were crisp and fat, the corncakes were good. In the dark beyond the wagon, Pet and Patty were eating, too. They bit off bites of grass with sharply crunching sounds.

'We'll camp here a day or two,' said Pa. 'Maybe we'll stay here. There's good land, timber in the bottoms, plenty of game—everything a man could want. What do you say, Caroline?'

'We might go farther and fare worse,' Ma replied.

'Anyway, I'll look around tomorrow,' Pa said. 'I'll take my gun and get us some good fresh meat.'

He lighted his pipe with a hot coal, and stretched out his legs comfortably. The warm, brown smell of tobacco smoke mixed with the warmth of the fire. Mary yawned, and slid off the wagon tongue to sit on the grass. Laura yawned, too. Ma quickly washed the tin plates, the tin cups, the knives and forks. She washed the bake-oven and the spider, and rinsed the dish-cloth.

For an instant she was still, listening to the long, wailing howl from the dark prairie. They all knew what it was. But that sound always ran cold up Laura's backbone and crinkled over the back of her head.

Ma shook the dish-cloth, and then she walked into the dark and spread the cloth on the tall grass to dry. When she came back Pa said: 'Wolves. Half a mile away, I'd judge. Well, where there's deer there will be wolves. I wish——'

He didn't say what he wished, but Laura knew. He wished Jack were there. When wolves howled in the Big Woods, Laura had always known that Jack would not let them hurt her. A lump swelled hard in her throat and her nose smarted. She winked fast and did not cry. That wolf, or perhaps another wolf, howled again.

'Bedtime for little girls!' Ma said, cheerfully. Mary got up and turned around so that Ma could unbutton her. But Laura jumped up and stood still. She saw something. Deep in the dark beyond the firelight, two green lights were shining near the ground. They were eyes.

Cold ran up Laura's backbone, her scalp crinkled, her hair stood up. The green lights moved; one winked out, then the other winked out, then both shone steadily, coming nearer. Very rapidly they were coming nearer.

'Look, Pa, look!' Laura said. 'A wolf!'

Pa did not seem to move quickly, but he did. In an instant he took his gun out of the wagon and was ready to fire at those green eyes. The eyes stopped coming. They were still in the dark, looking at him.

'It can't be a wolf. Unless it's a mad wolf,' Pa said. Ma lifted Mary into the wagon. 'And it's not that,' said Pa. 'Listen to the horses.' Pet and Patty were still biting off bites of grass.

'A lynx?' said Ma.

'Or a coyote?' Pa picked up a stick of wood; he shouted, and threw it. The green eyes went close to the ground, as if the animal crouched to spring. Pa held the gun ready. The creature did not move.

'Don't, Charles,' Ma said. But Pa slowly walked towards those eyes. And slowly along the ground the eyes crawled towards him. Laura could see the animal in the edge of the dark. It was a tawny animal and brindled. Then Pa shouted and Laura screamed.

The next thing she knew she was trying to hug a jumping, panting, wriggling Jack, who lapped her face and hands with his warm wet tongue. She couldn't hold him. He leaped and wriggled from her to Pa to Ma and back to her again.

'Well, I'm beat!' Pa said.

'So am I,' said Ma. 'But did you have to wake the baby?' She rocked Carrie in her arms, hushing her.

Jack was perfectly well. But soon he lay down close to Laura and sighed a long sigh. His eyes were red with tiredness, and all the under part of him was caked with mud. Ma gave him a cornmeal cake and he licked it and wagged politely, but he could not eat. He was too tired.

'No telling how long he kept swimming,' Pa said. 'Nor how far he was carried downstream before he landed.' And when at last he reached them, Laura called him a wolf, and Pa threatened to shoot him.

But Jack knew they didn't mean it. Laura asked him, 'You knew we didn't mean it, didn't you, Jack?' Jack wagged his stump of a tail; he knew.

It was past bedtime. Pa chained Pet and Patty to the feed-box at the back of the wagon and fed them their corn. Carrie slept again, and Ma helped Mary and Laura undress. She put their long nightgowns over their heads while they stuck their arms into the sleeves. They buttoned the neckbands themselves, and tied the strings of their nightcaps beneath their chins. Under the wagon Jack wearily turned around three times, and lay down to sleep.

In the wagon Laura and Mary said their prayers and crawled into their little bed. Ma kissed them good night.

On the other side of the canvas, Pet and Patty were eating their corn. When Patty whooshed into the feed-box, the whoosh was right at Laura's ear. There were little scurrying sounds in the grass. In the trees by the creek an owl called, 'Who-oo? who-oo?' Farther away another owl answered, 'Oo-oo, oo-oo.' Far away on the prairie the wolves howled, and under the wagon Jack growled low in his chest. In the wagon everything was safe and snug.

Thickly in front of the open wagon-top hung the large, glittering stars. Pa could reach them, Laura thought. She wished he would pick the largest one from the thread on which it hung from the sky, and give it to her. She was wide awake, she was not sleepy at all, but suddenly she was very much surprised. The large star winked at her!

Then she was waking up, next morning.

4

Prairie Day

SOFT WHICKERINGS WERE close to Laura's ear, and grain rattled into the feed-box. Pa was giving Pet and Patty their breakfasts.

'Back, Pet! Don't be greedy,' he said. 'You know it's Patty's turn.'

Pet stamped her foot and nickered.

'Now, Patty, keep your own end of the box,' said Pa. 'This is for Pet.'

Then a little squeal from Patty.

'Hah! Got nipped, didn't you?' Pa said. 'And serve you right. I told you to eat your own corn.'

Mary and Laura looked at each other and laughed. They could smell bacon and coffee and hear pancakes sizzling, and they scrambled out of bed.

Mary could dress herself, all but the middle button. Laura buttoned that one for her, then Mary buttoned Laura all the way up the back. They washed their hands and faces in the tin wash-basin on the wagon-step. Ma combed every tangle out of their hair, while Pa brought fresh water from the creek.

Then they sat on the clean grass and ate pancakes and bacon and molasses from the tin plates in their laps.

All around them shadows were moving over the waving grasses, while the sun rose. Meadow larks were springing straight up from the billows of grass into the high, clear sky, singing as they went. Small pearly clouds drifted in the immense blueness overhead. In all the weed-tops tiny birds were swinging and singing in tiny voices. Pa said they were dickcissels.

'Dickie, dickie!' Laura called back to them. 'Dickie bird!'

'Eat your breakfast, Laura,' Ma said. 'You must mind your manners, even if we are a hundred miles from anywhere.'

Pa said, mildly, 'It's only forty miles to Independence, Caroline, and no doubt there's a neighbour or so nearer than that.'

'Forty miles, then,' Ma agreed. 'But whether or not, it isn't good manners to sing at table. Or when you're eating,' she added, because there was no table.

There was only the enormous, empty prairie, with grasses blowing in waves of light and shadow across it, and the great blue sky above it, and birds flying up from it and singing with joy because the sun was rising. And on the whole enormous prairie there was no sign that any other human being had ever been there.

In all that space of land and sky stood the lonely, small, covered wagon. And close to it sat Pa and Ma and Laura and Mary and Baby Carrie, eating their breakfasts. The mustangs munched their corn, and Jack sat still, trying hard not to beg. Laura was not allowed to feed him while she ate, but she saved bits for him. And Ma made a big pancake for him, of the last of the batter.

Rabbits were everywhere in the grass, and thousands of prairie chickens, but Jack could not hunt his breakfast that day. Pa was going hunting, and Jack must guard the camp.

First Pa put Pet and Patty on their picket-lines. Then he took the wooden tub from the side of the wagon and filled it with water from the creek. Ma was going to do the washing.

Then Pa stuck his sharp hatchet in his belt, he hung his powder-horn beside the hatchet, he put the patch-box and the bullet-pouch in his pocket, and he took his gun on his arm.

He said to Ma: 'Take your time, Caroline. We won't move the wagon till we want to. We've got all the time there is.'

He went away. For a little while they could see the upper part of him above the tall grasses, going away and growing smaller. Then he went out of sight and the prairie was empty.

Mary and Laura washed the dishes while Ma made the beds in the wagon. They put the clean dishes neatly in their box; they picked up every scattered twig and put it in the fire; they stacked the wood against a wagon wheel. Then everything about the camp was tidy.

Ma brought the wooden pannikin of soft soap from the wagon. She kilted up her skirts and rolled up her sleeves, and she knelt by the tub on the grass. She washed sheets and pillow-cases and white underthings, she washed dresses and shirts, and she rinsed them in clear water and spread them on the clean grass, to dry in the sun.

Mary and Laura were exploring. They must not go far from the wagon, but it was fun to run through the tall grass, in the sunshine and wind. Huge rabbits bounded away before them, birds fluttered up and settled again. The tiny dickie-birds were everywhere, and their tiny nests were in the tall weeds. And everywhere were little brown-striped gophers.

These little creatures looked soft as velvet. They had bright round eyes and crinkling noses and wee paws. They popped out of holes in the ground, and stood up to look at Mary and Laura. Their hind legs folded under their haunches, their little paws folded tight to their chests, and they looked exactly like bits of dead wood sticking out of the ground. Only their bright eyes glittered.

Mary and Laura wanted to catch one to take to Ma. Again and again they almost had one. The gopher would stand perfectly still until you were sure you had him this time, then just as you touched him, he wasn't there. There was only his round hole in the ground.

Laura ran and ran, and couldn't catch one. Mary sat perfectly still beside a hole, waiting for one to come up, and just beyond her reach gophers scampered merrily, and gophers sat up and looked at her. But not one ever came out of that hole.

Once a shadow floated across the grass, and every gopher vanished. A hawk was sailing overhead. It was so close that Laura saw its cruel round eye turned downward to look at her. She saw its sharp beak and its savage claws curled ready to pounce. But the hawk saw nothing but Laura and Mary and round, empty holes in the ground. It sailed away, looking somewhere else for its dinner.

Then all the little gophers came up again.

It was nearly noon then. The sun was almost overhead. So Laura and Mary picked flowers from the weeds, and they took the flowers to Ma, instead of a gopher.

Ma was folding the dry clothes. The little panties and petticoats were whiter than snow, warm from the sun, and smelling like the grass. Ma laid them in the wagon, and took the flowers. She admired equally the flowers that Laura gave her and the flowers that Mary gave her, and she put them together in a tin cup full of water. She set them on the wagon-step, to make the camp pretty.

Then she split two cold corn-cakes and spread them with molasses. She gave one to Mary and one to Laura. That was their dinner, and it was very good.

'Where is a papoose, Ma?' Laura asked.

'Don't speak with your mouth full, Laura,' said Ma.

So Laura chewed and swallowed, and she said, 'I want to see a papoose.'

'Mercy on us!' Ma said. 'Whatever makes you want to see Indians? We will see enough of them. More than we want to, I wouldn't wonder.'

'They wouldn't hurt us, would they?' Mary asked. Mary was always good; she never spoke with her mouth full.

'No!' Ma said. 'Don't get such an idea into your head.'

'Why don't you like Indians, Ma?' Laura asked, and she caught a drip of molasses with her tongue.

'I just don't like them; and don't lick your fingers, Laura,' said Ma.

'This is Indian country, isn't it?' Laura said. 'What did we come to their country for, if you don't like them?'

Ma said she didn't know whether this was Indian country or not. She didn't know where the Kansas line was. But whether or no, the Indians would not be here long. Pa had word from a man in Washington that the Indian Territory would be open to settlement soon. It might already be open to settlement. They could not know, because Washington was so far away.

Then Ma took the flat-iron out of the wagon and heated it by the fire. She sprinkled a dress for Mary and a dress for Laura and a little dress for Baby Carrie, and her own sprigged calico. She spread a blanket and a sheet on the wagon seat, and she ironed the dresses.

Baby Carrie slept in the wagon. Laura and Mary and Jack lay on the shady grass beside it, because now the sunshine was hot. Jack's mouth was open and his red tongue hung out, his eyes blinked sleepily. Ma hummed softly to herself while the iron smoothed all the wrinkles out of the little dresses. All around them, to the very edge of the world, there was nothing but grasses waving in the wind. Far overhead, a few white puffs of cloud sailed in the thin blue air.

Laura was very happy. The wind sang a low, rustling song in the grass. Grasshoppers' rasping quivered up from all the immense prairie. A buzzing came faintly from all the trees in the creek bottoms. But all these sounds made a great, warm, happy silence. Laura had never seen a place she liked so much as this place.

She didn't know she had gone to sleep until she woke up. Jack was on his feet, wagging his stump tail. The sun was low, and Pa was coming across the prairie. Laura

jumped up and ran, and his long shadow stretched to meet her in the waving grasses.

He held up the game in his hand, for her to see. He had a rabbit, the largest rabbit she had ever seen, and two plump prairie hens. Laura jumped up and down and clapped her hands and squealed. Then she caught hold of his other sleeve and hippety-hopped through the tall grasses beside him.

'This country's cram-jammed with game,' he told her. 'I saw fifty deer if I saw one, and antelope, squirrels, rabbits, birds of all kinds. The creek's full of fish.' He said to Ma, 'I tell you, Caroline, there's everything we want here. We can live like kings!'

That was a wonderful supper. They sat by the camp fire and ate the tender, savoury, flavoury meat till they could eat no more. When at last Laura set down her plate, she sighed with contentment. She didn't want anything more in the world.

The last colour was fading from the enormous sky and all the level land was shadowy. The warmth of the fire was pleasant because the night wind was cool. Phoebe-birds called sadly from the woods down by the creek. For a little while a mocking-bird sang, then the stars came out and the birds were still.

Softly Pa's fiddle sang in the starlight. Sometimes he sang a little and sometimes the fiddle sang alone. Sweet and thin and far away, the fiddle went on singing:

'None knew thee but to love thee,
Thou dear one of my heart. . . .'

The large, bright stars hung down from the sky. Lower and lower they came, quivering with music.

Laura gasped, and Ma came quickly. 'What is it,

Laura?' she asked, and Laura whispered, 'The stars were singing.'

'You've been asleep,' Ma said. 'It is only the fiddle. And it's time little girls were in bed.'

She undressed Laura in the firelight and put her nightgown on and tied her nightcap, and tucked her into bed. But the fiddle was still singing in the starlight. The night was full of music, and Laura was sure that part of it came from the great, bright stars swinging so low above the prairie.

5

The House on the Prairie

LAURA AND MARY were up next morning earlier than the sun. They ate their breakfast of cornmeal mush with prairie-hen gravy, and hurried to help Ma wash the dishes. Pa was loading everything else into the wagon and hitching up Pet and Patty.

When the sun rose, they were driving on across the prairie. There was no road now. Pet and Patty waded through the grasses, and the wagon left behind it only the tracks of its wheels.

Before noon, Pa said, 'Whoa!' The wagon stopped.

'Here we are, Caroline!' he said. 'Right here we'll build our house.'

Laura and Mary scrambled over the feed-box and dropped to the ground in a hurry. All around them there was nothing but grassy prairie spreading to the edge of the sky.

Quite near them, to the north, the creek bottoms lay below the prairie. Some darker green tree-tops showed, and beyond them bits of the rim of earthen bluffs held up the prairie's grasses. Far away to the east, a broken line of different greens lay on the prairie, and Pa said that was the river.

'That's the Verdigris River,' he said, pointing it out to Ma.

Right away, he and Ma began to unload the wagon. They took out everything and piled it on the ground.

Then they took off the wagon-cover and put it over the pile. Then they took even the wagon-box off, while Laura and Mary and Jack watched.

The wagon had been home for a long time. Now there was nothing left of it but the four wheels and the parts that connected them. Pet and Patty were still hitched to the tongue. Pa took a bucket and his axe, and sitting on this skeleton wagon, he drove away. He drove right down into the prairie, out of sight.

'Where's Pa going?' Laura asked, and Ma said, 'He's going to get a load of logs from the creek bottoms.'

It was strange and frightening to be left without the wagon on the High Prairie. The land and the sky seemed too large, and Laura felt small. She wanted to hide and be still in the tall grass, like a little prairie chicken. But she didn't. She helped Ma, while Mary sat on the grass and minded Baby Carrie.

First Laura and Ma made the beds, under the wagon-cover tent. Then Ma arranged the boxes and bundles, while Laura pulled all the grass from a space in front of the tent. That made a bare place for the fire. They couldn't start the fire until Pa brought wood.

There was nothing more to do, so Laura explored a little. She did not go far from the tent. But she found a queer little kind of tunnel in the grass. You'd never notice it if you looked across the waving grass-tops. But when you

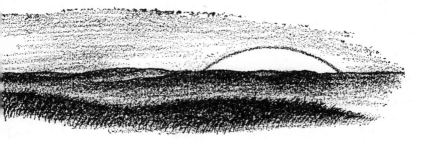

came to it, there it was—a narrow, straight, hard path down between the grass stems. It went out into the endless prairie.

Laura went along it a little way. She went slowly, and more slowly, and then she stood still and felt queer. So she turned around and came back quickly. When she looked over her shoulder there wasn't anything there. But she hurried.

When Pa came riding back on a load of logs, Laura told him about that path. He said he had seen it yesterday. 'It's some old trail,' he said.

That night by the fire Laura asked again when she would see a papoose, but Pa didn't know. He said you never saw Indians unless they wanted you to see them. He had seen Indians when he was a boy in New York State, but Laura never had. She knew they were wild men with red skins, and their hatchets were called tomahawks.

Pa knew all about wild animals, so he must know about wild men, too. Laura thought he would show her a papoose some day, just as he had shown her fawns, and little bears, and wolves.

For days Pa hauled logs. He made two piles of them, one for the house and one for the stable. There began to be a road where he drove back and forth to the creek bottoms. And at night on their picket-lines Pet and Patty ate the grass, till it was short and stubby all around the log-piles.

Pa began the house first. He paced off the size of it on the ground, then with his spade he dug a shallow little hollow along two sides of that space. Into these hollows he rolled two of the biggest logs. They were sound, strong logs, because they must hold up the house. They were called sills.

Then Pa chose two more strong, big logs, and he rolled these logs on to the ends of the sills, so that they made a hollow square. Now with his axe he cut a wide, deep notch near each end of these logs. He cut these notches out of the top of the log, but with his eye he measured the sills, and he cut the notches so that they would fit around half of the sill.

When the notches were cut, he rolled the log over. And the notches fitted down over the sill.

That finished the foundation of the house. It was one

log high. The sills were half buried in the ground, and the logs on their ends fitted snugly to the ground. At the corners, where they crossed, the notches let them fit together so that they were no thicker than one log. And the two ends stuck out beyond the notches.

Next day Pa began the walls. From each side he rolled up a log, and he notched its ends so that it fitted down over the end logs. Then he rolled up logs from the ends, and notched them so that they fitted down over the side logs. Now the whole house was two logs high.

The logs fitted solidly together at the corners. But no log is ever perfectly straight, and all logs are bigger at one end than at the other end, so cracks were left between them all along the walls. But that did not matter, because Pa would chink those cracks.

All by himself, he built the house three logs high. Then Ma helped him. Pa lifted one end of a log on to the wall, then Ma held it while he lifted the other end. He stood up on the wall to cut the notches, and Ma helped roll and hold the log while he settled it where it should be to make the corner perfectly square.

So, log by log, they built the walls higher, till they were pretty high, and Laura couldn't get over them any more. She was tired of watching Pa and Ma build the house, and she went into the tall grass, exploring. Suddenly she heard Pa shout, 'Let go! Get out from under!'

The big, heavy log was sliding. Pa was trying to hold up his end of it, to keep it from falling on Ma. He couldn't. It crashed down. Laura saw Ma huddled on the ground.

She got to Ma almost as quickly as Pa did. Pa knelt down and called Ma in a dreadful voice, and Ma gasped, 'I'm all right.'

The log was on her foot. Pa lifted the log and Ma pulled

her foot from under it, Pa felt her to see if any bones were broken.

'Move your arms,' he said. 'Is your back hurt? Can you turn your head?' Ma moved her arms and turned her head.

'Thank God,' Pa said. He helped Ma to sit up. She said again, 'I'm all right, Charles. It's just my foot.'

Quickly Pa took off her shoe and stocking. He felt her foot all over, moving the ankle and the instep and every toe. 'Does it hurt much?' he asked.

Ma's face was grey and her mouth was a tight line. 'Not much,' she said.

'No bones broken,' said Pa. 'It's only a bad sprain.'

Ma said cheerfully: 'Well, a sprain's soon mended. Don't be so upset, Charles.'

'I blame myself,' said Pa. 'I should have used skids.'

He helped Ma to the tent. He built up the fire and heated water. When the water was as hot as Ma could bear, she put her swollen foot into it.

It was providential that the foot was not crushed. Only a little hollow in the ground had saved it.

Pa kept pouring more hot water into the tub in which Ma's foot was soaking. Her foot was red from the heat and the puffed ankle began to turn purple. Ma took her foot out of the water and bound strips of rag tightly round and round the ankle. 'I can manage,' she said.

She could not get her shoe on. But she tied more rags around her foot, and she hobbled on it. She got supper as usual, only a little more slowly. But Pa said she could not help to build the house until her ankle was well.

He hewed out skids. These were long, flat slabs. One end rested on the ground, and the other end rested on the log wall. He was not going to lift any more logs; he and Ma would roll them up these skids.

But Ma's ankle was not well yet. When she unwrapped it in the evenings, to soak it in hot water, it was all purple and black and green and yellow. The house must wait.

Then one afternoon Pa came merrily whistling up the creek road. They had not expected him home from hunting so soon. As soon as he saw them he shouted, 'Good news!'

They had a neighbour, only two miles away on the other side of the creek. Pa had met him in the woods. They were going to trade work and that would make it easier for everyone.

'He's a bachelor,' said Pa, 'and he says he can get along without a house better than you and the girls can. So he's going to help me first. Then as soon as he gets his logs ready, I'll go over and help him.'

They need not wait any longer for the house, and Ma need not do any more work on it.

'How do you like that, Caroline?' Pa asked, joyfully; and Ma said, 'That's good, Charles. I'm glad.'

Early next morning Mr Edwards came. He was lean and tall and brown. He bowed to Ma and called her 'Ma'am' politely. But he told Laura that he was a wild-cat from Tennessee. He wore tall boots and a ragged jumper, and a coon-skin cap, and he could spit tobacco juice farther than Laura had ever imagined that anyone could spit tobacco juice. He could hit anything he spat at, too. Laura tried and tried, but she could never spit so far or so well as Mr Edwards could.

He was a fast worker. In one day he and Pa built those walls as high as Pa wanted them. They joked and sang while they worked, and their axes made the chips fly.

On top of the walls they set up a skeleton roof of slender poles. Then in the south wall they cut a tall hole for a door, and in the west wall and the east wall they cut square holes for windows.

Laura couldn't wait to see the inside of the house. As soon as the tall hole was cut, she ran inside. Everything was striped there. Stripes of sunshine came through the cracks in the west wall, and stripes of shadow came down from the poles overhead. The stripes of shade and sunshine were all across Laura's hands and her arms and her bare feet. And through the cracks between the logs she could see stripes of prairie. The sweet smell of the prairie mixed with the sweet smell of cut wood.

Then, as Pa cut away the logs to make the window hole in the west wall, chunks of sunshine came in. When he finished, a big block of sunshine lay on the ground inside the house.

Around the door hole and the window holes Pa and Mr Edwards nailed thin slabs against the cut ends of the logs. And the house was finished, all but the roof. The walls were solid and the house was large, much larger than the tent. It was a nice house.

Mr Edwards said he would go home now, but Pa and Ma said he must stay to supper. Ma had cooked an especially good supper because they had company.

There was stewed jack rabbit with white-flour dumplings and plenty of gravy. There was a steaming hot, thick cornbread flavoured with bacon fat. There was molasses to eat on the cornbread, but because this was a company supper they did not sweeten their coffee with molasses. Ma brought out the little paper sack of pale brown store sugar.

Mr. Edwards said he surely did appreciate that supper. Then Pa brought out his fiddle.

Mr Edwards stretched out on the ground, to listen. But first Pa played for Laura and Mary. He played their very favourite song, and he sang it. Laura liked it best of all because Pa's voice went down deep, deep, deeper in that song.

> 'Oh, I am a Gipsy King!
> I come and go as I please!
> I pull my old nightcap down,
> And take the world at my ease.'

Then his voice went deep, deep down, deeper than the very oldest bullfrog's.

> 'Oh!
>   I am
>   a
>   Gyp-
>   sy
>   KING!'

They all laughed. Laura could hardly stop laughing. 'Oh, sing it again, Pa! Sing it again!' she cried, before she remembered that children must be seen and not heard. Then she was quiet.

Pa went on playing, and everything began to dance. Mr Edwards rose up on one elbow, then he sat up, then he jumped up and he danced. He danced like a jumping-jack in the moonlight, while Pa's fiddle kept on rollicking and his foot kept tapping the ground, and Laura's hands and Mary's hands were clapping together and their feet were patting, too.

'You're the fiddlin'est fool that ever I see!' Mr Edwards shouted admiringly to Pa. He didn't stop dancing, Pa didn't stop playing. He played 'Money Musk' and 'Arkansas Traveller', 'Irish Washerwoman' and the 'Devil's Hornpipe'.

Baby Carrie couldn't sleep in all that music. She sat up in Ma's lap, looking at Mr Edwards with round eyes, and clapping her little hands and laughing.

Even the firelight danced, and all around its edge the shadows were dancing. Only the new house stood still and quiet in the dark, till the big moon rose and shone on its grey walls and the yellow chips around it.

Mr Edwards said he must go. It was a long way back to his camp on the other side of the woods and the creek. He took his gun, and said good night to Laura and Mary and Ma. He said a bachelor got mighty lonesome, and he surely had enjoyed this evening of home life.

'Play, Ingalls!' he said. 'Play me down the road!' So while he went down the creek road and out of sight, Pa played, and Pa and Mr Edwards and Laura sang with all their might.

> 'Old Dan Tucker was a fine old man;
> He washed his face in the frying-pan,
> He combed his hair with a wagon wheel,
> And died of the toothache in his heel.

> 'Git out of the way for old Dan Tucker!
> He's too late to get his supper!
> Supper's over and the dishes washed,
> Nothing left but a piece of squash!

> 'Old Dan Tucker went to town,
> Riding a mule, leading a houn' . . .'

Far over the prairie rang Pa's big voice and Laura's little one, and faintly from the creek bottoms came a last whoop from Mr Edwards.

> 'Git out of the way for old Dan Tucker!
> He's too late to get his supper!'

When Pa's fiddle stopped, they could not hear Mr Edwards any more. Only the wind rustled in the prairie grasses. The big, yellow moon was sailing high overhead. The sky was so full of light that not one star twinkled in it, and all the prairie was a shadowy mellowness.

Then from the woods by the creek a nightingale began to sing.

Everything was silent, listening to the nightingale's song. The bird sang on and on. The cool wind moved over the prairie and the song was round and clear above the grasses' whispering. The sky was like a bowl of light overturned on the flat black land.

The song ended. No one moved or spoke. Laura and Mary were quiet, Pa and Ma sat motionless. Only the wind stirred and the grasses sighed. Then Pa lifted the fiddle to his shoulder and softly touched the bow to the strings. A few notes fell like clear drops of water into the stillness. A pause, and Pa began to play the nightingale's song. The nightingale answered him. The nightingale began to sing again. It was singing with Pa's fiddle.

When the strings were silent, the nightingale went on singing. When it paused, the fiddle called to it and it sang again. The bird and the fiddle were talking to each other in the cool night under the moon.

6

Moving In

'THE WALLS ARE up,' Pa was saying to Ma in the morning. 'We'd better move in and get along as best we can without a floor or other fixings. I must build the stable as fast as I can, so Pet and Patty can be inside walls, too. Last night I could hear wolves howling from every direction, seemed like, and close, too.'

'Well, you have your gun, so I'll not worry,' said Ma.

'Yes, and there's Jack. But I'll feel easier in my mind when you and the girls have good solid walls around you.'

'Why do you suppose we haven't seen any Indians?' Ma asked.

'Oh, I don't know,' Pa replied, carelessly. 'I've seen their camping-places among the bluffs. They're away on a hunting-trip now, I guess.'

Then Ma called: 'Girls! The sun's up!' and Laura and Mary scrambled out of bed and into their clothes.

'Eat your breakfasts quickly,' Ma said, putting the last of the rabbit stew on their tin plates. 'We're moving into the house today, and all the chips must be out.'

So they ate quickly, and hurried to carry all the chips out of the house. They ran back and forth as fast as they could, gathering their skirts full of chips and dumping them in a pile near the fire. But there were still chips on the ground inside the house when Ma began to sweep it with her willow-bough broom.

Ma limped, though her sprained ankle was beginning

to get well. But she soon swept the earthen floor, and then Mary and Laura began to help her carry things into the house.

Pa was on top of the walls, stretching the canvas wagon-top over the skeleton roof of saplings. The canvas billowed in the wind, Pa's beard blew wildly and his hair stood up from his head as if it were trying to pull itself out. He held on to the canvas and fought it. Once it jerked so hard that Laura thought he must let go or sail into the air like a bird. But he held tight to the wall with his legs, and tight to the canvas with his hands, and he tied it down.

'There!' he said to it. 'Stay where you are, and be——'

'Charles!' Ma said. She stood with her arms full of quilts and looked up at him reprovingly.

'——and be good,' Pa said to the canvas. 'Why, Caroline, what did you think I was going to say?'

'Oh, Charles!' Ma said. 'You scallawag!'

Pa came right down the corner of the house. The ends

of the logs stuck out, and he used them for a ladder. He ran his hand through his hair so that it stood up even more wildly, and Ma burst out laughing. Then he hugged her, quilts and all.

Then they looked at the house and Pa said, 'How's that for a snug house!'

'I'll be thankful to get into it,' said Ma.

There was no door and there were no windows. There was no floor except the ground and no roof except the canvas. But that house had good stout walls, and it would stay where it was. It was not like the wagon, that every morning went on to some other place.

'We're going to do well here, Caroline,' Pa said. 'This is a great country. This is a country I'll be contented to stay in the rest of my life.'

'Even when it's settled up?' Ma asked.

'Even when it's settled up. No matter how thick and close the neighbours get, this country'll never feel crowded. Look at that sky!'

Laura knew what he meant. She liked this place, too. She liked the enormous sky and the winds, and the land that you couldn't see to the end of. Everything was so fresh and clean and big and splendid.

By dinner-time the house was in order. The beds were neatly made on the floor. The wagon-seat and two ends of logs were brought in for chairs. Pa's gun lay on its peg above the doorway. Boxes and bundles were neat against the walls. It was a pleasant house. A soft light came through the canvas roof, wind and sunshine came through the window holes, and every crack in the four walls glowed a little because the sun was overhead.

Only the camp fire stayed where it had been. Pa said he would build a fireplace in the house as soon as he could. He would hew out slabs to make a solid roof, too.

before winter came. He would lay a puncheon floor, and make beds and tables and chairs. But all that work must wait until he had helped Mr Edwards and had built a stable for Pet and Patty.

'When that's all done,' said Ma, 'I want a clothes-line.'

Pa laughed. 'Yes, and I want a well.'

After dinner he hitched Pet and Patty to the wagon and he hauled a tubful of water from the creek, so that Ma could do the washing. 'You could wash clothes in the creek,' he told her. 'Indian women do.'

'If we wanted to live like Indians, you could make a hole in the roof to let the smoke out, and we'd have the fire on the floor inside the house,' said Ma. 'Indians do.'

That afternoon she washed the clothes in the tub and spread them on the grass to dry.

After supper they sat for a while by the camp fire. That night they would sleep in the house; they would never sleep beside a camp fire again. Pa and Ma talked about the folks in Wisconsin, and Ma wished she could send them a letter. But Independence was forty miles away, and no letter could go until Pa made the long trip to the post-office there.

Back in the Big Woods so far away, Grandpa and Grandma and the aunts and uncles and cousins did not know where Pa and Ma and Laura and Mary and Baby Carrie were. And sitting there by the camp fire, no one knew what might have happened in the Big Woods. There was no way to find out.

'Well, it's bedtime,' Ma said. Baby Carrie was already asleep. Ma carried her into the house and undressed her, while Mary unbuttoned Laura's dress and petticoat waist down the back, and Pa hung a quilt over the door hole. The quilt would be better than no door. Then Pa went out to bring Pet and Patty close to the house.

He called back, softly, 'Come out here, Caroline, and look at the moon.'

Mary and Laura lay in their little bed on the ground inside the new house, and watched the sky through the window hole to the east. The edge of the big, bright moon glittered at the bottom of the window space, and Laura sat up. She looked at the great moon, sailing silently higher in the clear sky.

Its light made silvery lines in all the cracks on that side of the house. The light poured through the window hole

and made a square of soft radiance on the floor. It was so bright that Laura saw Ma plainly when she lifted the quilt at the door and came in.

Then Laura very quickly lay down, before Ma saw her naughtily sitting up in bed.

She heard Pet and Patty whinnying softly to Pa. Then the faint thuds of their feet came into her ear from the floor. Pet and Patty and Pa were coming towards the house, and Laura heard Pa singing:

> 'Sail on, silver moon!
> Shed your radiance o'er the sky——'

His voice was like a part of the night and the moonlight and the stillness of the prairie. He came to the doorway, singing,

> 'By the pale, silver light of the moon——'

Softly Ma said, 'Hush, Charles. You'll wake the children.'

So Pa came in without a sound. Jack followed at his heels and lay down across the doorway. Now they were all inside the stout walls of their new home, and they were snug and safe. Drowsily Laura heard a long wolf-howl rising from far away on the prairie, but only a little shiver went up her backbone and she fell asleep.

7

The Wolf-Pack

ALL IN ONE day Pa and Mr Edwards built the stable for Pet and Patty. They even put the roof on, working so late that Ma had to keep supper waiting for them.

There was no stable door, but in the moonlight Pa drove two stout posts well into the ground, one on either side of the doorway. He put Pet and Patty inside the stable, and then he laid small, split logs one above another, across the door space. The posts held them, and they made a solid wall.

'Now!' said Pa. 'Let those wolves howl! I'll sleep, tonight.'

In the morning, when he lifted the split logs from behind the posts, Laura was amazed. Beside Pet stood a long-legged, long-eared, wobbly little colt.

When Laura ran towards it, gentle Pet laid back her ears and snapped her teeth at Laura.

'Keep back, Laura!' Pa said, sharply. He said to Pet, 'Now, Pet, you know we won't hurt your little colt.' Pet answered him with a soft whinny. She would let Pa stroke her colt, but she would not let Laura or Mary come near it. When they even peeked at it through the cracks in the stable wall, Pet rolled the whites of her eyes at them and showed them her teeth. They had never seen a colt with ears so long. Pa said it was a little mule, but Laura said it looked like a jack rabbit. So they named the little colt Bunny.

When Pet was on the picket-line, with Bunny frisking around her and wondering at the big world, Laura must watch Baby Carrie carefully. If anyone but Pa came near Bunny, Pet squealed with rage and dashed to bite that little girl.

Early that Sunday afternoon Pa rode Patty away across the prairie to see what he should see. There was plenty of meat in the house, so he did not take his gun.

He rode away through the tall grass, along the rim of the creek bluffs. Birds flew up before him and circled and sank into the grasses. Pa was looking down into the creek bottoms as he rode; perhaps he was watching deer browsing there. Then Patty broke into a gallop, and swiftly she and Pa grew smaller. Soon there was only waving grass where they had been.

Late that afternoon Pa had not come home. Ma stirred the coals of the fire and laid chips on them, and began to get supper. Mary was in the house, minding the baby, and Laura asked Ma, 'What's the matter with Jack?'

Jack was walking up and down, looking worried. He wrinkled his nose at the wind, and the hair rose up on his neck and lay down, and then rose up again. Pet's hoofs suddenly thudded. She ran around the circle of her picket-rope and stood still, whickering a low whicker. Bunny came close to her.

'What's the matter, Jack?' Ma asked. He looked up at

her, but he couldn't say anything. Ma gazed around the whole circle of earth and sky. She could not see anything unusual.

'Likely it isn't anything, Laura,' she said. She raked coals around the coffee-pot and the spider and on to the top of the bake-oven. The prairie hen sizzled in the spider and the corncakes began to smell good. But all the time Ma kept glancing at the prairie all around. Jack walked about restlessly, and Pet did not graze. She faced the north-west, where Pa had gone, and kept her colt close beside her.

All at once Patty came running across the prairie. She was stretched out, running with all her might, and Pa was leaning almost flat on her neck.

She ran right past the stable before Pa could stop her. He stopped her so hard that she almost sat down. She was trembling all over and her black coat was streaked with sweat and foam. Pa swung off her. He was breathing hard, too.

'What is the matter, Charles?' Ma asked him.

Pa was looking towards the creek, so Ma and Laura looked at it, too. But they could see only the space above the bottom lands, with a few tree-tops in it, and the distant tops of the earthen bluffs under the High Prairie's grasses.

'What is it?' Ma asked again. 'Why did you ride Patty like that?'

Pa breathed a long breath. 'I was afraid the wolves would beat me here. But I see everything's all right.'

'Wolves!' she cried. 'What wolves?'

'Everything's all right, Caroline,' said Pa. 'Let a fellow get his breath.'

When he had got some breath, he said, 'I didn't ride Patty like that. It was all I could do to hold her at all. Fifty wolves, Caroline, the biggest wolves I ever saw. I wouldn't go through such a thing again, not for a mint of money.'

A shadow came over the prairie just then because the sun had gone down, and Pa said, 'I'll tell you about it later.'

'We'll eat supper in the house,' said Ma.

'No need of that,' he told her. 'Jack will give us warning in plenty of time.'

He brought Pet and her colt from the picket-line. He didn't take them and Patty to drink from the creek, as he usually did. He gave them the water in Ma's washtub, which was standing full, ready for the washing next morning. He rubbed down Patty's sweaty sides and legs and put her in the barn with Pet and Bunny.

Supper was ready. The camp fire made a circle of light in the dark. Laura and Mary stayed close to the fire, and kept Baby Carrie with them. They could feel the dark all around them, and they kept looking behind them at the place where the dark mixed with the edge of the firelight. Shadows moved there, as if they were alive.

Jack sat on his haunches beside Laura. The edges of his ears were lifted, listening to the dark. Now and then he walked a little way into it. He walked all around the camp fire, and came back to sit beside Laura. The hair lay flat on his thick neck and he did not growl. His teeth showed a little, but that was because he was a bulldog.

Laura and Mary ate their corncakes and the prairie hen's drumsticks, and they listened to Pa while he told Ma about the wolves.

He had found some more neighbours. Settlers were coming in and settling along both sides of the creek. Less than three miles away, in a hollow on the High Prairie, a man and his wife were building a house. Their name was Scott, and Pa said they were nice folks. Six miles beyond them, two bachelors were living in one house. They had taken two farms, and built the house on the line between them. One man's bunk was against one wall of the house, and the other man's bunk was against the other wall. So each man slept on his own farm, although they were in the same house and the house was only eight feet wide. They cooked and ate together in the middle of the house.

Pa had not said anything about the wolves yet. Laura wished he would. But she knew that she must not interrupt when Pa was talking.

He said that these bachelors did not know that anyone else was in the country. They had seen nobody but Indians. So they were glad to see Pa, and he stayed there longer than he had meant to.

Then he rode on, and from a little rise in the prairie he saw a white speck down in the creek bottoms. He thought it was a covered wagon, and it was. When he came to it, he found a man and his wife and five children. They had come from Iowa, and they had camped in the bottoms because one of their horses was sick. The horse was better now, but the bad night air so near the creek had given them fever 'n' ague. The man and his wife and the three oldest children were too sick to stand up. The little boy and girl, no bigger than Mary and Laura, were taking care of them.

So Pa did what he could for them, and then he rode back to tell the bachelors about them. One of them rode right away to fetch that family up on the High Prairie, where they would soon get well in the good air.

One thing had led to another, until Pa was starting home later than he had meant. He took a short cut across the prairie, and as he was loping along on Patty, suddenly out of a little draw came a pack of wolves. They were all around Pa in a moment.

'It was a big pack,' Pa said. 'All of fifty wolves, and the biggest wolves I ever saw in my life. Must be what they call buffalo wolves. Their leader's a big grey brute that stands three feet at the shoulder, if an inch. I tell you my hair stood straight on end.'

'And you didn't have your gun,' said Ma.

'I thought of that. But my gun would have been no use if I'd had it. You can't fight fifty wolves with one gun. And Patty couldn't outrun them.'

'What did you do?' Ma asked.

'Nothing,' said Pa. 'Patty tried to run. I never wanted

anything worse than I wanted to get away from there. But I knew if Patty even started, those wolves would be on us in a minute, pulling us down. So I held Patty to a walk.'

'Goodness, Charles!' Ma said under her breath.

'Yes. I wouldn't go through such a thing again for any money. Caroline, I never saw such wolves. One big fellow trotted along, right by my stirrup. I could have kicked him in the ribs. They didn't pay any attention to me at all. They must have just made a kill and eaten all they could.

'I tell you, Caroline, those wolves just closed in around Patty and me and trotted along with us. In broad daylight. For all the world like a pack of dogs going along with a horse. They were all around us, trotting along, and jumping and playing and snapping at each other, just like dogs.'

'Goodness, Charles!' Ma said again. Laura's heart was thumping fast, and her mouth and her eyes were wide open, staring at Pa.

'Patty was shaking all over, and fighting the bit,' said Pa. 'Sweat ran off her, she was so scared. I was sweating, too. But I held her down to a walk, and we went walking along among those wolves. They came right along with us, a quarter of a mile or more. That big fellow trotted by my tsirrup as if he were there to stay.

'Then we came to the head of a draw, running down into the creek bottoms. The big grey leader went down it, and all the rest of the pack trotted down into it, behind him. As soon as the last one was in the draw, I let Patty go.

'She headed straight for home, across the prairie. And she couldn't have run faster if I'd been cutting into her with a rawhide whip. I was scared the whole way. I thought the wolves might be coming this way and they might be making better time than I was. I was glad you had the gun, Caroline. And glad the house is built. I knew you could keep the wolves out of the house, with the gun. But Pet and the colt were outside.'

'You need not have worried, Charles,' Ma said. 'I guess I would manage to save our horses.'

'I was not fully reasonable, at the time,' said Pa. 'I know you would save the horses, Caroline. Those wolves wouldn't bother you, anyway. If they had been hungry, I wouldn't be here to——'

'Little pitchers have big ears,' Ma said. She meant that he must not frighten Mary and Laura.

'Well, all's well that ends well,' Pa replied. 'And those wolves are miles from here by now.'

'What made them act like that?' Laura asked him.

'I don't know, Laura,' he said. 'I guess they had just eaten all they could hold, and they were on their way to the creek to get a drink. Or perhaps they were out playing on the prairie, and not paying any attention to anything but their play, like little girls do sometimes. Perhaps they saw that I didn't have my gun and couldn't do them any harm. Or perhaps they had never seen a man before and didn't know that men can do them any harm. So they didn't think about me at all.'

Pet and Patty were restlessly walking round and round, inside the barn. Jack walked around the camp fire. When he stood still to smell the air and listen, the hair lifted on his neck.

'Bedtime for little girls!' Ma said, cheerfully. Not even Baby Carrie was sleepy yet, but Ma took them all into the house. She told Mary and Laura to go to bed, and she put Baby Carrie's little nightgown on and laid her in the big bed. Then she went outdoors to do the dishes. Laura wanted Pa and Ma in the house. They seemed so far away outside.

Mary and Laura were good and lay still, but Carrie sat up and played by herself in the dark. In the dark Pa's arm came from behind the quilt in the doorway and quietly took away his gun. Out by the camp fire the tin plates rattled. Then a knife scraped the spider. Ma and Pa were talking together and Laura smelled tobacco smoke.

The house was safe, but it did not feel safe because Pa's gun was not over the door and there was no door; there was only the quilt.

After a long time Ma lifted the quilt. Baby Carrie was asleep then. Ma and Pa came in very quietly and very quietly went to bed. Jack lay across the doorway, but his chin was not on his paws. His head was up, listening. Ma breathed softly, Pa breathed heavily, and Mary was asleep, too. But Laura strained her eyes in the dark to watch Jack. She could not tell whether the hair was standing up on his neck.

Suddenly she was sitting straight up in bed. She had been asleep. The dark was gone. Moonlight streamed through the window hole and streaks of moonlight came through every crack in that wall. Pa stood black in the moonlight at the window. He had his gun.

Right in Laura's ear a wolf howled.

She scringed away from the wall. The wolf was on the other side of it. Laura was too scared to make a sound. The cold was not in her backbone only, it was all through her. Mary pulled the quilt over her head. Jack growled and showed his teeth at the quilt in the doorway.

'Be still, Jack,' Pa said.

Terrible howls curled all around inside the house, and Laura rose out of bed. She wanted to go to Pa, but she knew better than to bother him now. He turned his head and saw her standing in her nightgown.

'Want to see them, Laura?' he asked softly. Laura couldn't say anything, but she nodded, and padded across the ground to him. He stood his gun against the wall and lifted her up to the window hole.

There in the moonlight sat half a circle of wolves. They sat on their haunches and looked at Laura in the window, and she looked at them. She had never seen such big wolves. The biggest one was taller than Laura. He was taller even than Mary. He sat in the middle, exactly opposite Laura. Everything about him was big—his pointed ears, and his pointed mouth with the tongue hanging out, and his strong shoulders and legs, and his two paws side by side, and his tail curled around the squatting haunch. His coat was shaggy grey and his eyes were glittering green.

Laura clutched her toes into a crack of the wall and she folded her arms on the window slab, and she looked and looked at that wolf. But she did not put her head through the empty window space into the outdoors where all those wolves sat so near her, shifting their paws and licking their chops. Pa stood firm against her back and kept his arm tight around her middle.

'He's awful big,' Laura whispered.

'Yes, and see how his coat shines,' Pa whispered into her hair. The moonlight made little glitters in the edges of the shaggy fur, all around the big wolf.

'They are in a ring clear around the house,' Pa whispered. Laura pattered beside him to the other window. He leaned his gun against that wall and lifted her up again. There, sure enough, was the other half of the circle of wolves. All their eyes glittered green in the shadow of the house. Laura could hear their breathing. When they saw Pa and Laura looking out, the middle of the circle moved back a little way.

Pet and Patty were squealing and running inside the barn. Their hoofs pounded the ground and crashed against the walls.

After a moment Pa went back to the other window, and Laura went, too. They were just in time to see the big wolf lift his nose till it pointed straight at the sky. His mouth opened, and a long howl rose towards the moon.

Then all around the house the circle of wolves pointed their noses towards the sky and answered him. Their howls shuddered through the house and filled the moonlight and quavered away across the vast silence of the prairie.

'Now go back to bed, little half-pint,' Pa said. 'Go to sleep. Jack and I will take care of you all.'

So Laura went back to bed. But for a long time she did not sleep. She lay and listened to the breathing of the wolves on the other side of the log wall. She heard the scratch of their claws on the ground, and the snuffling of a nose at a crack. She heard the big grey leader howl again, and all the others answering him.

But Pa was walking quietly from one window hole to the other, and Jack did not stop pacing up and down before the quilt that hung in the doorway. The wolves might howl, but they could not get in while Pa and Jack were there. So at last Laura fell asleep.

8

Two Stout Doors

LAURA FELT A soft warmth on her face and opened
her eyes into morning sunshine. Mary was talking
to Ma by the camp fire. Laura ran outdoors, all
bare inside her nightgown. There were no wolves to be
seen; only their tracks were thick around the house and
the stable.

Pa came whistling up the creek road. He put his gun on
its pegs and led Pet and Patty to the creek to drink as
usual. He had followed the wolf tracks so far that he knew
they were far away now, following a herd of deer.

The mustangs shied at the wolves' tracks and pricked
their ears nervously, and Pet kept her colt close at her side.
But they went willingly with Pa, who knew there was
nothing to fear.

Breakfast was ready. When Pa came back from the
creek they all sat by the fire and ate fried mush and

prairie-chicken hash. Pa said he would make a door that very day. He wanted more than a quilt between them and the wolves, next time.

'I have no more nails, but I'll not keep on waiting till I can make a trip to Independence,' he said. 'A man doesn't need nails to build a house or make a door.'

After breakfast he hitched up Pet and Patty, and taking his axe he went to get timber for the door. Laura helped wash the dishes and make the beds, but that day Mary minded the baby. Laura helped Pa make the door. Mary watched, but Laura handed him his tools.

With the saw he sawed logs the right length for a door. He sawed shorter lengths for cross-pieces. Then with the axe he split the logs into slabs, and smoothed them nicely. He laid the long slabs together on the ground and placed the shorter slabs across them. Then with the auger he bored holes through the cross-pieces into the long slabs. Into every hole he drove a wooden peg that fitted tightly.

That made the door. It was a good oak door, solid and strong.

For the hinges he cut three long straps. One hinge was to be near the top of the door, one near the bottom, and one in the middle.

He fastened them first on the door, in this way: he laid a little piece of wood on the door, and bored a hole through it into the door. Then he doubled one end of a strap around the little piece of wood, and with his knife cut round holes through the strap. He laid the little piece of wood on the door again, with the strap doubled around it, and all the holes making one hole. Then Laura gave him a peg and the hammer, and he drove the peg into the hole. The peg went through the strap and the little piece of wood and through the strap again and into the door. That held the strap so that it couldn't get loose.

'I told you a fellow doesn't need nails!' Pa said.

When he had fastened the three hinges to the door, he set the door in the doorway. It fitted. Then he pegged strips of wood to the old slabs on either side of the doorway, to keep the door from swinging outward. He set the door in place again, and Laura stood against it to hold it there, while Pa fastened the hinges to the doorframe.

But before he did this he had made the latch on the door, because, of course, there must be some way to keep a door shut.

This was the way he made the latch: first he hewed a short, thick piece of oak. From one side of this, in the middle, he cut a wide, deep notch. He pegged this stick to the inside of the door, up and down and near the edge. He put the notched side against the door, so that the notch made a little slot.

Then he hewed and whittled a longer, smaller stick. This stick was small enough to slip easily through the slot. He slid one end of it through the slot, and he pegged the other end to the door.

But he did not peg it tightly. The peg was solid and firm in the door, but the hole in the stick was larger than the peg. The only thing that held the stick on the door was the slot.

This stick was the latch. It turned easily on the peg, and its loose end moved up and down in the slot. And the loose end of it was long enough to go through the slot and across the crack between the door and the wall, and to lie against the wall when the door was shut.

When Pa and Laura had hung the door in the doorway, Pa marked the spot on the wall where the end of the latch came. Over that spot he pegged to the wall a stout piece of oak. This piece of oak was cut out at the top, so that the latch could drop between it and the wall.

Now Laura pushed the door shut, and while she pushed she lifted the end of the latch as high as it would go in the slot. Then she let it fall into its place behind the stout piece of oak. That held the latch against the wall, and the up-and-down strip held the latch in its slot against the door.

Nobody could break in without breaking the strong latch in two.

But there must be a way to lift the latch from the outside. So Pa made the latch-string. He cut it from a long strip of good leather. He tied one end to the latch, between the peg and the slot. Above the latch he bored a small hole through the door, and he pushed the end of the latch-string through the hole.

Laura stood outside, and when the end of the latch-string came through the hole she took hold of it and pulled. She could pull it hard enough to lift the latch and let herself in.

The door was finished. It was strong and solid, made of thick oak with oak slabs across it, all pegged together with good stout pegs. The latch-string was out; if you wanted to come in, you pulled the latch-string. But if you were inside and wanted to keep anyone out, then you pulled the latch-string in through its hole and nobody could get in. There was no doorknob on that door, and there was no keyhole and no key. But it was a good door.

'I call that a good day's work!' said Pa. 'And I had a fine little helper!'

He hugged the top of Laura's head with his hand. Then he gathered up his tools and put them away, whistling, and he went to take Pet and Patty from their picket-lines to water. The sun was setting, the breeze was cooler, and supper cooking on the fire made the best supper-smells that Laura had ever smelled.

There was salt pork for supper. It was the last of the salt pork, so next day Pa went hunting. But the day after that he and Laura made the barn door.

It was exactly like the house door, except that it had no latch. Pet and Patty did not understand door-latches and would not pull a latch-string in at night. So instead of a latch Pa made a hole through the door, and he put a chain through the hole.

At night he would pull an end of the chain through a crack between the logs in the stable wall, and he would padlock the two ends of the chain together. Then nobody could get into that stable.

'Now we're all snug!' Pa said. When neighbours began to come into a country, it was best to lock up your horses at night, because, where there are deer there will be wolves, and where there are horses, there will be horse-thieves.

That night at supper Pa said to Ma, 'Now, Caroline, as soon as we get Edwards' house up, I'm going to build you a fireplace, so you can do your cooking in the house, out of the wind and the storms. It seems like I never did see a place with so much sunshine, but I suppose it's bound to rain sometime.'

'Yes, Charles,' Ma said. 'Good weather never lasts for ever on this earth.'

9

A Fire on the Hearth

OUTSIDE THE HOUSE, close to the log wall opposite the door, Pa cut away the grass and scraped the ground smooth. He was getting ready to build the fireplace.

Then he and Ma put the wagon-box on the wheels again, and Pa hitched up Pet and Patty.

The rising sun was shortening all the shadows. Hundreds of meadow larks were rising from the prairie, singing higher and higher in the air. Their songs came down from the great clear sky like a rain of music. And all over the land, where the grasses waved and murmured under the wind, thousands of little dickie-birds clung with their tiny claws to the blossoming weeds and sang their thousands of little songs.

Pet and Patty sniffed the wind and whinnied with joy. They arched their necks and pawed at the ground because they were eager to go. Pa was whistling while he climbed to the wagon-seat and took up the reins. Then he looked down at Laura, who was looking up at him, and he stopped whistling and said: 'Want to go along, Laura? You and Mary?'

Ma said they could. They climbed up the wheels, clinging to the spokes with their bare toes, and they sat on the high wagon-seat beside Pa. Pet and Patty started with a little jump, and the wagon went jolting down the road that Pa's wagon wheels had made.

They went down between the bare, reddish-yellow walls of earth, all ridged and wrinkled by forgotten rains. Then they went on, across the rolling land of the creek bottoms. Masses of trees covered some of the low, rounded hills, and some of them were grassy, open spaces. Deer were lying in the shadows of the trees, and deer were grazing in the sunshine on the green grass. They lifted their heads and pricked their ears, and stood chewing and watching the wagon with their soft, large eyes.

All along the road the wild larkspur was blossoming pink and blue and white, birds balanced on yellow plumes of goldenrod, and butterflies were fluttering. Starry daisies lighted the shadows under trees, squirrels chattered on branches overhead, white-tailed rabbits hopped along the road, and snakes wriggled quickly across it when they heard the wagon coming.

Deep in the lowest valley the creek was running, in the shadow of dirt bluffs. When Laura looked up those bluffs, she couldn't see the prairie grass at all. Trees grew up the bluffs where the earth had crumbled, and where the bare dirt was so steep that trees couldn't grow on it bushes held on desperately with their roots. Half-naked roots were high above Laura's head.

'Where are the Indian camps?' Laura asked Pa. He had seen the Indians' deserted camps, here among the bluffs. But he was too busy to show them to her now. He must get the rocks to build the fireplace.

'You girls can play,' he said, 'but don't go out of my sight and don't go into the water. And don't play with snakes. Some of the snakes down here are poison.'

So Laura and Mary played by the creek, while Pa dug the rocks he wanted and loaded them into the wagon.

They watched long-legged water-bugs skate over the glassy-still pools. They ran along the bank to scare the frogs, and laughed when the green-coated frogs with their white vests plopped into the water. They listened to the wood-pigeons call among the trees, and the brown thrush singing. They saw the little minnows swimming all together in the shallow places where the creek ran sparkling. The minnows were thin grey shadows in the rippling water, only now and again one minnow flashed the sunshine from its silvery belly.

There was no wind along the creek. The air was still and drowsy-warm. It smelled of damp roots and mud, and it was full of the sound of rustling leaves and of the water running.

In the muddy places where deer's tracks were thick and every hoofprint held water, swarms of mosquitoes rose up with a keen, sharp buzzing. Laura and Mary slapped at mosquitoes on their faces and necks and hands and legs, and wished they could go wading. They were so hot and the water looked so cool. Laura was sure that it would do no harm just to dip one foot in, and when Pa's back was turned she almost did it.

'Laura,' said Pa, and she snatched the naughty foot back.

'If you girls want to go wading,' Pa said, 'you can do it in that shallow place. Don't go in over your ankles.'

Mary waded only a little while. She said the gravel hurt her feet, and she sat on a log and patiently slapped at mosquitoes. But Laura slapped and kept on wading. When she stepped, the gravel hurt her feet. When she stood still, the tiny minnows swarmed about her toes and nibbled them with their tiny mouths. It was a funny, squiggling feeling. Laura tried and tried to catch a minnow, but she only got the hem of her dress wet.

Then the wagon was loaded. Pa called, 'Come along, girls!' and they climbed to the wagon-seat again and rode away from the creek. Up through the woods and hills they rode again, to the High Prairie where the winds were always blowing and the grasses seemed to sing and whisper and laugh.

They had had a wonderful time in the creek bottoms. But Laura liked the High Prairie best. The prairie was so wide and sweet and clean.

That afternoon Ma sat sewing in the shade of the house, and Baby Carrie played on the quilt beside her, while Laura and Mary watched Pa build the fireplace.

First he mixed clay and water to a beautiful thick mud, in the mustangs' water bucket. He let Laura stir the mud while he laid a row of rocks around three sides of the space he had cleared by the house-wall. Then with a wooden paddle he spread the mud over the rocks. In the mud he laid another row of rocks, and plastered them over the top and down on the inside with more mud.

He made a box on the ground; three sides of the box

were made of rocks and mud, and the other side was the log wall of the house.

With rocks and mud and more rocks and more mud, he built the walls as high as Laura's chin. Then on the walls, close against the house, he laid a log. He plastered the log all over with mud.

After that, he built up rocks and mud on top of that log. He was making the chimney now, and he made it smaller and smaller.

He had to go to the creek for more rocks. Laura and Mary could not go again, because Ma said the damp air might give them a fever. Mary sat beside Ma and sewed

another block of her nine-patch quilt, but Laura mixed another bucketful of mud.

Next day Pa built the chimney as high as the house-wall. Then he stood and looked at it. He ran his fingers through his hair.

'You look like a wild man, Charles,' Ma said. 'You're standing your hair all on end.'

'It stands on end, anyway, Caroline,' Pa answered. 'When I was courting you, it never would lie down, no matter how much I slicked it with bear grease.'

He threw himself down on the grass at her feet. 'I'm plumb tuckered out, lifting rocks up there.'

'You've done well to build that chimney up so high, all by yourself,' Ma said. She ran her hand through his hair and stood it up more than ever. 'Why don't you make it stick-and-daub the rest of the way?' she asked him.

'Well, it would be easier,' he admitted. 'I'm blamed if I don't believe I will!'

He jumped up. Ma said, 'Oh, stay here in the shade and rest awhile.' But he shook his head.

'No use lazing here while there's work to be done, Caroline. The sooner I get the fireplace done, the sooner you can do your cooking inside, out of the wind.'

He hauled saplings from the woods, and he cut and notched them and laid them up like the walls of the house, on top of the stone chimney. As he laid them, he plastered them well with mud. And that finished the chimney.

Then he went into the house, and with his axe and saw he cut a hole in the wall. He cut away the logs that had made the fourth wall at the bottom of the chimney. And there was the fireplace.

It was large enough for Laura and Mary and Baby

Carrie to sit in. Its bottom was the ground that Pa had cleared of grass, and its front was the space where Pa had cut away the logs. Across the top of that space was the log that Pa had plastered all over with mud.

On each side Pa pegged a thick slab of green oak against the cut ends of the logs. Then by the upper corners of the fireplace he pegged chunks of oak to the wall, and on these he laid an oak slab and pegged it firmly. That was the mantel-shelf.

As soon as it was done, Ma set in the middle of the mantel-shelf the little china woman she had brought from the Big Woods. The little china woman had come all the way and had not been broken. She stood on the mantel-shelf with her little china shoes and her wide china skirts

and her tight china bodice, and her pink cheeks and blue eyes and golden hair all made of china.

Then Pa and Ma and Mary and Laura stood and admired that fireplace. Only Carrie did not care about it. She pointed at the little china woman and yelled when Mary and Laura told her that no one but Ma could touch it.

'You'll have to be careful with your fire, Caroline,' Pa said. 'We don't want sparks going up the chimney to set the roof on fire. That cloth would burn, easy. I'll split out some clapboards as soon as I can, and make a roof you won't have to worry about.'

So Ma carefully built a little fire in the new fireplace, and she roasted a prairie hen for supper. And that evening they ate in the house.

They sat at table, by the western window. Pa had quickly made the table of two slabs of oak. One end of the slabs stuck in a crack of the wall, and the other ends rested on short, upright logs. Pa had smoothed the slabs with his axe, and the table was very nice when Ma spread a cloth over it.

The chairs were chunks of big logs. The floor was the earth that Ma had swept clean with her willow-bough broom. On the floor, in the corners, the beds were neat under their patchwork quilts. The rays of the setting sun came through the window and filled the house with golden light.

Outside, and far, far away to the pink edge of the sky, the wind went blowing and the wild grasses waved.

Inside, the house was pleasant. The good roast chicken was juicy in Laura's mouth. Her hands and face were washed, her hair was combed, her napkin was tied around her neck. She sat up straight on the round end of log and used her knife and fork nicely, as Ma had taught her. She did not say anything, because children must not speak at table until they are spoken to, but she looked at Pa and Ma and Mary and at Baby Carrie in Ma's lap, and she felt contented. It was nice to be living in a house again.

10

A Roof and a Floor

ALL DAY LONG, every day, Laura and Mary were busy. When the dishes were washed and the beds made, there was always plenty to do and to see and to listen to.

They hunted for birds' nests in the tall grass, and when they found them the mother birds squawked and scolded. Sometimes they touched a nest gently, and all in an instant a nest full of downiness became a nest full of wide-gaping beaks, hungrily squawking. Then the mother bird scolded like anything, and Mary and Laura quietly went away because they did not want to worry her too much.

In the tall grass they lay still as mice and watched flocks of little prairie chickens running and pecking around their anxiously clucking, smooth brown mothers. They watched striped snakes rippling between the grass stems or lying so still that only their tiny flickering tongues and glittering eyes showed that they were alive. They were

garter snakes and would not hurt anybody, but Laura
and Mary did not touch them. Ma said snakes were best
left alone, because some snakes would bite, and it was
better to be safe than sorry.

And sometimes there'd be a great grey rabbit, so still
in the lights and shadows of a grass clump that you were
near enough to touch him before you saw him. Then, if
you were very quiet, you might stand a long time looking
at him. His round eyes stared at yours without meaning
anything. His nose wiggled, and sunlight was rosy through
his long ears, that had delicate veins in them and the softest
short fur on their outsides. The rest of his fur was so thick
and soft that at last you couldn't help trying, very carefully, to touch it.

Then he was gone in a flash and the place where he had
been sitting was hollowed and smooth and still warm from
his warm behind.

All the time, of course, Laura or Mary was minding
Baby Carrie, except when she had her afternoon nap.
Then they sat and soaked in the sunshine and the wind
until Laura forgot that the baby was sleeping. She jumped
up and ran and shouted till Ma came to the door and said,
'Dear me, Laura, must you yell like an Indian? I declare,'
Ma said, 'if you girls aren't getting to look like Indians!
Can I never teach you to keep your sun-bonnets on?'

Pa was up on the house wall, beginning the roof. He looked down at them and laughed.

'One little Indian, two little Indians, three little Indians,' he sang softly. 'No, only two.'

'You make three,' Mary said to him. 'You're brown, too.'

'But you aren't little, Pa,' said Laura. 'Pa, when are we going to see a papoose?'

'Goodness!' Ma exclaimed. 'What do you want to see an Indian baby for? Put on your sun-bonnet, now, and forget such nonsense.'

Laura's sun-bonnet hung down her back. She pulled it up by its strings, and its sides came past her cheeks. When her sun-bonnet was on she could see only what was in front of her, and that was why she was always pushing it back and letting it hang by its strings tied around her throat. She put her sun-bonnet on when Ma told her to, but she did not forget the papoose.

This was Indian country and she didn't know why she didn't see Indians. She knew she would see them sometime, though. Pa said so, but she was getting tired of waiting.

Pa had taken the canvas wagon-top off the house, and now he was ready to put the roof on. For days and days he had been hauling logs from the creek bottoms and splitting them into thin, long slabs. Piles of slabs lay all around the house and slabs stood against it.

'Come out of the house, Caroline,' he said. 'I don't want to risk anything falling on you or Carrie.'

'Wait, Charles, till I put away the china shepherdess,' Ma answered. In a minute she came out, with a quilt and her mending and Baby Carrie. She spread the quilt on the shady grass by the stable, and sat there to do her mending and watch Carrie play.

Pa reached down and pulled up a slab. He laid it

across the ends of the sapling rafters. Its edge stuck out beyond the wall. Then Pa put some nails in his mouth and took his hammer out of his belt, and he began to nail the slab to the rafters.

Mr Edwards had lent him the nails. They had met in the woods, where they were both chopping down trees, and Mr Edwards had insisted that Pa borrow nails for the roof.

'That's what I call a good neighbour!' Pa said when he told Ma about it.

'Yes,' said Ma. 'But I don't like to be beholden, not even to the best of neighbours.'

'Nor I,' Pa replied. 'I've never been beholden to any man yet, and I never will be. But neighbourliness is another matter, and I'll pay him back every nail as soon as I can make the trip to Independence.'

Now Pa carefully took the nails one by one from his mouth, and with ringing blows of the hammer he drove them into the slab. It was much quicker than drilling holes and whittling pegs and driving them into the holes. But every now and then a nail sprang away from the tough oak when the hammer hit it, and if Pa was not holding it firmly, it went sailing through the air.

Then Mary and Laura watched it fall, and they searched in the grass till they found it. Sometimes it was bent. Then Pa carefully pounded it straight again. It would never do to lose or waste a nail.

When Pa had nailed down two slabs, he got up on them. He laid and nailed more slabs, all the way up to the top of the rafters. The edge of each slab lapped over the edge of the slab below it.

Then he began again on the other side of the house, and he laid the roof all the way up from that side. A little crack was left between the highest slabs. So Pa made a little trough of two slabs, and he nailed this trough firmly, upside down over the crack.

The roof was done. The house was darker than it had been, because no light came through the slabs. There was not one single crack that would let rain come in.

'You have done a splendid job, Charles,' Ma said, 'and I'm thankful to have a good roof over my head.'

'You shall have furniture, too, as fine as I can make it,' Pa replied. 'I'll make a bedstead as soon as the floor is laid.'

He began again to haul logs. Day after day he hauled logs. He did not even stop hauling logs to go hunting; he took his gun on the wagon and brought back at night whatever meat he had shot from the wagon-seat.

When he had hauled enough logs to make the floor, he began to split them. He split each log straight down the middle. Laura liked to sit on the woodpile and watch him.

First, with a mighty blow of his axe he split the butt of the log. Into the crack he slipped the thin edge of an iron wedge. Then he wrenched the axe out of the log, and he drove the wedge deeper into the crack. The tough wood split a little farther.

All the way up the log Pa fought that tough oak. He struck with his axe into the crack. He drove blocks of wood into it, and moved the iron wedge higher. Little by little he followed the crack up the log.

He swung the axe high, and brought it down with a great swing and a grunt from his chest. 'Ugh!' The axe whizzed and struck, plung! It always struck exactly where Pa wanted it to.

At last, with a tearing, cracking sound, the whole log split. Its two halves lay on the ground, showing the tree's pale insides and the darker streak up its middle. Then Pa wiped the sweat from his forehead, he took a fresh grip on the axe, and he tackled another log.

One day the last log was split, and next morning Pa began to lay the floor. He dragged the logs into the house and laid them one by one, flat side up. With his spade he scraped the ground underneath, and fitted the round side of the log firmly down into it. With his axe he trimmed away the edge of bark and cut the wood straight, so that each log fitted against the next, with hardly a crack between them.

Then he took the head of the axe in his hand, and with

little, careful blows he smoothed the wood. He squinted along the log to see that the surface was straight and true. He took off last little bits, here and there. Finally he ran his hand over the smoothness, and nodded.

'Not a splinter!' he said. 'That'll be all right for little bare feet to run over.'

He left that log fitted into its place, and dragged in another.

When he came to the fireplace, he used shorter logs. He left a space of bare earth for a hearth, so that when sparks or coals popped out of the fire they would not burn the floor.

One day the floor was done. It was smooth and firm and

hard, a good floor of solid oak that would last, Pa said, for ever.

'You can't beat a good puncheon floor,' he said, and Ma said she was glad to be up off the dirt. She put the little china woman on the mantel-shelf, and spread a red-checked cloth on the table.

'There,' she said. 'Now we're living like civilized folks again.'

After that Pa filled the cracks in the walls. He drove thin strips of wood into them, and plastered them well with mud, filling every chink.

'That's a good job,' Ma said. 'That chinking will keep out the wind, no matter how hard it blows.'

Pa stopped whistling to smile at her. He slapped the last bit of mud between the logs and smoothed it and set down the bucket. At last the house was finished.

'I wish we had glass for the windows,' Pa said.

'We don't need glass, Charles,' said Ma.

'Just the same, if I do well with my hunting and trapping this winter, I'm going to get some glass in Independence next spring,' said Pa. 'And hang the expense!'

'Glass windows would be nice if we can afford them,' Ma said. 'But we'll cross that bridge when we come to it.'

They were all happy that night. The fire on the hearth was pleasant, for on the High Prairie even the summer nights were cool. The red-checked cloth was on the table, the little china woman glimmered on the mantel-shelf, and the new floor was golden in the flickering firelight. Outside, the night was large and full of stars. Pa sat for a long time in the doorway and played his fiddle and sang to Ma and Mary and Laura in the house and to the starry night outside.

11

Indians in the House

EARLY ONE MORNING Pa took his gun and went hunting. He had meant to make the bedstead that day. He had brought in the slabs, when Ma said she had no meat for dinner. So he stood the slabs against the wall and took down his gun.

Jack wanted to go hunting, too. His eyes begged Pa to take him, and whines came up from his chest and quivered in his throat till Laura almost cried with him. But Pa chained him to the stable.

'No, Jack,' Pa said. 'You must stay here and guard the place.' Then he said to Mary and Laura, 'Don't let him loose, girls.'

Poor Jack lay down. It was a disgrace to be chained, and he felt it deeply. He turned his head from Pa and would not watch him going away with the gun on his

shoulder. Pa went farther and farther away, till the prairies swallowed him and he was gone.

Laura tried to comfort Jack, but he would not be comforted. The more he thought about the chain, the worse he felt. Laura tried to cheer him up to frisk and play, but he only grew more sullen.

Both Mary and Laura felt that they could not leave Jack while he was so unhappy. So all that morning they stayed by the stable. They stroked Jack's smooth, brindled head and scratched around his ears, and told him how sorry they were that he must be chained. He licked their hands a little bit, but he was very sad and angry.

His head was on Laura's knee and she was talking to him, when suddenly he stood up and growled a fierce, deep growl. The hair on his neck stood straight up and his eyes glared red.

Laura was frightened. Jack had never growled at her before. Then she looked over her shoulder, where Jack was looking, and she saw two naked, wild men coming, one behind the other, on the Indian trail.

'Mary! Look!' she cried. Mary looked and saw them, too.

They were tall, thin, fierce-looking men. Their skin was brownish-red. Their heads seemed to go up to a peak, and the peak was a tuft of hair that stood straight up and ended in feathers. Their eyes were black and still and glittering, like snakes' eyes.

They came closer and closer. Then they went out of sight, on the other side of the house.

Laura's head turned and so did Mary's, and they looked at the place where those terrible men would appear when they came past the house.

'Indians!' Mary whispered. Laura was shivery; there was a queer feeling in her middle and the bones in her legs felt weak. She wanted to sit down. But she stood and looked and waited for those Indians to come out from beyond the house. The Indians did not do that.

All this time Jack had been growling. Now he stopped growling and was lunging against the chain. His eyes were red and his lips curled back and all the hair on his back was bristling. He bounded and bounded, clear off the

ground, trying to get loose from the chain. Laura was glad that the chain kept him right there with her.

'Jack's here,' she whispered to Mary. 'Jack won't let them hurt us. We'll be safe if we stay close to Jack.'

'They are in the house,' Mary whispered. 'They are in the house with Ma and Carrie.'

Then Laura began to shake all over. She knew she must do something. She did not know what those Indians

were doing to Ma and Baby Carrie. There was no sound at all from the house.

'Oh, what are they doing to Ma!' she screamed, in a whisper.

'Oh, I don't know!' Mary whispered.

'I'm going to let Jack loose,' Laura whispered hoarsely. 'Jack will kill them.'

'Pa said not to,' Mary answered. They were too scared to speak out loud. They put their heads together and watched the house and whispered.

'He didn't know Indians would come,' Laura said.

'He said not to let Jack loose.' Mary was almost crying.

Laura thought of little Baby Carrie and Ma, shut in the house with those Indians. She said, 'I'm going in to help Ma!'

She ran two steps, and walked a step, then she turned and flew back to Jack. She clutched him wildly and hung on to his strong, panting neck. Jack wouldn't let anything hurt her.

'We mustn't leave Ma in there alone,' Mary whispered. She stood still and trembled. Mary never could move when she was frightened. Laura hid her face against Jack and held on to him tightly.

Then she made her arms let go. Her hands balled into fists and her eyes shut tight and she ran towards the house as fast as she could run.

She stumbled and fell down and her eyes popped open. She was up again and running before she could think. Mary was close behind her. They came to the door. It was open, and they slipped into the house without a sound.

The naked wild men stood by the fireplace. Ma was bending over the fire, cooking something. Carrie clung to Ma's skirts with both hands and her head was hidden in the folds.

Laura ran towards Ma, but just as she reached the hearth she smelled a horribly bad smell and she looked up at the Indians. Quick as a flash, she ducked behind the long, narrow slab that leaned against the wall.

The slab was just wide enough to cover both her eyes. If she held her head perfectly still and pressed her nose against the slab, she couldn't see the Indians. And she felt safer. But she couldn't help moving her head just a little, so that one eye peeped out and she could see the wild men.

First she saw their leather moccasins. Then their stringy, bare, red-brown legs, all the way up. Around their waists each of the Indians wore a leather thong, and the furry skin of a small animal hung down in front. The fur was striped black and white, and now Laura knew what made that smell. The skins were fresh skunk skins.

A knife like Pa's hunting-knife, and a hatchet like Pa's hatchet, were stuck into each skunk skin.

The Indian's ribs made little ridges up their bare sides. Their arms were folded on their chests. At last Laura looked again at their faces, and she dodged quickly behind the slab.

Their faces were bold and fierce and terrible. Their black eyes glittered. High on their foreheads and above their ears where hair grows, these wild men had no hair. But on top of their heads a tuft of hair stood straight up. It was wound around with string, and feathers were stuck in it.

When Laura peeked out from behind the slab again, both Indians were looking straight at her. Her heart jumped into her throat and choked her with its pounding. Two black eyes glittered down into her eyes. The Indian did not move, not one muscle of his face moved. Only his eyes shone and sparkled at her. Laura didn't move, either. She didn't even breathe.

The Indian made two short, harsh sounds in his throat. The other Indian made one sound, like 'Hah!' Laura hid her eyes behind the slab again.

She heard Ma take the cover off the bake-oven. She heard the Indians squat down on the hearth. After a while she heard them eating.

Laura peeked, and hid, and peeked again, while the Indians ate the cornbread that Ma had baked. They ate every morsel of it, and even picked up the crumbs from the hearth. Ma stood and watched them and stroked Baby Carrie's head. Mary stood close behind Ma and held on to her sleeve.

Faintly Laura heard Jack's chain rattling. Jack was still trying to get loose.

When every crumb of the cornbread was gone, the Indians rose up. The skunk smell was stronger when they moved. One of them made harsh sounds in his throat again. Ma looked at him with big eyes; she did not say anything. The Indian turned around, the other Indian turned, too, and they walked across the floor and out through the door. Their feet made no sound at all.

Ma sighed a long, long sigh. She hugged Laura tight in one arm and Mary tight in the other arm, and through the window they watched those Indians going away, one behind the other, on the dim trail towards the west. Then Ma sat down on the bed and hugged Laura and Mary tighter, and trembled. She looked sick.

'Do you feel sick, Ma?' Mary asked her.

'No,' said Ma. 'I'm just thankful they're gone.'

Laura wrinkled her nose and said, 'They smell awful.'

'That was the skunk skins they wore,' Ma said.

Then they told her how they had left Jack and had come into the house because they were afraid the Indians would hurt her and Baby Carrie. Ma said they were her brave little girls.

'Now we must get dinner,' she said. 'Pa will be here soon and we must have dinner ready for him. Mary, bring me some wood. Laura, you may set the table.'

Ma rolled up her sleeves and washed her hands and mixed cornbread, while Mary brought the wood and Laura set the table. She set a tin plate and knife and fork and cup for Pa, and the same for Ma, with Carrie's little tin cup beside Ma's. And she set tin plates and knives and forks for her and Mary, but only their one cup between the plates.

Ma made the cornmeal and water into two thin loaves, each shaped in a half circle. She laid the loaves with their straight sides together in the bake-oven, and she pressed her hand flat on top of each loaf. Pa always said he did not ask any other sweetening, when Ma put the prints of her hands on the loaves.

Laura had hardly set the table when Pa was there. He left a big rabbit and two prairie hens outside the door, and stepped in and laid his gun on its pegs. Laura and Mary ran and clutched him, both talking at once.

'What's all this? What's all this?' he said, rumpling their hair. 'Indians? So you've seen Indians at last, have you, Laura? I noticed they have a camp in a little valley west of here. Did Indians come to the house, Caroline?'

'Yes, Charles, two of them,' Ma said. 'I'm sorry, but they took all your tobacco, and they ate a lot of cornbread. They pointed to the cornmeal and made signs for me to cook some. I was afraid not to. Oh Charles! I was afraid!'

'You did the right thing,' Pa told her. 'We don't want to make enemies of any Indians.' Then he said, 'Whew! what a smell.'

'They wore fresh skunk skins,' said Ma. 'And that was all they wore.'

'Must have been thick while they were here,' Pa said.

'It was, Charles. We were short of cornmeal, too.'

'Oh well. We have enough to hold out a while yet. And our meat is running all over the country. Don't worry, Caroline.'

'But they took all your tobacco.'

'Never mind,' Pa said. 'I'll get along without tobacco till I can make that trip to Independence. The main thing is to be on good terms with the Indians. We don't want to wake up some night with a band of screeching dev——'

He stopped. Laura dreadfully wanted to know what he had been going to say. But Ma's lips were pressed together and she shook a little shake of her head at Pa.

'Come on, Mary and Laura!' Pa said. 'We'll skin that rabbit and dress the prairie hens while that cornbread bakes. Hurry! I'm hungry as a wolf!'

They sat on the woodpile in the wind and sunshine and watched Pa work with his hunting-knife. The big rabbit was shot through the eye, and the prairie hens' heads were shot clean away. They never knew what hit them, Pa said.

Laura held the edge of the rabbit skin while Pa's keen knife ripped it off the rabbit meat. 'I'll salt this skin and peg it out on the house wall to dry,' he said. 'It will make a warm fur cap for some little girl to wear next winter.'

But Laura could not forget the Indians. She said to Pa that if they had turned Jack loose, he would have eaten those Indians right up.

Pa laid down the knife. 'Did you girls even think of turning Jack loose?' he asked, in a dreadful voice.

Laura's head bowed down and she whispered, 'Yes, Pa.'

'After I told you not to?' Pa said, in a more dreadful voice.

Laura couldn't speak, but Mary choked, 'Yes, Pa.'

For a moment Pa was silent. He sighed a long sigh like Ma's sigh after the Indians went away.

'After this,' he said, in a terrible voice, 'you girls remember always to do as you're told. Don't you even think of disobeying me. Do you hear?'

'Yes, Pa,' Laura and Mary whispered.

'Do you know what would have happened if you had turned Jack loose?' Pa asked.

'No, Pa,' they whispered.

'He would have bitten those Indians,' said Pa. 'Then there would have been trouble. Bad trouble. Do you understand?'

'Yes, Pa,' they said. But they did not understand.

'Would they have killed Jack?' Laura asked.

'Yes. And that's not all. You girls remember this: you do as you're told, no matter what happens.'

'Yes, Pa,' Laura said, and Mary said, 'Yes, Pa.' They were glad they had not turned Jack loose.

'Do as you're told,' said Pa, 'and no harm will come to you.'

12

Fresh Water to Drink

P A HAD MADE the bedstead. He had smoothed the oak slabs till there was not a splinter on them. Then he pegged them firmly together. Four slabs made a box to hold the straw-tick. Across the bottom of it Pa stretched a rope, zigzagged from side to side and pulled tight.

One end of the bedstead Pa pegged solidly to the wall, in a corner of the house. Only one corner of the bed was not against a wall. At this corner, Pa set up a tall slab. He pegged it to the bedstead. As high up as he could reach, he pegged two strips of oak to the walls and to the tall slab. Then he climbed up on them, and pegged the top of the tall slab solidly to a rafter. And on the strips of oak he laid a shelf, above the bed.

'There you are, Caroline!' he said.

'I can't wait to see it made up,' said Ma. 'Help me bring in the straw-tick.'

She had filled the straw-tick that morning. There was no straw on the High Prairie, so she had filled it with dry, clean, dead grass. It was hot from the sunshine and it had a grassy, sweet smell. Pa helped her bring it into the house and lay it in the bedstead. She tucked the sheets in, and spread her prettiest patchwork quilt over them. At the head of the bed she set up the goose-feather pillows, and spread the pillow-shams against them. On each white pillow-sham two little birds were outlined with red thread.

Then Pa and Ma and Laura and Mary stood and looked at the bed. It was a very nice bed. The zigzag rope was softer than the floor to sleep on. The straw-tick was plump with the sweet-smelling grass, the quilt lay smooth, and the pretty pillow-shams stood up crisply. The shelf was a good place to store things. The whole house had quite an air, with such a bed in it.

That night when Ma went to bed, she settled into the crackling straw-tick and said to Pa, 'I declare, I'm so comfortable it's almost sinful.'

Mary and Laura still slept on the floor, but Pa would make a little bed for them as soon as he could. He had made the big bed, and he had made a stout cupboard and padlocked it, so the Indians could not take all the corn-meal if they came again. Now he had only to dig a well, and then he would make that trip to town. He must dig the well first, so that Ma could have water while he was gone.

Next morning he marked a large circle in the grass near the corner of the house. With his spade he cut the sod inside the circle, and lifted it up in large pieces. Then he began to shovel out the earth, digging himself deeper and deeper down.

Mary and Laura must not go near the well while Pa was digging. Even when they couldn't see his head any more, shovelfuls of earth came flying up. At last the spade flew up and fell in the grass. Then Pa jumped. His hands caught hold of the sod, then one elbow gripped it, and then the other elbow, and with a heave Pa came rolling out. 'I can't throw the dirt out from any deeper,' he said.

He had to have help, now. So he took his gun and rode away on Patty. When he came back he brought a plump rabbit, and he had traded work with Mr Scott. Mr Scott would help him dig this well, and then he would help dig Mr Scott's well.

Ma and Laura and Mary had not seen Mr and Mrs Scott. Their house was hidden somewhere in a little valley on the prairie. Laura had seen the smoke rising up from it, and that was all.

At dawn next morning Mr Scott came. He was short and stout. His hair was bleached by the sun and his skin was bright red and scaly. He did not tan; he peeled.

'It's this blasted sun and wind,' he said. 'Beg your pardon, ma'am, but it's enough to make a saint use strong language. I might as well be a snake, the way I keep on shedding my skin in this country.'

Laura liked him. Every morning, as soon as the dishes were washed and the beds made, she ran out to watch Mr Scott and Pa working at the well. The sunshine was blistering, even the winds were hot, and the prairie grasses were turning yellow. Mary preferred to stay in the house and sew on her patchwork quilt. But Laura liked the fierce light and the sun and the wind, and she couldn't stay away from the well. But she was not allowed to go near its edge.

Pa and Mr Scott had made a stout windlass. It stood over the well, and two buckets hung from it on the ends of a rope. When the windlass was turned, one bucket went down into the well and the other bucket came up. In the morning Mr Scott slid down the rope and dug. He filled the buckets with earth, almost as fast as Pa could haul them up and empty them. After dinner, Pa slid down the rope into the well, and Mr Scott hauled up the buckets.

Every morning, before Pa would let Mr Scott go down the rope, he set a candle in a bucket and lighted it and lowered it to the bottom. Once Laura peeped over the edge and she saw the candle brightly burning, far down in the dark hole in the ground.

Then Pa would say, 'Seems to be all right,' and he would pull up the bucket and blow out the candle.

'That's all foolishness, Ingalls,' Mr Scott said. 'The well was all right yesterday.'

'You can't ever tell,' Pa replied. 'Better be safe than sorry.'

Laura did not know what danger Pa was looking for by that candle-light. She did not ask, because Pa and Mr Scott were busy. She meant to ask later, but she forgot.

One morning Mr Scott came while Pa was eating break-fast. They heard him shout: 'Hi, Ingalls! It's sunup. Let's go!' Pa drank his coffee and went out.

The windlass began to creak and Pa began to whistle. Laura and Mary were washing the dishes and Ma was making the big bed, when Pa's whistling stopped. They heard him say, 'Scott!' He shouted, 'Scott! Scott!' Then he called: 'Caroline! Come quick!'

Ma ran out of the house. Laura ran after her.

'Scott's fainted, or something, down there,' Pa said. 'I've got to go down after him.'

'Did you send down the candle?' Ma asked.

'No. I thought he had. I asked him if it was all right, and he said it was.' Pa cut the empty bucket off the rope and tied the rope firmly to the windlass.

'Charles, you can't. You mustn't,' Ma said.

'Caroline, I've got to.'

'You can't. Oh, Charles, no!'

'I'll make it all right. I won't breathe till I get out. We can't let him die down there.'

Ma said, fiercely: 'Laura, keep back!' So Laura kept back. She stood against the house and shivered.

'No, no, Charles! I can't let you,' Ma said. 'Get on Patty and go for help.'

'There isn't time.'

'Charles, if I can't pull you up—if you keel over down there and I can't pull you up——'

'Caroline, I've got to,' Pa said. He swung into the well. His head slid out of sight, down the rope.

Ma crouched and shaded her eyes, staring down into the well.

All over the prairie meadowlarks were rising, singing, flying straight up into the sky. The wind was blowing warmer, but Laura was cold.

Suddenly Ma jumped up and seized the handle of the windlass. She tugged at it with all her might. The rope strained and the windlass creaked. Laura thought that

Pa had keeled over, down in the dark bottom of the well, and Ma couldn't pull him up. But the windlass turned a little, and then a little more.

Pa's hand came up, holding to the rope. His other hand reached above it and took hold of the rope. Then Pa's head came up. His arm held on to the windlass. Then somehow he got to the ground and sat there.

The windlass whirled around and there was a thud deep down in the well. Pa struggled to get up and Ma said: 'Sit still, Charles! Laura, get some water. Quick!'

Laura ran. She came hurrying back, lugging the pail of water. Pa and Ma were both turning the windlass. The rope slowly wound itself up, and the bucket came up out of the well, and tied to the bucket and the rope was Mr Scott. His arms and his legs and his head hung and wobbled, his mouth was partly open and his eyes half shut.

Pa tugged him on to the grass. Pa rolled him over and he flopped where he was rolled. Pa felt his wrist and listened at his chest, and then Pa lay down beside him.

'He's breathing,' Pa said. 'He'll be all right, in the air. I'm all right, Caroline. I'm plumb tuckered out, that's all.'

'Well!' Ma scolded. 'I should think you would be! Of all the senseless performances! My goodness gracious! scaring a body to death, all for want of a little reasonable care! My goodness! I——' She covered her face with her apron and burst out crying.

That was a terrible day.

'I don't want a well,' Ma sobbed. 'It isn't worth it. I won't have you running such risks!'

Mr Scott had breathed a kind of gas that stays deep in the ground. It stays at the bottom of wells because it is heavier than the air. It cannot be seen or smelled, but no one can breathe it very long and live. Pa had gone down into that gas to tie Mr Scott to the rope so that he could be pulled up out of the gas.

When Mr Scott was able, he went home. Before he went he said to Pa: 'You were right about that candle business, Ingalls. I thought it was all foolishness and I would not bother with it, but I've found out my mistake.'

'Well,' said Pa, 'where a light can't live, I know I can't. And I like to be safe when I can be. But all's well that ends well.'

Pa rested awhile. He had breathed a little of the gas and he felt like resting. But that afternoon he unravelled a thread from a tow sack, and he took a little powder from his powder-horn. He tied the powder in a piece of cloth with one end of the tow string in the powder.

'Come along, Laura,' he said, 'and I'll show you something.'

They went to the well. Pa lighted the end of the string and waited till the spark was crawling quickly along it. Then he dropped the little bundle into the well.

In a minute they heard a muffled bang! and a puff of smoke came out of the well. 'That will bring the gas,' Pa said.

When the smoke was all gone, he let Laura light the candle and stand beside him while he let it down. All the way down in the dark hole the little candle kept on burning like a star.

So next day Pa and Mr Scott went on digging the well. But they always sent the candle down every morning.

There began to be a little water in the well, but it was not enough. The buckets came up full of mud, and Pa and Mr Scott worked every day in deeper mud. In the mornings when the candle went down, it lighted oozing-wet walls, and candlelight sparkled in rings over the water when the bucket struck bottom.

Pa stood knee deep in water and bailed out bucketfuls before he could begin digging in the mud.

One day when he was digging, a loud shout came echoing up. Ma ran out of the house and Laura ran to the well. 'Pull, Scott! Pull!' Pa yelled. A swishing, gurgling sound echoed down there. Mr Scott turned the windlass as fast as he could, and Pa came up climbing hand over hand up the rope.

'I'm blamed if that's not quicksand!' Pa gasped, as he stepped on to the ground, muddy and dripping. 'I was pushing down hard on the spade, when all of a sudden it went down, the whole length of the handle. And water came pouring up all around me.'

'A good six feet of this rope's wet,' Mr Scott said, winding it up. The bucket was full of water. 'You showed sense in getting out of that hand over hand, Ingalls. That water came up faster than I could pull you out.' Then Mr Scott slapped his thigh and shouted, 'I'm blasted if you didn't bring up the spade!'

Sure enough, Pa had saved his spade.

In a little while the well was almost full of water. A circle of blue sky lay not far down in the ground, and when Laura looked at it, a little girl's head looked up at her. When she waved her hand, a hand on the water's surface waved, too.

The water was clear and cold and good. Laura thought she had never tasted anything so good as those long, cold drinks of water. Pa hauled no more stale, warm water from the creek. He built a solid platform over the well, and a heavy cover for the hole that let the water-bucket through. Laura must never touch that cover. But whenever she or Mary was thirsty, Ma lifted the cover and drew a dripping bucket of cold, fresh water from that well.

13

Texas Longhorns

ONE EVENING LAURA and Pa were sitting on the doorstep. The moon shone over the dark prairie, the winds were still, and softly Pa played his fiddle.

He let a last note quiver far, far away, until it dissolved in the moonlight. Everything was so beautiful that Laura wanted it to stay so for ever. But Pa said it was time for little girls to go to bed.

Then Laura heard a strange, low, distant sound. 'What's that?' she said.

Pa listened. 'Cattle, by George!' he said. 'Must be the cattle herds going north to Fort Dodge.'

After she was undressed, Laura stood in her nightgown at the window. The air was very still, not a grass blade rustled, and far away and faint she could hear that sound. It was almost a rumble and almost a song.

'Is that singing, Pa?' she asked.

'Yes,' Pa said. 'The cowboys are singing the cattle to sleep. Now hop into bed, you little scallawag!'

Laura thought of cattle lying on the dark ground in the moonlight, and of cowboys softly singing lullabies.

Next morning when she ran out of the house two strange men were sitting on horses by the stable. They were talking to Pa. They were as red-brown as Indians, but their eyes were narrow slits between squinting eyelids. They wore flaps of leather over their legs, and spurs, and wide-brimmed hats. Handkerchiefs were knotted around their necks, and pistols were on their hips.

They said, 'So long,' to Pa, and 'Hi! Yip!' to their horses, and they galloped away.

'Here's a piece of luck!' Pa said to Ma. Those men were cowboys. They wanted Pa to help them keep the cattle out of the ravines among the bluffs of the creek bottoms. Pa would not charge them any money, but he told them he would take a piece of beef. 'How would you like a good piece of beef?' Pa asked.

'Oh, Charles!' said Ma, and her eyes shone.

Pa tied his biggest handkerchief around his neck. He showed Laura how he could pull it up over his mouth and nose to keep the dust out. Then he rode Patty west along the Indian trail, till Laura and Mary couldn't see him any more.

All day the hot sun blazed and the hot winds blew, and the sound of the cattle herds came nearer. It was a faint, mournful sound of cattle lowing. At noon dust was blowing along the horizon. Ma said that so many cattle trampled the grasses flat and stirred up dust from the prairie.

Pa came riding home at sunset, covered with dust. There was dust in his beard and in his hair and on the rims of his eyelids, and dust fell off his clothes. He did not bring any beef, because the cattle were not across the creek yet. The cattle went very slowly, eating grass as they went. They had to eat enough grass to be fat when they came to the cities where people ate them.

Pa did not talk much that night, and he didn't play the fiddle. He went to bed soon after supper.

The herds were so near now that Laura could hear them plainly. The mournful lowing sounded over the prairie till the night was dark. Then the cattle were quieter and the cowboys began to sing. Their songs were not like lullabies. They were high, lonely, wailing songs, almost like the howling of wolves.

Laura lay awake, listening to the lonely songs wandering in the night. Farther away, real wolves howled. Sometimes the cattle lowed. But the cowboys' songs went on, rising and falling and wailing away under the moon. When everyone else was asleep, Laura stole softly to the window, and she saw three fires gleaming like red eyes from the dark edge of the land. Overhead the sky was big and still and full of moonlight. The lonely songs seemed to be crying for the moon. They made Laura's throat ache.

All next day Laura and Mary watched the west. They could hear the far-away bawling of the cattle, they could see dust blowing. Sometimes they thinly heard a shrill yell.

Suddenly a dozen long-horned cattle burst out of the prairie, not far from the stable. They had come up out of a draw going down to the creek bottoms. Their tails stood up and their fierce horns tossed and their feet pounded the ground. A cowboy on a spotted mustang galloped madly to get in front of them. He waved his big hat and yelled sharp, high yells. 'Hi! Yi-yi-yi! Hi!' The cattle wheeled, clashing their long horns together. With lifted tails they galloped lumbering away, and behind them the mustang ran and whirled and ran, herding them together. They all went over a rise of ground and down out of sight.

Laura ran back and forth, waving her sun-bonnet and yelling, 'Hi! Yi-yi-yi!' till Ma told her to stop. It was not ladylike to yell like that. Laura wished she could be a cowboy.

Late that afternoon three riders came out of the west, driving one lone cow. One of the riders was Pa, on Patty. Slowly they came nearer, and Laura saw that with the cow was a little spotted calf.

The cow came lunging and plunging. Two cowboys rode well apart in front of her. Two ropes around her long horns were fastened to the cowboys' saddles. When the cow lunged with her horns towards either cowboy the other cowboy's pony braced its feet and held her. The cow bawled and the little calf bleated thinner bawls.

Ma watched from the window, while Mary and Laura stood against the house and stared.

The cowboys held the cow with their ropes while Pa tied her to the stable. Then they said good-bye to him and rode away.

Ma could not believe that Pa had actually brought home a cow. But it really was their own cow. The calf was too small to travel, Pa said, and the cow would be too thin to sell, so the cowboys had given them to Pa. They had given him the beef, too; a big chunk was tied to his saddle-horn.

Pa and Ma and Mary and Laura and even Baby Carrie laughed for joy. Pa always laughed out loud and his laugh was like great bells ringing. When Ma was pleased she smiled a gentle smile that made Laura feel warm all over. But now she was laughing because they had a cow.

'Give me a bucket, Caroline,' said Pa. He was going to milk the cow, right away.

He took the bucket, he pushed back his hat, and he squatted by the cow to milk her. And that cow hunched herself and kicked Pa flat on his back.

Pa jumped up. His face was blazing red and his eyes snapped blue sparks.

'Now, by the Great Horn Spoon, I'll milk her!' he said.

He got his axe and he sharpened two stout slabs of oak. He pushed the cow against the stable, and he drove those slabs deep into the ground beside her. The cow bawled and the little calf squalled. Pa tied poles firmly to the posts and stuck their ends into the cracks of the stable, to make a fence.

Now the cow could not move forward nor backward nor sideways. But the little calf could nudge its way between its mother and the stable. So the baby calf felt safe and stopped bawling. It stood on that side of the cow and drank its supper, and Pa put his hand through the fence and milked from the other side. He got a tin cup almost full of milk.

'We'll try again in the morning,' he said. 'The poor thing's as wild as a deer. But we'll gentle her, we'll gentle her.'

The dark was coming on. Nighthawks were chasing insects in the dark air. Bullfrogs were croaking in the creek bottoms. A bird called, 'Whip! Whip! Whip-poor-Will!'

'Who? Who-oo?' said an owl. Far away the wolves howled, and Jack was growling.

'The wolves are following the herds,' Pa said. 'To-morrow I'll build a strong high yard for the cow, that wolves can't get into.'

So they all went into the house with the beef. Pa and Ma and Mary and Laura all agreed to give the milk to Baby Carrie. They watched her drink it. The tin cup hid her face, but Laura could see the gulps of milk going down her throat. Gulp by gulp, she swallowed all that good milk. Then she licked the foam from her lips with her red tongue, and laughed.

It seemed a long time before the cornbread and the sizzling beef steaks were done. But nothing had ever tasted so good as that tough, juicy beef. And everyone was happy because now there would be milk to drink, and perhaps even butter for the cornbread.

The lowing of the cattle herds was far away again, and the songs of the cowboys were almost too faint to be heard. All those cattle were on the other side of the creek bottoms now, in Kansas. Tomorrow they would slowly go farther on their long way northward to Fort Dodge, where the soldiers were.

14

Indian Camp

DAY AFTER DAY was hotter than the day before. The wind was hot. 'As if it came out of an oven,' Ma said.

The grass was turning yellow. The whole world was rippling green and gold under the blazing sky.

At noon the wind died. No birds sang. Everything was so still that Laura could hear the squirrels chattering in the trees down by the creek. Suddenly black crows flew overhead, cawing their rough, sharp caws. Then everything was still again.

Ma said that this was midsummer.

Pa wondered where the Indians had gone. He said they had left their little camp on the prairie. And one day he asked Laura and Mary if they would like to see that camp.

Laura jumped up and down and clapped her hands, but Ma objected.

'It is so far, Charles,' she said. 'And in this heat.'

Pa's blue eyes twinkled. 'This heat doesn't hurt the Indians and it won't hurt us,' he said. 'Come on, girls!'

'Please, can't Jack come, too?' Laura begged. Pa had taken his gun, but he looked at Laura and he looked at Jack, then he looked at Ma, and he put the gun up on its pegs again.

'All right, Laura,' he said. 'I'll take Jack, Caroline, and leave you the gun.'

Jack jumped around them, wagging his stump of a tail. As soon as he saw which way they were going, he set off, trotting ahead. Pa came next, and behind him came Mary, and then Laura. Mary kept her sun-bonnet on, but Laura let hers dangle down her back.

The ground was hot under their bare feet. The sunshine pierced through their faded dresses and tingled on their arms and backs. The air was really as hot as the air in an oven, and it smelled faintly like baking bread. Pa said the smell came from all the grass seeds parching in the heat.

They went farther and farther into the vast prairie. Laura felt smaller and smaller. Even Pa did not seem as big as he really was. At last they went down into the little hollow where the Indians had camped.

Jack started up a big rabbit. When it bounded out o the grass Laura jumped. Pa said quickly: 'Let him go, Jack! We have meat enough.' So Jack sat down and watched the big rabbit go bounding away down the hollow.

Laura and Mary looked around them. They stayed close to Pa. Low bushes grew on the sides of the hollow—buck-brush with sprays of berries faintly pink, and sumac holding up green cones but showing here and there a bright red leaf. The goldenrod's plumes were turning grey, and the ox-eyed daisies' yellow petals hung down from the crown centres.

All this was hidden in the secret little hollow. From the house Laura had seen nothing but grasses, and now from this hollow she could not see the house. The prairie seemed to be level, but it was not level.

Laura asked Pa if there were lots of hollows on the prairie, like this one. He said there were.

'Are Indians in them?' she almost whispered. He said he didn't know. There might be.

She held tight to his hand and Mary held to his other hand, and they looked at the Indians' camp. There were ashes where Indian camp fires had been. There were holes in the ground where tent-poles had been driven. Bones were scattered where Indian dogs had gnawed them. All along the sides of the hollow, Indian ponies had bitten the grasses short.

Tracks of big moccasins and smaller moccasins were everywhere, and tracks of little bare toes. And over these tracks were tracks of rabbits and tracks of birds, and wolves' tracks.

Pa read the tracks for Mary and Laura. He showed them tracks of two middle-sized moccasins by the edge of a camp fire's ashes. An Indian woman had squatted there. She wore a leather skirt with fringes; the tiny marks of the fringe were in the dust. The track of her toes inside the moccasins was deeper than the track of her heels, because she had leaned forward to stir something cooking in a pot on the fire.

Then Pa picked up a smoke-blackened forked stick. And he said that the pot had hung from a stick laid across the top of two upright, forked sticks. He showed Mary and Laura the holes where the forked sticks had been driven into the ground. Then he told them to look at the bones around that camp fire and tell him what had cooked in that pot.

They looked, and they said, 'Rabbit.' That was right; the bones were rabbits' bones.

Suddenly Laura shouted, 'Look! Look!' Something bright blue glittered in the dust. She picked it up, and it was a beautiful blue bead. Laura shouted with joy.

Then Mary saw a red bead, and Laura saw a green one, and they forgot everything but beads. Pa helped them look. They found white beads and brown beads,

and more and more red and blue beads. All that afternoon they hunted for beads in the dust of the Indian
camp. Now and then Pa walked up to the edge of the
hollow and looked towards home, then he came back
and helped to hunt for more beads. They looked all the
ground over carefully.

When they couldn't find any more, it was almost
sunset. Laura had a handful of beads, and so did Mary.
Pa tied them carefully in his handkerchief, Laura's beads
in one corner and Mary's in another corner. He put the
handkerchief in his pocket, and they started home.

The sun was low behind their backs when they came out
of the hollow. Home was small and very far away. And
Pa did not have his gun.

Pa walked so swiftly that Laura could hardly keep up.
She trotted as fast as she could, but the sun sank faster.
Home seemed farther and farther away. The prairie
seemed larger, and a wind ran over it, whispering something frightening. All the grasses shook as if they were
scared.

Then Pa turned around and his blue eyes twinkled at
Laura. He said: 'Getting tired, little half-pint? It's a
long way for little legs.'

He picked her up, big girl that she was, and he settled
her safe against his shoulder. He took Mary by the hand,
and so they all came home together.

Supper was cooking on the fire, Ma was setting the
table, and Baby Carrie played with little pieces of wood
on the floor. Pa tossed the handkerchief to Ma.

'I'm later than I meant, Caroline,' he said. 'But look
what the girls found.' He took the milk-bucket and went
quickly to bring Pet and Patty from their picket-lines and
to milk the cow.

Ma untied the handkerchief and exclaimed at what she

found. The beads were even prettier than they had been in the Indian camp.

Laura stirred her beads with her finger and watched them sparkle and shine. 'These are mine,' she said.

Then Mary said, 'Carrie can have mine.'

Ma waited to hear what Laura would say. Laura didn't want to say anything. She wanted to keep those pretty beads. Her chest felt all hot inside, and she wished with all her might that Mary wouldn't always be such a good little girl. But she couldn't let Mary be better than she was.

So she said, slowly, 'Carrie can have mine, too.'

'That's my unselfish, good little girls,' said Ma.

She poured Mary's beads into Mary's hands, and Laura's into Laura's hands, and she said she would give them a thread to string them on. The beads would make a pretty necklace for Carrie to wear around her neck.

Mary and Laura sat side by side on their bed, and they strung those pretty beads on the thread that Ma gave them. Each wet her end of the thread in her mouth and twisted it tightly. Then Mary put her end of the thread through the small hole in each of the beads, and Laura put her end through her beads, one by one.

They didn't say anything. Perhaps Mary felt sweet and good inside, but Laura didn't. When she looked at Mary she wanted to slap her. So she dared not look at Mary again.

The beads made a beautiful string. Carrie clapped her hands and laughed when she saw it. Then Ma tied it around Carrie's little neck, and it glittered there. Laura felt a little bit better. After all, her beads were not enough beads to make a whole string, and neither were Mary's, but together they made a whole string of beads for Carrie.

When Carrie felt the beads on her neck, she grabbed at them. She was so little that she did not know any better than to break the string. So Ma untied it, and she put the beads away until Carrie should be old enough to wear them. And often after that Laura thought of those pretty beads and she was still naughty enough to want her beads for herself.

But it had been a wonderful day. She could always think about that long walk across the prairie, and about all they had seen in the Indian camp.

15

Fever 'n' Ague

NOW BLACKBERRIES WERE ripe, and in the hot afternoons Laura went with Ma to pick them. The big, black, juicy berries hung thick in brier-patches in the creek bottoms. Some were in the shade of trees and some were in the sun, but the sun was so hot that Laura and Ma stayed in the shade. There were plenty of berries.

Deer lay in the shady groves and watched Ma and Laura. Blue jays flew at their sun-bonnets and scolded because they were taking the berries. Snakes hurriedly crawled away from them, and in the trees the squirrels woke up and chattered at them. Wherever they went among the scratchy briers, mosquitoes rose up in buzzing swarms.

Mosquitoes were thick on the big, ripe berries, sucking the sweet juice. But they liked to bite Laura and Ma as much as they liked to eat blackberries.

Laura's fingers and her mouth were purple-black with berry juice. Her face and her hands and her bare feet were covered with brier scratches and mosquito bites. And they were spattered with purple stains, too, where she had slapped at the mosquitoes. But every day they brought home pails full of berries, and Ma spread them in the sun to dry.

Every day they ate all the blackberries they wanted,

and next winter they would have dried blackberries to stew.

Mary hardly ever went to pick blackberries. She stayed in the house to mind Baby Carrie, because she was older. In the daytime there were only one or two mosquitoes in the house. But at night, if the wind wasn't blowing hard, mosquitoes came in thick swarms. On still nights Pa kept piles of damp grass burning all around the house and the stable. The damp grass made a smudge of smoke, to keep the mosquitoes away. But a good many mosquitoes came, anyway.

Pa could not play his fiddle in the evenings because so many mosquitoes bit him. Mr Edwards did not come visiting after supper any more, because the mosquitoes were so thick in the bottoms. All night Pet and Patty and the colt and the calf and the cow were stamping and swishing their tails in the stable. And in the morning Laura's forehead was speckled with mosquito bites.

'This won't last long,' Pa said. 'Fall's not far away, and the first cold wind will settle 'em!'

Laura did not feel very well. One day she felt cold even in the hot sunshine, and she could not get warm by the fire.

Ma asked why she and Mary did not go out to play, and Laura said she didn't feel like playing. She was tired and she ached. Ma stopped her work and asked, 'Where do you ache?'

Laura didn't exactly know. She said: 'I just ache. My legs ache.'

'I ache, too,' Mary said.

Ma looked at them and said they looked healthy enough. But she said something must be wrong or they wouldn't be so quiet. She pulled up Laura's skirt and petticoats to see where her legs ached, and suddenly

Laura shivered all over. She shivered so that her teeth rattled in her mouth.

Ma put her hand against Laura's cheek. 'You can't be cold,' she said. 'Your face is hot as fire.'

Laura felt like crying, but of course she didn't. Only little babies cried. 'I'm hot now,' she said. 'And my back aches.'

Ma called Pa, and he came in. 'Charles, do look at the girls,' she said. 'I do believe they are sick.'

'Well, I don't feel any too well myself,' said Pa. 'First I'm hot and then I'm cold, and I ache all over. Is that the way you feel, girls? Do your very bones ache?'

Mary and Laura said that was the way they felt. Then Ma and Pa looked a long time at each other and Ma said, 'The place for you girls is bed.'

It was so queer to be put to bed in the daytime, and Laura was so hot that everything seemed wavering. She held on to Ma's neck while Ma was undressing her, and she begged Ma to tell her what was wrong with her.

'You will be all right. Don't worry,' Ma said, cheerfully. Laura crawled into bed and Ma tucked her in. It felt good to be in bed. Ma smoothed her forehead with her cool, soft hand and said, 'There, now. Go to sleep.'

Laura did not exactly go to sleep, but she didn't really wake up again for a long, long time. Strange things seemed to keep happening in a haze. She would see Pa crouching by the fire in the middle of the night, then suddenly sunshine hurt her eyes and Ma fed her broth from a spoon. Something dwindled slowly, smaller and smaller, till it was tinier than the tiniest thing. Then slowly it swelled till it was larger than anything could be. Two voices jabbered faster and faster, then a slow voice drawled more slowly than Laura could bear. There were no words, only voices.

Mary was hot in the bed beside her. Mary threw off the covers, and Laura cried because she was so cold. Then she was burning up, and Pa's hand shook the cup of water. Water spilled down her neck. The tin cup rattled against her teeth till she could hardly drink. Then Ma tucked in the covers and Ma's hand burned against Laura's cheek.

She heard Pa say, 'Go to bed, Caroline.'

Ma said, 'You're sicker than I am, Charles.'

Laura opened her eyes and saw bright sunshine. Mary was sobbing, 'I want a drink of water! I want a drink of water! I want a drink of water!' Jack went back and forth between the big bed and the little bed. Laura saw Pa lying on the floor by the big bed.

Jack pawed at Pa and whined. He took hold of Pa's sleeve with his teeth and shook it. Pa's head lifted up a little and he said, 'I must get up, I must. Caroline and the girls.' Then his head fell back and he lay still. Jack lifted up his nose and howled.

Laura tried to get up, but she was too tired. Then she saw Ma's red face looking over the edge of the big bed. Mary was all the time crying for water. Ma looked at Mary and then she looked at Laura, and she whispered, 'Laura, can you?'

'Yes, Ma,' Laura said. This time she got out of bed. But when she tried to stand up, the floor rocked and she fell down. Jack's tongue lapped and lapped at her face, and he quivered and whined. But he stood still and firm when she took hold of him and sat up against him.

She knew she must get water to stop Mary's crying, and she did. She crawled all the way across the floor to the water-bucket. There was only a little water in it.

She shook so with cold that she could hardly get hold of the dipper. But she did get hold of it. She dipped up some water, and she set out to cross that enormous floor again. Jack stayed beside her all the way.

Mary's eyes didn't open. Her hands held on to the dipper and her mouth swallowed all the water out of it. Then she stopped crying. The dipper fell on the floor, and Laura crawled under the covers. It was a long time before she began to get warm again.

Sometimes she heard Jack sobbing. Sometimes he howled and she thought he was a wolf, but she was not afraid. She lay burning up and hearing him howl. She heard the voices jabbering again, and the slow voice drawling, and she opened her eyes and saw a big, black face close above her face.

It was coal-black and shiny. Its eyes were black and soft. Its teeth shone white in a thick, big mouth. This face smiled, and a deep voice said, softly, 'Drink this, little girl.'

An arm lifted under her shoulders, and a black hand held a cup to her mouth. Laura swallowed a bitter

swallow and tried to turn her head away, but the cup followed her mouth. The mellow, deep voice said again, 'Drink it. It will make you well.' So Laura swallowed the whole bitter dose.

When she woke up, a fat woman was stirring the fire. Laura looked at her carefully and she was not black. She was tanned, like Ma.

'I want a drink of water, please,' Laura said.

The fat woman brought it at once. The good, cold water made Laura feel better. She looked at Mary asleep beside her; she looked at Pa and Ma asleep in the big bed. Jack lay half asleep on the floor. Laura looked again at the fat woman and asked, 'Who are you?'

'I'm Mrs Scott,' the woman said, smiling. 'There now, you feel better, don't you?'

'Yes, thank you,' Laura said politely. The fat woman brought her a cup of hot prairie-chicken broth.

'Drink it all up, like a good child,' she said. Laura drank every drop of the good broth. 'Now go to sleep,' said Mrs Scott. 'I'm here to take care of everything till you're all well.'

Next morning Laura felt so much better that she wanted to get up, but Mrs Scott said she must stay in bed until the doctor came. She lay and watched Mrs Scott tidy the house and give medicine to Pa and Ma and Mary. Then it was Laura's turn. She opened her mouth, and Mrs Scott poured a dreadful bitterness out of a small folded paper on to Laura's tongue. Laura drank water and swallowed and swallowed and drank again. She could swallow the powder but she couldn't swallow the bitterness.

Then the doctor came. And he was the black man. Laura had never seen a black man before and she could not take her eyes off Dr Tan. He was so very black. She would have been afraid of him if she had not liked him so much. He smiled at her with all his white teeth. He talked with Pa and Ma, and laughed a rolling, jolly laugh. They all wanted him to stay longer, but he had to hurry away.

Mrs Scott said that all the settlers, up and down the creek, had fever 'n' ague. There were not enough well people to take care of the sick, and she had been going from house to house, working night and day.

'It's a wonder you ever lived through,' she said. 'All of you down at once.' What might have happened if Dr Tan hadn't found them, she didn't know.

Dr Tan was a doctor with the Indians. He was on his way north to Independence when he came to Pa's house. It was a strange thing that Jack, who hated strangers and never let one come near the house until Pa or Ma told him to, had gone to meet Dr Tan and begged him to come in.

'And here you all were, more dead than alive,' Mrs Scott said. Dr Tan had stayed with them a day and a night before Mrs Scott came. Now he was doctoring all the sick settlers.

Mrs Scott said that all this sickness came from eating water-melons. She said, 'I've said a hundred times, if I have once, that water-melons——'

'What's that?' Pa exclaimed. 'Who's got water-melons?'

Mrs Scott said that one of the settlers had planted water-melons in the creek bottoms. And every soul who had eaten one of those melons was down sick that very minute. She said she had warned them. 'But, no,' she said. 'There was no arguing with them. They would eat those melons, and now they're paying for it.'

'I haven't tasted a good slice of water-melon since Hector was a pup,' said Pa.

Next day he was out of bed. The next day, Laura was

up. Then Ma got up, and then Mary. They were all thin and shaky, but they could take care of themselves. So Mrs Scott went home.

Ma said she didn't know how they could ever thank her, and Mrs Scott said, 'Pshaw! What are neighbours for but to help each other out?'

Pa's cheeks were hollows and he walked slowly. Ma often sat down to rest. Laura and Mary didn't feel like playing. Every morning they all took those bitter powders. But Ma still smiled her lovely smile, and Pa whistled cheerfully.

'It's an ill wind that doesn't blow some good,' he said. He wasn't able to work, so he could make a rocking-chair for Ma.

He brought some slender willows from the creek bot-toms, and he made the chair in the house. He could stop any time to put wood on the fire or lift a kettle for Ma.

First he made four stout legs and braced them firmly with cross-pieces. Then he cut thin strips of the tough willow-skin, just under the bark. He wove these strips back and forth, under and over, till they made a seat for the chair.

He split a long, straight sapling down the middle. He pegged one end of half of it to the side of the seat, and curved it up and over and down, and pegged the other end to the other side of the seat. That made a high, curved back to the chair. He braced it firmly, and then he wove the thin willow-strips across and up and down, under and over each other, till they filled in the chair-back.

With the other half of the split sapling Pa made arms for the chair. He curved them from the front of the seat to the chair-back, and he filled them in with woven strips.

Last of all, he split a larger willow which had grown in a curve. He turned the chair upside down, and he pegged the curved pieces to its legs, to make the rockers. And the chair was done.

Then they made a celebration. Ma took off her apron and smoothed her smooth brown hair. She pinned her gold pin in the front of her collar. Mary tied the string of beads around Carrie's neck. Pa and Laura put Mary's pillow on the chair-seat, and set Laura's pillow against its back. Over the pillows Pa spread the quilt from the little bed. Then he took Ma's hand and led her to the chair, and he put Baby Carrie in her arms.

Ma leaned back in the softness. Her thin cheeks flushed and her eyes sparkled with tears, but her smile was beautiful. The chair rocked her gently and she said, 'Oh, Charles! I haven't been so comfortable since I don't know when.'

Then Pa took his fiddle, and he played and sang to Ma in the firelight. Ma rocked and Baby Carrie went to

sleep, and Mary and Laura sat on their bench and were happy.

The very next day, without saying where he was going, Pa rode away on Patty. Ma wondered and wondered where he had gone. And when Pa came back he was balancing a water-melon in front of him on the saddle.

He could hardly carry it into the house. He let it fall on the floor, and dropped down beside it.

'I thought I'd never get it here,' he said. 'It must weigh forty pounds, and I'm as weak as water. Hand me the butcher knife.'

'But, Charles!' Ma said. 'You mustn't. Mrs Scott said——'

Pa laughed his big, pealing laugh again. 'But that's not reasonable,' he said. 'This is a good melon. Why should it have fever 'n' ague? Everybody knows that fever 'n' ague comes from breathing the night air.'

'This water-melon grew in the night air,' said Ma.

'Nonsense!' Pa said. 'Give me the butcher knife. I'd eat this melon if I knew it would give me chills and fever.'

'I do believe you would,' said Ma, handing him the knife.

It went into the melon with a luscious sound. The green rind split open, and there was the bright red inside, flecked with black seeds. The red heart actually looked frosty. Nothing had ever been so tempting as that water-melon, on that hot day.

Ma would not taste it. She would not let Laura and Mary eat one bite. But Pa ate slice after slice after slice, until at last he sighed and said the cow could have the rest of it.

Next day he had a little chill and a little fever. Ma blamed the water-melon. But next day she had a chill and a little fever. So, they did not know what could have caused their fever 'n' ague.

No one knew, in those days, that fever 'n' ague was malaria, and that some mosquitoes give it to people when they bite them.

16

Fire in the Chimney

THE PRAIRIE HAD changed. Now it was a dark yellow, almost brown, and red streaks of sumac lay across it. The wind wailed in the tall grass, and it whispered sadly across the curly, short buffalo grass. At night the wind sounded like someone crying.

Pa said again that this was a great country. In the Big Woods he had had to cut hay and cure it and stack it and put it in the barn for winter. Here on the High Prairie, the sun had cured the wild grass where it stood, and all winter the mustangs and the cow could mow their own hay. He needed only a small stack, for stormy days.

Now the weather was cooler and he would go to town. He had not gone while the summer was hot, because the heat would be too hard on Pet and Patty. They must pull the wagon twenty miles a day, to get to town in two days. And he did not want to be away from home any longer than he had to.

He stacked the small stack of hay by the barn. He cut the winter's wood and corded it in a long cord against the house. Now he had only to get meat enough to last while he was gone, so he took his gun and went hunting.

Laura and Mary played in the wind outdoors. When they heard a shot echo in the woods along the creek, they knew that Pa had got some meat.

The wind was cooler now, and all along the creek bottoms flocks of wild ducks were rising, flying, settling again.

Up from the creek came long lines of wild geese, forming in V's for their flight farther south. The leader in front called to those behind him. 'Honk?' he called. All down the lines the wild geese answered, one after another. 'Honk.' 'Honk'. 'Honk'. Then he cried, 'Honk!' And, 'Honk-honk! Honk-honk!' the others answered him. Straight away south he flew on his strong wings, and the long lines evenly followed him.

The tree-tops along the creek were coloured now. Oaks were reds and yellows and browns and greens. Cotton-woods and sycamores and walnuts were sunshiny yellow. The sky was not so brightly blue, and the wind was rough.

That afternoon the wind blew fiercely and it was cold. Ma called Mary and Laura into the house. She built up the fire and drew her rocker near it, and she sat rocking Baby Carrie and singing softly to her:

'By lo, baby bunting.
Papa's gone a-hunting,
To get a rabbit skin
To wrap the baby bunting in.'

Laura heard a little crackling in the chimney. Ma stopped singing. She bent forward and looked up the chimney. Then she got up quietly, put Carrie in Mary's arms, pushed Mary down into the rocking-chair, and hurried outdoors. Laura ran after her.

The whole top of the chimney was on fire. The sticks that made it were burning up. The fire was roaring in the wind and licking towards the helpless roof. Ma seized a long pole and struck and struck at the roaring fire, and burning sticks fell all around her.

Laura didn't know what to do. She grabbed a pole, too, but Ma told her to stay away. The roaring fire was terrible.

It could burn the whole house and Laura couldn't do anything.

She ran into the house. Burning sticks and coals were falling down the chimney and rolling out on the hearth. The house was full of smoke. One big, blazing stick rolled on the floor, under Mary's skirts. Mary couldn't move, she was so scared.

Laura was too scared to think. She grabbed the back of the heavy rocking-chair and pulled with all her might. The chair with Mary and Carrie in it came sliding back across the floor. Laura grabbed up the burning stick and flung it into the fireplace just as Ma came in.

'That's a good girl, Laura, to remember I told you never to leave fire on the floor,' Ma said. She took the water-pail and quickly and quietly poured water on the fire in the fireplace. Clouds of steam came out.

Then Ma said, 'Did you burn your hands?' She looked at Laura's hands, but they were not burned, because she had thrown the burning stick so quickly.

Laura was not really crying. She was too big to cry. Only one tear ran out of each eye and her throat choked up, but that was not crying. She hid her face against Ma and hung on to her tight. She was so glad the fire had not hurt Ma.

'Don't cry, Laura,' Ma said, stroking her hair. 'Were you afraid?'

'Yes,' Laura said. 'I was afraid Mary and Carrie would burn up. I was afraid the house would burn up and we wouldn't have any house. I'm—I'm scared now!'

Mary could talk now. She told Ma how Laura had pulled the chair away from the fire. Laura was so little, and the chair so big and so heavy with Mary and Carrie in it, that Ma was surprised. She said she didn't know how Laura had done it.

'You were a brave girl, Laura,' she said. But Laura had really been terribly scared.

'And no harm's done,' Ma said. 'The house didn't burn up, and Mary's skirts didn't catch fire and burn her and Carrie. So everything is all right.'

When Pa came home he found the fire out. The wind was roaring over the low stone top of the chimney and the house was cold. But Pa said he would build up the chimney with green sticks and fresh clay, and plaster it so well that it wouldn't catch fire again.

He had brought four fat ducks, and he said he could have killed hundreds. But four were all they needed. He said to Ma, 'You save the feathers from the ducks and geese we eat, and I'll shoot you a feather bed.'

He could, of course, have got a deer, but the weather was not yet cold enough to freeze the meat and keep it from spoiling before they could eat it. And he had found the place where a flock of wild turkeys roosted. 'Our Thanksgiving and Christmas turkeys,' he said. 'Great, big, fat fellows. I'll get them when the time comes.'

Pa went whistling to mix mud and cut green sticks and build the chimney up again, while Ma cleaned the ducks. Then the fire merrily crackled, a fat duck roasted, and the cornbread baked. Everything was snug and cosy again.

After supper Pa said he supposed he'd better start to town early next morning. 'Might as well go and get it over with,' he said.

'Yes, Charles, you'd better go,' Ma said.

'We could get along all right, if I didn't,' said Pa. 'There's no need of running to town all the time, for every little thing. I have smoked better tobacco than that stuff Scott raised back in Indiana, but it will do. I'll raise some next summer and pay him back. I wish I hadn't borrowed those nails from Edwards.'

'You did borrow them, Charles,' Ma replied. 'And as for the tobacco, you don't like borrowing any more than I do. We need more quinine. I've been sparing with the corn-meal, but it's almost gone and so is the sugar. You could find a bee-tree, but there's no cornmeal tree to be found, so far as I know, and we'll raise no corn till next year. A little salt pork would taste good, too, after all this wild game. And, Charles, I'd like to write to the folks in Wis-consin. If you mail a letter now, they can write this winter, and then we can hear from them next spring.'

'You're right, Caroline. You always are,' Pa said. Then he turned to Mary and Laura and said it was bedtime. If he was going to start early in the morning, he'd better start sleeping early tonight.

He pulled off his boots while Mary and Laura got into their nightgowns. But when they were in bed he took down his fiddle. Softly he played and softly sang,

> 'So green grows the laurel,
>   And so does the rue,
> So woeful, my love,
>   At the parting with you.'

Ma turned towards him and smiled. 'Take care of yourself on the trip, Charles, and don't worry about us,' she told him. 'We will be all right.'

17

Pa Goes to Town

BEFORE DAWN, PA went away. When Laura and
Mary woke, he was gone and everything was empty
and lonely. It was not as though Pa had only gone
hunting. He was going to town, and he would not be back
for four long days.

Bunny had been shut in the stable, so she couldn't
follow her mother. The trip was too long for a colt. Bunny
whinnied lonesomely. Laura and Mary stayed in the
house with Ma. Outdoors was too large and empty to
play in when Pa was away. Jack was uneasy, too, and
watchful.

At noon Laura went with Ma to water Bunny and to
move the cow's picket-pin to fresh grass. The cow was
quite gentle now. She followed where Ma led, and she
would even let Ma milk her.

At milking-time Ma was putting on her bonnet, when

suddenly all Jack's hair stood up stiff on his neck and back, and he rushed out of the house. They heard a yell and a scramble and a shout: 'Call off your dog! Call off your dog!'

Mr Edwards was on top of the woodpile, and Jack was climbing up after him.

'He's got me treed,' Mr Edwards said, backing along the top of the woodpile. Ma could hardly make Jack come away. Jack grinned savagely and his eyes were red. He had to let Mr Edwards come down from the woodpile, but he watched him every minute.

Ma said, 'I declare, he seems to know that Mr Ingalls isn't here.'

Mr Edwards said that dogs knew more than most folks gave them credit for.

On his way to town that morning, Pa had stopped at Mr Edwards' house and asked him to come over every day to see that everything was all right. And Mr Edwards was such a good neighbour that he had come at chore-time, to do the chores for Ma. But Jack had made up his mind not to let anyone but Ma go near the cow or Bunny while Pa was gone. He had to be shut in the house while Mr Edwards did the chores.

When Mr Edwards went away he said to Ma, 'Keep

that dog in the house tonight, and you'll be safe enough.'

The dark crept slowly all around the house. The wind cried mournfully and owls said, 'Who-oo? Oo-oo.' A wolf howled, and Jack growled low in his throat. Mary and Laura sat close to Ma in the firelight. They knew they were safe in the house, because Jack was there and Ma had pulled the latch-string in.

Next day was empty like the first. Jack paced around the stable and around the house, then around the stable and back to the house. He would not pay any attention to Laura.

That afternoon Mrs Scott came to visit with Ma. While they visited, Laura and Mary sat politely, as still as mice. Mrs Scott admired the new rocking-chair. The more she rocked in it, the more she enjoyed it, and she said how neat and comfortable and pretty the house was.

She said she hoped to goodness they would have no trouble with Indians. Mr Scott had heard rumours of trouble. She said, 'Land knows, they'd never do anything with this country themselves. All they do is roam around over it like wild animals. Treaties or no treaties, the land belongs to folks that'll farm it. That's only common sense and justice.'

She did not know why the government made treaties with Indians. The only good Indian was a dead Indian. The very thought of Indians made her blood run cold. She said, 'I can't forget the Minnesota massacre. My Pa and my brothers went out with the rest of the settlers, and stopped them only fifteen miles west of us. I've heard Pa tell often enough how they——'

Ma made a sharp sound in her throat, and Mrs Scott stopped. Whatever a massacre was, it was something that grown-ups would not talk about when little girls were listening.

After Mrs Scott had gone, Laura asked Ma what a massacre was. Ma said she could not explain that now; it was something that Laura would understand when she was older.

Mr Edwards came to do the chores again that evening, and again Jack treed him on the woodpile. Ma had to drag him off. She told Mr Edwards she couldn't think what had got into that dog. Maybe it was the wind that upset him.

The wind had a strange, wild howl in it, and it went through Laura's clothes as if the clothes weren't there. Her teeth and Mary's teeth chattered while they carried many armfuls of wood into the house.

That night they thought of Pa, in Independence. If nothing had delayed him, he would be camping there now, near the houses and the people. Tomorrow he would be in the store, buying things. Then, if he could get an early start, he could come part way home and camp on the prairie tomorrow night. And the next night he might come home.

In the morning the wind was blowing fiercely and it was so cold that Ma kept the door shut. Laura and Mary stayed by the fire and listened to the wind, screaming around the house and howling in the chimney. That afternoon they wondered if Pa was leaving Independence and coming towards them, against that wind.

Then, when it was dark, they wondered where he was camping. The wind was bitterly cold. It came even into the snug house and made their backs shiver while their faces roasted in the heat of the fire. Somewhere on the big, dark, lonesome prairie Pa was camping in that wind.

The next day was very long. They could not expect Pa in the morning, but they were waiting till they could expect him. In the afternoon they began to watch the creek road. Jack was watching it, too. He whined to go out, and he went all around the stable and the house, stopping to look towards the creek bottoms and show his teeth. The wind almost blew him off his feet.

When he came in he would not lie down. He walked about, and worried. The hair rose on his neck, and flattened, and rose again. He tried to look out of the window, and then whined at the door. But when Ma opened it, he changed his mind and would not go out.

'Jack's afraid of something,' Mary said.

'Jack's not afraid of anything, ever!' Laura contradicted.

'Laura, Laura,' Ma said. 'It isn't nice to contradict.'

In a minute Jack decided to go out. He went to see that the cow and calf and Bunny were safe in the stable. And Laura wanted to tell Mary, 'I told you so!' She didn't, but she wanted to.

At chore-time Ma kept Jack in the house so he could not tree Mr Edwards on the woodpile. Pa had not come yet. The wind blew Mr Edwards in through the door. He was breathless, and stiff with cold. He warmed himself

by the fire before he did the chores, and when he had done them he sat down to warm himself again.

He told Ma that Indians were camping in the shelter of the bluffs. He had seen the smoke from their fires when he crossed the bottoms. He asked Ma if she had a gun.

Ma said she had Pa's pistol, and Mr Edwards said, 'I reckon they'll stay close in camp, a night like this.'

'Yes,' Ma said.

Mr Edwards said he could make himself right comfortable with hay in the stable, and he would spend the night there if Ma said so. Ma thanked him nicely, but said she would not put him to that trouble. They would be safe enough with Jack.

'I am expecting Mr Ingalls any minute now,' she told him. So Mr Edwards put on his coat and cap and muffler and mittens and picked up his gun. He said he didn't guess that anything would bother her, anyway.

'No,' Ma said.

When she shut the door behind him, she pulled the latch-string in, though darkness had not yet come. Laura and Mary could see the creek road plainly, and they watched it until the dark hid it. Then Ma closed and barred the wooden window shutter. Pa had not come.

They ate supper. They washed the dishes and swept the hearth, and still he had not come. Out in the dark where he was, the wind shrieked and wailed and howled. It rattled the door-latch and shook the shutters. It screamed down the chimney and the fire roared and flared.

All the time Laura and Mary strained their ears to hear the sound of wagon wheels. They knew Ma was listening, too, though she was rocking and singing Carrie to sleep.

Carrie fell asleep and Ma went on gently rocking. At last she undressed Carrie and put her to bed. Laura and

Mary looked at each other; they didn't want to go to bed.

'Bedtime, girls!' Ma said. Then Laura begged to be allowed to sit up till Pa came, and Mary backed her up, till Ma said they might.

For a long, long time they sat up. Mary yawned, then Laura yawned, then they both yawned. But they kept their eyes wide open. Laura's eyes saw things grow very large and then very small, and sometimes she saw two Marys and sometimes she couldn't see at all, but she was going to sit up till Pa came. Suddenly a fearful crash scared her and Ma picked her up. She had fallen off the bench, smack on the floor.

She tried to tell Ma that she wasn't sleepy enough to have to go to bed, but an enormous yawn almost split her head in two.

In the middle of the night she sat straight up. Ma was sitting still in the rocking-chair by the fire. The door-latch rattled, the shutters shook, the wind was howling. Mary's eyes were open and Jack walked up and down. Then Laura heard again a wild howl that rose and fell and rose again.

'Lie down, Laura, and go to sleep,' Ma said gently.

'What's that howling?' Laura asked.

'The wind is howling,' said Ma. 'Now mind me, Laura.'

Laura lay down, but her eyes would not shut. She knew that Pa was out in the dark, where that terrible howling was. The wild men were in the bluffs along the creek bottoms, and Pa would have to cross the creek bottoms in the dark. Jack growled.

Then Ma began to sway gently in the comfortable rocking-chair. Firelight ran up and down, up and down the barrel of Pa's pistol in her lap. And Ma sang, softly and sweetly:

'There is a happy land,
　Far, far away,
Where saints in glory stand,
　Bright, bright as day.

'Oh, to hear the angels sing,
　Glory to the Lord, our King——'

Laura didn't know that she had gone to sleep. She thought the shining angels began to sing with Ma, and she lay listening to their heavenly singing until suddenly her eyes opened and she saw Pa standing by the fire.

She jumped out of bed, shouting, 'Oh Pa! Pa!'

Pa's boots were caked with frozen mud, his nose was red with cold, his hair wildly stood up on his head. He was so cold that coldness came through Laura's night-gown when she reached him.

'Wait!' he said. He wrapped Laura in Ma's big shawl, and then he hugged her. Everything was all right. The house was cosy with firelight, there was the warm, brown smell of coffee, Ma was smiling, and Pa was there.

The shawl was so large that Mary wrapped the other end of it around her. Pa pulled off his stiff boots and warmed his stiff, cold hands. Then he sat on the bench and he took Mary on one knee and Laura on the other and he hugged them against him, all snuggled in the shawl. Their bare toes toasted in the heat from the fire.

'Ah!' Pa sighed. 'I thought I never would get here.'

Ma rummaged among the stores he had brought, and spooned brown sugar into a tin cup. Pa had brought sugar from Independence. 'Your coffee will be ready in a minute, Charles,' she said.

'It rained between here and Independence, going,' Pa told them. 'And coming back, the mud froze between the spokes till the wheels were nearly solid. I had to get out and knock it loose, so the horses could pull the wagon. And seemed like we'd no more than started, when I had to get out and do it again. It was all I could do to keep Pet and Patty coming against that wind. They're so worn out they can hardly stagger. I never saw such a wind; it cuts like a knife.'

The wind had begun while he was in town. People there told him he had better wait until it blew itself out, but he wanted to get home.

'It beats me,' he said, 'why they call a south wind a norther, and how a wind from the south can be so tarnation cold. I never saw anything like it. Down here in this country, the north end of a south wind is the coldest wind I ever heard of.'

He drank his coffee and wiped his moustache with his handkerchief, and said: 'Ah! That hits the spot, Caroline! Now I'm beginning to thaw out.'

Then his eyes twinkled at Ma and he told her to open the square package on the table. 'Be careful,' he said. 'Don't drop it.'

Ma stopped unwrapping it and said: 'Oh, Charles! You didn't!'

'Open it,' Pa said.

In that square package there were eight small squares of window-glass. They would have glass windows in their house.

Not one of the squares was broken. Pa had brought them safely all the way home. Ma shook her head and said he shouldn't have spent so much, but her whole face was smiling and Pa laughed with joy. They were all so pleased. All winter long they could look out of the windows as much as they liked, and the sunshine could come in.

Pa said he thought that Ma and Mary and Laura would like glass windows better than any other present, and he was right. They did. But the windows were not all he had brought them. There was a little paper sack full of pure white sugar. Ma opened it and Mary and Laura looked at the sparkling whiteness of that beautiful sugar, and they each had a taste of it from a spoon. Then Ma tied it carefully up. They would have white sugar when company came.

Best of all, Pa was safely home again.

Laura and Mary went back to sleep, very comfortable all over. Everything was all right when Pa was there. And now he had nails, and cornmeal, and fat pork, and salt, and everything. He would not have to go to town again for a long time.

18

The Tall Indian

IN THOSE THREE days the norther had howled and screeched across the prairie till it blew itself out. Now the sun was warm and the wind was mild, but there was a feeling of autumn in the air.

Indians came riding on the path that passed so close to the house. They went by as though it were not there.

They were thin and brown and bare. They rode their little ponies without saddle or bridle. They sat up straight on the naked ponies and did not look to right or left. But their black eyes glittered.

Laura and Mary backed against the house and looked up at them. And they saw red-brown skin bright against the blue sky, and scalplocks wound with coloured string, and feathers quivering. The Indians' faces were like the red-brown wood that Pa had carved to make a bracket for Ma.

'I thought that trail was an old one they didn't use any more,' Pa said. 'I wouldn't have built the house so close to it if I'd known it's a highroad.'

Jack hated Indians, and Ma said she didn't blame him. She said, 'I declare, Indians are getting so thick around here that I can't look up without seeing one.'

As she spoke she looked up, and there stood an Indian. He stood in the doorway, looking at them, and they had not heard a sound.

'Goodness!' Ma gasped.

Silently Jack jumped at the Indian. Pa caught him by the collar, just in time. The Indian hadn't moved; he stood as still as if Jack hadn't been there at all.

'How!' he said to Pa.

Pa held on to Jack and replied, 'How!' He dragged Jack to the bedpost and tied him there. While he was doing it, the Indian came in and squatted down by the fire.

Then Pa squatted down by the Indian, and they sat there, friendly but not saying a word, while Ma finished cooking dinner.

Laura and Mary were close together and quiet on their bed in the corner. They couldn't take their eyes from that Indian. He was so still that the beautiful eagle-feathers in his scalplock didn't stir. Only his bare chest and the leanness under his ribs moved a little to his breathing. He wore fringed leather leggings, and his moccasins were covered with beads.

Ma gave Pa and the Indian their dinners on two tin plates, and they ate silently. Then Pa gave the Indian some tobacco for his pipe. They filled their pipes, and they lighted the tobacco with coals from the fire, and they silently smoked until the pipes were empty.

All this time nobody had said anything. But now the Indian said something to Pa. Pa shook his head and said, 'No speak.'

A while longer they all sat silent. Then the Indian rose up and went away without a sound.

'My goodness gracious!' Ma said.

Laura and Mary ran to the window. They saw the Indian's straight back, riding away on a pony. He held a gun across his knees, its ends stuck out on either side of him.

Pa said that Indian was no common trash. He guessed by the scalplock that he was an Osage.

'Unless I miss my guess,' Pa said, 'that was French he spoke. I wish I had picked up some of that lingo.'

'Let Indians keep themselves to themselves,' said Ma, 'and we will do the same. I don't like Indians around underfoot.'

Pa told her not to worry.

'That Indian was perfectly friendly,' he said. 'And their camps down among the bluffs are peaceable enough. If we treat them well and watch Jack, we won't have any trouble.'

The very next morning, when Pa opened the door to go to the stable, Laura saw Jack standing in the Indian trail. He stood stiff, his back bristled, and all his teeth showed. Before him in the path the tall Indian sat on his pony.

Indian and pony were still as still. Jack was telling them plainly that he would spring if they moved. Only the eagle feathers that stood up from the Indian's scalplock were waving and spinning in the wind.

When the Indian saw Pa, he lifted his gun and pointed it straight at Jack.

Laura ran to the door, but Pa was quicker. He stepped between Jack and that gun, and he reached down and grabbed Jack by the collar. He dragged Jack out of the Indian's way, and the Indian rode on, along the trail.

Pa stood with his feet wide apart, his hands in his pockets, and watched the Indian riding farther and farther away across the prairie.

'That was a darned close call!' Pa said. 'Well, it's his path. An Indian trail, long before we came.'

He drove an iron ring into a log of the house wall, and he chained Jack to it. After that, Jack was always chained. He was chained to the house in the daytime, and at night he was chained to the stable door, because horse-thieves were in the country now. They had stolen Mr Edwards' horses.

Jack grew crosser and crosser because he was chained. But it could not be helped. He would not admit that the trail was the Indians' trail, he thought it belonged to Pa.

And Laura knew that something terrible would happen if Jack hurt an Indian.

Winter was coming now. The grasses were a dull colour under a dull sky. The winds wailed as if they were looking for something they could not find. Wild animals were wearing their thick winter fur, and Pa set his traps in the creek bottoms. Every day he visited them, and ever day he went hunting. Now that the nights were freezing cold, he shot deer for meat. He shot wolves and foxes for their fur, and his traps caught beaver and muskrat and mink.

He stretched the skins on the outside of the house and carefully tacked them there, to dry. In the evenings he worked the dried skins between his hands to make them soft, and he added them to the bundle in the corner. Every day the bundle of furs grew bigger.

Laura loved to stroke the thick fur of red foxes. She liked the brown, soft fur of beaver, too, and the shaggy wolf's fur. But best of all she loved the silky mink. Those were all furs that Pa saved to trade next spring in Independence. Laura and Mary had rabbit-skin caps, and Pa's cap was musk-rat.

One day when Pa was hunting, two Indians came. They came into the house, because Jack was chained.

Those Indians were dirty and scowling and mean. They acted as if the house belonged to them. One of them looked through Ma's cupboard and took all the corn-bread. The other took Pa's tobacco-pouch. They looked at the pegs where Pa's gun belonged. Then one of them picked up the bundle of furs.

Ma held Baby Carrie in her arms, and Mary and Laura stood close to her. They looked at that Indian taking Pa's furs. They couldn't do anything to stop him.

He carried them as far as the door. Then the other Indian said something to him. They made harsh sounds at each other in their throats, and he dropped the furs. They went away.

Ma sat down. She hugged Mary and Laura close to her and Laura felt Ma's heart beating.

'Well,' Ma said, smiling, 'I'm thankful they didn't take the plough and seeds.'

Laura was surprised. She asked, 'What plough?'

'The plough and all our seeds for next year are in that bundle of furs,' said Ma.

When Pa came home they told him about those Indians, and he looked sober. But he said that all was well that ended well.

That evening when Mary and Laura were in bed, Pa

played his fiddle. Ma was rocking in the rocking-chair, holding Baby Carrie against her breast, and she began to sing softly with the fiddle:

'Wild roved an Indian maid,
    Bright Alfarata,
Where flow the waters
    Of the blue Juniata.
Strong and true my arrows are
    In my painted quiver,
Swift goes my light canoe
    A-down the rapid river.

'Bold is my warrior good,
    The love of Alfarata,
Proud wave his sunny plumes
    Along the Juniata.
Soft and low he speaks to me,
    And then his war-cry sounding
Rings his voice in thunder loud
    From height to height resounding.

'So sang the Indian maid,
    Bright Alfarata,
Where sweep the waters
    Of the blue Juniata.
Fleeting years have borne away
    The voice of Alfarata,
Still flow the waters
    Of the blue Juniata.'

Ma's voice and the fiddle's music softly died away. And Laura asked, 'Where did the voice of Alfarata go, Ma?'

'Goodness!' Ma said. 'Aren't you asleep yet?'

'I'm going to sleep,' Laura said. 'But please tell me where the voice of Alfarata went?'

'Oh I suppose she went west,' Ma answered. 'That's what the Indians do.'

'Why do they do that, Ma?' Laura asked. 'Why do they go west?'

'They have to,' Ma said.

'Why do they have to?'

'The government makes them, Laura,' said Pa. 'Now go to sleep.'

He played the fiddle softly for a while. Then Laura asked, 'Please, Pa, can I ask just one more question?'

'May I,' said Ma.

Laura began again. 'Pa, please, may I——'

'What is it?' Pa asked. It was not polite for little girls to interrupt, but of course Pa could do it.

'Will the government make these Indians go west?'

'Yes,' Pa said. 'When white settlers come into a country, the Indians have to move on. The government is going to move these Indians farther west, any time now. That's why we're here, Laura. White people are going to settle all this country, and we get the best land because we get here first and take our pick. Now do you understand?'

'Yes, Pa,' Laura said. 'But, Pa, I thought this was Indian Territory. Won't it make the Indians mad to have to——'

'No more questions, Laura,' Pa said, firmly. 'Go to sleep.'

19

Mr Edwards Meets Santa Claus

THE DAYS WERE short and cold, the wind whistled sharply, but there was no snow. Cold rains were falling. Day after day the rain fell, pattering on the roof and pouring from the eaves.

Mary and Laura stayed close by the fire, sewing their nine-patch quilt blocks, or cutting paper dolls from scraps of wrapping-paper, and hearing the wet sound of the rain. Every night was so cold that they expected to see snow next morning, but in the morning they saw only sad, wet grass.

They pressed their noses against the squares of glass in the windows that Pa had made, and they were glad they could see out. But they wished they could see snow.

Laura was anxious because Christmas was near, and Santa Claus and his reindeer could not travel without snow. Mary was afraid that, even if it snowed, Santa Claus

could not find them, so far away in Indian Territory. When they asked Ma about this, she said she didn't know.

'What day is it?' they asked her, anxiously. 'How many more days till Christmas?' And they counted off the days on their fingers, till there was only one more day left.

Rain was still falling that morning. There was not one crack in the grey sky. They felt almost sure there would be no Christmas. Still, they kept hoping.

Just before noon the light changed. The clouds broke and drifted apart, shining white in a clear blue sky. The sun shone, birds sang, and thousands of drops of water sparkled on the grasses. But when Ma opened the door to let in the fresh, cold air, they heard the creek roaring.

They had not thought about the creek. Now they knew they would have no Christmas, because Santa Claus could not cross that roaring creek.

Pa came in, bringing a big fat turkey. If it weighed less than twenty pounds, he said, he'd eat it, feathers and all. He asked Laura, 'How's that for a Christmas dinner? Think you can manage one of those drumsticks?'

She said, yes, she could. But she was sober. Then Mary asked him if the creek was going down, and he said it was still rising.

Ma said it was too bad. She hated to think of Mr Edwards eating his bachelor cooking all alone on Christmas day. Mr Edwards had been asked to eat Christmas dinner with them, but Pa shook his head and said a man would risk his neck, trying to cross that creek now.

'No,' he said. 'That current's too strong. We'll just have to make up our minds that Edwards won't be here tomorrow.'

Of course that meant that Santa Claus could not come, either.

Laura and Mary tried not to mind too much. They watched Ma dress the wild turkey, and it was a very fat turkey. They were lucky little girls, to have a good house to live in, and a warm fire to sit by, and such a turkey for their Christmas dinner. Ma said so, and it was true. Ma said it was too bad that Santa Claus couldn't come this year, but they were such good girls that he hadn't forgotten them; he would surely come next year.

Still, they were not happy.

After supper that night they washed their hands and faces, buttoned their red-flannel nightgowns, tied their nightcap strings, and soberly said their prayers. They lay down in bed and pulled the covers up. It did not seem at all like Christmas time.

Pa and Ma sat silent by the fire. After a while Ma asked why Pa didn't play the fiddle, and he said, 'I don't seem to have the heart to, Caroline.'

After a longer while, Ma suddenly stood up.

'I'm going to hang up your stockings, girls,' she said. 'Maybe something will happen.'

Laura's heart jumped. But then she thought again of the creek and she knew nothing could happen.

Ma took one of Mary's clean stockings and one of Laura's, and she hung them from the mantel-shelf, on either side of the fireplace. Laura and Mary watched her over the edge of their bed-covers.

'Now go to sleep,' Ma said, kissing them good night. 'Morning will come quicker if you're asleep.'

She sat down again by the fire and Laura almost went to sleep. She woke up a little when she heard Pa say, 'You've only made it worse, Caroline.' And she thought she heard Ma say: 'No, Charles. There's the white sugar.' But perhaps she was dreaming.

Then she heard Jack growl savagely. The door-latch rattled and some one said, 'Ingalls! Ingalls!' Pa was stirring up the fire, and when he opened the door Laura saw that it was morning. The outdoors was grey.

'Great fish-hooks, Edwards! Come in, man! What's happened?' Pa exclaimed.

Laura saw the stockings limply dangling, and she scrooged her shut eyes into the pillow. She heard Pa piling wood on the fire, and she heard Mr Edwards say he had carried his clothes on his head when he swam the creek. His teeth rattled and his voice quivered. He would be all right, he said, as soon as he got warm.

'It was too big a risk, Edwards,' Pa said. 'We're glad you're here, but that was too big a risk for a Christmas dinner.'

'Your little ones had to have a Christmas,' Mr Edwards replied. 'No creek could stop me, after I fetched them their gifts from Independence.'

Laura sat straight up in bed. 'Did you see Santa Claus?' she shouted.

'I sure did,' Mr Edwards said.

'Where? When? What did he look like? What did he say? Did he really give you something for us?' Mary and Laura cried.

'Wait, wait a minute!' Mr Edwards laughed. And Ma said she would put the presents in the stockings, as Santa Claus intended. She said they mustn't look.

Mr Edwards came and sat on the floor by their bed, and he answered every question they asked him. They honestly tried not to look at Ma, and they didn't quite see what she was doing.

When he saw the creek rising, Mr Edwards said, he had known that Santa Claus could not get across it. ('But you crossed it,' Laura said. 'Yes,' Mr Edwards replied, 'but Santa Claus is too old and fat. He couldn't make it, where a long, lean razor-back like me could do so.') And Mr Edwards reasoned that if Santa Claus couldn't cross the creek, likely he would come no farther south than Independence. Why should he come forty miles across the prairie, only to be turned back? Of course he wouldn't do that!

So Mr Edwards had walked to Independence. ('In the rain?' Mary asked. Mr Edwards said he wore his rubber coat.) And there, coming down the street in Independence, he had met Santa Claus. ('In the daytime?' Laura asked. She hadn't thought that anyone could see Santa Claus in the daytime. No, Mr Edwards said; it was night, but light shone out across the street from the saloons.)

Well, the first thing Santa Claus said was, 'Hello, Edwards!' ('Did he know you?' Mary asked, and Laura asked, 'How did you know he was really Santa Claus?' Mr Edwards said that Santa Claus knew everybody. And he had recognized Santa at once by his whiskers. Santa Claus had the longest, thickest, whitest set of whiskers west of the Mississippi.)

So Santa Claus said, 'Hello, Edwards! Last time I saw you you were sleeping on a corn-shuck bed in Tennessee.' And Mr Edwards well remembered the little pair of red-yarn mittens that Santa Claus had left for him that time.

Then Santa Claus said: 'I understand you're living now down along the Verdigris River. Have you ever met up, down yonder, with two little young girls named Mary and Laura?'

'I surely am acquainted with them,' Mr Edwards replied.

'It rests heavy on my mind,' said Santa Claus. 'They are both of them sweet, pretty, good little young things, and I know they are expecting me. I surely do hate to disappoint two good little girls like them. Yet with the water up the way it is, I can't ever make it across that creek. I can figure no way whatsoever to get to their cabin this year. Edwards, would you do me the favour to fetch them their gifts this one time?'

'I'll do that, and with pleasure,' Mr Edwards told him.

Then Santa Claus and Mr Edwards stepped across the street to the hitching-posts where the pack-mule was tied. ('Didn't he have his reindeer?' Laura asked. 'You know he couldn't,' Mary said. 'There isn't any snow.' 'Exactly,' said Mr Edwards. Santa Claus travelled with a pack-mule in the south-west.)

And Santa Claus uncinched the pack and looked through it, and he took out the presents for Mary and Laura.

'Oh, what are they?' Laura cried; but Mary asked, 'Then what did he do?'

Then he shook hands with Mr Edwards, and he swung up on his fine bay horse. Santa Claus rode well, for a man of his weight and build. And he tucked his long, white whiskers under his bandana. 'So long, Edwards,' he said, and he rode away on the Fort Dodge trail, leading his pack-mule and whistling.

Laura and Mary were silent an instant, thinking of that.

Then Ma said, 'You may look now, girls.'

Something was shining bright in the top of Laura's

stocking. She squealed and jumped out of bed. So did Mary, but Laura beat her to the fireplace. And the shining thing was a glittering new tin cup.

Mary had one exactly like it.

These new tin cups were their very own. Now they each had a cup to drink out of. Laura jumped up and down and shouted and laughed, but Mary stood still and looked with shining eyes at her own tin cup.

Then they plunged their hands into the stockings again. And they pulled out two long, long sticks of candy. It was peppermint candy, striped red and white. They looked and looked at that beautiful candy, and Laura licked her stick, just one lick. But Mary was not so greedy. She didn't take even one lick of her stick.

Those stockings weren't empty yet. Mary and Laura pulled out two small packages. They unwrapped them, and each found a little heart-shaped cake. Over their delicate brown tops was sprinkled white sugar. The sparkling grains lay like tiny drifts of snow.

The cakes were too pretty to eat. Mary and Laura just looked at them. But at last Laura turned hers over, and she nibbled a tiny nibble from underneath, where it wouldn't show. And the inside of that little cake was white!

It had been made of pure white flour, and sweetened with white sugar.

Laura and Mary never would have looked in their stockings again. The cups and the cakes and the candy were almost too much. They were too happy to speak. But Ma asked if they were sure the stockings were empty.

Then they put their arms down inside them, to make sure.

And in the very toe of each stocking was a shining bright, new penny!

They had never even thought of such a thing as having a penny. Think of having a whole penny for your very own. Think of having a cup and a cake and a stick of candy *and* a penny.

There never had been such a Christmas.

Now, of course, right away Laura and Mary should have thanked Mr Edwards for bringing those lovely presents all the way from Independence. But they had forgotten all about Mr Edwards. They had even forgotten Santa Claus. In a minute they would have remembered, but before they did, Ma said, gently, 'Aren't you going to thank Mr Edwards?'

'Oh, thank you, Mr Edwards! Thank you!' they said, and they meant it with all their hearts. Pa shook Mr Edwards' hand, too, and shook it again. Pa and Ma and Mr Edwards acted as if they were almost crying, Laura didn't know why. So she gazed again at her beautiful presents.

She looked up again when Ma gasped. And Mr Edwards was taking sweet potatoes out of his pockets. He said they had helped to balance the package on his head when he swam across the creek. He thought Pa and Ma might like them, with the Christmas turkey.

There were nine sweet potatoes. Mr Edwards had brought them all the way from town, too. It was just too much. Pa said so. 'It's too much, Edwards,' he said. They never could thank him enough.

Mary and Laura were much too excited to eat breakfast. They drank the milk from their shining new cups, but they could not swallow the rabbit stew and the cornmeal mush.

'Don't make them, Charles,' Ma said. 'It will soon be dinner-time.'

For Christmas dinner there was the tender, juicy, roasted turkey. There were the sweet potatoes, baked in the ashes and carefully wiped so that you could eat the good skins, too. There was a loaf of salt-rising bread made from the last of the white flour.

And after all that there were stewed dried blackberries and little cakes. But these little cakes were made with brown sugar and they did not have white sugar sprinkled over their tops.

Then Pa and Ma and Mr Edwards sat by the fire and talked about Christmas times back in Tennessee and up north in the Big Woods. But Mary and Laura looked at their beautiful cakes and played with their pennies and drank water out of their new cups. And little by little they licked and sucked their sticks of candy, till each stick was sharp-pointed on one end.

That was a happy Christmas.

20

A Scream in the Night

T HE DAYS WERE short and grey now, the nights
were very dark and cold. Clouds hung low above
the little house and spread low and far over the
bleak prairie. Rain fell, and sometimes snow was driven
on the wind. Hard little bits of snow whirled in the air
and scurried over the humped backs of miserable grasses.
And next day the snow was gone.

Every day Pa went hunting and trapping. In the cosy,
firelit house Mary and Laura helped Ma with the work.
Then they sewed quilt-patches. They played Pat-a-Cake
with Carrie, and they played Hide the Thimble. With a
piece of string and their fingers, they played Cat's Cradle.
And they played Bean Porridge Hot. Facing each other,
they clapped their hands together and against each other's
hands, keeping time while they said,

'Bean porridge hot,
　Bean porridge cold,
Bean porridge in the pot,
　Nine days old.

'Some like it hot,
　Some like it cold,
Some like it in the pot,
　Nine days old.

'I like it hot,
　I like it cold,
I like it in the pot,
　Nine days old.'

That was true. No supper was so good as the thick bean porridge, flavoured with a small bit of salt pork, that Ma dipped on to the tin plates when Pa had come home cold and tired from his hunting. Laura liked it hot, and she liked it cold, and it was always good as long as it lasted. But it never really lasted nine days. They ate it up before that.

All the time the wind blew, shrieking, howling, wailing, screaming, and mournfully sobbing. They were used to hearing the wind. All day they heard it, and at night in their sleep they knew it was blowing. But one night they heard such a terrible scream that they all woke up.

Pa jumped out of bed, and Ma said: 'Charles! What was it?'

'It's a woman screaming,' Pa said. He was dressing as fast as he could. 'Sounded like it came from Scott's.'

'Oh, what can be wrong!' Ma exclaimed.

Pa was putting on his boots. He put his foot in, and he put his fingers through the strap-ears at the top of the long boot leg. Then he gave a mighty pull, and he stamped hard on the floor, and that boot was on.

'Maybe Scott is sick,' pulling on the other boot.

'You don't suppose——?' Ma asked, low.

'No,' said Pa. 'I keep telling you they won't make any trouble. They're perfectly quiet and peaceable down in those camps among the bluffs.'

Laura began to climb out of bed, but Ma said, 'Lie down and be still, Laura.' So she lay down.

Pa put on his warm, bright plaid coat, and his fur cap, and his muffler. He lighted the candle in the lantern, took his gun, and hurried outdoors.

Before he shut the door behind him, Laura saw the night outside. It was black dark. Not one star was shining. Laura had never seen such solid darkness.

'Ma?' she said.

'What, Laura?'

'What makes it so dark?'

'It's going to storm,' Ma answered. She pulled the latch-string in and put a stick of wood on the fire. Then she went back to bed. 'Go to sleep, Mary and Laura,' she said.

But Ma did not go to sleep, and neither did Mary and Laura. They lay wide awake and listened. They could not hear anything but the wind.

Mary put her head under the quilt and whispered to Laura, 'I wish Pa'd come back.'

Laura nodded her head on the pillow, but she couldn't say anything. She seemed to see Pa striding along the top of the bluff, on the path that went towards Mr Scott's house. Tiny bright spots of candlelight darted here and there from the holes cut in the tin lantern. The little flickering lights seemed to be lost in the black dark.

After a long time Laura whispered, 'It must be 'most morning.' And Mary nodded. All that time they had been lying and listening to the wind, and Pa had not come back

Then, high above the shrieking of the wind they heard again that terrible scream. It seemed quite close to the house.

Laura screamed, too, and leaped out of bed. Mary ducked under the covers. Ma got up and began to dress in a hurry. She put another stick of wood on the fire and told Laura to go back to bed. But Laura begged so hard that Ma said she could stay up. 'Wrap yourself in the shawl,' Ma said.

They stood by the fire and listened. They couldn't hear anything but the wind. And they could not do anything. But at least they were not lying down in bed.

Suddenly fists pounded on the door and Pa shouted: 'Let me in! Quick, Caroline!'

Ma opened the door and Pa slammed it quickly behind him. He was out of breath. He pushed back his cap and said: 'Whew! I'm scared yet.'

'What was it, Charles?' said Ma.

'A panther,' Pa said.

He had hurried as fast as he could go to Mr Scott's. When he got there, the house was dark and everything was quiet. Pa went all around the house, listening, and looking with the lantern. He could not find a sign of anything wrong. So he felt like a fool, to think he had got up and dressed in the middle of the night and walked two miles, all because he heard the wind howl.

He did not want Mr and Mrs Scott to know about it. So he did not wake them up. He came home as fast as he could because the wind was bitter cold. And he was hurrying along the path, where it went on the edge of the bluff, when all of a sudden he heard that scream right under his feet.

'I tell you my hair stood up till it lifted my cap,' he told Laura. 'I lit out for home like a scared rabbit.'

'Where was that panther, Pa?' she asked him.

'In a tree-top,' said Pa. 'In the top of that big cotton-wood that grows against the bluff there.'

'Pa, did it come after you?' Laura asked, and he said, 'I don't know, Laura.'

'Well, you're safe now, Charles,' said Ma.

'Yes, and I'm glad of it. This is too dark a night to be out with panthers,' Pa said. 'Now, Laura, where's my bootjack?'

Laura brought it to him. The bootjack was a thin oak slab with a notch in one end and a cleat across the middle of it. Laura laid it on the floor with the cleat down, and the cleat lifted up the notched end. Then Pa stood on it with one foot; he put the other foot into the notch, and the notch held the boot by the heel while Pa pulled his foot out. Then he pulled off his other boot, the same way. The boots clung tightly, but they had to come off.

Laura watched him do this, and then she asked, 'Would a panther carry off a little girl, Pa?'

'Yes,' said Pa. 'And kill her and eat her, too. You and Mary must stay in the house till I shoot that panther. As soon as daylight comes I will take my gun and go after him.'

All the next day Pa hunted that panther. And he hunted the next day and the next day. He found the panther's tracks, and he found the hide and bones of an antelope that the panther had eaten, but he did not find the panther anywhere. The panther went swiftly through tree-tops, where it left no tracks.

Pa said he would not stop till he killed that panther. He said, 'We can't have panthers running around in a country where there are little girls.'

But he did not kill that panther, and he did stop hunting it. One day in the woods he met an Indian. They stood in the wet, cold woods and looked at each other, and they could not talk because they did not know each other's words. But the Indian pointed to the panther's tracks, and he made motions with his gun to show Pa that he had killed that panther. He pointed to the tree-tops and to the ground, to show that he had shot it out of a tree. And he motioned to the sky, and west and east, to say that he had killed it the day before.

So that was all right. The panther was dead.

Laura asked if a panther would carry off a little papoose and kill and eat her, too, and Pa said yes. Probably that was why the Indian had killed that panther.

21

Indian Jamboree

WINTER ENDED AT LAST. There was a softer note in the sound of the wind, and the bitter cold was gone. One day Pa said he had seen a flock of wild geese flying north. It was time to take his furs to Independence.

Ma said, 'The Indians are so near!'

'They are perfectly friendly,' said Pa. He often met Indians in the woods where he was hunting. There was nothing to fear from Indians.

'No,' Ma said. But Laura knew that Ma was afraid of Indians. 'You must go, Charles,' she said. 'We must have a plough and seeds. And you will soon be back again.'

Before dawn next morning Pa hitched Pet and Patty to the wagon, loaded his furs into it, and drove away.

Laura and Mary counted the long, empty days. One, two, three, four, and still Pa had not come home. In the morning of the fifth day they began earnestly to watch for him.

It was a sunny day. There was still a little chill in the wind, but it smelled of spring. The vast blue sky resounded to the quacks of wild ducks and the honk-honk-honking of wild geese. The long, black-dotted lines of them were all flying north.

Laura and Mary played outdoors in the wild, sweet weather. And poor Jack watched them and sighed. He couldn't run and play any more, because he was chained. Laura and Mary tried to comfort him, but he didn't want petting. He wanted to be free again, as he used to be.

Pa didn't come that morning; he didn't come that afternoon. Ma said it must have taken him a long time to trade his furs.

That afternoon Laura and Mary were playing hopscotch. They marked the lines with a stick in the muddy yard. Mary really didn't want to hop; she was almost eight years old and she didn't think that hop-scotch was a ladylike play. But Laura teased and coaxed, and said that if they stayed outdoors they would be sure to see Pa the minute he came from the creek bottoms. So Mary was hopping.

Suddenly she stopped on one foot and said, 'What's that?'

Laura had already heard the queer sound and she was listening to it. She said, 'It's the Indians.'

Mary's other foot dropped and she stood frozen still. She was scared. Laura was not exactly scared, but that sound made her feel funny. It was the sound of quite a lot of Indians, chopping with their voices. It was something like the sound of an axe chopping, and something like a dog barking, and it was something like a song, but not like any song that Laura had ever heard. It was a wild, fierce sound, but it didn't seem angry.

Laura tried to hear it more clearly. She couldn't hear it very well, because hills and trees and the wind were in the way, and Jack was savagely growling.

Ma came outdoors and listened a minute. Then she told Mary and Laura to come into the house. Ma took Jack inside, too, and pulled in the latch-string.

They didn't play any more. They watched at the window, and listened to that sound. It was harder to hear, in the house. Sometimes they couldn't hear it; then they heard it again. It hadn't stopped.

Ma and Laura did the chores earlier than usual. They locked Bunny and the cow and calf in the stable, and took the milk to the house. Ma strained it and set it away. She drew a bucket of fresh water from the well, while Laura and Mary carried in wood. All the time that sound went on; it was louder, now, and faster. It made Laura's heart beat fast.

They all went into the house and Ma barred the door. The latch-string was already in. They wouldn't go out of the house till morning.

The sun slowly sank. All around the edge of the prairie the edge of the sky flushed pink. Firelight flickered in the dusky house and Ma was getting supper, but Laura and Mary silently watched from the window. They saw the colours fade from everything. The land was shadowy and the sky was clear, pale grey. All the time that sound came from the creek bottoms, louder and louder, faster and faster. And Laura's heart beat faster and louder.

How she shouted when she heard the wagon! She ran to the door and jumped up and down, but she couldn't unbar it. Ma wouldn't let her go out. Ma went out, to help Pa bring in the bundles.

He came in with his arms full, and Laura and Mary clung to his sleeves and jumped on his feet. Pa laughed his jolly big laugh. 'Hey! hey! don't upset me!' he laughed. 'What do you think I am? A tree to climb?'

He dropped the bundles on the table, he hugged Laura in a big bear hug, and tossed her and hugged her again. Then he hugged Mary snugly in his other arm.

'Listen, Pa,' Laura said. 'Listen to the Indians. Why are they making that funny noise?'

'Oh, they're having some kind of jamboree,' Pa said.
'I heard them when I crossed the creek bottoms.'

Then he went out to unhitch the horses and bring in
the rest of the bundles. He had got the plough; he left
it in the stable, but he brought all the seeds into the house
for safety. He had sugar, not any white sugar this time,
but brown. White sugar cost too much. But he had
brought a little white flour. There were cornmeal and
salt and coffee and all the seeds they needed. Pa had even
got seed potatoes. Laura wished they might eat the
potatoes but they must be saved to plant.

Then Pa's face beamed and he opened a small paper

sack. It was full of crackers. He set it on the table, and he unwrapped and set beside it a glass jar full of little green cucumber pickles.

'I thought we'd all have a treat,' he said.

Laura's mouth watered, and Ma's eyes shone softly at Pa. He had remembered how she longed for pickles.

That wasn't all. He gave Ma a package and watched her unwrap it and in it was enough pretty calico to make her a dress.

'Oh, Charles, you shouldn't! It's too much!' she said. But her face and Pa's were two beams of joy.

Now he hung up his cap and his plaid coat on their pegs. His eyes looked sideways at Laura and Mary, but that was all. He sat down and stretched out his legs to the fire.

Mary sat down, too, and folded her hands in her lap. But Laura climbed on to Pa's knee and beat him with her fists. 'Where is it? Where is it? Where's my present?' she said, beating him.

Pa laughed his big laugh, like great bells ringing, and he said, 'Why, I do believe there is something in my blouse pocket.'

He took out an oddly shaped package, and very, very slowly he opened it.

'You first, Mary,' he said, 'because you are so patient.' And he gave Mary a comb for her hair. 'And here, flutterbudget! this is for you,' he said to Laura.

The combs were exactly alike. They were made of black rubber and curved to fit over the top of a little girl's head. And over the top of the comb lay a flat piece of black rubber, with curving slits cut in it, and in the very middle of it a little five-pointed star was cut out. A bright coloured ribbon was drawn underneath, and the colour showed through.

The ribbon in Mary's comb was blue, and the ribbon in Laura's comb was red.

Ma smoothed back their hair and slid the combs into it, and there in the golden hair, exactly over the middle of Mary's forehead, was a little blue star. And in Laura's brown hair, over the middle of her forehead, was a little red star.

Laura looked at Mary's star, and Mary looked at Laura's, and they laughed with joy. They had never had anything so pretty.

Ma said, 'But, Charles, you didn't get yourself a thing!'

'Oh, I got myself a plough,' said Pa. 'Warm weather'll be here soon now, and I'll be ploughing.'

That was the happiest supper they had had for a long time. Pa was safely home again. The fried salt pork was very good, after so many months of eating ducks and geese and turkeys and venison. And nothing had ever tasted so good as those crackers and the little green sour pickles.

Pa told them about all the seeds. He had got seeds of turnips and carrots and onions and cabbage. He had got peas and beans. And corn and wheat and tobacco and the seed potatoes. And water-melon seeds. He said to Ma, 'I tell you, Caroline, when we begin getting crops off this rich land of ours, we'll be living like kings!'

They had almost forgotten the noise from the Indian camp. The window shutters were closed now, and the wind was moaning in the chimney and whining around the house. They were so used to the wind that they did not hear it. But when the wind was silent an instant, Laura heard again that wild, shrill, fast-beating sound from the Indian camps.

Then Pa said something to Ma that made Laura sit very still and listen carefully. He said that folks in Independence said that the government was going to put the white settlers out of the Indian territory. He said the Indians had been complaining and they had got that answer from Washington.

'Oh, Charles, no!' Ma said. 'Not when we have done so much.'

Pa said he didn't believe it. He said, 'They always have let settlers keep the land. They'll make the Indians move on again. Didn't I get word straight from Washington that this country's going to be opened for settlement any time now?'

'I wish they'd settle it and stop talking about it,' Ma said.

After Laura was in bed she lay awake a long time, and so did Mary. Pa and Ma sat in the firelight and candlelight, reading. Pa had brought a newspaper from Kansas, and he read it to Ma. It proved that he was right, the government would not do anything to the white settlers.

Whenever the sound of the wind died away, Laura could faintly hear the noise of that wild jamboree in the Indian camp. Sometimes even above the howling of the wind she thought she still heard those fierce yells of jubilation. Faster, faster, faster they made her heart beat. 'Hi! Hi! Hi-yi! Hah! Hi! Hah!'

22

Prairie Fire

SPRING HAD COME. The warm winds smelled exciting, and all outdoors was large and bright and
sweet. Big white shining clouds floated high up in
clear space. Their shadows floated over the prairie. The
shadows were thin and brown, and all the rest of the
prairie was the pale, soft colours of dead grasses.

Pa was breaking the prairie sod, with Pet and Patty
hitched to the breaking-plough. The sod was a tough,
thick mass of grass-roots. Pet and Patty slowly pulled
with all their might and the sharp plough slowly turned
over a long, unbroken strip of that sod.

The dead grass was so tall and thick that it held up
the sod. Where Pa had ploughed, he didn't have a
ploughed field. The long strips of grass-roots lay on top
of grass, and grass stuck out between them.

But Pa and Pet and Patty kept on working. He said that sod potatoes and sod corn would grow this year, and next year the roots and the dead grasses would be rotted. In two or three years he would have nicely ploughed fields. Pa liked the land because it was so rich, and there wasn't a tree or a stump or a rock in it.

Now a great many Indians came riding along the Indian trail. Indians were everywhere. Their guns echoed in the creek bottoms where they were hunting. No one knew how many Indians were hidden in the prairie which seemed so level but wasn't. Often Laura saw an Indian where no one had been an instant before.

Indians often came to the house. Some were friendly, some were surly and cross. All of them wanted food and tobacco, and Ma gave them what they wanted. She was afraid not to. When an Indian pointed at something and grunted, Ma gave him that thing. But most of the food was kept hidden and locked up.

Jack was cross all the time, even with Laura. He was never let off the chain, and all the time he lay and hated the Indians. Laura and Mary were quite used to seeing them now. Indians didn't surprise them at all. But they always felt safer near Pa or Jack.

One day they were helping Ma get dinner. Baby Carrie

was playing on the floor in the sunshine, and suddenly the sunshine was gone.

'I do believe it is going to storm,' Ma said, looking out of the window. Laura looked, too, and great black clouds were billowing up in the south, across the sun.

Pet and Patty were coming running from the field, Pa holding to the heavy plough and bounding in long leaps behind it.

'Prairie fire!' he shouted. 'Get the tub full of water! Put sacks in it! Hurry!'

Ma ran to the well, Laura ran to tug the tub to it. Pa tied Pet to the house. He brought the cow and calf from the picket-line and shut them in the stable. He caught Bunny and tied her fast to the north corner of the house. Ma was pulling up buckets of water as fast as she could. Laura ran to get the sacks that Pa had flung out of the stable.

Pa was ploughing, shouting at Pet and Patty to make them hurry. The sky was black now, the air was as dark as if the sun had set. Pa ploughed a long furrow west of the house and south of the house, and back again east of the house. Rabbits came bounding past him as if he wasn't there.

Pet and Patty came galloping, the plough and Pa bounding behind them. Pa tied them to the other north corner of the house. The tub was full of water. Laura helped Ma push the sacks under the water to soak them.

'I couldn't plough but one furrow; there isn't time,' Pa said. 'Hurry, Caroline. That fire's coming faster than a horse can run.'

A big rabbit bounded right over the tub while Pa and Ma were lifting it. Ma told Laura to stay at the house. Pa and Ma ran staggering to the furrow with the tub.

Laura stayed close to the house. She could see the red

fire coming under the billows of smoke. More rabbits
went leaping by. They paid no attention to Jack and he
didn't think about them; he stared at the red undersides
of the rolling smoke and shivered and whined while he
crowded close to Laura.

The wind was rising and wildly screaming. Thousands
of birds flew before the fire, thousands of rabbits were
running.

Pa was going along the furrow, setting fire to the grass on the other side of it. Ma followed with a wet sack, beating at the flames that tried to cross the furrow. The whole prairie was hopping with rabbits. Snakes rippled across the yard. Prairie hens ran silently, their necks outstretched and their wings spread. Birds screamed in the screaming wind.

Pa's little fire was all around the house now, and he helped Ma fight it with the wet sacks. The fire blew wildly, snatching at the dry grass inside the furrow. Pa and Ma thrashed at it with the sacks, when it got across the furrow they stamped it with their feet. They ran back and forth in the smoke, fighting that fire.

The prairie fire was roaring now, roaring louder and louder in the screaming wind. Great flames came roaring, flaring and twisting high. Twists of flame broke loose and came down on the wind to blaze up in the grasses far ahead of the roaring wall of fire. A red light came from the rolling black clouds of smoke overhead.

Mary and Laura stood against the house and held hands

and trembled. Baby Carrie was in the house. Laura
wanted to do something, but inside her head was a roaring
and whirling like the fire. Her middle shook, and tears
poured out of her stinging eyes. Her eyes and her nose and
her throat stung with smoke.

Jack howled. Bunny and Pet and Patty were jerking
at the ropes and squealing horribly. The orange, yellow,
terrible flames were coming faster than horses can run,
and their quivering light danced over everything.

Pa's little fire had made a burned black strip. The little
fire went backing slowly away against the wind, it went
slowly crawling to meet the racing furious big fire. And
suddenly the big fire swallowed the little one.

The wind rose to a high, crackling, rushing shriek,
flames climbed into the crackling air. Fire was all around
the house.

Then it was over. The fire went roaring past and away.

Pa and Ma were beating out little fires here and there
in the yard. When they were all out, Ma came to the

house to wash her hands and face. She was all streaked with smoke and sweat, and she was trembling.

She said there was nothing to worry about. 'The back-fire saved us,' she said, 'and all's well that ends well.'

The air smelled scorched. And to the very edge of the sky, the prairie was burned naked and black. Threads of smoke rose from it. Ashes blew on the wind. Everything felt different and miserable. But Pa and Ma were cheerful because the fire was gone and it had not done any harm.

Pa said that the fire had not missed them far, but a miss is as good as a mile. He asked Ma, 'If it had come while I was in Independence, what would you have done?'

'We would have gone to the creek with the birds and the rabbits, of course,' Ma said.

All the wild things on the prairie had known what to do. They ran and flew and hopped and crawled as fast as they could go, to the water that would keep them safe from fire. Only the little soft striped gophers had gone down deep into their holes, and they were the first to come up and look around at the bare, smoking prairie.

Then out of the creek bottoms the birds came flying over it, and a rabbit cautiously hopped and looked. It was a long, long time before the snakes crawled out of the bottoms and the prairie hens came walking.

The fire had gone out among the bluffs. It had never reached the creek bottoms or the Indian camps.

That night Mr Edwards and Mr Scott came to see Pa. They were worried because they thought that perhaps the Indians had started that fire on purpose to burn out the white settlers.

Pa didn't believe it. He said the Indians had always burned the prairie to make green grass grow more quickly, and travelling easier. Their ponies couldn't gallop through the thick, tall, dead grass. Now the ground was clear. And he was glad of it, because ploughing would be easier.

While they were talking, they could hear drums beating in the Indian camps, and shouts. Laura sat still as a mouse on the doorstep and listened to the talk and to the Indians. The stars hung low and large and quivering over the burned prairie, and the wind blew gently in Laura's hair.

Mr Edwards said there were too many Indians in those camps; he didn't like it. Mr Scott said he didn't know why so many of those savages were coming together, if they didn't mean devilment.

'The only good Indian is a dead Indian,' Mr Scott said.

Pa said he didn't know about that. He figured that Indians would be as peaceable as anybody else if they were let alone. On the other hand, they had been moved west so many times that naturally they hated white folks. But an Indian ought to have sense enough to know when he was licked. With soldiers at Fort Gibson and Fort Dodge, Pa didn't believe these Indians would make any trouble.

'As to why they are congregating in these camps, Scott, I can tell you that,' he said. 'They're getting ready for their big spring buffalo hunt.'

He said there were half a dozen tribes down in those camps. Usually the tribes were fighting each other, but every spring they made peace and all came together for the big hunt.

'They're sworn to peace among themselves,' he said, 'and they're thinking about hunting the buffalo. So it's not likely they'll start on the warpath against us. They'll have their talks and their feasts, and then one day they'll all hit the trail after the buffalo herds. The buffalo will be working their way north pretty soon, following the green grass. By George! I'd like to go on a hunt like that myself. It must be a sight to see.'

'Well, maybe you're right about it, Ingalls,' Mr Scott said slowly. 'Anyway, I'll be glad to tell Mrs Scott what you say. She can't get the Minnesota massacres out of her head.'

23

Indian War-Cry

NEXT MORNING PA went whistling to his ploughing. He came in at noon black with soot from the
burned prairie, but he was pleased. The tall grass
didn't bother him any more.

But there was an uneasiness about the Indians. More
and more Indians were in the creek bottoms. Mary and
Laura saw the smoke from their fires by day, and at
night they heard the savage voices shouting.

Pa came early from the field. He did the chores early,
and shut Pet and Patty, Bunny and the cow and calf into
the stable. They could not stay out in the yard to graze
in the cool moonlight.

When shadows began to gather on the prairie and the
wind was quiet, the noises from the Indian camps grew
louder and wilder. Pa brought Jack into the house. The
door was shut and the latch-string pulled in. No one could
go outdoors till morning.

Night crept towards the little house, and the darkness
was frightening. It yelped with Indian yells, and one night
it began to throb with Indian drums.

In her sleep Laura heard all the time that savage yipping and the wild, throbbing drums. She heard Jack's
claws clicking, and his low growl. Sometimes Pa sat up in
bed, listening.

One evening he took his bullet-mould from the box
under the bed. He sat for a long time on the hearth,

melting lead and making bullets. He did not stop till he had used the last bit of lead.

Laura and Mary lay awake and watched him. He had never made so many bullets at one time before. Mary asked, 'What makes you do that, Pa?'

'Oh, I haven't anything else to do,' Pa said, and he began to whistle cheerfully. But he had been ploughing all day. He was too tired to play the fiddle. He might have gone to bed, instead of sitting up so late, making bullets.

No more Indians came to the house. For days, Mary and Laura had not seen a single Indian. Mary did not like to go out of the house any more. Laura had to play out-doors by herself, and she had a queer feeling about the prairie. It didn't feel safe. It seemed to be hiding something. Sometimes Laura had a feeling that something was watching her, something was creeping up behind her. She turned around quickly, and nothing was there.

Mr Scott and Mr Edwards, with their guns, came and talked to Pa in the field. They talked quite a while, then they went away together. Laura was disappointed because Mr Edwards did not come to the house.

At dinner Pa said to Ma that some of the settlers were talking about a stockade. Laura didn't know what a stockade was. Pa had told Mr Scott and Mr Edwards that it was a foolish notion. He told Ma, 'If we need one, we'd need it before we could get it built. And the last thing we want to do is to act like we're afraid.'

Mary and Laura looked at each other. They knew it was no use to ask questions. They would only be told again that children must not speak at table until they were spoken to. Or that children should be seen and not heard.

That afternoon Laura asked Ma what a stockade was.

Ma said it was something to make little girls ask questions. That meant that grown-ups would not tell you what it was. And Mary looked a look at Laura that said, 'I told you so.'

Laura didn't know why Pa said he must not act as if he were afraid. Pa was never afraid. Laura didn't want to act as if she were afraid, but she was. She was afraid of the Indians.

Jack never laid back his ears and smiled at Laura any more. Even while she petted him, his ears were lifted, his neck bristled, and his lips twitched back from his teeth. His eyes were angry. Every night he growled more fiercely, and every night the Indian drums beat faster, faster, and the wild yipping rose higher and higher, faster, wilder.

In the middle of the night Laura sat straight up and screamed. Some terrible sound had made cold sweat come out all over her.

Ma came to her quickly and said in her gentle way: 'Be quiet, Laura. You mustn't frighten Carrie.'

Laura clung to Ma, and Ma was wearing her dress. The fire was covered with ashes and the house was dark, but Ma had not gone to bed. Moonlight came through the window. The shutter was open, and Pa stood in the dark by the window, looking out. He had his gun.

Out in the night the drums were beating and the Indians were wildly yelling.

Then that terrible sound came again. Laura felt as if she were falling; she couldn't hold on to anything; there was nothing solid anywhere. It seemed a long time before she could see or think or speak.

She screamed: 'What is it? What is it? Oh, Pa, what is it?'

She was shaking all over and she felt sick in her middle. She heard the drums pounding and the wild yipping yells and she felt Ma holding her safe. Pa said, 'It's the Indian war-cry, Laura.'

Ma made a soft sound, and he said to her, 'They might as well know, Caroline.'

He explained to Laura that that was the Indian way of talking about war. The Indians were only talking about it, and dancing around their fires. Mary and Laura must not be afraid, because Pa was there, and Jack was there, and soldiers were at Fort Gibson and Fort Dodge.

'So don't be afraid, Mary and Laura,' he said again.

Laura gasped and said, 'No, Pa.' But she was horribly afraid. Mary couldn't say anything; she lay shivering under the covers.

Then Carrie began to cry, so Ma carried her to the

rocking-chair and gently rocked her. Laura crept out of bed and huddled against Ma's knee. And Mary, left all alone, crept after her and huddled close, too. Pa stayed by the window, watching.

The drums seemed to beat in Laura's head. They seemed to beat deep inside her. The wild, fast yipping yells were worse than wolves. Something worse was coming, Laura knew it. Then it came—the Indian war-cry.

A nightmare is not so terrible as that night was. A nightmare is only a dream, and when it is worst you wake up. But this was real and Laura could not wake up. She could not get away from it.

When the war-cry was over, Laura knew it had not got her yet. She was still in the dark house and she was pressed

close against Ma. Ma was trembling all over. Jack's howling ended in a sobbing growl. Carrie began to scream again, and Pa wiped his forehead and said, 'Whew!'

'I never heard anything like it,' Pa said. He asked, 'How do you suppose they learned to do it?' but nobody answered that.

'They don't need guns. That yell's enough to scare anybody to death,' he said. 'My mouth's so dry I couldn't whistle a tune to save my life. Bring me some water, Laura.'

That made Laura feel better. She carried a dipper full of water to Pa at the window. He took it and smiled at her, and that made her feel very much better. He drank a little and smiled again and said, 'There! now I can whistle!'

He whistled a few notes to show her that he could.

Then he listened. And Laura, too, heard far away the soft pitter-pat, pat-pat, pitter-pat pat, of a pony's galloping. It came nearer.

From one side of the house came the drum-throbbing and the fast, shrill, yapping yells, and from the other side came the lonely sound of the rider's galloping.

Nearer and nearer it came. Now the hoofs clattered loudly and suddenly they were going by. The galloping went by and grew fainter, down the creek road.

In the moonlight Laura saw the behind of a little black Indian pony, and an Indian on its back. She saw a huddle of blanket and a naked head and a flutter of feathers above it, and moonlight on a gun barrel and then it was all gone. Nothing was there but empty prairie.

Pa said he was durned if he knew what to make of it. He said that was the Osage who had tried to talk French to him.

He asked, 'What's he doing, out at this hour, riding hell bent for leather?'

Nobody answered because nobody knew.

The drums throbbed and the Indians went on yelling. The terrible war-cry came again and again.

Little by little, after a long time, the yells grew fainter and fewer. At last Carrie cried herself to sleep. Ma sent Mary and Laura back to bed.

Next day they could not go out of the house. Pa stayed close by. There was not one sound from the Indian camps. The whole vast prairie was still. Only the wind blew over the blackened earth where there was no grass to rustle. The wind blew past the house with a rushing sound like running water.

That night the noise in the Indian camps was worse than the night before. Again the war-cries were more terrible than the most dreadful nightmare. Laura and Mary huddled close against Ma, poor little Baby Carrie cried, Pa watched at the window with his gun. And all night long Jack paced and growled, and screamed when the war-cries came.

The next night, and the next night, and the next night, were worse and worse. Mary and Laura were so tired that they fell asleep while the drums pounded and the Indians yelled. But a war-cry always jerked them wide awake in terror.

And the silent days were even worse than the nights. Pa watched and listened all the time. The plough was in the field where he had left it; Pet and Patty and the colt and the cow and calf stayed in the barn. Mary and Laura could not go out of the house. And Pa never stopped looking at the prairie all around, and turning his head quickly towards the smallest noise. He ate hardly any dinner; he kept getting up and going outdoors to look all around at the prairie.

One day his head nodded down to the table and he slept

there. Ma and Mary and Laura were still to let him sleep. He was so tired. But in a minute he woke up with a jump and said, sharply, to Ma, 'Don't let me do that again!'

'Jack was on guard,' Ma said gently.

That night was worst of all. The drums were faster and the yells were louder and fiercer. All up and down the creek war-cries answered war-cries and the bluffs echoed. There was no rest. Laura ached all over and there was a terrible ache in her very middle.

At the window Pa said, 'Caroline, they are quarrelling among themselves. Maybe they will fight each other.'

'Oh, Charles, if they only will!' Ma said.

All night there was not a minute's rest. Just before dawn a last war-cry ended and Laura slept against Ma's knee.

She woke up in bed. Mary was sleeping beside her. The door was open, and by the sunshine on the floor Laura knew it was almost noon. Ma was cooking dinner. Pa sat on the doorstep.

He said to Ma, 'There's another big party, going off to the south.'

Laura went to the door in her nightgown, and she saw a long line of Indians far away. The line came up out of the black prairie and it went farther away southward. The Indians on their ponies were so small in the distance that they looked not much bigger than ants.

Pa said that two big parties of Indians had gone west that morning. Now this one was going south. It meant that the Indians had quarrelled among themselves. They were going away from their camps in the creek bottoms. They would not go all together to their big buffalo-hunt.

That night the darkness came quietly. There was no sound except the rushing of the wind.

'Tonight we'll sleep!' Pa said, and they did. All night

long they did not even dream. And in the morning Jack was still sleeping limp and flat on the same spot where he had been sleeping when Laura went to bed.

The next night was still, too, and again they all slept soundly. That morning Pa said he felt as fresh as a daisy, and he was going to do a little scouting along the creek.

He chained Jack to the ring in the house wall, and he took his gun and went out of sight down the creek road.

Laura and Mary and Ma could not do anything but wait until he came back. They stayed in the house and wished he would come. The sunshine had never moved so slowly on the floor as it did that day.

But he did come back. Late in the afternoon he came. And everything was all right. He had gone far up and down the creek and had seen many deserted Indian camps. All the Indians had gone away, except a tribe called the Osages.

In the woods Pa had met an Osage who could talk to him. This Indian told him that all the tribes except the Osages had made up their minds to kill the white people who had come into the Indian country. And they were getting ready to do it when the lone Indian came riding into their big pow-wow.

That Indian had come riding so far and fast because he did not want them to kill the white people. He was an Osage, and they called him a name that meant he was a great soldier.

'Soldat du Chêne', Pa said his name was.

'He kept arguing with them day and night,' Pa said, 'till all the other Osages agreed with him. Then he stood up and told the other tribes that if they started to massacre us, the Osages would fight them.'

That was what had made so much noise, that last terrible night. The other tribes were howling at the Osages,

13

and the Osages were howling back at them. The other tribes did not dare fight Soldat du Chêne and all his Osages, so next day they went away.

'That's one good Indian!' Pa said. No matter what Mr Scott said, Pa did not believe that the only good Indian was a dead Indian.

24

Indians Ride Away

THERE WAS ANOTHER long night of sleep. It was so good to lie down and sleep soundly. Everything was safe and quiet. Only the owls called 'Who-oo? Who-oo?' in the woods along the creek, while the great moon sailed slowly over the curve of the sky above the endless prairie.

In the morning the sun shone warmly. Down by the creek the frogs were croaking. 'Garrump! Garrump!' they cried by the edge of the pools. 'Knee deep! Knee deep! Better go 'round.'

Ever since Ma had told them what the frogs were saying, Mary and Laura could hear the words plainly.

The door was open to let in the warm spring air. After breakfast Pa went out, whistling merrily. He was going to hitch Pet and Patty to the plough again. But his whistling suddenly stopped. He stood on the doorstep, looking towards the east, and he said, 'Come here, Caroline. And you, Mary and Laura.'

Laura ran out first, and she was surprised. The Indians were coming.

They did not come on the creek road. They came riding up out of the creek bottoms far to the east.

First came the tall Indian who had gone riding by the house in the moonlight. Jack was growling and Laura's heart beat fast. She was glad to be close to Pa. But she

knew this was the good Indian, the Osage chief who had stopped the terrible war-cries.

His black pony came trotting willingly, sniffing the wind that blew its mane and tail like fluttering banners. The pony's nose and head were free; it wore no bridle. Not even one strap was on it anywhere. There was nothing to make it do anything it didn't want to do. Willingly it came trotting along the old Indian trail as it it liked to carry the Indian on its back.

Jack growled savagely, trying to get loose from his chain. He remembered this Indian who had pointed a gun at him. Pa said, 'Be still, Jack.' Jack growled again, and for the first time in their lives Pa struck him. 'Lie down! Be still!' Pa said. Jack cowered down and was still.

The pony was very near now, and Laura's heart beat faster and faster. She looked at the Indian's beaded moccasin, she looked up along the fringed legging that clung to the pony's bare side. A bright-coloured blanket was wrapped around the Indian. One bare brown-red arm carried a rifle lightly across the pony's naked shoulders. Then Laura looked up at the Indian's fierce, still, brown face.

It was a proud, still face. No matter what happened, it would always be like that. Nothing would change it. Only the eyes were alive in that face, and they gazed

steadily far away to the west. They did not move. Nothing moved or changed, except the eagle feathers standing straight up from the scalplock on the shaved head. The long feathers swayed and dipped, waving and spinning in the wind as the tall Indian on the black pony passed on into the distance.

'Du Chêne himself,' Pa said, under his breath, and he lifted his hand in salute.

But the happy pony and the motionless Indian went by. They went by as if the house and stable and Pa and Ma and Mary and Laura were not there at all.

Pa and Ma and Mary and Laura slowly turned and looked at that Indian's proud straight back. Then other ponies and other blankets and shaved heads and eagle feathers came between. One by one on the path, more and more savage warriors were riding behind Du Chêne. Brown face after brown face went by. Ponies' manes and tails blew in the wind, beads glittered, fringe flapped, eagle feathers were waving on all the naked heads. Rifles lying on the ponies' shoulders bristled all along the line.

Laura was excited about the ponies. There were black ponies, bay ponies, grey and brown and spotted ponies. Their little feet went trippety-trip-trip, trippety-trip, pat-patter, pat-patter, trippety pat-patter, all along the Indian trail. Their nostrils widened at Jack and their bodies shied away from him, but they came on bravely, looking with their bright eyes at Laura.

'Oh, the pretty ponies! See the pretty ponies!' she cried, clapping her hands. 'Look at the spotted one.'

She thought she would never be tired of watching those ponies coming by, but after a while she began to look at the women and children on their backs. The women and children came riding behind the Indian men. Little naked brown Indians, no bigger than Mary and Laura, were riding the pretty ponies. The ponies did not have to wear bridles or saddles, and the little Indians did not have to wear clothes. All their skin was out in the fresh air and the sunshine. Their straight black hair blew in the wind and their black eyes sparkled with joy. They sat on their ponies stiff and still like grown-up Indians.

Laura looked and looked at the Indian children, and they looked at her. She had a naughty wish to be a little Indian girl. Of course she did not really mean it. She only wanted to be bare naked in the wind and the sunshine, and riding one of those gay little ponies.

The Indian children's mothers were riding ponies, too. Leather fringe dangled about their legs and blankets were wrapped around their bodies, but the only thing on their heads was their black, smooth hair. Their faces were brown and placid. Some had narrow bundles tied on their backs, and tiny babies' heads stuck out of the top of the bundles. And some babies and some small children rode in baskets hanging at the ponies' sides, beside their mothers.

More and more and more ponies passed, and more children, and more babies on their mothers' backs, and more babies in baskets on the ponies' sides. Then came a mother riding, with a baby in a basket on each side of her pony.

Laura looked straight into the bright eyes of the little baby nearer her. Only its small head showed above the basket's rim. Its hair was as black as a crow and its eyes were black as a night when no stars shine.

Those black eyes looked deep into Laura's eyes and she looked deep down into the blackness of that little baby's eyes, and she wanted that one little baby.

'Pa,' she said, 'get me that little Indian baby!'

'Hush, Laura!' Pa told her sternly.

The little baby was going by. Its head turned and its eyes kept looking into Laura's eyes.

'Oh, I want it! I want it!' Laura begged. The baby was going farther and farther away, but it did not stop looking back at Laura. 'It wants to stay with me,' Laura begged. 'Please, Pa, please!'

'Hush, Laura,' Pa said. 'The Indian woman wants to keep her baby.'

'Oh, Pa!' Laura pleaded, and then she began to cry. It was shameful to cry, but she couldn't help it. The little Indian baby was gone. She knew she would never see it any more.

Ma said she had never heard of such a thing. 'For shame, Laura,' she said, but Laura could not stop crying. 'Why on earth do you want an Indian baby, of all things?' Ma asked her.

'Its eyes are so black,' Laura sobbed. She could not say what she meant.

'Why, Laura,' Ma said, 'you don't want another baby. We have a baby, our own baby.'

'I want the other one, too!' Laura sobbed, loudly.

'Well, I declare!' Ma exclaimed.

'Look at the Indians, Laura,' said Pa. 'Look west, and then look east, and see what you see.'

Laura could hardly see at first. Her eyes were full of

tears and sobs kept jerking out of her throat. But she obeyed Pa as best she could, and in a moment she was still. As far as she could see to the west and as far as she could see to the east there were Indians. There was no end to that long, long line.

'That's an awful lot of Indians,' Pa said.

More and more and more Indians came riding by. Baby Carrie grew tired of looking at Indians and played by herself on the floor. But Laura sat on the doorstep, Pa stood close beside her, and Ma and Mary stood in the doorway. They looked and looked and looked at Indians riding by.

It was dinner-time, and no one thought of dinner. Indian ponies were still going by, carrying bundles of skins and tent-poles and dangling baskets and cooking pots. There were a few more women and a few more naked Indian children. Then the very last pony went by. But Pa and Ma and Laura and Mary still stayed in the doorway, looking, till that long line of Indians slowly pulled itself over the western edge of the world. And nothing was left but silence and emptiness. All the world seemed very quiet and lonely.

Ma said she didn't feel like doing anything, she was so let down. Pa told her not to do anything but rest.

'You must eat something, Charles,' Ma said.

'No,' said Pa. 'I don't feel hungry.' He went soberly to hitch up Pet and Patty, and he began again to break the tough sod with the plough.

Laura could not eat anything, either. She sat a long time on the doorstep, looking into the empty west where the Indians had gone. She seemed still to see waving feathers and black eyes and to hear the sound of ponies' feet.

25

Soldiers

AFTER THE INDIANS had gone, a great peace settled on the prairie. And one morning the whole land was green.

'When did that grass grow?' Ma asked, in amazement. 'I thought the whole country was black, and now there's nothing but green grass as far as the eye can see.'

The whole sky was filled with lines of wild ducks and wild geese flying north. Crows cawed above the trees along the creek. The winds whispered in the new grass, bringing scents of earth and of growing things.

In the mornings the meadow larks rose singing into the sky. All day the curlews and killdeers and sandpipers chirped and sang in the creek bottoms. Often in the early evening the mocking-birds were singing.

One night Pa and Mary and Laura sat still on the doorstep, watching little rabbits playing in the grass in the starlight. Three rabbit mothers hopped about with lopping ears and watched their little rabbits playing, too.

In the daytime everyone was busy. Pa hurried with his ploughing, and Mary and Laura helped Ma plant the early garden seeds. With the hoe Ma dug small holes in the matted grass roots that the plough had turned up, and Laura and Mary carefully dropped the seeds. Then Ma covered them snugly with earth. They planted onions and carrots and peas and beans and turnips. And they were all so happy because spring had come, and pretty

soon they would have vegetables to eat. They were growing very tired of just bread and meat.

One evening Pa came from the field before sunset and he helped Ma set out the cabbage plants and the sweet-potato plants. Ma had sowed the cabbage seed in a flat box and kept it in the house. She watered it carefully, and carried it every day from the morning sunshine to the afternoon sunshine that came through the windows. And she had saved one of the Christmas sweet potatoes, and planted it in another box. The cabbage seeds were now little grey-green plants, and the sweet potato had sent up a stem and green leaves from every one of its eyes.

Pa and Ma took each tiny plant very carefully and settled its roots comfortably in holes made for them. They watered the roots and pressed earth upon them firmly. It was dark before the last plant was in its place, and Pa and Ma were tired. But they were glad, too, because this year they'd have cabbages and sweet potatoes.

Every day they all looked at that garden. It was rough and grassy because it was made in the prairie sod, but all the tiny plants were growing. Little crumpled leaves of peas came up, and tiny spears of onions. The beans themselves popped out of the ground. But it was a little yellow

bean-stem, coiled like a spring, that pushed them up. Then the bean was cracked open and dropped by two baby bean-leaves, and the leaves unfolded flat to the sunshine.

Pretty soon they would all begin to live like kings.

Every morning Pa went cheerfully whistling to the field. He had planted some early sod potatoes, and some potatoes were saved to plant later. Now he carried a sack of corn fastened to his belt, and as he ploughed he threw grains of corn into the furrow beside the plough's point. The plough turned over a strip of sod on top of the seed corn. But the corn would fight its way up through the matted roots, and there would be a cornfield.

There would be green corn for dinner some day. And next winter there would be ripe corn for Pet and Patty to eat.

One morning Mary and Laura were washing the dishes and Ma was making the beds. She was humming softly to herself and Laura and Mary were talking about the garden. Laura liked peas best, and Mary liked beans. Suddenly they heard Pa's voice, loud and angry.

Ma went quickly to the door, and Laura and Mary peeped out on either side of her.

Pa was driving Pet and Patty from the field, dragging the plough behind them. Mr Scott and Mr Edwards were with Pa, and Mr Scott was talking earnestly.

'No, Scott!' Pa answered him. 'I'll not stay here to be taken away by the soldiers like an outlaw! If some blasted politicians in Washington hadn't sent out word it would be all right to settle here, I'd never have been three miles over the line into Indian Territory. But I'll not wait for the soldiers to take us out. We're going now!'

'What is the matter, Charles? Where are we going?' Ma asked.

'Durned if I know! But we're going. We're leaving here!' Pa said. 'Scott and Edwards say the government is sending soldiers to take all us settlers out of Indian Territory.'

His face was very red and his eyes were like blue fire. Laura was frightened; she had never seen Pa look like that. She pressed close against Ma and was still, looking at Pa.

Mr Scott started to speak, but Pa stopped him. 'Save your breath, Scott. It's no use to say another word. You can stay till the soldiers come if you want to. I'm going out now.'

Mr Edwards said he was going, too. He would not stay to be driven across the line like an ornery yellow hound.

'Ride out to Independence with us, Edwards,' Pa said. But Mr Edwards answered that he didn't care to go north. He would make a boat and go on down the river to some settlement farther south.

'Better come out with us,' Pa urged him, 'and go down on foot through Missouri. It's a risky trip, one man alone in a boat, going down the Verdigris among the wild Indian tribes.'

But Mr Edwards said he had already seen Missouri and he had plenty of powder and lead.

Then Pa told Mr Scott to take the cow and calf. 'We can't take them with us,' Pa said. 'You've been a good neighbour, Scott, and I'm sorry to leave you. But we're going out in the morning.'

Laura heard all this, but she had not believed it until she saw Mr Scott leading away the cow. The gentle cow went meekly away with the rope around her long horns, and the calf frisked and jumped behind. There went all the milk and butter.

Mr Edwards said he would be too busy to see them again. He shook hands with Pa, saying, 'Good-bye, Ingalls, and good luck.' He shook hands with Ma and said, 'Good-bye, ma'am. I won't be seeing you all again, but I sure will never forget your kindness.'

Then he turned to Mary and Laura, and he shook their hands as if they were grown up. 'Good-bye,' he said.

Mary said, politely, 'Good-bye, Mr Edwards.' But Laura forgot to be polite. She said: 'Oh, Mr Edwards, I wish you wouldn't go away! Oh, Mr Edwards, thank you, thank you for going all the way to Independence to find Santa Claus for us.'

Mr Edwards' eyes shone very bright, and he went away without saying another word.

Pa began to unhitch Pet and Patty in the middle of the morning, and Laura and Mary knew it was really true; they really were going away from there. Ma didn't say anything. She went into the house and looked around, at the dishes not washed and the bed only partly made, and she lifted up both hands and sat down.

Mary and Laura went on doing the dishes. They were careful not to let them make a sound. They turned around quickly when Pa came in.

He looked like himself again, and he was carrying the potato-sack.

'Here you are, Caroline!' he said, and his voice sounded natural. 'Cook a plenty for dinner! We've been going without potatoes, saving them for seed. Now we'll eat 'em up!'

So that day for dinner they ate the seed potatoes. They were very good, and Laura knew that Pa was right when he said, 'There's no great loss without some small gain.'

After dinner he took the wagon bows from their pegs in the barn. He put them on the wagon, one end of each bow in its iron strap on one side of the wagon box, and the other end in its iron strap on the other side. When all the bows were standing up in their places, Pa and Ma spread the wagon cover over them and tied it down tightly. Then Pa pulled the rope in the end of the wagon cover till it puckered together and left only a tiny round hole in the middle of the back.

There stood the covered wagon, all ready to load in the morning.

Everyone was quiet that night. Even Jack felt that something was wrong, and he lay down close to Laura when she went to bed.

It was now too warm for a fire, but Pa and Ma sat looking at the ashes in the fireplace.

Ma sighed gently and said, 'A whole year gone, Charles.' But Pa answered cheerfully: 'What's a year amount to? We have all the time there is.'

26

Going Out

AFTER BREAKFAST NEXT morning, Pa and Ma packed the wagon. First of all the bedding was made into two beds, laid on top of each other across the back of the wagon, and carefully covered with a pretty plaid blanket. Mary and Laura and Baby Carrie would ride there in the daytime. At night the top bed would be put in the front of the wagon, for Pa and Ma to sleep in. And Mary and Laura would sleep in the bottom bed, where it was.

Next Pa took the small cupboard from the wall, and in it Ma packed the food and the dishes. Pa put the cupboard under the wagon-seat, and in front of it he laid a sack of corn for the horses.

'It will make a good rest for our feet, Caroline,' he said to Ma.

Ma packed all the clothing in two carpet-bags, and Pa hung them to the wagon bows inside the wagon. Opposite them he hung his rifle in its straps, and his bullet-pouch and powder-horn hung beneath it. His fiddle in its box he laid on one end of the bed, where it would ride softly.

Ma wrapped the black iron spider, the bake-oven, and the coffee-pot in sacks, and put them in the wagon, while Pa tied the rocking-chair and the tub outside, and hung the water-bucket and the horse-bucket underneath. And he put the tin lantern carefully in the front corner of the wagon-box, where the sack of corn held it still.

Now the wagon was loaded. The only thing they could not take was the plough. Well, that could not be helped. There was no room for it. When they came to wherever they were going, Pa could get more furs to trade for another plough.

Laura and Mary climbed into the wagon and sat on the bed in the back. Ma put Baby Carrie between them. They were all freshly washed and combed. Pa said they were clean as a hound's tooth, and Ma told them they were bright as new pins.

Then Pa hitched Pet and Patty to the wagon. Ma climbed to her place on the seat and held the lines. And suddenly Laura wanted to see the house again. She asked Pa please to let her look out. So he loosened the rope in the back of the wagon-cover, and that made a large round hole. Laura and Mary could look out of it, but still the rope held up enough canvas to keep Carrie from tumbling into the feed-box.

The snug log house looked just as it always had. It did not seem to know they were going away. Pa stood a moment in the doorway and looked all around inside; he looked at the bedstead and the fireplace and the glass windows. Then he closed the door carefully, leaving the latch-string out.

'Someone might need shelter,' he said.

He climbed to his place beside Ma, gathered the reins into his own hands, and chirruped to Pet and Patty.

Jack went under the wagon. Pet whinnied to Bunny, who came to walk beside her. And they were off.

Just before the creek road went down into the bottoms, Pa stopped the mustangs, and they all looked back.

As far as they could see, to the east and to the south and to the west, nothing was moving on all the vastness of the High Prairie. Only the green grass was rippling in the wind, and white clouds drifted in the high, clear sky.

'It's a great country, Caroline,' Pa said. 'But there will be wild Indians and wolves here for many a long day.'

The little log house and the little stable sat lonely in the stillness.

Then Pet and Patty briskly started onward. The wagon went down from the bluffs into the wooded creek bottoms, and high in a tree-top a mocking-bird began to sing.

'I never heard a mocking-bird sing so early,' said Ma, and Pa answered softly, 'He is telling us good-bye.'

They rode down through the low hills to the creek. The ford was low, an easy crossing. On they went, across the bottoms where antlered deer stood up to watch them passing, and mother deer with their fawns bounded into the shadows of the woods. And up between the steep red-earth cliffs the wagon climbed to prairie again.

Pet and Patty were eager to go. Their hoofs had made a muffled sound in the bottoms, but now they rang on the hard prairie. And the wind sang shrill against the fore-most wagon bows.

Pa and Ma were still and silent on the wagon-seat, and Mary and Laura were quiet, too. But Laura felt all excited inside. You never know what will happen next, nor where you'll be tomorrow, when you are travelling in a covered wagon.

At noon Pa stopped beside a little spring to let the mustangs eat and drink and rest. The spring would soon be dry in the summer's heat, but there was plenty of water now.

Ma took cold cornbread and meat from the food-box, and they all ate, sitting on the clean grass in the shade of the wagon. They drank from the spring, and Laura and Mary ran around in the grass, picking wild flowers, while Ma tidied the food-box and Pa hitched up Pet and Patty again.

Then for a long time they went on, across the prairie. There was nothing to be seen but the blowing grass, the sky, and the endless wagon track. Now and then a rabbit bounded away. Sometimes a prairie hen with her brood of prairie chicks scuttled out of sight in the grass. Baby Carrie slept, and Mary and Laura were almost asleep when they heard Pa say, 'Something's wrong there.'

Laura jumped up, and far ahead on the prairie she saw a small, light-coloured bump. She couldn't see anything else unusual.

'Where?' she asked Pa.

'There,' Pa said, nodding towards that bump. 'It isn't moving.'

Laura didn't say any more. She kept on looking, and she saw that that bump was a covered wagon. Slowly it grew bigger. She saw that no horses were hitched to it. Nothing moved, anywhere around it. Then she saw something dark in front of it.

The dark thing was two people sitting on the wagon tongue. They were a man and a woman. They sat looking down at their feet, and they moved only their heads to look up when Pet and Patty stopped in front of them.

'What's wrong? Where are your horses?' Pa asked.

'I don't know,' the man said. 'I tied them to the wagon last night, and this morning they were gone. Somebody cut the ropes and took them away in the night.'

'What about your dog?' said Pa.

'Haven't got a dog,' the man said.

Jack stayed under the wagon. He didn't growl, but he didn't come out. He was a sensible dog, and knew what to do when he met strangers.

'Well, your horses are gone,' Pa told the man. 'You'll never see them again. Hanging's too good for horse-thieves.'

'Yes,' the man said.

Pa looked at Ma, and Ma barely nodded. Then Pa said, 'Come ride with us to Independence.'

'No,' said the man. 'All we've got is in this wagon. We won't leave it.'

'Why, man! What will you do?' Pa exclaimed. 'There may be nobody along here for days, weeks. You can't stay here.'

'I don't know,' the man said.

'We'll stay with our wagon,' the woman said. She was looking down at her hands clasped in her lap, and Laura couldn't see her face; she could see only the side of the sun-bonnet.

'Better come,' Pa told them. 'You can come back for your wagon.'

'No,' the woman said.

They wouldn't leave the wagon; everything they owned in the world was in it. So at last Pa drove on, leaving them sitting on the wagon tongue, all alone on the prairie.

Pa muttered to himself: 'Tenderfeet! Everything they own, and no dog to watch it. Didn't keep watch himself. And tied his horses with ropes!' Pa snorted. 'Tenderfeet!' he said again. 'Shouldn't be allowed loose west of the Mississippi!'

'But, Charles! Whatever will become of them?' Ma asked him.

'There are soldiers at Independence,' said Pa. 'I'll tell the captain, and he'll send out men to bring them in. They can hold out that long. But it's durned lucky for them that we came by. If we hadn't, there's no telling when they would have been found.'

Laura watched that lonely wagon until it was only a small lump on the prairie. Then it was a speck. Then it was gone.

All the rest of that day Pa drove on and on. They didn't see anybody else.

When the sun was setting, Pa stopped by a well. A house had once been there, but it was burned. The well held plenty of good water, and Laura and Mary gathered bits of half-burned wood to make the fire, while Pa unhitched and watered the horses and put them on picket-lines. Then Pa took the seat down from the wagon and lifted out the food-box. The fire burned beautifully, and Ma quickly got supper.

Everything was just as it used to be before they built the house. Pa and Ma and Carrie were on the wagon-seat, Laura and Mary sat on the wagon tongue. They ate the good supper, hot from the camp fire. Pet and Patty and

Bunny munched the good grass, and Laura saved bits for Jack, who mustn't beg but could eat his fill as soon as supper was over.

Then the sun went down, far away in the west, and it was time to make the camp ready for night.

Pa chained Pet and Patty to the feed-box at the end of the wagon. He chained Bunny to the side. And he fed them all their supper of corn. Then he sat by the fire and smoked his pipe, while Ma tucked Mary and Laura into bed and laid Baby Carrie beside them.

She sat down beside Pa at the fire, and Pa took his fiddle out of its box and began to play.

'Oh, Susanna, don't you cry for me,' the fiddle wailed, and Pa began to sing.

> 'I went to California
>   With my wash-pan on my knee,
>   And every time I thought of home,
>   I wished it wasn't me.'

'Do you know, Caroline,' Pa stopped singing to say, 'I've been thinking what fun the rabbits will have, eating that garden we planted.'

'Don't, Charles,' Ma said.

'Never mind, Caroline!' Pa told her. 'We'll make a better garden. Anyway, we're taking more out of Indian Territory than we took in.'

'I don't know what,' Ma said, and Pa answered, 'Why, there's the mule!' Then Ma laughed, and Pa and the fiddle sang again.

> 'In Dixie land I'll take my stand,
>   And live and die in Dixie!
>   Away, away, away, away,
>   Away down south in Dixie!'

They sang with a lilt and a swing that almost lifted Laura right out of bed. She must lie still and not wake Carrie. Mary was sleeping, too, but Laura had never been wider awake.

She heard Jack making his bed under the wagon. He was turning round and round, trampling down the grass. Then he curled into that round nest with a flop and a sigh of satisfaction.

Pet and Patty were munching the last of their corn, and their chains rattled. Bunny lay down beside the wagon.

They were all there together, safe and comfortable for the night, under the wide, starlit sky. Once more the covered wagon was home.

The fiddle began to play a marching tune, and Pa's clear voice was singing like a deep-toned bell.

> 'And we'll rally round the flag, boys,
>   We'll rally once again,
>   Shouting the battle-cry of Freedom!'

Laura felt that she must shout, too. But softly Ma looked in through the round hole in the wagon-cover.

'Charles,' Ma said, 'Laura is wide awake. She can't go to sleep on such music as that.'

Pa didn't answer, but the voice of the fiddle changed. Softly and slurringly it began a long, swinging rhythm that seemed to rock Laura gently.

She felt her eyelids closing. She began to drift over endless waves of prairie grasses, and Pa's voice went with her, singing.

> 'Row away, row o'er the waters so blue,
>   Like a feather we sail in our gum-tree canoe.
>   Row the boat lightly, love, over the sea;
>   Daily and nightly I'll wander with thee.'

On the Banks of Plum Creek

Contents

On the Banks
of Plum Creek

The Door in the Ground

THE DIM WAGON track went no farther on the prairie, and Pa stopped the horses.

When the wagon wheels stopped turning, Jack dropped down in the shade between them. His belly sank on the grass and his front legs stretched out. His nose fitted in the furry hollow. All of him rested, except his ears.

All day long for many, many days, Jack had been trotting under the wagon. He had trotted all the way from the little log house in Indian Territory, across Kansas, across Missouri, across Iowa, and a long way into Minnesota. He had learned to take his rest whenever the wagon stopped.

In the wagon Laura jumped up, and so did Mary. Their legs were tired of not moving.

'This must be the place,' Pa said. 'It's half a mile up the creek from Nelson's. We've come a good half-mile, and there's the creek.'

Laura could not see a creek. She saw a grassy bank, and beyond it a line of willow-tree tops, waving in the gentle wind. Everywhere else the prairie grasses were rippling far away to the sky's straight edge.

'Seems to be some kind of stable over there,' said Pa, looking around the edge of the canvas wagon-cover. 'But where's the house?'

Laura jumped inside her skin. A man was standing

beside the horses. No one had been in sight anywhere, but suddenly that man was there. His hair was pale yellow, his round face was as red as an Indian's, and his eyes were so pale that they looked like a mistake. Jack growled.

'Be still, Jack!' said Pa. He asked the man, 'Are you Mr. Hanson?'

'Yah,' the man said.

Pa spoke slowly and loudly. 'I heard you want to go West. You trade your place?'

The man looked slowly at the wagon. He looked at the mustangs, Pet and Patty. After a while he said again, 'Yah.'

Pa got out of the wagon, and Ma said, 'You can climb out and run around, girls, I know you are tired, sitting still.'

Jack got up when Laura climbed down the wagon wheel, but he had to stay under the wagon until Pa said he might go. He looked out at Laura while she ran along a little path that was there.

The path went across short sunny grass, to the edge of the bank. Down below it was the creek, rippling and glistening in the sunshine. The willow trees grew up beyond the creek.

Over the edge of the bank, the path turned and went slanting down, close against the grassy bank that rose up like a wall.

Laura went down it cautiously. The bank rose up beside her till she could not see the wagon. There was only the high sky above her, and down below her the water was talking to itself. Laura went a step farther, then one more step. The path stopped at a wider, flat place, where it turned and dropped down to the creek in stair-steps. Then Laura saw the door.

The door stood straight up in the grassy bank, where the path turned. It was like a house door, but whatever was behind it was under the ground. The door was shut.

In front of it lay two big dogs with ugly faces. They saw Laura and slowly rose up.

Laura ran very fast, up the path to the safe wagon. Mary was standing there, and Laura whispered to her, 'There's a door in the ground, and two big dogs—' She looked behind her. The two dogs were coming.

Jack's deep growl rolled from under the wagon. He showed those dogs his fierce teeth.

'These your dogs?' Pa said to Mr. Hanson. Mr. Hanson turned and spoke words that Laura could not understand. But the dogs understood. One behind the other, they slunk over the edge of that bank, down out of sight.

Pa and Mr. Hanson walked slowly away towards the stable. The stable was small and it was not made of logs. Grass grew on its walls and its roof was covered with growing grasses, blowing in the wind.

Laura and Mary stayed near the wagon, where Jack was. They looked at the prairie grasses swaying and bending, and yellow flowers nodding. Birds rose and flew and sank into the grasses. The sky curved very high and its rim came neatly down to the faraway edge of the round earth.

When Pa and Mr. Hanson came back, they heard Pa say: 'All right, Hanson. We'll go to town tomorrow and fix up the papers. Tonight we'll camp here.'

'Yah, yah!' Mr. Hanson agreed.

Pa boosted Mary and Laura into the wagon and drove out on the prairie. He told Ma that he had traded Pet and Patty for Mr. Hanson's land. He had traded Bunny, the mule-colt, and the wagon-cover for Mr. Hanson's crops and his oxen.

He unhitched Pet and Patty and led them to the creek to drink. He put them on their picket-lines and helped Ma make camp for the night. Laura was quiet. She did not want to play and she was not hungry when they all sat eating supper by the camp fire.

'The last night out,' said Pa. 'Tomorrow we'll be settled again. The house is in the creek bank, Caroline.'

'Oh, Charles!' said Ma. 'A dugout. We've never had to live in a dugout yet.'

'I think you'll find it very clean,' Pa told her. 'Norwegians are clean people. It will be snug for winter, and that's not far away.'

'Yes, it will be nice to be settled before snow flies,' Ma agreed.

'It's only till I harvest the first wheat crop,' said Pa. 'Then you'll have a fine house and I'll have horses and maybe even a buggy. This is great wheat country, Caroline! Rich, level land, with not a tree or a rock to contend with. I can't make out why Hanson sowed such a small field. It must have been a dry season, or Hanson's no farmer, his wheat is so thin and light.'

Beyond the firelight, Pet and Patty and Bunny were eating grass. They bit it off with sharp, pulling crunches, and then stood chewing it and looking through the dark at the low stars shining. They switched their tails peacefully. They did not know they had been traded.

Laura was a big girl, seven years old. She was too big to cry. But she could not help asking, 'Pa, did you have to give him Pet and Patty? Did you, Pa?'

Pa's arm drew her close to him in a cuddly hug.

'Why, little half-pint,' Pa said. 'Pet and Patty like to travel. They are little Indian ponies, Laura, and ploughing is too hard work for them. They will be much happier, travelling out West. You wouldn't want to keep them here, breaking their hearts on a plough. Pet and Patty will go on travelling, and with those big oxen I can break up a great big field and have it ready for wheat next spring.

'A good crop of wheat will bring us more money than we've ever had, Laura. Then we'll have horses, and new dresses, and everything you can want.'

Laura did not say anything. She felt better with Pa's arm around her, but she did not want anything except to keep Pet and Patty and Bunny, the long-eared colt.

The House in the Ground

ARLY IN THE morning Pa helped Mr. Hanson move the wagon bows and cover on to Mr. Hanson's wagon. Then they brought everything out of the dugout house, up the bank, and they packed it in the covered wagon.

Mr. Hanson offered to help move the things from Pa's wagon into the dugout, but Ma said, 'No, Charles. We will move in when you come back.'

So Pa hitched Pet and Patty to Mr. Hanson's wagon. He tied Bunny behind it, and he rode away to town with Mr. Hanson.

Laura watched Pet and Patty and Bunny going away. Her eyes smarted and her throat ached. Pet and Patty arched their necks, and their manes and tails rippled in the wind. They went away gaily, not knowing that they were never coming back.

The creek was singing to itself down among the willows, and the soft wind bent the grasses over the top of the bank. The sun was shining and all around the wagon was clean, wide space to be explored.

The first thing was to untie Jack from the wagon wheel. Mr. Hanson's two dogs had gone away, and Jack could run about as he pleased. He was so glad that he jumped up against Laura to lick her face and made her sit down hard. Then he ran down the path and Laura ran after him.

Ma picked up Carrie and said: 'Come, Mary. Let's go look at the dugout.'

Jack got to the door first. It was open. He looked in, and then he waited for Laura.

All around that door green vines were growing out of the grassy bank, and they were full of flowers. Red and blue and purple and rosy-pink and white and striped flowers all had their throats wide open as if they were singing glory to the morning. They were morning-glory flowers.

Laura went under those singing flowers into the dug-

out. It was one room, all white. The earth walls had
been smoothed and whitewashed. The earth floor was
smooth and hard.

When Ma and Mary stood in the doorway the light
went dim. There was a small greased-paper window
beside the door. But the wall was so thick that the light
from the window stayed near the window.

That front wall was built of sod. Mr. Hanson had
dug out his house, and then he had cut long strips of
prairie sod and laid them on top of one another, to make
the front wall. It was a good, thick wall with not one
crack in it. No cold could get through that wall.

Ma was pleased. She said, 'It's small, but it's clean and
pleasant.' Then she looked up at the ceiling and said,
'Look, girls!'

The ceiling was made of hay. Willow boughs had
been laid across and their branches woven together, but
here and there the hay that had been spread on them
showed through.

'Well!' Ma said.

They all went up the path and stood on the roof of
that house. No one could have guessed it was a roof.
Grass grew on it and waved in the wind just like all the
grasses along the creek bank.

'Goodness,' said Ma. 'Anybody could walk over this
house and never know it's here.'

But Laura spied something. She bent over and parted
the grasses with her hands, and then she cried: 'I've
found the stovepipe hole! Look, Mary! Look!'

Ma and Mary stopped to look, and Carrie leaned
out from Ma's arm and looked, and Jack came pushing
to look. They could look right down into the whitewashed
room under the grass.

They looked at it till Ma said, 'We'll brush out the

place and move in what we can before Pa comes back. Mary and Laura, you bring the water-pails.'

Mary carried the large pail and Laura carried the small one, and they went down the path again. Jack ran ahead and took his place by the door.

Ma found a willow-twig broom in a corner, and she brushed the walls carefully. Mary watched Carrie to keep her from falling down into the creek, and Laura took the little pail and went for water.

She hoppity-skipped down the stair-steps to the end of a little bridge across the creek. The bridge was one wide plank. Its other end was under a willow tree.

The tall willows fluttered slender leaves up against the sky, and little willows grew around them in clumps. They shaded all the ground, and it was cool and bare. The path went across it to a little spring, where cold, clear water fell into a tiny pool and then ran trickling to the creek.

Laura filled the little pail and went back across the sunny footbridge and up the steps. She went back and forth, fetching water in the little pail and pouring it into the big pail set on a bench inside the doorway.

Then she helped Ma bring down from the wagon everything they could carry. They had moved nearly everything into the dugout when Pa came rattling down the path. He was carrying a little tin stove and two pieces of stovepipe.

'Whew!' he said, setting them down, 'I'm glad I had to carry them only three miles. Think of it, Caroline! Town's only three miles away! Just a nice walk. Well, Hanson's on his way West and the place is ours. How do you like it, Caroline?'

'I like it,' said Ma. 'But I don't know what to do about the beds. I don't want to put them on the floor.'

2

'What's the matter with that?' Pa asked her. 'We've been sleeping on the ground.'

'That's different,' Ma said. 'I don't like to sleep on the floor in a house.'

'Well, that's soon fixed,' said Pa. 'I'll cut some willow boughs to spread the beds on, for tonight. Tomorrow I'll find some straight willow poles, and make a couple of bedsteads.'

He took his axe and went whistling up the path, over the top of the house and down the slope beyond it to the creek. There lay a tiny valley where willows grew thick all along beside the water.

Laura ran at his heels. 'Let me help, Pa!' she panted. 'I can carry some.'

'Why, so you can,' said Pa, looking down at her with his eyes twinkling. 'There's nothing like help when a man has a big job to do.'

Pa often said he did not know how he could manage without Laura. She had helped him make the door for the log house in Indian Territory. Now she helped him carry the leafy willow boughs and spread them in the dugout. Then she went with him to the stable.

All four walls of the stable were built of sods, and the roof was willow-boughs and hay, with sods laid over it. The roof was so low that Pa's head touched it when he stood up straight. There was a manger of willow poles, and two oxen were tied there. One was a huge grey ox with short horns and gentle eyes. The other was smaller, with fierce, long horns and wild eyes. He was bright red-brown all over.

'Hello, Bright,' Pa said to him.

'And how are you, Pete, old fellow?' he asked the big ox, slapping him gently.

'Stand back out of the way, Laura,' he said, 'till we

see how these cattle act. We've got to take them to water.'

He put ropes around their horns and led them out of the stable. They followed him slowly down the slope to a level path that went through green rushes to the flat edge of the creek. Laura slowly tagged after them. Their legs were clumsy and their big feet split in the middle. Their noses were broad and slimy.

Laura stayed outside the stable while Pa tied them to the manger. She walked with him towards the dugout.

'Pa,' she asked, in a little voice, 'did Pet and Patty truly want to go out West?'

'Yes, Laura,' Pa told her.

'Oh, Pa,' she said, and there was a tremble in her voice, 'I don't think I like cattle—much.'

Pa took her hand and comforted it in his big one. He said, 'We must do the best we can, Laura, and not grumble. What must be done is best done cheerfully. And some day we will have horses again.'

'When, Pa?' she asked him, and he said, 'When we raise our first crop of wheat.'

Then they went into the dugout. Ma was cheerful, Mary and Carrie were already washed and combed, and everything was neat. The beds were made on the willow boughs and supper was ready.

After supper they all sat on the path before the door. Pa and Ma had boxes to sit on. Carrie cuddled sleepily in Ma's lap, and Mary and Laura sat on the hard path, their legs hanging over its sharp edge. Jack turned around three times and lay down with his head against Laura's knee.

They all sat quiet, looking across Plum Creek and the willows, watching the sun sink far away in the west, far away over the prairie lands.

At last Ma drew a long breath. 'It is all so tame and peaceful,' she said. 'There will be no wolves or Indians howling tonight. I haven't felt so safe and at rest since I don't know when.'

Pa's slow voice answered, 'We're safe enough, all right. Nothing can happen here.'

The peaceful colours went all around the rim of the sky. The willows breathed and the water talked to itself in the dusk. The land was dark grey. The sky was light grey and stars prickled through it.

'It's bedtime,' Ma said. 'And here is something new, anyway. We've never slept in a dugout before.' She was laughing, and Pa laughed softly with her.

Laura lay in bed and listened to the water talking and the willows whispering. She would rather sleep outdoors, even if she heard wolves, than be so safe in this house dug under the ground.

3

Rushes and Flags

EVERY MORNING AFTER Mary and Laura had done the dishes, made their bed and swept the floor, they could go out to play.

All around the door the morning-glory flowers were fresh and new, springing with all their might out of the green leaves. All along Plum Creek the birds were talking. Sometimes a bird sang, but mostly they talked. Tweet, tweet, oh twitter twee twit! one said. Then another said, Chee, Chee, Chee, and another laughed, Ha ha ha, tiraloo!

Laura and Mary went over the top of their house and down along the path where Pa led the oxen to water.

There along the creek rushes were growing, and blue flags. Every morning the blue flags were new. They stood up dark blue and proud among the green rushes.

Each blue flag had three velvet petals that curved down like a lady's dress over hoops. From its waist three ruffled silky petals stood up and curved together. When Laura looked down inside them, she saw three narrow pale tongues, and each tongue had a strip of golden fur on it.

Sometimes a fat bumble-bee, all black velvet and gold, was bumbling and butting there.

The flat creek bank was warm, soft mud. Little pale-yellow and pale-blue butterflies hovered there, and alighted and sipped. Bright dragonflies flew on blurry

wings. The mud squeezed up between Laura's toes.
Where she stepped, and where Mary stepped, and where
the oxen had walked, there were tiny pools of water in
their footprints.

Where they waded in the shallow water a footprint
would not stay. First a swirl like smoke came up from it
and wavered away in the clear water. Then the footprint slowly melted. The toes smoothed out and the heel
was only a small hollow.   There were tiny fishes in the
water. They were so small that you could hardly see them.
Only when they went swiftly sometimes a silvery belly
flashed. When Laura and Mary stood still these little
fishes swarmed around their feet and nibbled. It was a
tickly feeling.

On top of the water the water-bugs skated. They had
tall legs, and each of their feet made a wee dent in the
water. It was hard to see a water-bug; he skated so fast
that before you saw him he was somewhere else.

The rushes in the wind made a wild, lonely sound.
They were not soft and flat like grass; they were hard and
round and sleek and jointed. One day when Laura was
wading in a deep place by the rushes, she took hold of a
big one to pull herself up on the bank. It squeaked.

For a minute Laura could hardly breathe. Then she
pulled another. It squeaked, and came in two.

The rushes were little hollow tubes, fitted together at
the joints. The tubes squeaked when you pulled them
apart. They squeaked when you pushed them together
again.

Laura and Mary pulled them apart to hear them
squeak. Then they put little ones together to make
necklaces. They put big ones together to make long tubes.
They blew through the tubes into the creek and made it
bubble. They blew at the little fishes and scared them.

Whenever they were thirsty, they could draw up long drinks of water through those tubes.

Ma laughed when Laura and Mary came to dinner and supper, all splashed and muddy, with green necklaces around their necks and the long green tubes in their hands. They brought her bouquets of the blue flags and she put them on the table to make it pretty.

'I declare,' she said, 'you two play in the creek so much, you'll be turning to water-bugs!'

Pa and Ma did not care how much they played in the creek. Only they must never go upstream beyond the little willow valley. The creek came around a curve there. It came out of a hole full of deep, dark water. They must never go near enough to that hole, even to see it.

'Some day I'll take you there,' Pa promised them. And one Sunday afternoon he told them that this was the day.

4

Deep Water

IN THE DUGOUT Laura and Mary took off all their clothes, and over their bare skins they put on old patched dresses. Ma tied on her sunbonnet, Pa took Carrie on his arm, and they all set out.

They went past the cattle path and the rushes, past the willow valley and the plum thickets. They went down a steep, grassy bank, and then across a level place where the grass was tall and coarse. They passed a high, almost straight-up wall of earth where no grass grew.

'What is that, Pa?' asked Laura; and Pa said, 'That is a tableland, Laura.'

He pushed on through the thick, tall grass, making a path for Ma and Mary and Laura. Suddenly they came out of the high grass and the creek was there.

It ran twinkling over white gravel into a wide pool, curved against a low bank where the grass was short. Tall willows stood up on the other side of the pool. Flat on the water lay a shimmery picture of those willows, with every green leaf fluttering.

Ma sat on the bank and kept Carrie with her, while Laura and Mary waded into the pool. 'Stay near the edge, girls!' Ma told them. 'Don't go in where it's deep.'

The water came up under their skirts and made them float. Then the calico got wet and stuck to their legs. Laura went in deeper and deeper. The water came up and up, almost to her waist. She squatted down, and it came to her chin.

Everything was watery, cool, and unsteady. Laura felt very light. Her feet were so light that they almost lifted off the creek bottom. She hopped, and splashed with her arms.

'Oo, Laura, don't!' Mary cried.

'Don't go in any farther, Laura,' said Ma.

Laura kept on splashing. One big splash lifted both feet. Her feet came up, her arms did as they pleased, her head went under the water. She was scared. There was nothing to hold on to, nothing solid anywhere. Then she was standing up, streaming water all over. But her feet were solid.

Nobody had seen that. Mary was tucking up her skirts, Ma was playing with Carrie. Pa was out of sight among the willows. Laura walked as fast as she could in the water. She stepped down deeper and deeper. The water came up past her middle, up to her arms.

Suddenly, deep down in the water, something grabbed her foot.

The thing jerked, and down she went into the deep water. She couldn't breathe, she couldn't see. She grabbed and could not get hold of anything. Water filled her ears and her eyes and her mouth.

Then her head came out of the water close to Pa's head. Pa was holding her.

'Well, young lady,' Pa said, 'you went out too far, and how did you like it?'

Laura could not speak; she had to breathe.

'You heard Ma tell you to stay close to the bank,' said Pa. 'Why didn't you obey her? You deserved a ducking, and I ducked you. Next time you'll do as you're told.'

'Y-yes, Pa!' Laura spluttered. 'Oh, Pa, p-please do it again!'

Pa said, 'Well, I'll—!' Then his great laughter rang among the willows.

'Why didn't you holler when I ducked you?' he asked Laura. 'Weren't you scared?'

'I w-was—awful scared!' Laura gasped. 'But p-please do it again!' Then she asked him, 'How did you get down there, Pa?'

Pa told her he had swum under water from the willows. But they could not stay in the deep water; they must go near the bank and play with Mary.

All that afternoon Pa and Laura and Mary played in the water. They waded and they fought water fights, and whenever Laura or Mary went near the deep water, Pa ducked them. Mary was a good girl after one ducking, but Laura was ducked many times.

Then it was almost chore time and they had to go home. They went dripping along the path through the tall grass, and when they came to the tableland Laura wanted to climb it.

Pa climbed part way up, and Laura and Mary climbed holding to his hands. The dry dirt slipped and slid. Tangled grass roots hung down from the bulging edge overhead. Then Pa lifted Laura up and set her on the tableland.

It really was like a table. That ground rose up high above the tall grasses, and it was round, and flat on top. The grass there was short and soft.

Pa and Laura and Mary stood up on top of that tableland, and looked over the grass tops and the pool to the prairie beyond. They looked all around at prairies stretching to the rim of the sky.

Then they had to slide down again to the lowland and go on home. That had been a wonderful afternoon.

'It's been lots of fun,' Pa said. 'But you girls remember what I tell you. Don't you ever go near that swimming-hole unless I am with you.'

5

Strange Animal

ALL THE NEXT day Laura remembered. She remembered the cool, deep water in the shade of the tall willows. She remembered that she must not go near it.

Pa was away. Mary stayed with Ma in the dugout. Laura played all alone in the hot sunshine. The blue flags were withering among the dull rushes. She went past the willow valley and played in the prairie grasses among the black-eyed Susans and goldenrod. The sunshine was very hot and the wind was scorching.

Then Laura thought of the tableland. She wanted to climb it again. She wondered if she could climb it all by herself. Pa had not said that she could not go to the tableland.

She ran down the steep bank and went across the lowland, through the tall, coarse grasses. The tableland stood up straight and high. It was very hard to climb. The dry earth slid under Laura's feet, her dress was dirty where her knees dug in while she held on to the grasses and pulled herself up. Dust itched on her sweaty skin. But at last she got her stomach on the edge; she heaved and rolled and she was on top of the tableland.

She jumped up, and she could see the deep, shady pool under the willows. It was cool and wet, and her whole skin felt thirsty. But she remembered that she must not go there.

The tableland seemed big and empty and not interesting. It had been exciting when Pa was there, but now it was just flat land, and Laura thought she would go home and get a drink. She was very thirsty.

She slid down the side of the tableland and slowly started back along the way she had come. Down among the tall grasses the air was smothery and very hot. The dugout was far away and Laura was terribly thirsty.

She remembered with all her might that she must not go near that deep, shady swimming-pool, and suddenly she turned around and hurried towards it. She thought she would only look at it. Just looking at it would make her feel better. Then she thought she might wade in the edge of it but she would not go into the deep water.

She came into the path that Pa had made, and she trotted faster.

Right in the middle of the path before her stood an animal.

Laura jumped back, and stood and stared at it. She had never seen such an animal. It was almost as long as Jack, but its legs were very short. Long grey fur bristled all over it. It had a flat head and small ears. Its flat head slowly tilted up and it stared at Laura.

She stared back at its funny face. And while they stood still and staring, that animal widened and shortened and spread flat on the ground. It grew flatter and flatter, till it was a grey fur laid there. It was not like a whole animal at all. Only it had eyes staring up.

Slowly and carefully Laura stooped and reached and picked up a willow stick. She felt better then. She stayed bent over, looking at that flat grey fur.

It did not move and neither did Laura. She wondered what would happen if she poked it. It might change to some other shape. She poked it gently with the short stick.

A frightful snarl came out of it. Its eyes sparkled mad, and fierce white teeth snapped almost on Laura's nose.

Laura ran with all her might. She could run fast. She did not stop running till she was in the dugout.

'Goodness, Laura!' Ma said. 'You'll make yourself sick, tearing around so in this heat.'

All that time, Mary had been sitting like a little lady,

spelling out words in the book that Ma was teaching her to read. Mary was a good little girl.

Laura had been bad and she knew it. She had broken her promise to Pa. But no one had seen her. No one knew that she had started to go to the swimming-hole. If she did not tell, no one would ever know. Only that strange animal knew, and it could not tell on her. But she felt worse and worse inside.

That night she lay awake beside Mary. Pa and Ma sat in the starlight outside the door and Pa was playing his fiddle.

'Go to sleep, Laura,' Ma said, softly, and softly the fiddle sang to her. Pa was a shadow against the sky and his bow danced among the great stars.

Everything was beautiful and good, except Laura. She had broken her promise to Pa. Breaking a promise was bad as telling a lie. Laura wished she had not done it. But she had done it, and if Pa knew, he would punish her.

Pa went on playing softly in the starlight. His fiddle sang to her sweetly and happily. He thought she was a good little girl. At last Laura could bear it no longer.

She slid out of bed and her bare feet stole across the cool earthen floor. In her nightgown and nightcap she stood beside Pa. He drew the last notes from the strings with his bow and she could feel him smiling down at her.

'What is it, little half-pint?' he asked her. 'You look like a little ghost, all white in the dark.'

'Pa,' Laura said, in a quivery small voice, 'I—I— started to go to the swimming-hole.'

'You did!' Pa exclaimed. Then he asked, 'Well, what stopped you?'

'I don't know,' Laura whispered. 'It had grey fur and it—it flattened out flat. It snarled.'

'How big was it?' Pa asked.

Laura told him all about that strange animal.

Pa said, 'It must have been a badger.'

Then for a long time he did not say anything and Laura waited. Laura could not see his face in the dark, but she leaned against his knee and she could feel how strong and kind he was.

'Well,' he said at last, 'I hardly know what to do, Laura. You see, I trusted you. It is hard to know what to do with a person you can't trust. But do you know what people have to do to anyone they can't trust?'

'Wh-at?' Laura quavered.

'They have to watch him,' said Pa. 'So I guess you must be watched. Your Ma will have to do it because I must work at Nelson's. So tomorrow you stay where Ma can watch you. You are not to go out of her sight all day. If you are good all day, then we will let you try again to be a little girl we can trust.

'How about it, Caroline?' he asked Ma.

'Very well, Charles,' Ma said out of the dark. 'I will watch her tomorrow. But I am sure she will be good. Now back to bed, Laura, and go to sleep.'

The next day was a dreadful day.

Ma was mending, and Laura had to stay in the dugout. She could not even fetch water from the spring, for that was going out of Ma's sight. Mary fetched the water, Mary took Carrie to walk on the prairie. Laura had to stay in.

Jack laid his nose on his paws and waggled, he jumped out on the path and looked back at her, smiling with his ears, begging her to come out. He could not understand why she did not.

Laura helped Ma. She washed the dishes and made both beds and swept the floor and set the table. At dinner she sat bowed on her bench and ate what Ma set before her. Then she wiped the dishes. After that she ripped a sheet that was worn in the middle. Ma turned the strips of muslin and pinned them together, and Laura whipped the new seam, over and over with tiny stitches.

She thought that seam and that day would never end.

But at last Ma rolled up her mending and it was time to get supper.

'You have been a good girl, Laura,' Ma said. 'We

will tell Pa so. And tomorrow morning you and I are going to look for that badger. I am sure he saved you from drowning, for if you had gone to that deep water you would have gone into it. Once you begin being naughty, it is easier to go on and on, and sooner or later something dreadful happens.'

'Yes, Ma,' Laura said. She knew that now.

The whole day was gone. Laura had not seen that sunrise, nor the shadows of clouds on the prairie. The morning-glories were withered and that day's blue flags were dead. All day Laura had not seen the water running in the creek, the little fishes in it, and the water-bugs skating over it. She was sure that being good could never be as hard as being watched.

Next day she went with Ma to look for the badger. In the path she showed Ma the place where he had flattened himself on the grass. Ma found the hole where he lived. It was a round hole under a clump of grass on the prairie bank. Laura called to him and she poked a stick into the hole.

If the badger was at home, he would not come out. Laura never saw that old grey badger again.

6

Wreath of Roses

OUT ON THE prairie beyond the stable there was a long grey rock. It rose up above the waving grasses and nodding wild flowers. On top it was flat and almost smooth, so wide that Laura and Mary could run on it side by side, and so long that they could race each other. It was a wonderful place to play.

Grey-green lichens with ruffled edges grew flat on it. Wandering ants crossed it. Often a butterfly stopped to rest there. Then Laura watched the velvety wings slowly opening and closing, as if the butterfly breathed with them. She saw the tiny feet on the rock, and the feelers quivering, and even the round, lidless eyes.

She never tried to catch a butterfly. She knew that its wings were covered with feathers too tiny to see. A touch would brush off those tiny feathers and hurt the butterfly.

The sun was always warm on the big grey rock. Sunshine was always on the waving prairie grasses, and birds and butterflies in the sunshine. Breezes always blew there, warm and perfumed from the sun-warmed grasses. Far away, towards the place where the sky came down to the land, small dark things moved on the prairie. They were cattle, grazing.

Laura and Mary never went to play on the grey rock in the mornings, and they did not stay there when the sun was going down, because morning and evening the cattle went by.

They went by in a herd, with trampling hoofs and tossing horns. Johnny Johnson, the herd boy, walked behind them. He had a round red face, and round blue eyes, and pale, whitey-yellow hair. He grinned, and did not say anything. He couldn't. He did not know any words that Laura and Mary knew.

Late one afternoon Pa called them from the creek. He was going to the big rock to see Johnny Johnson bring the cattle home, and Laura and Mary could go with him.

Laura skipped with joy. She had never been so close to a herd of cattle, and she would not be afraid when Pa was there. Mary came slowly, staying close to Pa.

The cattle were already quite near. Their bawling was growing louder. Their horns tossed above the herd, and a thin, golden dust rose up around them.

'Here they come!' Pa said. 'Scramble up!' He boosted Mary and Laura on to the big rock. Then they looked at the cattle.

Red backs and brown backs, black and white and spotted backs, surged by. Eyes rolled and tongues licked flat noses; heads tipped wickedly to gouge with fierce horns. But Laura and Mary were safe on the high grey rock, and Pa stood against it, watching.

The last of the herd was going by, when both Laura and Mary caught sight of the prettiest cow they had ever seen.

She was a small white cow. She had red ears, and in the middle of her forehead there was a red spot. Her small white horns curved inward, pointing to that red spot. And on her white side, right in the middle, there was a perfect circle of red spots as big as roses.

Even Mary jumped up and down.

'Oh look! Oh, look!' Laura shouted. 'Pa, see the cow with the wreath of roses!'

Pa laughed. He was helping Johnny Johnson drive that cow away from the others. He called back: 'Come along, girls! Help me drive her into the stable!'

Laura jumped off the rock and ran to help him, shouting, 'Why, Pa, why? Oh, Pa, are we going to keep her?'

The little white cow went into the stable, and Pa answered, 'She's our cow!'

Laura turned and ran as fast as she could. She pounded down the path and rushed into the dugout, yelling: 'Oh, Ma, Ma! Come see the cow! We've got a cow! Oh, Ma, the prettiest cow!'

Ma took Carrie on her arm and came to see.

'Charles!' she said.

'She's ours, Caroline!' said Pa. 'How do you like her?'

'But, Charles!' Ma said.

'I got her from Nelson,' Pa told her. 'I'm paying him by day's work. Nelson's got to have help, haying and harvesting. Look at her. She's a good little milch cow. Caroline, we're going to have milk and butter.'

'Oh, Charles!' said Ma.

Laura did not wait to hear any more. She turned around and ran again, as fast as she could go, along the path and down into the dugout. She grabbed her tin cup from the supper table and she rushed back again.

Pa had tied the pretty white cow in her own little stall, beside Pete and Bright. She stood quietly chewing her cud. Laura squatted down beside her and, holding the tin cup carefully in one hand, she took hold of that cow with her other hand and squeezed just as she had seen Pa do when he milked. And sure enough a streak of warm white milk went straight into the tin cup.

'My goodness! what is that child doing!' Ma exclaimed.

'I'm milking, Ma,' said Laura.

'Not on that side,' Ma told her, quickly. 'She'll kick you.'

But the gentle cow only turned her head and looked at Laura with gentle eyes. She looked surprised, but she did not kick.

'Always milk a cow from the right side, Laura,' said Ma. But Pa said: 'Look at the little half-pint! Who taught you to milk?'

Nobody had taught Laura. She knew how to milk a cow; she had watched Pa do it. Now they all watched her. Streak after streak of milk zinged into the tin cup; then streak after streak purred and foamed, till the white foam rose up almost to the cup's brim.

Then Pa and Ma and Mary and Laura each took a

big swallow of that warm, delicious milk, and what was left Carrie drank up. They felt good inside and they all stood looking at that beautiful cow.

'What is her name?' Mary asked.

Pa's big laugh rang out and he said, 'Her name is Reet.'

'Reet?' Ma repeated. 'What outlandish name is that?'

'The Nelsons called her some Norwegian name,' said Pa. 'When I asked what it meant, Mrs. Nelson said it was a reet.'

'What on earth is a reet?' Ma asked him.

'That's what I asked Mrs. Nelson,' said Pa. 'She kept on saying, "a reet," and I guess I looked as foolish as I felt, for finally she said, "a reet of roses." '

'A wreath!' Laura shouted. 'A wreath of roses!'

Then they all laughed till they could not laugh any more, and Pa said: 'It does beat all. In Wisconsin we lived among Swedes and Germans. In Indian Territory we lived among the Indians. Now here in Minnesota all the neighbours are Norwegians. They're good neighbours, too. But I guess our kind of folks is pretty scarce.'

'Well,' said Ma, 'we're not going to call this cow Reet, nor yet Wreath of Roses. Her name is Spot.'

7

Ox on the Roof

NOW LAURA AND Mary had chores to do.
Every morning before the sun was up they had to
drive Spot to the big grey rock to meet the herd,
so that Johnny could take her with the other cattle to
eat grass all day. And every afternoon they had to remember to meet the herd and put Spot in the stable.

In the mornings they ran through the dewy chill
grass that wet their feet and dabbled the hems of their
dresses. They liked to splash their bare feet through the
grass all strung with dewdrops. They liked to watch the
sun rise over the edge of the world.

First everything was grey and still. The sky was grey,
the grass was grey with dew, the light was grey and the
wind held its breath.

Then sharp streaks of green came into the eastern
sky. If there was a little cloud, it turned pink. Laura
and Mary sat on the damp, cold rock, hugging their
chilly legs. They rested their chins on their knees and
watched, and in the grass below them Jack sat, watching,
too. But they never could see when the sky first began to
be pink.

The sky was very faintly pink, then it was pinker.
The colour went higher up the sky. It grew brighter and
deeper. It blazed like fire, and suddenly the little cloud
was glittering gold. In the centre of the blazing colour,
on the flat edge of the earth, a tiny sliver of sun appeared.

It was a short streak of white fire. Suddenly the whole sun bounded up, round and huge, far bigger than the ordinary sun and throbbing with so much light that its roundness almost burst.

Laura couldn't help blinking. While she blinked just once, the sky turned blue, the golden cloud vanished. The everyday sun shone over the prairie grasses where thousands of birds were flying and twittering.

In the evenings when the cattle came home, Laura and Mary always ran fast to get up on the big rock before all those heads and horns and trampling legs reached them.

Pa was working for Mr. Nelson now, and Pete and Bright had no work to do. They went with Spot and the other cattle to eat grass. Laura was never afraid of gentle, white Spot, but Pete and Bright were so big that they would scare anybody.

One evening all the cattle were angry. They came bellowing and pawing, and when they reached the big rock they did not go by. They ran around it, bawling and fighting. Their eyes rolled, their horns tossed and slashed at each other. Their hoofs raised a smudge of dust and their clashing horns were frightful.

Mary was so scared that she could not move. Laura was so scared that she jumped right off the rock. She knew she had to drive Spot and Pete and Bright into the stable.

The cattle towered up in the dust. Their feet trampled and their horns slashed and they bawled. But Johnny helped to head Pete and Bright and Spot towards the stable. Jack helped, too. Jack growled at their heels and Laura ran yelling behind them. And with his big stick Johnny drove the herd away.

Spot went into the stable. Then Bright went in. Pete

was going in, and Laura was not scared now, when suddenly big Pete wheeled around. His horns hooked and his tail stood up, and he galloped after the herd.

Laura ran in front of him. She waved her arms and

yelled. He bellowed, and went thundering towards the creek bank.

Laura ran with all her might, to get in front of him again. But her legs were short and Pete's were long. Jack came running as fast as he could, but he only made Pete jump longer jumps.

Pete jumped right on top of the dugout. Laura saw

his hind leg go down, down through the roof. She saw him sit on it. That big ox was going to fall on Ma and Carrie, and it was Laura's fault because she had not stopped him.

He heaved and pulled his leg up. Laura had not stopped running. She was in front of Pete now and Jack was in front of him, too.

They chased Pete into the stable and Laura put up the bars. She was shaking all over and her legs were weak. Her knees kept hitting together.

Ma had come running up the path, carrying Carrie. But no harm had been done. There was only a hole through the roof where Pete's leg had come down and gone up again. Ma said it had given her a turn to see it coming down through the ceiling.

'But there's no great damage done,' she said.

She stuffed the hole full of grass, and swept out the earth that had fallen into the dugout. Then she and Laura laughed because it was funny to live in a house where a steer could step through the roof. It was like being rabbits.

Next morning while Laura was doing dishes, she saw some little dark things rolling down the whitewashed wall. They were crumbs of earth. She looked up to see where they came from, and she jumped away from there quicker than a rabbit. A big rock smashed down, and the whole ceiling poured down over it.

The sun shone down into the house and the air was full of dust. Ma and Mary and Laura choked and sneezed looking up at the sky where a ceiling should have been. Carrie sat sneezing in Ma's arms. Jack rushed in, and when he saw the sky overhead he growled at it. Then he sneezed.

'Well, that settles it,' said Ma.

'What does, Ma?' Laura asked. She thought Ma meant that something was settling the dust.

'This does,' Ma said. 'Pa will have to mend that roof tomorrow.'

Then they carried out the rock and the earth and the bunches of hay that had fallen. Ma swept and swept again with the willow-twig broom.

That night they slept in their house, under the starry sky. Such a thing had never happened before.

Next day Pa had to stay at home to build a new roof. Laura helped him carry fresh willow boughs and she handed them to him while he wedged them into place. They put clean fresh grass thick over the willows. They piled earth on the grass. Then over the top Pa laid strips of sod cut from the prairie.

He fitted them together and Laura helped him stamp them down.

'That grass will never know it's been moved,' Pa said. 'In a few days you won't be able to tell this new roof from the prairie.'

He did not scold Laura for letting Pete get away. He only said, 'It's no place for a big ox to be running, right over our roof!'

8

Straw-Stack

WHEN MR. NELSON's harvesting was done, Pa had paid for Spot. He could do his own harvesting now. He sharpened the long, dangerous scythe that little girls must never touch, and he cut down the wheat in the small field beyond the stable. He bound it in bundles and stacked them.

Then every morning he went to work on the level land across the creek. He cut the prairie grass and left it to dry in the sunshine. He raked it into piles with a wooden rake. He yoked Pete and Bright to the wagon, and hauled the hay and made six big stacks of it over there.

At night he was always too tired, now, to play the fiddle. But he was glad because when the hay was stacked he could plough that stubble land, and that would be the wheat-field.

One morning at daylight three strange men came with a threshing-machine. They threshed Pa's stack of wheat. Laura heard the harsh machinery noises while she drove Spot through the dewy grass, and when the sun rose chaff flew golden in the wind.

The threshing was done and the men went away with the machine before breakfast. Pa said he wished Hanson had sown more wheat.

'But there's enough to make us some flour,' he said. 'And the straw, with what hay I've cut, will feed the

35

stock through the winter. Next year,' he said, 'we'll have a crop of wheat that will amount to something!'

When Laura and Mary went up on the prairie to play, that morning, the first thing they saw was a beautiful golden straw-stack.

It was tall and shining bright in the sunshine. It smelled sweeter than hay.

Laura's feet slid in the sliding, slippery straw, but she could climb faster than straw slid. In a minute she was high on top of that stack.

She looked across the willow tops and away beyond the creek at the far land. She could see the whole, great, round prairie. She was high up in the sky, almost as high as birds. Her arms waved and her feet bounced on the springy straw. She was almost flying, 'way high up in the windy sky.

'I'm flying! I'm flying!' she called down to Mary. Mary climbed up to her.

'Jump! Jump!' Laura said. They held hands and jumped, round and round, higher and higher. The wind blew and their skirts flapped and their sunbonnets swung at the ends of the sunbonnet strings around their necks.

'Higher! Higher!' Laura sang, jumping. Suddenly the straw slid under her. Over the edge of the stack she went, sitting in straw, sliding faster and faster. Bump! She landed at the bottom. Plump! Mary landed on her.

They rolled and laughed in the crackling straw. Then they climbed the stack, and slid down it again. They had never had so much fun.

They climbed up and slid, climbed and slid, until there was hardly any stack left in the middle of loose heaps of straw.

Then they were sober. Pa had made that straw-stack and now it was not at all as he had left it. Laura looked at Mary and Mary looked at her, and they looked at what was left of that straw-stack. Then Mary said she was going into the dugout, and Laura went quietly with her. They were very good, helping Ma and playing nicely with Carrie, until Pa came to dinner.

When he came in he looked straight at Laura, and Laura looked at the floor.

'You girls mustn't slide down the straw-stack any more,' Pa said. 'I had to stop and pitch up all that loose straw.'

'We won't, Pa,' Laura said, earnestly, and Mary said, 'No, Pa, we won't.'

After dinner Mary washed the dishes and Laura dried them. Then they put on their sunbonnets and went up the path to the prairie. The straw-stack was golden-bright in the sunshine.

'Laura! What are you doing!' said Mary.

'I'm not doing anything!' said Laura. 'I'm not even hardly touching it!'

'You come right away from there, or I'll tell Ma!' said Mary.

'Pa didn't say I couldn't smell it,' said Laura.

She stood close to the golden stack and sniffed long, deep sniffs. The straw was warmed by the sun. It smelled better than wheat kernels taste when you chew them. Laura burrowed her face in it, shutting her eyes and smelling deeper and ·deeper.

'Mmm!' she said.

Mary came and smelled it and said, 'Mmm!'

Laura looked up the glistening, prickly, golden stack. She had never seen the sky so blue as it was above that gold. She could not stay on the ground. She had to be high up in the blue sky.

'Laura!' Mary cried. 'Pa said we mustn't!'

Laura was climbing. 'He did not, either!' she contradicted. 'He did not say we must not climb up it. He said we must not slide down it. I'm only climbing.'

'You come right straight down from there,' said Mary.

Laura was on top of the stack. She looked down at Mary and said, like a very good little girl, 'I am not going to slide down. Pa said not to.'

Nothing but the blue sky was higher than she was. The wind was blowing. The green prairie was wide and far. Laura spread her arms and jumped, and the straw bounded her high.

'I'm flying! I'm flying!' she sang. Mary climbed up, and Mary began to fly, too.

They bounced until they could bounce no higher. Then they flopped flat on the sweet warm straw. Bulges of straw rose up on both sides of Laura. She rolled on to a bulge and it sank, but another rose up. She rolled on to that bulge, and then she was rolling faster and faster; she could not stop.

'Laura!' Mary screamed. 'Pa said—' But Laura was rolling. Over, over, over, right down that straw-stack she rolled and thumped in straw on the ground.

She jumped up and climbed that straw-stack again as fast as she could. She flopped and began to roll again. 'Come on, Mary!' she shouted. 'Pa didn't say we can't roll!'

Mary stayed on top of the stack and argued. 'I know Pa didn't say we can't roll, but——'

'Well, then!' Laura rolled down again. 'Come on!' she called up. 'It's lots of fun!'

'Well, but I—' said Mary. Then she came rolling down.

It was great fun. It was more fun than sliding. They climbed and rolled and climbed and rolled, laughing harder all the time. More and more straw rolled down with them. They waded in it and rolled each other in it and climbed and rolled down again, till there was hardly anything left to climb.

Then they brushed every bit of straw off their dresses, they picked every bit out of their hair, and they went quietly into the dugout.

When Pa came from the hay-field that night, Mary was busily setting the table for supper. Laura was behind the door, busy with the box of paper dolls.

'Laura,' Pa said, dreadfully, 'come here.'

Slowly Laura went out from behind the door.

'Come here,' said Pa, 'right over here by Mary.'

He sat down and he stood them before him, side by side. But it was Laura he looked at.

He said, sternly, 'You girls have been sliding down the straw-stack again.'

'No, Pa,' said Laura.

'Mary!' said Pa. 'Did you slide down the straw-stack?'

'N-no, Pa,' Mary said.

'Laura!' Pa's voice was terrible. 'Tell me again, DID YOU SLIDE DOWN THE STRAW-STACK?'

'No, Pa,' Laura answered again. She looked straight into Pa's shocked eyes. She did not know why he looked like that.

'Laura!' Pa said.

'We did not slide, Pa,' Laura explained. 'But we did roll down it.'

Pa got up quickly and went to the door and stood looking out. His back quivered. Laura and Mary did not know what to think.

When Pa turned around, his face was stern but his eyes were twinkling.

'All right, Laura,' he said. 'But now I want you girls to stay away from that straw-stack. Pete and Bright and Spot will have nothing but hay and straw to eat this winter. They need every bite of it. You don't want them to be hungry, do you?'

'Oh no, Pa!' they said.

'Well, if that straw's to be fit to feed them, it MUST— STAY—STACKED. Do you understand?'

'Yes, Pa,' said Laura and Mary.

That was the end of their playing on the straw-stack.

9

Grasshopper Weather

NOW PLUMS WERE ripening in the wild-plum thickets all along Plum Creek. Plum trees were low trees. They grew close together, with many little scraggly branches all strung with thin-skinned, juicy plums. Around the air was sweet and sleepy, and wings hummed.

Pa was ploughing all the land across the creek, where he had cut the hay. Early before the sun came up, when Laura went to drive Spot to meet the cattle at the grey boulder, Pete and Bright were gone from the stable. Pa had yoked them to the plough and gone to work.

When Laura and Mary had washed the breakfast dishes, they took tin pails and went to pick plums. From the top of their house, they could see Pa ploughing. The oxen and the plough and Pa crawled slowly along a curve of the prairie. They looked very small, and a little smoke of dust blew away from the plough.

Every day the velvety brown-dark patch of ploughed land grew bigger. It ate up the silvery-gold stubble field beyond the hay-stacks. It spread over the prairie waves. It was going to be a very big wheat-field, and when some day Pa cut the wheat, he and Ma and Laura and Mary would have everything they could think of.

They would have a house, and horses, and candy every day, when Pa made a wheat crop.

Laura went wading through the tall grasses to the plum

thickets by the creek. Her sunbonnet hung down her back and she swung her tin pail. The grasses were crisping yellow now, and dozens of little grasshoppers jumped crackling from Laura's swishing feet. Mary came walking behind in the path Laura made and she kept her sunbonnet on.

When they came to a plum thicket they set down their big pails. They filled their little pails with plums and emptied them into the big pails till they were full. Then they carried the big pails back to the roof of the dugout. On the clean grass Ma spread clean cloths, and Laura and Mary laid the plums on the cloths, to dry in the sun. Next winter they would have dried plums to eat.

The shade of the plum thickets was a thin shade. Sunshine flickered between the narrow leaves overhead. The little branches sagged with their weight of plums, and plums had fallen and rolled together between drifts of long grass underfoot.

Some were smashed, some were smooth and perfect, and some had cracked open, showing the juicy yellow inside.

Bees and hornets stood thick along the cracks, sucking up the juices with all their might. Their scaly tails wiggled with joy. They were too busy and too happy to sting. When Laura poked them with a blade of grass, they only moved a step and did not stop sucking up the good plum juice.

Laura put all the good plums in her pail. But she flicked the hornets off the cracked plums with her finger nail and quickly popped the plum into her mouth. It was sweet and warm and juicy. The hornets buzzed around her in dismay; they did not know what had become of their plum. But in a minute they pushed into the crowds sucking at another one.

'I declare, you eat more plums than you pick up,' Mary said.

'I don't either any such a thing,' Laura contradicted. 'I pick up every plum I eat.'

'You know very well what I mean,' Mary said, crossly. 'You just play around while I work.'

But Laura filled her big pail as quickly as Mary filled hers. Mary was cross because she would rather sew or read than pick plums. But Laura hated to sit still; she liked picking plums.

She liked to shake the trees. You must know exactly how to shake a plum tree. If you shake it too hard, the green plums fall, and that wastes them. If you shake it too softly, you do not get all the ripe plums. In the night they will fall, and some will smash and be wasted.

Laura learned exactly how to shake a plum tree. She held its scaling-rough bole and shook it, one quick, gentle shake. Every plum swung on its stem and all around her they fell pattering. Then one more jerk while the plums were swinging, and the last ripe ones fell plum-plump! plum-plump! plump! plump!

There were many kinds of plums. When the red ones were all picked, the yellow ones were ripe. Then the blue ones. The largest of all were the very last. They were the frost plums, that would not ripen until after frost.

One morning the whole world was delicately silvered. Every blade of grass was silvery and the path had a thin sheen. It was hot like fire under Laura's bare feet, and they left dark footprints in it. The air was cold in her nose and her breath steamed. So did Spot's. When the sun came up, the whole prairie sparkled. Millions of tiny, tiny sparks of colour blazed on the grasses.

That day the frost plums were ripe. They were large,

purple plums and all over their purple was a silvery thin sheen like frost.

The sun was not so hot now and the nights were chilly. The prairie was almost the tawny colour of the hay-stacks. The smell of the air was different and the sky was not so sharply blue.

Still the sunshine was warm at noon. There was no rain and no more frosts. It was almost Thanksgiving time, and there was no snow.

'I don't know what to make of it,' Pa said. 'I never saw weather like this. Nelson says the oldtimers call it grasshopper weather.'

'Whatever do they mean by that?' Ma asked him.

Pa shook his head. 'You can't prove it by me. "Grasshopper weather," was what Nelson said. I couldn't make out what he meant by it.'

'Likely it's some old Norwegian saying,' Ma said.

Laura liked the sound of the words and when she ran through the crackling prairie grasses and saw the grasshoppers jumping she sang to herself: 'Grasshopper weather! Grasshopper weather!'

10

Cattle in the Hay

SUMMER WAS GONE, winter was coming, and now it was time for Pa to make a trip to town. Here in Minnesota, town was so near that Pa would be gone only one day, and Ma was going with him.

She took Carrie, because Carrie was too little to be left far from Ma. But Mary and Laura were big girls. Mary was going on nine and Laura was going on eight, and they could stay at home and take care of everything while Pa and Ma were gone.

For going-to-town, Ma made a new dress for Carrie, from the pink calico that Laura had worn when she was little. There was enough of it to make Carrie a little pink sunbonnet. Carrie's hair had been in curl-papers all night. It hung in long, golden, round curls, and when Ma tied the pink sunbonnet strings under Carrie's chin, Carrie looked like a rose.

Ma wore her hoopskirts and her best dress, the beautiful challis with little strawberries on it, that she had worn to the sugaring-dance at Grandma's, long ago in the Big Woods.

'Now be good girls, Laura and Mary,' was the last thing she said. She was on the wagon seat, with Carrie beside her. Their lunch was in the wagon. Pa took up the ox goad.

'We'll be back before sundown,' he promised. 'Hi-oop!' he said to Pete and Bright. The big ox and the little one leaned into their yoke and the wagon started.

'Good-bye, Pa! Good-bye, Ma! Good-bye, Carrie, good-bye!' Laura and Mary called after it.

Slowly the wagon went away. Pa walked beside the oxen. Ma and Carrie, the wagon, and Pa all grew smaller, till they were gone into the prairie.

The prairie seemed big and empty then, but there was nothing to be afraid of. There were no wolves and no Indians. Besides, Jack stayed close to Laura. Jack was a responsible dog. He knew that he must take care of everything when Pa was away.

That morning Mary and Laura played by the creek, among the rushes. They did not go near the swimming-hole. They did not touch the straw-stack. At noon they ate the corn dodgers and molasses and drank the milk that Ma had left for them. They washed their tin cups and put them away.

Then Laura wanted to play on the big rock, but Mary wanted to stay in the dugout. She said that Laura must stay there, too.

'Ma can make me,' Laura said, 'but you can't.'

'I can so,' said Mary. 'When Ma's not here, you have to do what I say because I'm older.'

'You have to let me have my way because I'm littler,' said Laura.

'That's Carrie, it isn't you,' Mary told her. 'If you don't do what I say, I'll tell Ma.'

'I guess I can play where I want to!' said Laura.

Mary grabbed at her, but Laura was too quick. She darted out, and she would have run up the path, but Jack was in the way. He stood stiff, looking across the creek. Laura looked too, and she screeched, 'Mary!'

The cattle were all around Pa's hay-stacks. They were eating the hay. They were tearing into the stacks with their horns, gouging out hay, eating it and trampling over it.

There would be nothing left to feed Pete and Bright and Spot in the winter-time.

Jack knew what to do. He ran growling down the steps to the foot-bridge. Pa was not there to save the hay-stacks; they must drive those cattle away.

'Oh, we can't! We can't!' Mary said scared. But Laura ran behind Jack and Mary came after her. They went over the creek and past the spring. They came up on the prairie and now they saw the fierce, big cattle quite near. The long horns were gouging, the thick legs trampling and jostling, the wide mouths bawling.

Mary was too scared to move. Laura was too scared to stand still. She jerked Mary along. She saw a stick, and grabbed it up and ran yelling at the cattle. Jack ran at them, growling. A big red cow swiped at him with her horns, but he jumped behind her. She snorted and galloped. All the other cattle ran humping and jostling after her, and Jack and Laura and Mary ran after them.

But they could not chase those cattle away from the hay-stacks. The cattle ran around and around and in between the stacks, jostling and bawling, tearing off hay and trampling it. More and more hay slid off the stacks. Laura ran panting and yelling, waving her stick. The faster she ran, the faster the cattle went, black and brown and red, brindle and spotted cattle, big and with awful horns, and they would not stop wasting the hay. Some tried to climb over the toppling stacks.

Laura was hot and dizzy. Her hair unbraided and blew in her eyes. Her throat was rough from yelling, but she kept on yelling, running, and waving her stick. She was too scared to hit one of those big, horned cows. More and more hay kept coming down and faster and faster they trampled over it.

Suddenly Laura turned around and ran the other way. She faced the big red cow coming around a hay-stack.

The huge legs and shoulders and terrible horns were coming fast. Laura could not scream now. But she jumped at that cow and waved her stick. The cow tried to stop, but all the other cattle were coming behind her and she couldn't. She swerved and ran away across the ploughed ground, all the others galloping after her.

Jack and Laura and Mary chased them, farther and farther from the hay. Far into the high prairie grasses they chased those cattle.

Johnny Johnson rose out of the prairie, rubbing his eyes. He had been lying asleep in a warm hollow of grass.

'Johnny! Johnny!' Laura screeched. 'Wake up and watch the cattle!'

'You'd better!' Mary told him.

Johnny Johnson looked at the cattle grazing in the deep grass, and he looked at Laura and Mary and Jack. He did not know what had happened and they could not tell him because the only words he knew were Norwegian.

They went back through the high grass that dragged at their trembling legs. They were glad to drink at the spring. They were glad to be in the quiet dugout and sit down to rest.

11

Runaway

ALL THAT LONG, quiet afternoon they stayed in the dugout. The cattle did not come back to the hay-stacks. Slowly the sun went down the western sky. Soon it would be time to meet the cattle at the big grey rock, and Laura and Mary wished that Pa and Ma would come home.

Again and again they went up the path to look for the wagon. At last they sat waiting with Jack on the grassy top of their house. The lower the sun went, the more attentive Jack's ears were. Often he and Laura stood up to look at the edge of the sky where the wagon had gone, though they could see it just as well when they were sitting down.

Finally Jack turned one ear that way, then the other. Then he looked up at Laura and a waggle went from his neck to his stubby tail. The wagon was coming!

They all stood and watched till it came out of the prairie. When Laura saw the oxen, and Ma and Carrie on the wagon seat, she jumped up and down swinging her sunbonnet and shouting, 'They're coming! They're coming!'

'They're coming awful fast,' Mary said.

Laura was still. She heard the wagon rattling loudly. Pete and Bright were coming very fast. They were running. They were running away.

The wagon came bumpity-banging and bouncing.

Laura saw Ma down in a corner of the wagon box, hanging on to it and hugging Carrie. Pa came bounding in long jumps beside Bright, shouting and hitting at Bright with the goad.

He was trying to turn Bright back from the creek bank. He could not do it. The big oxen galloped nearer and nearer the steep edge. Bright was pushing Pa off it. They were all going over. The wagon, Ma and Carrie, were going to fall down the bank, all the way down to the creek.

Pa shouted a terrible shout. He struck Bright's head with all his might, and Bright swerved. Laura ran screaming. Jack jumped at Bright's nose. Then the wagon, Ma, and Carrie flashed by. Bright crashed against the stable and suddenly everything was still.

Pa ran after the wagon and Laura ran behind him.

'Whoa, Bright! Whoa, Pete,' Pa said. He held on to the wagon box and looked at Ma.

'We're all right, Charles,' Ma said. Her face was grey and she was shaking all over.

Pete was trying to go on through the doorway into the stable, but he was yoked to Bright and Bright was headed against the stable wall. Pa lifted Ma and Carrie out of the wagon, and Ma said, 'Don't cry, Carrie. See, we're all right.'

Carrie's pink dress was torn down the front. She snuffled against Ma's neck and tried to stop crying as Ma told her.

'Oh, Caroline! I thought you were going over the bank.' Pa said.

'I thought so, too, for a minute,' Ma answered. 'But I might have known you wouldn't let that happen.'

'Pshaw!' said Pa. 'It was good old Pete. He wasn't running away. Bright was, but Pete was only going along. He saw the stable and wanted his supper.'

But Laura knew that Ma and Carrie would have

fallen down into the creek with the wagon and oxen, if Pa had not run so fast and hit Bright so hard. She crowded against Ma's hoopskirt and hugged her tight and said, 'Oh, Ma! Oh, Ma!' So did Mary.

'There there,' said Ma. 'All's well that ends well. Now, girls, help bring in the packages while Pa puts up the oxen.'

They carried all the little packages into the dugout. They met the cattle at the grey rock and put Spot into the stable, and Laura helped milk her while Mary helped Ma get supper.

At supper, they told how the cattle had got into the hay-stacks and how they had driven them away. Pa said they had done exactly the right thing. He said, 'We knew we could depend on you to take care of everything. Didn't we, Caroline?'

They had completely forgotten that Pa always brought them presents from town, until after supper he pushed back his bench and looked as if he expected something. Then Laura jumped on his knee, and Mary sat on the other, and Laura bounced and asked, 'What did you bring us, Pa? What? What?'

'Guess,' Pa said.

They could not guess. But Laura felt something crackle in his jumper pocket and she pounced on it. She pulled out a paper bag, beautifully striped with tiny red and green stripes. And in the bag were two sticks of candy, one for Mary and one for Laura!

They were maple-sugar-coloured, and they were flat on one side.

Mary licked hers. But Laura bit her stick, and the outside of it came off, crumbly. The inside was hard and clear and dark brown. And it had a rich, brown, tangy taste. Pa said it was hoarhound candy.

After the dishes were done, Laura and Mary each took her stick of candy and they sat on Pa's knees, outside the door in the cool dusk. Ma sat just inside the dugout, humming to Carrie in her arms.

The creek was talking to itself under the yellow willows. One by one the great stars swung low and seemed to quiver and flicker in the little wind.

Laura was snug in Pa's arm. His beard softly tickled her cheek and the delicious candy-taste melted on her tongue.

After a while she said, 'Pa.'

'What, little half-pint?' Pa's voice asked against her hair.

'I think I like wolves better than cattle,' she said.

'Cattle are more useful, Laura,' Pa said.

She thought about that a while. Then she said, 'Anyway, I like wolves better.'

She was not contradicting; she was only saying what she thought.

'Well, Laura, we're going to have a good team of horses before long,' Pa said. She knew when that would be. It would be when they had a wheat crop.

12

The Christmas Horses

GRASSHOPPER WEATHER WAS strange weather. Even at Thanksgiving, there was no snow. The door of the dugout was wide open while they ate Thanksgiving dinner. Laura could see across the bare willow-tops, far over the prairie to the place where the sun would go down. There was not one speck of snow. The prairie was like soft yellow fur. The line where it met the sky was not sharp now; it was smudged and blurry.

'Grasshopper weather,' Laura thought to herself. She thought of grasshoppers' long, folded wings and their high-jointed hind legs. Their feet were thin and scratchy. Their heads were hard, with large eyes on the corners, and their jaws were tiny and nibbling.

If you caught a grasshopper and held him, and gently poked a green blade of grass into his jaws, they nibbled it fast. They swiftly nibbled in the whole grass blade, till the tip of it went into them and was gone.

Thanksgiving dinner was good. Pa had shot a wild goose for it. Ma had to stew the goose because there was no fireplace, and no oven in the little stove. But she made dumplings in the gravy. There were corn dodgers and mashed potatoes. There were butter, and milk, and stewed dried plums. And three grains of parched corn lay beside each tin plate.

At the first Thanksgiving dinner the poor Pilgrims had

had nothing to eat but three parched grains of corn. Then the Indians came and brought them turkeys, so the Pilgrims were thankful.

Now, after they had eaten their good, big Thanksgiving dinner, Laura and Mary could eat their grains of corn and remember the Pilgrims. Parched corn was good. It crackled and crunched, and its taste was sweet and brown.

Then Thanksgiving was past and it was time to think of Christmas. Still there was no snow and no rain. The sky was grey, the prairie was dull, and the winds were cold. But the cold winds blew over the top of the dugout.

'A dugout is snug and cosy,' said Ma. 'But I do feel like an animal penned up for the winter.'

'Never mind, Caroline,' Pa said. 'We'll have a good house next year.' His eyes shone and his voice was like singing. 'And good horses, and a buggy to boot! I'll take you riding, dressed up in silks! Think, Caroline—this level, rich land, not a stone or stump to contend with, and only three miles from a railroad! We can sell every grain of wheat we raise!'

Then he ran his fingers through his hair and said. 'I do wish I had a team of horses.'

'Now, Charles,' said Ma. 'Here we are, all healthy and safe and snug, with food for the winter. Let's be thankful for what we have.'

'I am,' Pa said. 'But Pete and Bright are too slow for harrowing and harvesting. I've broken up that big field with them, but I can't put it all in wheat, without horses.'

Then Laura had a chance to speak without interrupting. She said, 'There isn't any fireplace.'

'Whatever are you talking about?' Ma asked her.

'Santa Claus,' Laura answered.

'Eat your supper, Laura, and let's not cross bridges till we come to them,' said Ma.

Laura and Mary knew that Santa Claus could not come down a chimney when there was no chimney. One day Mary asked Ma how Santa Claus could come. Ma did not answer. Instead, she asked, 'What do you girls want for Christmas?'

She was ironing. One end of the ironing-board was on the table and the other on the bedstead. Pa had made the bedstead that high, on purpose. Carrie was playing on the bed and Laura and Mary sat at the table. Mary was sorting quilt blocks and Laura was making a little apron for the rag doll, Charlotte. The wind howled overhead and whined in the stovepipe, but there was no snow yet.

Laura said, 'I want candy.'

'So do I,' said Mary, and Carrie cried, 'Tandy?'

'And a new winter dress, and a coat, and a hood,' said Mary.

'So do I,' said Laura. 'And a dress for Charlotte, and——'

Ma lifted the iron from the stove and held it out to them. They could test the iron. They licked their fingers and touched them, quicker than quick, to the smooth hot bottom. If it crackled, the iron was hot enough.

'Thank you, Mary and Laura,' Ma said. She began carefully ironing around and over the patches on Pa's shirt. 'Do you know what Pa wants for Christmas?'

They did not know.

'Horses,' Ma said. 'Would you girls like horses?'

Laura and Mary looked at each other.

'I only thought,' Ma went on, 'if we all wished for horses, and nothing but horses, then maybe——'

Laura felt queer. Horses were everyday; they were not Christmas. If Pa got horses, he would trade for them.

Laura could not think of Santa Claus and horses at the same time.

'Ma!' she cried. 'There IS a Santa Claus, isn't there?'

'Of course there's a Santa Claus,' said Ma. She set the iron on the stove to heat again.

'The older you are, the more you know about Santa Claus,' she said. 'You are so big now, you know he can't be just one man, don't you? You know he is everywhere on Christmas Eve. He is in the Big Woods, and in Indian Territory, and far away in York State, and here. He comes down all the chimneys at the same time. You know that, don't you?'

'Yes, Ma,' said Mary and Laura.

'Well,' said Ma. 'Then you see——'

'I guess he is like angels,' Mary said, slowly. And Laura could see that, just as well as Mary could.

Then Ma told them something else about Santa Claus. He was everywhere, and besides that, he was all the time.

Whenever anyone was unselfish, that was Santa Claus.

Christmas Eve was the time when everybody was unselfish. On that one night, Santa Claus was everywhere, because everybody, all together stopped being selfish and wanted other people to be happy. And in the morning you saw what that had done.

'If everybody wanted everybody else to be happy, all the time, then would it be Christmas all the time?' Laura asked, and Ma said, 'Yes, Laura.'

Laura thought about that. So did Mary. They thought and they looked at each other, and they knew what Ma wanted them to do. She wanted them to wish for nothing but horses for Pa. They looked at each other again and they looked away quickly and they did not say anything. Even Mary, who was always so good, did not say a word.

That night after supper Pa drew Laura and Mary close

5

to him in the crook of his arms. Laura looked up at his face, and then she snuggled against him and said, 'Pa.'

'What is it, little half-pint of sweet cider?' Pa asked, and Laura said,

'Pa, I want Santa Claus—to bring——'

'What?' Pa asked.

'Horses,' said Laura. 'If you will let me ride them sometimes.'

'So do I!' said Mary. But Laura had said it first.

Pa was surprised. His eyes shone soft and bright at them. 'Would you girls really like horses?' he asked them.

'Oh yes, Pa!' they said.

'In that case,' said Pa, smiling, 'I have an idea that Santa Claus will bring us all a fine team of horses.'

That settled it. They would not have any Christmas, only horses. Laura and Mary soberly undressed and soberly buttoned up their nightgowns and tied their nighcap strings. They knelt down together and said,

'Now I lay me down to sleep,
I pray the Lord my soul to keep.
If I should die before I wake
I pray the Lord my soul to take,

and please bless Pa and Ma and Carrie and everybody and make me a good girl for ever'n'ever. Amen.'

Quickly Laura added, in her own head, 'And please make me only glad about the Christmas horses, for ever'n'ever amen again.'

She climbed into bed and almost right away she was glad. She thought of horses sleek and shining, of how their manes and tails blew in the wind, how they picked up their swift feet and sniffed the air with velvety noses and looked at everything with bright, soft eyes. And Pa would let her ride them.

Pa had tuned his fiddle and now he set it against his shoulder. Overhead the wind went wailing lonely in the cold dark. But in the dugout everything was snug and cosy.

Bits of firelight came through the seams of the stove and twinkled on Ma's steel knitting-needles and tried to catch Pa's elbow. In the shadows the bow was dancing, on the floor Pa's toe was tapping, and the merry music hid the lonely crying of the wind.

13

A Merry Christmas

NEXT MORNING, SNOW was in the air. Hard bits of snow were leaping and whirling in the howling wind.

Laura could not go out to play. In the stable, Spot and Pete and Bright stood all day long, eating the hay and straw. In the dugout, Pa mended his boots while Ma read to him again the story called *Millbank*. Mary sewed and Laura played with Charlotte. She could let Carrie hold Charlotte, but Carrie was too little to play with paper dolls; she might tear one.

That afternoon, when Carrie was asleep, Ma beckoned Mary and Laura. Her face was shining with a secret. They put their heads close to hers, and she told them. They could make a button-string for Carrie's Christmas!

They climbed on to their bed and turned their backs to Carrie and spread their laps wide. Ma brought them her button-box.

The box was almost full. Ma had saved buttons since she was smaller than Laura, and she had buttons her mother had saved when her mother was a little girl. There were blue buttons and red buttons, silvery and goldy buttons, curved-in buttons with tiny raised castles and bridges and trees on them, and twinkling jet buttons, painted china buttons, striped buttons, buttons like juicy blackberries, and even one tiny dog-head button. Laura squealed when she saw it.

'Sh!' Ma shushed her. But Carrie did not wake up.

Ma gave them all those buttons to make a button-string for Carrie.

After that, Laura did not mind staying in the dugout. When she saw the outdoors, the wind was driving snow drifts across the bare frozen land. The creek was ice and the willow tops rattled. In the dugout she and Mary had their secret.

They played gently with Carrie and gave her everything she wanted. They cuddled her and sang to her and got her to sleep whenever they could. Then they worked on the button string.

Mary had one end of the string and Laura had the other. They picked out the buttons they wanted and strung them on the string. They held the string out and looked at it, and took off some buttons and put on others. Sometimes they took every button off, and started again. They were going to make the most beautiful button-string in the world.

One day Ma told them that this was the day before Christmas. They must finish the button-string that day.

They could not get Carrie to sleep. She ran and shouted, climbed on benches and jumped off, and skipped and sang. She did not get tired. Mary told her to sit still like a little lady, but she wouldn't. Laura let her hold Charlotte, and she jounced Charlotte up and down and flung her against the wall.

Finally Ma cuddled her and sang. Laura and Mary were perfectly still. Lower and lower Ma sang, and Carrie's eyes blinked till they shut. When softly Ma stopped singing, Carrie's eyes popped open and she shouted, 'More, Ma! More!'

But at last she fell asleep. Then quickly, quickly, Laura and Mary finished the button-string. Ma tied the ends together for them. It was done; they could not change one button more. It was a beautiful button-string.

That evening after supper, when Carrie was sound asleep, Ma hung her clean little pair of stockings from the table edge. Laura and Mary, in their nightgowns, slid the button-string into one stocking.

Then that was all. Mary and Laura were going to bed when Pa asked them, 'Aren't you girls going to hang your stockings?'

'But I thought,' Laura said, 'I thought Santa Claus was going to bring us horses.'

'Maybe he will,' said Pa. 'But little girls always hang up their stockings on Christmas Eve, don't they?'

Laura did not know what to think. Neither did Mary. Ma took two clean stockings out of the clothes-box, and Pa helped hang them beside Carrie's. Laura and Mary said their prayers and went to sleep, wondering.

In the morning Laura heard the fire crackling. She opened one eye the least bit, and saw lamplight, and a bulge in her Christmas stocking.

She yelled and jumped out of bed. Mary came running, too, and Carrie woke up. In Laura's stocking, and in Mary's stocking, there were little paper packages, just alike. In the packages was candy.

Laura had six pieces, and Mary had six. They had never seen such beautiful candy. It was too beautiful to eat. Some pieces were like ribbons, bent in waves. Some were short bits of round stick candy, and on their flat ends were coloured flowers that went all the way through. Some were perfectly round and striped.

In one of Carrie's stockings were four pieces of that beautiful candy. In the other was the button-string. Carrie's eyes and her mouth were perfectly round when she saw it. Then she squealed, and grabbed it and squealed again. She sat on Pa's knee, looking at her candy and her button-string and wriggling and laughing with joy.

Then it was time for Pa to do the chores. He said, 'Do you suppose there is anything for us in the stable?' And

Ma said, 'Dress as fast as you can, girls, and you can go to the stable and see what Pa finds.'

It was winter, so they had to put on stockings and shoes. But Ma helped them button up the shoes and she pinned their shawls under their chins. They ran out into the cold.

Everything was grey, except a long red streak in the

eastern sky. Its red light shone on the patches of grey-white snow. Snow was caught in the dead grass on the walls and roof of the stable and it was red. Pa stood waiting in the stable door. He laughed when he saw Laura and Mary, and he stepped outside to let them go in.

There, standing in Pete's and Bright's places, were two horses.

They were larger than Pet and Patty, and they were a soft, red-brown colour, shining like silk. Their manes and tails were black. Their eyes were bright and gentle. They put their velvety noses down to Laura and nibbled softly at her hand and breathed warm on it.

'Well, flutterbudget!' said Pa, 'and Mary. How do you girls like your Christmas?'

'Very much, Pa,' said Mary, but Laura could only say, 'Oh, Pa!'

Pa's eyes shone deep and he asked, 'Who wants to ride the Christmas horses to water?'

Laura could hardly wait while he lifted Mary up and showed her how to hold on to the mane, and told her not to be afraid. Then Pa's strong hands swung Laura up. She sat on the horse's big, gentle back and felt its aliveness carrying her.

All outdoors was glittering now with sunshine on snow and frost. Pa went ahead, leading the horses and carrying his axe to break the ice in the creek so they could drink. The horses lifted their heads and took deep breaths and whooshed the cold out of their noses. Their velvety ears pricked forward, then back and forward again.

14

Spring Floods

IN THE MIDDLE of the night Laura sat straight up in
bed. She never heard anything like the roaring at the
door.

'Pa! Pa, what's that?' she screamed.

'Sounds like the creek,' he said, jumping out of bed. He
opened the door, and the roaring came into the black
darkness of the dugout. It scared Laura.

She heard Pa shouting, 'Jiminy crickets! It's raining
fish-hooks and hammer handles!'

Ma said something that Laura could not hear.

'Can't see a thing!' Pa shouted. 'It's dark as a stack of
black cats! Don't worry, the creek can't get this high! It
will go over the low bank on the other side!'

He shut the door and the roaring was not so loud.

'Go to sleep, Laura,' he said. But Laura lay awake,
listening to that roaring thundering by the door.

Then she opened her eyes. The window was grey. Pa
was gone, Ma was getting breakfast, but the creek was
still roaring.

In a flash Laura was out of bed and opening the door.
Whoosh! Icy cold rain went all over her and took her
breath away. She jumped out, into cold water pouring
down her whole skin. Right at her feet the creek was rushing and roaring.

The path ended where she was. Angry water was leaping and rolling over the steps that used to go down to the

65

footbridge. The willow clumps were drowned and tree tops swirled in yellow foam. The noise crowded into Laura's ears. She could not hear the rain. She felt it beating on her sopping-wet nightgown, she felt it striking her head as if she had no hair, but she heard only the creek's wild roaring.

The fast, strong water was fearful and fascinating. It snarled foaming through the willow tops and swirled far out on the prairie. It came dashing high and white around the bend upstream. It was always changing and always the same, strong and terrible.

Suddenly Ma jerked Laura into the dugout, asking her, 'Didn't you hear me call you?'

'No, Ma,' Laura said.

'Well, no,' said Ma, 'I suppose you didn't.'

Water was streaming down Laura and making a puddle around her bare feet. Ma pulled off her sticking-wet nightgown and rubbed her hard all over with a towel.

'Now dress quickly,' Ma said, 'or you'll catch your death of cold.'

But Laura was glowing warm. She had never felt so fine and frisky. Mary said, 'I'm surprised at you, Laura. I wouldn't go out in the rain and get all wet like that.'

'Oh, Mary, you just ought to see the creek!' Laura cried, and she asked, 'Ma, may I go out and see it again after breakfast?'

'You may not,' said Ma. 'Not while it is raining.'

But while they were eating breakfast the rain stopped. The sun was shining, and Pa said that Laura and Mary might go with him to look at the creek.

The air was fresh and clean and damp. It smelled like spring. The sky was blue, with large clouds sailing in it. All the snow was gone from the soaking wet earth. Up on the high bank, Laura could still hear the creek roaring.

'This weather beats me,' said Pa. 'I never saw anything like it.'

'Is it still grasshopper weather?' Laura asked him, but Pa did not know.

They went along the high bank, looking at the strange sights. The roaring, foaming creek changed everything. The plum thickets were only foamy brushwood in the water. The tableland was a round island. All around it the water flowed smoothly, coming out of a wide, humping river and running back into it. Where the swimming-pool had been, the tall willows were short willows standing in a lake.

Beyond them, the land that Pa had ploughed lay black and wet. Pa looked at it and said, 'It won't be long now till I can get the wheat planted.'

15

The Footbridge

NEXT DAY LAURA was sure that Ma would not let
her go to play in the creek. It was still roaring, but
more softly. In the dugout she could hear it calling
her. So Laura quietly slipped outdoors without saying
anything to Ma.

The water was not so high now. It had gone down
from the steps and Laura could see it foaming against the
footbridge. Part of the plank was above the water.

All winter the creek had been covered with ice; it had
been motionless and still, never making a sound. Now it
was running swiftly and making a joyful noise. Where it
struck the edge of the plank it foamed up in white bubbles
and laughed to itself.

Laura took off her shoes and stockings and put them
safely on the bottom step. Then she walked out on the
plank and stood watching the noisy water.

Drops splashed her bare feet and thin little waves ran
around them. She dabbled one foot in the swirling foam.
Then down she sat on the plank and plumped both legs
into the water. The creek ran strong against them and she
kicked against it. That was fun!

Now she was wet almost all over, but her whole skin
wanted to be in the water. She lay on her stomach and
thrust her arms down on each side of the plank, deep into
the fast current. But that was not enough. She wanted to

be really in the roaring, joyous creek. She clasped her hands together under the plank and rolled off it.

In that very instant, she knew the creek was not playing. It was strong and terrible. It seized her whole body and pulled it under the plank. Only her head was out, and one arm desperately across the narrow plank.

The water was pulling her and it was pushing, too. It was trying to drag her head under the plank. Her chin held on to the edge and her arm clutched, while the water pulled hard at all the rest of her. It was not laughing now.

No one knew where she was. No one could hear her if she screamed for help. The water roared loud and tugged at her, stronger and stronger. Laura kicked, but the water was stronger than her legs. She got both arms across the plank and pulled, but the water pulled harder. It pulled the back of her head down and it jerked as if it would jerk her in two. It was cold. The coldness soaked into her.

This was not like wolves or cattle. The creek was not alive. It was only strong and terrible and never stopping. It would pull her down and whirl her away, rolling and tossing her like a willow branch. It would not care.

Her legs were tired, and her arms hardly felt the plank any more.

'I must get out. I must!' she thought. The creek's roaring was in her head. She kicked hard with both her feet and pulled hard with her arms, and then she was lying on the plank again.

The plank was solid under her stomach and under her face. She lay on it and breathed and was glad it was solid.

When she moved, her head whirled. She crawled off the plank. She took her shoes and her stockings and she climbed slowly up the muddy steps. At the door of the dugout she stopped. She did not know what to say to Ma.

After a while she went in. Just inside the door she stood still and water dripped off her. Ma was sewing.

'Where have you been, Laura?' Ma asked, looking up. Then she came quickly, saying: 'My goodness! Turn around, quick!' She began unbuttoning Laura down the back. 'What happened? Did you fall in the creek?'

'No, ma'am,' Laura said. 'I—I went in.'

Ma listened and went on undressing Laura and rubbing her hard all over with a towel. She did not say a word even when Laura had told her everything. Laura's teeth chattered, and Ma wrapped a quilt around her and sat her close to the stove.

At last Ma said: 'Well, Laura, you have been very

naughty and I think you knew it all the time. But I can't punish you. I can't even scold you. You came near being drowned.'

Laura did not say anything.

'You won't go near the creek again till Pa or I say you may, and that won't be till the water goes down,' said Ma.

'No'm,' Laura said.

The creek would go down. It would be a gentle, pleasant place to play in again. But nobody could make it do that. Nobody could make it do anything. Laura knew now that there were things stronger than anybody. But the creek had not got her. It had not made her scream and it could not make her cry.

16

The Wonderful House

THE CREEK WENT down. All at once the days were warm, and early every morning Pa went to work the wheat-field with Sam and David, the Christmas horses.

'I declare,' Ma said, 'you're working that ground to death and killing yourself.'

But Pa said the ground was dry because there had not been enough snow. He must plough deep and harrow well, and get the wheat sowed quickly. Every day he was working before the sun came up and he worked till dark. Laura waited in the dark till she heard Sam and David splashing into the ford. Then she ran into the dugout for the lantern and she hurried to the stable to hold it so that Pa could see to do the chores.

He was too tired to laugh or talk. He ate supper and went to bed.

At last the wheat was sowed. Then he sowed oats, and he made the potato patch and the garden. Ma and Mary and Laura helped plant the potatoes and sprinkle little seeds in the garden-rows, and they let Carrie think she was helping.

The whole world was green with grass now; the yellow-green willow leaves were uncurling. Violets and butter-cups were thick in the prairie hollows, and the sorrel's clover-like leaves and lavender blossoms were sour and good to eat. Only the wheat-field was bare and brown.

One evening Pa showed Laura a faint green mist on that brown field. The wheat was up! Each tiny sprout was so thin you could hardly see it, but so many of them all together made that misty green. Everyone was happy that night because the wheat was a good stand.

The next day Pa drove to town. Sam and David could go to town and come back in one afternoon. There was hardly time to miss Pa, and they were not even watching for him when he came home. Laura heard the wagon first, and she was the first one up the path.

Pa was sitting on the wagon seat. His face was one big shining of joy, and lumber was piled high in the wagon box behind him. He sang out, 'Here's your new house, Caroline!'

'But, Charles!' Ma gasped. Laura ran and climbed up over the wheel, up on to that pile of boards. She had never seen such smooth, straight beautiful boards. They had been sawed by machinery.

'But the wheat's hardly up yet!' Ma said.

'That's all right,' Pa told her. 'They let me have the lumber, and we'll pay for it when we sell the wheat.'

Laura asked him, 'Are we going to have a house made of boards?'

'Yes, flutterbudget,' said Pa. 'We're going to have a whole house built of sawed lumber. And it's going to have glass windows!'

It was really true. Next morning Mr. Nelson came to help Pa, and they began digging the cellar for that house. They were going to have that wonderful house, just because the wheat was growing.

Laura and Mary could hardly stay in the dugout long enough to do their work. But Ma made them do it.

'And I won't have you giving your work a lick and a promise,' said Ma. So they washed every breakfast dish

6

and put them all away. They made their bed neatly. They brushed the floor with the willow-twig broom and set the broom in its place. Then they could go.

They ran down the steps and over the footbridge, and under the willows, up to the prairie. They went through the prairie grasses and up to the top of a green knoll, where Pa and Mr. Nelson were building the new house.

It was fun to watch them set up the skeleton house. The timbers stood up slender and golden-new, and the sky was very blue between them. The hammers made a gay sound. The planes cut long curly shavings from the sweet-smelling boards.

Laura and Mary hung little shavings over their ears for earrings. They put them around their necks for necklaces. Laura tucked long ones in her hair and they hung down in golden curls, just the colour she had always wanted her hair to be.

Up on the skeleton roof Pa and Mr. Nelson hammered and sawed. Little blocks of wood fell down, and Laura and Mary gathered them in piles and built houses of their own. They had never had such a good time.

Pa and Mr. Nelson covered the skeleton walls with slanting boards nailed on. They shingled the roof with bought shingles. Bought shingles were thin and all the same size; they were far finer shingles than even Pa could hew with an axe. They made an even, tight roof, with not one crack in it.

Then Pa laid the floor of silky-smooth boards that were grooved along the edges and fitted together perfectly. Overhead he laid another floor for the upstairs, and made the ceiling of the downstairs.

Across the downstairs, Pa put up a partition. That house was going to have two rooms! One was the bed-room, and the other was only to live in. He put two shining-clear glass windows in that room; one looking toward the sunrise and the other beside the doorway to the south. In the bedroom walls he set two more windows, and they were glass windows, too.

Laura had never seen such wonderful windows. They were in halves. There were six panes of glass in each half, and the bottom half would push up, and stay up when a stick was set under it.

Opposite the front door Pa put a back door, and outside it he built a tiny room. That was a lean-to, because it leaned against the house. It would keep out the north winds in the winter-time, and it was a place where Ma could keep her broom and mop and washtub.

Now Mr. Nelson was not there and Laura asked questions all the time. Pa said the bedroom was for Ma and Carrie and him. He said the attic was for Mary and Laura, to sleep in and to play in. Laura wanted so much to see it that he stopped work on the lean-to and nailed strips of board up the wall, to make the attic ladder.

Laura skipped quickly up that ladder till her head came up through the hole in the attic floor. The attic was as big as both rooms downstairs. Its floor was smooth boards. Its slanting roof was the underside of the fresh, yellow shingles. There was a little window at each end of that attic, and those windows were glass windows!

At first Mary was scared to swing off the ladder to the attic floor. Then she was scared to step down through the floor-hole on to the ladder. Laura felt scared, too, but she pretended she didn't. And they soon got used to getting on and off the ladder.

Now they thought the house was done. But Pa nailed black tar-paper all over the outside of the house walls. Then he nailed more boards over that paper. They were long smooth boards, one lapping over the other all up the sides of the house. Then around the windows and the door-ways Pa nailed flat frames.

'This house is tight as a drum!' he said. There was not one single crack in the roof or the walls or the floor of that house, to let in rain or cold winds.

Then Pa put in the doors, and they were bought doors. They were smooth, and far thinner than slab doors hewed with an axe, and even thinner panels were set into them above and below their middles. Their hinges were bought hinges, and it was marvellous to see them open and shut. They did not rattle like wooden hinges or let the door drag like leather hinges.

Into those doors Pa set bought locks, with keys that went into small, shaped holes, and turned and clicked. These locks had white china door knobs.

Then one day Pa said, 'Laura and Mary, can you keep a secret?'

'Oh yes, Pa!' they said.

'Promise you won't tell Ma?' he asked, and they promised.

He opened the lean-to door. And there stood a shiny-black cookstove. Pa had brought it from town and hidden it there, to surprise Ma.

On top, that cookstove had four round holes and four round lids fitted them. Each lid had a grooved hole in it, and there was an iron handle that fitted into the holes, to lift the lid by. In front, there was a long, low door. There were slits in this door, and a piece of iron would slide back and forth, to close these slits or open them. That was the draught. Under it, a shelf like an oblong pan stuck out. That was to catch ashes and keep them from dropping on the floor. A lid swung flat over this hollowed-out shelf. And on the lid were raised iron letters in rows.

Mary put her finger on the bottom row and spelled

out, 'P A T. One seven seven nought.' She asked Pa, 'What's that spell, Pa?'

'It spells Pat,' Pa said.

Laura opened a big door on the side of that stove, and looked into a big square place with a shelf across it, 'Oh Pa, what's this for?' she asked him.

'It's the oven,' Pa told her.

He lifted that marvellous stove and set it in the living-room, and put up the stovepipe. Piece by piece, the stove-

pipe went up through the ceiling and the attic and through a hole he sawed in the roof. Then Pa climbed on to the roof and he set a larger tin pipe over the stovepipe. The tin pipe had a spread-out, flat bottom that covered the hole in the roof. Not a drop of rain could run down the stovepipe into the new house.

That was a prairie chimney.

'Well, it's done,' Pa said. 'Even to a prairie chimney.'

There was nothing more that a house could possibly

have. The glass windows made the inside of that house so light that you would hardly know you were in a house. It smelled clean and piny, from the yellow-new board walls and floor. The cookstove stood lordly in the corner by the lean-to door. A touch on the the white-china door knob swung the bought door on its bought hinges, and the door knob's little iron tongue clicked and held the door shut.

'We'll move in, tomorrow morning,' Pa said. 'This is the last night we'll sleep in a dugout.'

Laura and Mary took his hands and they went down the knoll. The wheat-field was a silky, shimmery green rippling over a curve of the prairie. Its sides were straight and its corners square, and all around it the prairie grasses looked coarser and darker green. Laura looked back at the wonderful house. In the sunshine on the knoll, it-sawed-lumber walls and roof were as golden as a straws stack.

17

Moving In

IN THE SUNNY morning Ma and Laura helped carry everything from the dugout up to the top of the bank and load it in the wagon. Laura hardly dared look at Pa; they were bursting with the secret surprise for Ma.

Ma did not suspect anything. She took the hot ashes out of the little old stove so that Pa could handle it. She asked Pa, 'Did you remember to get more stovepipe?'

'Yes, Caroline,' Pa said. Laura did not laugh, but she choked.

'Goodness, Laura,' Ma said, 'have you got a frog in your throat?'

David and Sam hauled the wagon away, across the ford and back over the prairie, up to the new house. Ma and Mary and Laura, with armfuls of things, and Carrie toddling ahead, went over the footbridge and up the grassy path. The sawed-lumber house with its bought-shingle roof was all golden on the knoll, and Pa jumped off the wagon and waited to be with Ma when she saw the cook-stove.

She walked into the house and stopped short. Her mouth opened and shut. Then she said, weakly, 'My land!'

Laura and Mary whooped and danced, and so did Carrie, though she did not know why.

'It's yours, Ma! It's your new cookstove!' they shouted. 'It's got an oven! And four lids, and a little handle!'

Mary said. 'It's got letters on it and I can read them! P A T, Pat!'

'Oh, Charles, you shouldn't!' Ma said.

Pa hugged her. 'Don't you worry, Caroline!' he told her.

'I never have worried, Charles,' Ma answered. 'But building such a house, and glass windows, and buying a stove—it's too much.'

'Nothing's too much for you,' said Pa. 'And don't worry about the expense. Just look through that glass at that wheat-field!'

But Laura and Mary pulled her to the cookstove. She lifted the lids as Laura showed her, she watched while Mary worked the draught, she looked at the oven.

'My!' she said. 'I don't know if I dare try to get dinner on such a big, beautiful stove!'

But she did get dinner on that wonderful stove and Mary and Laura set the table in the bright, airy room. The glass windows were open, air and light came in from every side, and sunshine was streaming in through the doorway and the shining window beside it.

It was such fun to eat in that big, airy, light house that after dinner they sat at the table, just enjoying being there.

'Now this is something like!' Pa said.

Then they put up the curtains. Glass windows must have curtains, and Ma had made them of pieces of worn-out sheets, starched crisp and white as snow. She had edged them with narrow strips of pretty calico. The curtains in the big room were edged with pink strips from Carrie's little dress that had been torn when the oxen ran away. The bedroom curtains were edged with strips from Mary's old blue dress. That was the pink calico and the blue calico that Pa brought home from town, long ago in the Big Woods.

While Pa was driving nails to hold the strings for the curtains, Ma brought out two long strips of brown wrapping-paper that she had saved. She folded them, and she showed Mary and Laura how to cut tiny bits out of the folded paper with the scissors. When each unfolded her paper, there was a row of stars.

Ma spread the paper on the shelves behind the stove. The stars hung over the edges of the shelves, and the light shone through them.

When the curtains were up, Ma hung two snowy-clean sheets across a corner of the bedroom. That made a nice place where Pa and Ma could hang their clothes. Up in the attic, Ma put up another sheet that Mary and Laura could hang their clothes behind.

The house was beautiful when Ma had finished. The pure-white curtains were looped back on each side of the clear glass windows. Between those pink-edged, snowy curtains the sunshine streamed in. The walls were all clean, piny-smelling boards, with the skeleton of the house against them, and the ladder going up to the attic. The cookstove and its stovepipe were glossy black, and in that corner were the starry shelves.

Ma spread the between-meals red-checked cloth on the table, and on it she set the shining-clean lamp. She laid there the paper-covered Bible, the big green *Wonders of the Animal World*, and the novel named *Millbank*. The two benches stood neatly by the table.

The last thing, Pa hung the bracket on the wall by the front window, and Ma stood the little china shepherdess on it.

That was the wood-brown bracket that Pa had carved with stars and vines and flowers, for Ma's Christmas long ago. That was the same smiling little shepherdess, with golden hair and blue eyes and pink cheeks, her little china bodice laced with china-gold ribbons and her little china apron and her little china shoes. She had travelled from the Big Woods all the way to Indian Territory, and all the way to Plum Creek in Minnesota, and there she stood smiling. She was not broken. She was not nicked nor even scratched. She was the same little shepherdess, smiling the same smile.

That night Mary and Laura climbed the ladder and went to bed by themselves in their large, airy, very own attic. They did not have curtains because Ma had no more old sheets. But each had a box to sit on, and each had a box to keep her treasures in. Charlotte and the paper dolls lived in Laura's box, and Mary's quilt blocks and her scrapbag were in Mary's box. Behind the curtain each had her nail, to take her nightgown off and hang her dress on. The single thing wrong with that room was that Jack could not climb up the ladder.

Laura went to sleep at once. She had been running in and out of the new house and up and down the ladder all day long. But she could not stay asleep. The new house was so still. She missed the sound of the creek singing to her in her sleep. The stillness kept waking her.

At last it was a sound that opened her eyes. She listened. It was a sound of many, many little feet running about overhead. It seemed to be thousands of little animals scampering on the roof. What could it be?

Why, it was raindrops! Laura had not heard rain pattering on the roof for so long that she had forgotten the sound of it. In the dugout she could not hear rain, there was so much earth and grass above her.

She was happy while she lay drowsing to sleep again, hearing the pitter-pat-patter of rain on the roof.

18

The Old Crab and the Bloodsuckers

WHEN LAURA JUMPED out of bed in the morning, her bare feet landed on a smooth, wooden floor. She smelled the piny smell of boards. Overhead was the slanting roof of yellow-bright shingles and the rafters holding them up.

From the eastern window she saw the little path going down the grassy knoll. She saw a square corner of the pale-green, silky wheat-field, and beyond it the grey-green oats. Far, far away was the edge of the great, green earth, and a silver streak of the sun's edge peeping over it. The willow creek and the dugout seemed far away and long ago.

Suddenly, warm yellow sunshine poured over her in her nightgown. On the clean wood-yellow floor the panes of the window were sunshine, the little bars between them were shadow, and Laura's head in the nightcap, her braids, and her hands with all the separate fingers when she held them up, were darker, solid shadow.

Downstairs the lids clattered on the new, fine cookstove. Ma's voice came up through the square hole where the ladder went down. 'Mary! Laura! Time to get up, girls!'

That was the way a new day began in the new house.

But while they were eating breakfast in the large, airy downstairs Laura wanted to see the creek. She asked Pa if she might go back to play there.

'No, Laura,' Pa said. 'I don't want you to go back to that creek, where the dark, deep holes are. But when your work is done, you and Mary run along that path that Nelson made coming to work, and see what you find!'

They hurried to do the work. And in the lean-to they found a bought broom! There seemed no end to the wonders in this house. This broom had a long, straight, perfectly round, smooth handle. The broom part was made of thousands of thin, stiff, greeny-yellow bristles. Ma said they were broom straws. They were cut absolutely straight across the bottom, and they curved at the top into flat, firm shoulders. Stitches of red string held them tight. This broom was nothing like the round, willow-bough brooms that Pa made. It seemed too fine to sweep with. And it glided over the smooth floor like magic.

Still, Laura and Mary could hardly wait to follow that path. They worked fast; they put away the broom, and they started. Laura was in such a hurry that she walked nicely only a few steps, then she began to run. Her bonnet slid back and hung by its strings around her neck and her bare feet flew over the dim, grassy path, down the knoll, across a bit of level land, up a low slope. And there was the creek!

Laura was astonished. This was such a different-looking creek, too, so gentle in the sun between its low, grassy banks.

The path stopped in the shade of a great willow tree. A footbridge went on across the water to level, sunny grass. Then the dim path wandered on until it curved around a tiny hill and went out of sight.

Laura thought that little path went on for ever wandering on sunny grass and crossing friendly streams and always going around low hills to see what was on the other side. She knew it really must go to Mr. Nelson's house, but it was a little path that did not want to stop anywhere. It wanted always to be going on.

The creek came flowing out of a thicket of plum trees. The low trees grew thickly on both sides of the narrow water, and their boughs almost touched above it. The water was dark in their shade.

Then it spread out and ran wide and shallow, dimpling and splashing over sand and gravel. It narrowed to slide under the footbridge and ran on gurgling till it stopped in a large pool. The pool was glassy-still by a clump of willows.

Laura waited till Mary came. Then they went wading in the shallow water over the sparkling sand and pebbles. Tiny minnows swam in swarms around their toes. When they stood still the minnows nibbled at their feet. Suddenly Laura saw a strange creature in the water.

He was almost as long as Laura's foot. He was sleek and greeny-brown. In front he had two long arms that ended in big, flat, pincer-claws. Along his sides were short legs, and his strong tail was flat and scaly, with a thin forked fin at the end. Bristles stuck out of his nose, and his eyes were round and bulging.

'What's that!' Mary said. She was scared.

Laura did not go any nearer him. She bent down cautiously to see him, and suddenly he was not there. Faster than a water-bug, he shot backward, and a little curl of muddy water came out from under a flat rock where he had gone.

In a minute he thrust out a claw and snapped it. Then he looked out.

When Laura waded nearer, he flipped backwards under the stone. But when she splashed water at his stone, he ran out, snapping his claws, trying to catch her bare toes.

Then Laura and Mary ran screaming and splashing away from his home.

They teased him with a long stick. His big claw snapped that stick right in two. They got a bigger stick, and he clamped his claw and did not let go till Laura lifted him out of the water. His eyes glared and his tail curled under him, and his other claw was snapping. Then he let go and dropped, and flipped under his stone again.

He always came out, fighting mad, when they splashed at his stone. And they always ran screaming away from his frightful claws.

They sat for a while on the footbridge in the shade of the big willow. They listened to the water running and watched its sparkles. Then they went wading again, all the way to the plum thicket.

Mary would not go into the dark water under the plum trees. The creek bottom was muddy there and she did not like to wade in mud. So she sat on the bank while Laura waded into the thicket.

The water was still there, with old leaves floating on its edges. The mud squelched between Laura's toes and came up in clouds till she could not see the bottom. The air smelled old and musty. So Laura turned around and waded back into the clean water and the sunshine.

There seemed to be some blobs of mud on her legs and feet. She splashed the clear water over them to wash them off. But they did not wash off. Her hand could not scrape them off.

They were the colour of mud, they were soft like mud. But they stuck as tight as Laura's skin.

Laura screamed. She stood there screaming, 'Oh, Mary, Mary! Come! Quick!'

Mary came, but she would not touch those horrible things. She said they were worms. Worms made her sick.

Laura felt sicker than Mary, but it was more awful to have those things on her than it was to touch them. She took hold of one, she dug her fingernails into it, and pulled.

The thing stretched out long, and longer, and longer, and still it hung on.

'Oh don't! Oh don't! Oh, you'll pull it in two!' Mary said. But Laura pulled it out longer, till it came off. Blood trickled down her leg from the place where it had been.

One by one, Laura pulled those things off. A little trickle of blood ran down where each one let go.

Laura did not feel like playing any more. She washed her hands and her legs in the clean water and she went to the house with Mary.

It was dinner-time and Pa was there. Laura told him about those mud-brown things without eyes or head or legs, that had fastened to her skin in the creek.

Ma said they were leeches and that doctors put them on sick people. But Pa called them bloodsuckers. He said they lived in the mud, in dark, still places in the water.

'I don't like them,' Laura said.

'Then stay out of the mud, flutterbudget,' said Pa. 'If you don't want trouble, don't go looking for it.'

Ma said, 'Well, you girls won't have much time for playing in the creek, anyway. Now we're nicely settled and only two and a half miles from town, you can go to school.'

Laura could not say a word. Neither could Mary. They looked at each other and thought, 'School?'

19

The Fish-Trap

THE MORE LAURA was told about school, the more
she did not want to go there. She did not know
how she could stay away from the creek all day
long. She asked, 'Oh, Ma, do I have to?'

Ma said that a great girl almost eight years old should
be learning to read instead of running wild on the banks
of Plum Creek.

'But I can read, Ma,' Laura begged. 'Please don't make
me go to school. I can read. Listen!'

She took the book named *Millbank*, and opened it, and
looking up anxiously at Ma she read, 'The doors and
windows of Millbank were closed. Crape streamed from
the door knob——'

'Oh, Laura,' Ma said, 'you are not reading! You are
only reciting what you've heard me read to Pa so often.
Besides, there are other things to learn—spelling and
writing and arithmetic. Don't say any more about it. You
will start to school with Mary Monday morning.'

Mary was sitting down to sew. She looked like a good
little girl who wanted to go to school.

Just outside the lean-to door Pa was hammering at
something. Laura went bounding out so quickly that his
hammer nearly hit her.

'Oop!' said Pa. 'Nearly hit you that time. I should have
expected you, flutterbudget. You're always on hand like a
sore thumb.'

'Oh, what are you doing, Pa?' Laura asked him. He was nailing together some narrow strips of board left from the house-building.

'Making a fish-trap,' said Pa. 'Want to help me? You can hand me the nails.'

One by one, Laura handed him the nails, and Pa drove them in. They were making a skeleton box. It was a long, narrow box without a top, and Pa left wide cracks between the strips of wood.

'How will that catch fish?' Laura asked. 'If you put it in the creek they will swim in through the cracks but they will swim right out again.'

'You wait and see,' said Pa.

Laura waited till Pa put away the nails and hammer. He put the fish-trap on his shoulder and said, 'You can come help me set it.'

Laura took his hand and skipped beside him down the knoll and across the level land to the creek. They went along the low bank, past the plum thicket. The banks were steeper here, the creek was narrower, and its noise was louder. Pa went crashing down through bushes, Laura climbed scrooging down under them, and there was a waterfall.

The water ran swift and smooth to the edge and fell over it with a loud, surprised crash-splashing. From the bottom it rushed up again and whirled around, then it jumped and hurried away.

Laura would never have tired of watching it. But she must help Pa set the fish-trap. They put it exactly under the waterfall. The whole waterfall went into the trap, and boiled up again more surprised than before. It could not jump out of the trap. It foamed out through the cracks.

'Now you see, Laura,' said Pa. 'The fish will come over the falls into the trap, and the little ones will go out

7

through the cracks, but the big ones can't. They can't climb back up the falls. So they'll have to stay swimming in the box till I come and take them out.'

At that very minute a big fish came slithering over the falls. Laura squealed and shouted, 'Look, Pa! Look!'

Pa's hands in the water grabbed the fish and lifted him

out, flopping. Laura almost fell into the waterfall. They looked at that silvery fat fish and then Pa dropped him into the trap again.

'Oh Pa, can't we please stay and catch enough fish for supper?' Laura asked.

'I've got to get to work on a sod barn, Laura,' said Pa. 'And plough the garden and dig a well and——' Then he looked at Laura and said, 'Well, little half-pint, maybe it won't take long.'

He sat on his heels and Laura sat on hers and they waited. The creek poured and splashed, always the same and always changing. Glints of sunshine danced on it. Cool air came up from it and warm air lay on Laura's neck. The bushes held up thousands of little leaves against the sky. They smelled warm and sweet in the sun.

'Oh, Pa,' Laura said, 'do I have to go to school?'

'You will like school, Laura,' said Pa.

'I like it better here,' Laura said, mournfully.

'I know, little half-pint,' said Pa, 'but it isn't everybody that gets a chance to learn to read and write and cipher. Your Ma was a school-teacher when we met, and when she came West with me I promised that our girls would have a chance to get book learning. That's why we stopped here, so close to a town that has a school. You're almost eight years old now, and Mary going on nine, and it's time you began. Be thankful you've got the chance, Laura.'

'Yes, Pa,' Laura sighed. Just then another big fish came over the falls. Before Pa could catch it, here came another!

Pa cut and peeled a forked stick. He took four big fish out of the trap and strung them on the stick. Laura and Pa went back to the house, carrying those flopping fish. Ma's eyes were round when she saw them. Pa cut off their heads and stripped out their insides and showed Laura how to scale fish. He scaled three, and she scaled almost all of one. Ma rolled them in meal and fried them in fat, and they all ate good fish for supper.

'You always think of something, Charles,' said Ma. 'Just when I'm wondering where our living is to come from, now it's spring.' Pa could not hunt in the spring-time, for then all the rabbits had little rabbits and the birds had little birds in their nests.

'Wait till I harvest that wheat!' Pa said. 'Then we'll have salt pork every day. Yes, by gravy, and fresh beef!'

Every morning after that, before he went to work, Pa brought fish from the trap. He never took more than they needed to eat. The others he lifted out of the trap and let swim away.

He brought buffalo fish and pickerel, and catfish, and shiners, and bullheads with two black horns. He brought some whose names he did not know. Every day there was fish for breakfast and fish for dinner and fish for supper.

20

School

MONDAY MORNING CAME. As soon as Laura and Mary had washed the breakfast dishes, they went up the ladder and put on their Sunday dresses. Mary's was a blue-sprigged calico, and Laura's was red-sprigged.

Ma braided their hair very tightly and bound the ends with thread. They could not wear their Sunday hair-ribbons because they might lose them. They put on their sunbonnets, freshly washed and ironed.

Then Ma took them into the bedroom. She knelt down by the box where she kept her best things, and she took out three books. They were the books she had studied when she was a little girl. One was a speller, and one was a reader, and one was a 'rithmetic.

She looked solemnly at Mary and Laura, and they were solemn, too.

'I am giving you these books for your very own, Mary and Laura,' Ma said. 'I know you will take care of them and study them faithfully.'

'Yes, Ma,' they said.

She gave Mary the books to carry. She gave Laura the little tin pail with their lunch in it, under a clean cloth.

'Good-bye,' she said. 'Be good girls.'

Ma and Carrie stood in the doorway, and Jack went with them down the knoll. He was puzzled. They went on across the grass where the tracks of Pa's wagon wheels went, and Jack stayed close beside Laura.

When they came to the ford of the creek, he sat down and whined anxiously. Laura had to explain to him that he must not come any farther. She stroked his big head and tried to smooth out the worried wrinkles. But he sat watching and frowning while they waded across the shallow, wide ford.

They waded carefully and did not splash their clean dresses. A blue heron rose from the water, flapping away with his long legs dangling. Laura and Mary stepped carefully on to the grass. They would not walk in the dusty wheel tracks until their feet were dry, because their feet must be clean when they came to town.

The new house looked small on its knoll with the great green prairie spreading far around it. Ma and Carrie had gone inside. Only Jack sat watching by the ford.

Mary and Laura walked on quietly.

Dew was sparkling on the grass. Meadow larks were singing. Snipes were walking on their long, thin legs. Prairie hens were clucking and tiny prairie chicks were peeping. Rabbits stood up with paws dangling, long ears twitching, and their round eyes staring at Mary and Laura.

Pa had said that town was only two and a half miles away, and the road would take them to it. They would know they were in town when they came to a house.

Large white clouds sailed in the enormous sky and their grey shadows trailed across the waving prairie grasses. The road always ended a little way ahead, but when they came to that ending, the road was going on. It was only the tracks of Pa's wagon through the grass.

'For pity's sake, Laura,' said Mary, 'keep your sunbonnet on! You'll be brown as an Indian, and what will the town girls think of us?'

'I don't care!' said Laura, loudly and bravely.

'You do, too!' said Mary.

'I don't either!' said Laura.

'You do!'

'I don't!'

'You're just as scared of town as I am,' said Mary.

Laura did not answer. After a while she took hold of her sunbonnet strings and pulled the bonnet up over her head.

'Anyway, there's two of us,' Mary said.

They went on and on. After a long time they saw town. It looked like small blocks of wood on the prairie. When the road dipped down, they saw only grasses again and the sky. Then they saw the town again, always larger. Smoke went up from its stovepipes.

The clean, grassy road ended in dust. This dusty road went by a small house and then past a store. The store had a porch with steps going up to it.

Beyond the store there was a blacksmith shop. It stood back from the road, with a bare place in front of it. Inside it a big man in a leather apron made a bellows puff! puff! at red coals. He took a white-hot iron out of the coals with tongs, and swung a big hammer down on it, whang! Dozens of sparks flew out tiny in the daylight.

Beyond the bare place was the back of a building. Mary and Laura walked close to the side of this building. The ground was hard there. There was no more grass to walk on.

In front of this building, another wide, dusty road crossed their road. Mary and Laura stopped. They looked across the dust at the fronts of two more stores. They heard a confused noise of children's voices. Pa's road did not go any farther.

'Come on,' said Mary, low. But she stood still. 'It's the school where we hear the hollering. Pa said we would hear it.'

Laura wanted to turn around and run all the way
home.

She and Mary went slowly walking out into the dust
and turned towards that noise of voices. They went
padding along between two stores. They passed piles of
boards and shingles; that must be the lumber-yard
where Pa got the boards for the new house. Then they
saw the schoolhouse.

It was out on the prairie beyond the end of the dusty
road. A long path went towards it through the grass.
Boys and girls were in front of it.

Laura went along the path towards them and Mary
came behind her. All those girls and boys stopped their
noise and looked. Laura kept on going nearer and nearer
all those eyes, and suddenly, without meaning to, she
swung the dinner-pail and called out, 'You all sounded
just like a flock of prairie chickens!'

They were surprised. But they were not as much surprised as Laura. She was ashamed, too. Mary gasped, 'Laura!' Then a freckled boy with fire-coloured hair yelled. 'Snipes, yourselves! Snipes! Snipes! Long-legged snipes!'

Laura wanted to sink down and hide her legs. Her dress was too short, it was much shorter than the town girls' dresses. So was Mary's. Before they came to Plum Creek, Ma had said they were outgrowing those dresses. Their bare legs did look long and spindly, like snipes' legs.

All the boys were pointing and yelling, 'Snipes! Snipes!'

Then a red-headed girl began pushing those boys and saying: 'Shut up! You make too much noise! Shut up, Sandy!' she said to the red-headed boy, and he shut up. She came close to Laura and said:

'My name is Christy Kennedy, and that horrid boy is my brother Sandy, but he doesn't mean any harm. What's your name?'

Her red hair was braided so tightly that the braids were stiff. Her eyes were dark blue, almost black, and her round cheeks were freckled. Her sunbonnet hung down her back.

'Is that your sister?' she said. 'Those are my sisters.' Some big girls were talking to Mary. 'The big one's Nettie, and the black-haired one's Cassie, and then there's Donald and me and Sandy. How many brothers and sisters have you?'

'Two,' Laura said. 'That's Mary, and Carrie's the baby. She has golden hair, too. And we have a bulldog named Jack. We live on Plum Creek. Where do you live?'

'Does your Pa drive two bay horses with black manes and tails?' Christy asked.

'Yes,' said Laura. 'They are Sam and David, our Christmas horses.'

'He comes by our house, so you came by it, too,' said Christy. 'It's the house before you came to Beadle's store and post-office, before you get to the blacksmith shop. Miss Eva Beadle's our teacher. That's Nellie Oleson.'

Nellie Oleson was very pretty. Her yellow hair hung in long curls, with two big blue ribbon bows on top. Her dress was thin white lawn, with little blue flowers scattered over it, and she wore shoes.

She looked at Laura and she looked at Mary, and she wrinkled up her nose.

'Hm!' she said. 'Country girls!'

Before anyone else could say anything, a bell rang. A young lady stood in the schoolhouse doorway, swinging the bell in her hand. All the boys and girls hurried by her into the schoolhouse.

She was a beautiful young lady. Her brown hair was frizzed in bangs over her brown eyes, and done in thick braids behind. Buttons sparkled all down the front of her bodice, and her skirts were drawn back tightly and fell down behind in big puffs and loops. Her face was sweet and her smile was lovely.

She laid her hand on Laura's shoulder and said, 'You're a new little girl, aren't you?'

'Yes, ma'am,' said Laura.

'And is this your sister?' Teacher asked, smiling at Mary.

'Yes, ma'am,' said Mary.

'Then come with me,' said Teacher, 'and I'll write your names in my book.'

They went with her the whole length of the schoolhouse, and stepped up on the platform.

The schoolhouse was a room made of new boards. Its ceiling was the underneath of shingles, like the attic ceiling. Long benches stood one behind another down the middle of the room. They were made of planed boards. Each bench had a back, and two shelves stuck out from the back, over the bench behind. Only the front bench did not have any shelves in front of it, and the last bench did not have any back.

There were two glass windows in each side of the school-house. They were open, and so was the door. The wind came in, and the sound of waving grasses, and the smell and the sight of the endless prairie and the great light of the sky.

Laura saw all this while she stood with Mary by Teacher's desk and they told her their names and how old they were. She did not move her head, but her eyes looked around.

A water-pail stood on a bench by the door. A bought broom stood in one corner. On the wall behind Teacher's desk there was a smooth space of boards painted black. Under it was a little trough. Some kind of short, white sticks lay in the trough, and a block of wood with a woolly bit of sheepskin pulled tightly around it and nailed down. Laura wondered what those things were.

Mary showed Teacher how much she could read and spell. But Laura looked at Ma's book and shook her head. She could not read. She was not even sure of all the letters.

'Well, you can begin at the beginning, Laura,' said Teacher, 'and Mary can study farther on. Have you a slate?'

They did not have a slate.

'I will lend you mine,' Teacher said. 'You cannot learn to write without a slate.'

She lifted up the top of her desk and took out the slate. The desk was made like a tall box, with one side cut out for her knees. The top rose up on bought hinges, and under it was the place where she kept things. Her books were there, and the ruler.

Laura did not know until later that the ruler was to punish anyone who fidgeted or whispered in school. Anyone who was so naughty had to walk up to Teacher's desk and hold out her hand while Teacher slapped it many times, hard, with the ruler.

But Laura and Mary never whispered in school, and they always tried not to fidget. They sat side by side on a bench and studied. Mary's feet rested on the floor, but Laura's dangled. They held their book open on the board shelf before them, Laura studying at the front of the book and Mary studying farther on, and the pages between standing straight up.

Laura was a whole class by herself, because she was the only pupil who could not read. Whenever Teacher had time, she called Laura to her desk and helped her read letters. Just before dinner-time that first day, Laura was able to read, C A T, cat. Suddenly she remembered and said, 'P A T, Pat!'

Teacher was surprised.

'R A T, rat!' said Teacher. 'M A T, mat!' And Laura was reading! She could read the whole first row in the speller.

At noon all the other children and Teacher went home to dinner. Laura and Mary took their dinner-pail and sat in the grass against the shady side of the empty schoolhouse. They ate their bread and butter and talked.

'I like school,' Mary said.

'So do I,' said Laura. 'Only it makes my legs tired. But I don't like that Nellie Oleson that called us country girls.'

'We are country girls,' said Mary.

'Yes, and she needn't wrinkle her nose!' Laura said.

21

Nellie Oleson

JACK WAS WAITING to meet them at the ford that night, and at supper they told Pa and Ma all about school. When they said they were using Teacher's slate, Pa shook his head. They must not be beholden for the loan of a slate.

Next morning he took his money out of the fiddle-box and counted it. He gave Mary a round silver piece to buy a slate.

'There's plenty of fish in the creek,' he said. 'We'll hold out till wheat-harvest.'

'There'll be potatoes pretty soon, too,' said Ma. She tied the money in a handkerchief and pinned it inside Mary's pocket.

Mary clutched that pocket all the way along the prairie road. The wind was blowing. Butterflies and birds were flying over the waving grasses and wild flowers. The rabbits loped before the wind and the great clear sky curved over it all. Laura swung the dinner-pail and hippety-hopped.

In town, they crossed dusty Main Street and climbed the steps to Mr. Oleson's store. Pa had said to buy the slate there.

Inside the store there was a long board counter. The wall behind it was covered with shelves, full of tin pans and pots and lamps and lanterns and bolts of coloured cloth. By the other wall stood ploughs and kegs of nails and rolls of wire, and on that wall hung saws and hammers and hatchets and knives.

A large, round, yellow cheese was on the counter, and on the floor in front of it was a barrel of molasses, and a whole keg of pickles, and a big wooden box full of crackers, and two tall wooden pails of candy. It was Christmas candy; two big pails full of it.

Suddenly the back door of the store burst open, and Nellie Oleson and her little brother Willie came bouncing in. Nellie's nose wrinkled at Laura and Mary, and Willie yahed at them: 'Yah! Yah! Long-legged snipes!'

'Shut up, Willie,' Mr. Oleson said. But Willie did not shut up. He went on saying: 'Snipes! Snipes!'

Nellie flounced by Mary and Laura, and dug her hands into a pail of candy. Willie dug into the other pail. They grabbed all the candy they could hold and stood cramming it into their mouths. They stood in front of Mary and Laura, looking at them, and did not offer them even one piece.

'Nellie! You and Willie go right back out of here!' Mr. Oleson said.

They went on stuffing candy into their mouths and staring at Mary and Laura. Mr. Oleson took no more notice of them. Mary gave him the money and he gave her the slate. He said: 'You'll want a slate pencil, too. Here it is. One penny.'

Nellie said, 'They haven't got a penny.'

'Well, take it along, and tell your Pa to give me the penny next time he comes to town,' said Mr. Oleson.

'No, sir. Thank you,' Mary said. She turned around and so did Laura, and they walked out of the store. At the door Laura looked back. And Nellie made a face at her. Nellie's tongue was streaked red and green from the candy.

'My goodness!' Mary said, 'I couldn't be as mean as that Nellie Oleson.'

Laura thought: 'I could. I could be meaner to her than she is to us, if Ma and Pa would let me.'

They looked at their slate's smooth, soft-grey surface, and its clean, flat wooden frame, cunningly fitted together at the corners. It was a handsome slate. But they must have a slate pencil.

Pa had already spent so much for the slate that they hated to tell him they must have another penny. They walked along soberly, till suddenly Laura remembered their Christmas pennies. They still had those pennies that they had found in their stockings on Christmas morning in Indian Territory.

Mary had a penny, and Laura had a penny, but they needed only one slate pencil. So they decided that Mary would spend her penny for the pencil and after that she would own half of Laura's penny. Next morning they bought the pencil, but they did not buy it from Mr. Oleson. They bought it at Mr. Beadle's store and post-office, where Teacher lived, and that morning they walked on to school with Teacher.

All through the long, hot weeks they went to school, and every day they liked it more. They liked reading, writing, and arithmetic. They liked spelling-down on Friday afternoons. And Laura loved recess, when the little girls rushed out into the sun and wind, picking wild flowers among the prairie grasses and playing games.

The boys played boys' games on one side of the school-house; the little girls played on the other side, and Mary sat with the other big girls, ladylike on the steps.

The little girls always played ring-around-a-rosy, because Nellie Oleson said to. They got tired of it, but they always played it, till one day, before Nellie could say anything, Laura said, 'Let's play Uncle John!'

'Let's! Let's!' the girls said, taking hold of hands. But Nellie grabbed both hands full of Laura's long hair and jerked her flat on the ground.

'No! No!' Nellie shouted. 'I want to play ring-around-a-rosy!'

Laura jumped up and her hand flashed out to slap Nellie. She stopped it just in time. Pa said she must never strike anybody.

'Come on, Laura,' Christy said, taking her hands Laura's face felt bursting and she could hardly see, but she went circling with the others around Nellie. Nellie tossed her curls and flounced her skirts because she had her way. Then Christy began singing and all the other. joined in:

'Uncle John is sick abed.
What shall we send him?'

'No! No! Ring-around-a-rosy!' Nellie screamed. 'Or I won't play!' She broke through the ring and no one went after her.

'All right, you get in the middle, Maud,' Christy said, They began again.

'Uncle John is sick abed.
What shall we send him?
A piece of pie, a piece of cake,
Apple and dumpling!
What shall we send it in?
A golden saucer.
Who shall we send it by?
The governor's daughter.
If the governor's daughter ain't at home,
Who shall we send it by?'

Then all the girls shouted,

'By Laura Ingalls!'

Laura stepped into the middle of the ring and they danced around her. They went on playing Uncle John till Teacher rang the bell. Nellie was in the schoolhouse, crying, and she said she was so mad that she was never going to speak to Laura or Christy again.

But the next week she asked all the girls to a party at her house on Saturday afternoon. She asked Christy and Laura, specially.

22

Town Party

LAURA AND MARY had never been to a party and did not quite know what it would be like. Ma said it was a pleasant time that friends had together.

After school on Friday she washed their dresses and sunbonnets. Saturday morning she ironed them, fresh and crisp. Laura and Mary bathed that morning, too, instead of that night.

'You look sweet and pretty as posies,' Ma said when they came down the ladder, dressed for the party. She tied on their hair-ribbons and warned them not to lose them. 'Now be good girls,' she said, 'and mind your manners.'

When they came to town they stopped for Cassie and Christy. Cassie and Christy had never been to a party, either. They all went timidly into Mr. Oleson's store, and Mr. Oleson told them, 'Go right on in!'

So they went past the candy and pickles and ploughs, to the back door of the store. It opened, and there stood Nellie all dressed up, and Mrs. Oleson asking them in.

Laura had never seen such a fine room. She could hardly say 'Good afternoon, Mrs. Oleson,' and 'Yes, ma'am,' and 'No, ma'am.'

The whole floor was covered with some kind of heavy cloth that felt rough under Laura's bare feet. It was brown and green, with red and yellow scrolls all over it.

The walls and the ceiling were narrow, smooth boards fitted together with a crease between them. The table and chairs were of a yellow wood that shone like glass, and their legs were perfectly round. There were coloured pictures on the walls.

'Go into the bedroom, girls, and leave your bonnets,' Mrs. Oleson said in a company voice.

The bedstead was shiny wood, too. There were two other pieces of furniture. One was made of drawers on top of each other, with two little drawers sitting on its top, and two curved pieces of wood went up and held a big looking-glass between them. On top of the other stood a china pitcher in a big china bowl, and a small china dish with a piece of soap on it.

There were glass windows in both rooms, and the curtains of those windows were white lace.

Behind the front room was a big lean-to with a cook-stove in it, like Ma's new one, and all kinds of tin pots and pans hanging on the walls.

All the girls were there now, and Mrs. Oleson's skirts went rustling among them. Laura wanted to be still and look at things, but Mrs. Oleson said, 'Now, Nellie, bring out your playthings.'

'They can play with Willie's playthings,' Nellie said.

'They can't ride on my velocipede!' Willie shouted.

'Well, they can play with your Noah's ark and your soldiers,' said Nellie, and Mrs. Oleson made Willie be quiet.

The Noah's ark was the most wonderful thing that Laura had ever seen. They all knelt down and squealed and shouted and laughed over it. There were zebras and elephants and tigers and horses; all kinds of animals, just as if the picture had come out of the paper-covered Bible at home.

And there were two whole armies of tin soldiers, with uniforms painted bright blue and bright red.

There was a jumping-jack. He was cut out of thin, flat wood; striped paper trousers and jacket were pasted on him, and his face was painted white with red cheeks and circles around his eyes, and his tall cap was pointed. He hung between two thin red strips of wood, and when you squeezed them he danced. His hands held on to twisted strings. He would turn a somersault over the strings; he would stand on his head with his toe on his nose.

Even the big girls were chattering and squealing over those animals and those soldiers, and they laughed at the jumping-jack till they cried.

Then Nellie walked among them, saying, 'You can look at my doll.'

The doll had a china head, with smooth red cheeks and red mouth. Her eyes were black and her china hair was black and waved. Her wee hands were china, and her feet were tiny china feet in black china shoes.

'Oh!' Laura said. 'Oh, what a beautiful doll! Oh, Nellie, what is her name?'

'She's nothing but an old doll,' Nellie said. 'I don't care about this old doll. You wait till you see my wax doll.'

She threw the china doll in a drawer, and she took out a long box. She put the box on the bed and took off its lid. All the girls leaned around her to look.

There lay a doll that seemed to be alive. Real golden hair lay in soft curls on her little pillow. Her lips were parted, showing two tiny white teeth. Her eyes were closed. The doll was sleeping there in the box.

Nellie lifted her up, and her eyes opened wide. They were big blue eyes. She seemed to laugh. Her arms stretched out and she said, 'Mamma!'

'She does that when I squeeze her stomach,' Nellie

said. 'Look!' She punched the doll's stomach hard with her fist, and the poor doll cried out, 'Mamma!'

She was dressed in blue silk. Her petticoats were real petticoats trimmed with ruffles and lace, and her panties were real little panties that would come off. On her feet were real little blue leather slippers.

All this time Laura had not said a word. She couldn't.

She did not think of actually touching that marvellous doll, but without meaning to, her finger reached out owards the blue silk.

'Don't you touch her!' Nellie screeched. 'You keep your hands off my doll, Laura Ingalls!'

She snatched the doll against her and turned her back so Laura could not see her putting her back in the box.

Laura's face burned hot and the other girls did not know what to do. Laura went and sat on a chair. The others watched Nellie put the box in a drawer and shut it. Then they looked at the animals and the soldiers again and squeezed the jumping-jack.

Mrs. Oleson came in and asked Laura why she was not playing. Laura said, 'I would rather sit here, thank you, ma'am.'

'Would you like to look at these?' Mrs. Oleson asked her, and she laid two books in Laura's lap.

'Thank you, ma'am,' Laura said.

She turned the pages of the books carefully. One was not exactly a book; it was thin and it had no covers. It was a little magazine, all for children. The other was a book with a thick, glossy cover, and on the cover was a picture of an old woman wearing a peaked cap and riding on a broom across a huge yellow moon. Over her head large letters said, MOTHER GOOSE.

Laura had not known there were such wonderful books in the world. On every page of that book there was a picture and a rhyme. Laura could read some of them. She forgot all about the party.

Suddenly Mrs. Oleson was saying: 'Come, little girl. You mustn't let the others eat all the cake, must you?'

'Yes, ma'am,' Laura said. 'No, ma'am.'

A glossy white cloth covered the table. On it was a beautiful sugar-white cake and tall glasses.

'I got the biggest piece!' Nellie shouted, grabbing a big piece out of that cake. The others sat waiting till Mrs. Oleson gave them their pieces. She put each piece on a china plate.

'Is your lemonade sweet enough?' Mrs. Oleson asked. So Laura knew that it was lemonade in the glasses. She had never tasted anything like it. At first it was sweet, but after she ate a bit of the sugar-white off her piece of cake, the lemonade was sour. But they all answered Mrs. Oleson politely, 'Yes, thank you, ma'am.'

They were careful not to let a crumb of cake fall on the tablecloth. They did not spill one drop of lemonade.

Then it was time to go home, and Laura remembered to say, as Ma had told them to: 'Thank you, Mrs. Oleson. I had a very good time at the party.' So did all the others.

When they were out of the store, Christy said to Laura, 'I wish you'd slapped that mean Nellie Oleson.'

'Oh no! I couldn't!' Laura said. 'But I'm going to get even with her. Sh! Don't let Mary know I said that.'

Jack was waiting lonesome at the ford. It was Saturday, and Laura had not played with him. It would be a whole week before they would have another day of playing along Plum Creek.

They told Ma all about the party, and she said. 'We must not accept hospitality without making some return. I've been thinking about it, girls, and you must ask Nellie Oleson and the others to a party here. I think a week from Saturday.'

23
Country Party

'WILL YOU COME to my party?' Laura asked Christy and Maud and Nellie Oleson. Mary asked the big girls. They all said they would come.

That Saturday morning the new house was specially pretty. Jack could not come in on the scrubbed floors. The windows were shining and the pink-edged curtains were freshly crisp and white. Laura and Mary made new starry papers for the shelves, and Ma made vanity cakes.

She made them with beaten eggs and white flour. She dropped them into a kettle of sizzling fat. Each one came up bobbing, and floated till it turned itself over, lifting up its honey-brown, puffy bottom. Then it swelled underneath till it was round, and Ma lifted it out with a fork.

She put every one of those cakes in the cupboard. They were for the party.

Laura and Mary and Ma and Carrie were dressed up and waiting when the guests came walking out from town. Laura had even brushed Jack, though he was always clean and handsome in his white and brown-spotted short fur.

He ran down with Laura to the ford. The girls came laughing and splashing through the sunny water, all except Nellie. She had to take off her shoes and stockings and she complained that the gravel hurt her feet. She said: 'I don't go barefooted. I have shoes and stockings.'

She was wearing a new dress and big, new hair-ribbon bows.

'Is that Jack?' Christy asked, and they all patted him and said what a good dog he was. But when he politely wagged to Nellie, she said: 'Go away! Don't you touch my dress!'

'Jack wouldn't touch your dress,' Laura said.

They went up the path between the blowing grasses and wild flowers, to the house where Ma was waiting. Mary told her the girls' names one by one, and she smiled her lovely smile and spoke to them. But Nellie smoothed down her new pretty dress and said to Ma:

'Of course I didn't wear my best dress to just a country party.'

Then Laura didn't care what Ma had taught her; she didn't care if Pa punished her. She was going to get even with Nellie for that. Nellie couldn't speak that way to Ma.

Ma only smiled and said: 'It's a very pretty dresst Nellie. We're glad you could come.' But Laura was not going to forgive Nellie.

The girls liked the pretty house. It was so clean and airy, with sweet-smelling breezes blowing through it and the grassy prairies all around. They climbed the ladder and looked at Laura's and Mary's very own attic; none of them had anything like that. But Nellie asked, 'Where are your dolls?'

Laura was not going to show her darling rag Charlotte to Nellie Oleson. She said: 'I don't play with dolls. I play in the creek.'

Then they went outdoors with Jack. Laura showed them the little chicks by the hay-stacks, and they looked at the green garden rows and the thick-growing wheat-field. They ran down the knoll to the low bank of Plum Creek. There was the willow and footbridge, and the water coming out of the plum thicket's shade, running wide and shallow over sparkling pebbles and gurgling under the bridge to the knee-deep pool.

Mary and the big girls came down slowly, bringing Carrie to play with. But Laura and Christy and Maud and Nellie held their skirts up above their knees and went wading into the cool, flowing water. Away through the shallows the minnows went swimming in crowds away from the shouts and splashing.

The big girls took Carrie wading where the water sparkled thin in the sunshine, and gathered pretty pebbles along the creek's edge. The little girls played tag across the footbridge. They ran on the warm grass, and played in the water again. And while they were playing, Laura suddenly thought of what she could do to Nellie.

She led the girls wading near the old crab's home. The noise and splashing had driven him under his rock. She saw his angry claws and browny-green head peeping out, and she crowded Nellie near him. Then she kicked a big splash of water on to his rock and she screamed,

'Oo, Nellie! Nellie, look out!'

The old crab rushed at Nellie's toes, snapping his claws to nip them.

'Run! Run!' Laura screamed, pushing Christy and Maud back towards the bridge, and then she ran after Nellie. Nellie ran screaming straight into the muddy water under the plum thicket. Laura stopped on the gravel and looked back at the crab's rock.

'Wait, Nellie,' she said. 'You stay there.'

'Oh, what was it? What was it? Is he coming?' Nellie asked. She had dropped her dress, and her skirt petticoats were in the muddy water.

'It's an old crab,' Laura told her. 'He cuts big sticks in two with his claws. He could cut our toes right off.'

'Oh, where is he? Is he coming?' Nellie asked.

'You stay there and I'll look,' said Laura, and she went wading slowly and stopping and looking. The old crab was under his rock again, but Laura did not say so. She waded very slowly all the way to the bridge, while Nellie watched from the plum thicket. Then she waded back and said, 'You can come out now.'

Nellie came out into the clean water. She said she didn't like that horried old creek and wasn't going to play any more. She tried to wash her muddy skirt and then she tried to wash her feet, and then she screamed.

Muddy-brown bloodsuckers were sticking to her legs and her feet. She couldn't wash them off. She tried to pick one off, and then she ran screaming up on the creek bank. There she stood kicking as hard as she could, first one foot and then the other, screaming all the time.

Laura laughed till she fell on the grass and rolled. 'Oh, look, look!' she shouted, laughing. 'See Nellie dance!'

All the girls came running. Mary told Laura to pick those bloodsuckers off Nellie, but Laura didn't listen. She kept on rolling and laughing.

'Laura!' Mary said. 'You get up and pull those things off, or I'll tell Ma.'

Then Laura began to pull the bloodsuckers off Nellie. All the girls watched and screamed while she pulled them out long, and longer, and longer. Nellie cried: 'I don't like your party!' she said. 'I want to go home!'

Ma came hurrying down to the creek to see why they were screaming. She told Nellie not to cry, a few leeches were nothing to cry about. She said it was time now for them all to come to the house.

The table was set prettily with Ma's best white cloth and the blue pitcher full of flowers. The benches were drawn up on either side of it. Shiny tin cups were full of

cold, creamy milk from the cellar, and the big platter
was heaped with honey-coloured vanity cakes.

The cakes were not sweet, but they were rich and crisp,
and hollow inside. Each one was like a great bubble. The
crisp bits of it melted on the tongue.

They ate and ate those vanity cakes. They said they
had never tasted anything so good, and they asked Ma
what they were.

'Vanity cakes,' said Ma. 'Because they are all puffed
up, like vanity, with nothing solid inside.'

There were so many vanity cakes that they ate till they
could eat no more, and they drank all the sweet, cold milk
they could hold. Then the party was over. All the girls but
Nellie said thank you for the party. Nellie was still mad.

Laura did not care. Christy squeezed her and said in her
ear, 'I never had such a good time! And it just served
Nellie right!'

Deep down inside her Laura felt satisfied when she
thought of Nellie dancing on the creek bank.

24

Going to Church

I T WAS SATURDAY night and Pa sat on the doorstep, smoking his after-supper pipe.

Laura and Mary sat close on either side of him. Ma h Carrie in her lap, rocked gently to and fro, just inside the doorway.

The winds were still. The stars hung low and bright. The dark sky was deep beyond the stars, and Plum Creek talked softly to itself.

'They told me in town this afternoon that there will be preaching in the new church tomorrow,' said Pa. 'I met the home missionary, Reverend Alden, and he wanted us to be sure to come. I told him we would.'

'Oh, Charles,' Ma exclaimed, 'we haven't been to church for so long!'

Laura and Mary had never seen a church. But they knew from Ma's voice that going to church must be better than a party. After a while Ma said, 'I am so glad I finished my new dress.'

'You will look sweet as a posy in it,' Pa told her. 'We must start early.'

Next morning was a hurry. Breakfast was a hurry, work was a hurry, and Ma hurried about dressing herself and Carrie. She called up the ladder in a hurrying voice: 'Come on down, girls. I'll tie your ribbons.'

They hurried down. Then they stood and stared at Ma. She was perfectly beautiful in her new dress. It was black-

and-white calico, a narrow stripe of white, then a wider stripe of black lines and white lines no wider than threads. Up the front it was buttoned with black buttons. And the skirt was pulled back and lifted up to puffs and shirrings behind.

Crocheted lace edged the little stand-up collar. Crocheted lace spread out in a bow on Ma's breast, and the gold breast-pin held the collar and the bow. Ma's face was lovely. Her cheeks were flushed and her eyes were bright.

She turned Laura and Mary around and quickly tied the ribbons on their braids. Then she took Carrie's hand. They all went out on the doorstep and Ma locked the door.

Carrie looked like one of the little angel-birds in the Bible. Her dress and her tiny sunbonnet were white and all trimmed with lace. Her eyes were big and solemn; her golden curls hung by her cheeks and peeped from under the bonnet behind.

Then Laura saw her own pink ribbons on Mary's braids. She clapped her hand over her mouth before a word came out. She twisted round and looked down her own back. Mary's blue ribbons were on her braids!

She and Mary looked at each other and did not say a word. Ma, in her hurry, had made a mistake. They hoped she would not notice. Laura was so tired of pink and Mary was so tired of blue. But Mary had to wear blue because her hair was golden and Laura had to wear pink because her hair was brown.

Pa came driving the wagon from the stable. He had brushed Sam and David till they shone in the morning sunshine. They stepped proudly, tossing their heads, and their manes and tails rippled.

There was a clean blanket on the wagon seat and another spread on the bottom of the wagon box. Pa carefully helped Ma climb up over the wheel. He lifted Carrie to Ma's lap. Then he tossed Laura into the wagon box and her braids flew out.

'Oh dear!' Ma exclaimed. 'I put the wrong ribbons on Laura's hair!'

'It'll never be noticed on a trotting horse!' said Pa. So Laura knew she could wear the blue ribbons.

Sitting beside Mary on the clean blanket in the wagon bottom, she pulled her braids over her shoulder. So did Mary, and they smiled at each other. Laura could see the blue whenever she looked down, and Mary could see the pink.

Pa was whistling, and when Sam and David started he began to sing.

> 'Oh, every Sunday morning
> My wife is by my side
> A-waiting for the wagon,
> And we'll all take a ride!'

'Charles,' Ma said, softly, to remind him that this was Sunday. Then they all sang together,

> 'There is a happy land,
> Far, far away,
> Where saints in glory stand,
> Bright, bright as day!'

Plum Creek came out from the willow shadows and spread wide and flat and twinkling in the sunshine. Sam and David trotted through the sparkling shallows. Glittering drops flew up, and waves splashed from the wheels. Then they were away on the endless prairie.

The wagon rolled softly along the road that hardly made a mark on the green grasses. Birds sang their morning songs. Bees hummed. Great yellow bumblebees went bumbling from flower to flower, and big grasshoppers flew up and away.

Too soon they came to town. The blacksmith shop was shut and still. The doors of the stores were closed. A few dressed-up men and women, with their dressed-up children, walked along the edges of dusty Main Street. They were all going towards the church.

The church was a new building not far from the schoolhouse. Pa drove towards it through the prairie grass. It was like the schoolhouse, except that on its roof was a tiny room no walls and nothing in it.

'What's that?' Laura asked.

'Don't point, Laura,' said Ma. 'It's a belfry.'

Pa stopped the wagon against the high porch of the church. He helped Ma out of the wagon, but Laura and Mary just stepped over the side of the wagon box. They all waited there while Pa drove into the shade of the church, unhitched Sam and David and tied them to the wagon box.

People were coming through the grass, climbing the steps and going into the church. There was a solemn, low rustling inside it.

At last Pa came. He took Carrie on his arm and walked with Ma into the church. Laura and Mary walked softly, close behind them. They all sat in a row on a long bench.

Church was exactly like a schoolhouse, except that it had a strange, large, hollow feeling. Every little noise was loud against the new board walls.

A tall, thin man stood up behind the tall desk on the platform. His clothes were black and his big cravat was black and his hair and the beard that went around his face were dark. His voice was gentle and kind. All the heads bowed down. The man's voice talked to God for a long time, while Laura sat perfectly still and looked at the blue ribbons on her braids.

Suddenly, right beside her, a voice said, 'Come with me.'

Laura almost jumped out of her skin. A pretty lady stood there, smiling out of soft blue eyes. The lady said again, 'Come with me, little girls. We are going to have a Sunday-school class.'

Ma nodded at them, so Laura and Mary slid down from the bench. They had not known there was going to be school on Sunday.

The lady led them to a corner. All the girls from school were there, looking questions at one another. The lady pulled benches around to make a square pen. She sat down and took Laura and Christy beside her. When the others were settled on the square of benches, the lady said her name was Mrs. Tower, and she asked their names. Then she said, 'Now, I'm going to tell you a story!'

Laura was very pleased. But Mrs. Tower began, 'It is all about a little baby, born long ago in Egypt. His name was Moses.'

So Laura did not listen any more. She knew all about Moses in the bulrushes. Even Carrie knew that.

After the story, Mrs. Tower smiled more than ever, and said. 'Now we'll all learn a Bible verse! Won't that be nice?'

'Yes, ma'am,' they all said. She told a Bible verse to each girl in turn. They were to remember the verses and repeat them to her next Sunday. That was their Sunday-school lesson.

When it was Laura's turn, Mrs. Tower cuddled her and smiled almost as warm and sweet as Ma. She said, 'My very littlest girl must have a very small lesson. It will be the shortest verse in the Bible!'

Then Laura knew what it was. But Mrs. Tower's eyes smiled and she said, 'It is just three words!' She said them, and asked, 'Now do you think you can remember that for a whole week?'

Laura was surprised at Mrs. Tower. Why, she remembered long Bible verses and whole songs! But she did not want to hurt Mrs. Tower's feelings. So she said, 'Yes, ma'am.'

'That's my little girl!' Mrs. Tower said. But Laura was

Ma's little girl. 'I'll tell you again, to help you remember. Just three words,' said Mrs. Tower. 'Now can you say them after me?'

Laura squirmed.

'Try,' Mrs. Tower urged her. Laura's head bowed lower and she whispered the verse.

'That's right!' Mrs. Tower said. 'Now will you do your best to remember, and tell me next Sunday?'

Laura nodded.

After that everyone stood up. They all opened their

mouths and tried to sing 'Jerusalem, the Golden.' Not
many of them knew the words or the tune. Miserable
squiggles went up Laura's backbone and the insides of her
ears crinkled. She was glad when they all sat down again.

Then the tall, thin man stood up and talked.

Laura thought he never would stop talking. She looked
through the open windows at butterflies going where they
pleased. She watched the grasses blowing in the wind. She
listened to the wind whining thin along the edges of the
roof. She looked at the blue hair ribbons. She looked at
each of her finger nails and admired how the fingers of her
hands would fit together. She struck her fingers out
straight, so they looked like the corner of a log house. She
looked at the underneath of shingles, overhead. Her legs
ached from dangling still.

At last every one stood up and tried again to sing. When
that was over, there was no more. They could go home.

The tall thin man was standing by the door. He was the
Reverend Alden. He shook Ma's hand and he shook Pa's
hand and they talked. Then he bent down, and he shook
Laura's hand.

His teeth smiled in his dark beard. His eyes were warm
and blue. He asked, 'Did you like Sunday-school, Laura?'

Suddenly Laura did like it. She said, 'Yes, sir.'

'Then you must come every Sunday!' he said. 'We'll
expect you.' And Laura knew he really would expect her.
He would not forget.

On the way home Pa said, 'Well, Caroline, it's pleasant
to be with a crowd of people all trying to do the right
thing, same as we are.'

'Yes, Charles,' Ma said, thankfully. 'It will be a pleasure
to look forward to, all week.'

Pa turned on the seat and asked, 'How do you girls like
the first time you ever went to church?'

'They can't sing,' said Laura.

Pa's great laugh rang out. Then he explained, 'There was nobody to pitch the hymn with a tuning-fork.'

'Nowadays, Charles,' said Ma, 'people have hymn books.'

'Well, maybe we'll be able to afford some, some day,' Pa said.

After that they went to Sunday-school every Sunday. Three or four Sundays they went to Sunday-school, and then again the Reverend Alden was there, and that was a church Sunday. The Reverend Alden lived at his real church, in the East. He could not travel all the way to this church every Sunday. This was his home missionary church, in the West.

There were no more long, dull, tiresome Sundays, because there was always Sunday-school to go to, and to talk about afterwards. The best Sundays were the Sundays when the Reverend Alden was there. He always remembered Laura, and she remembered him betweentimes. He called Laura and Mary his 'little country girls'.

Then one Sunday while Pa and Ma and Mary and Laura were all sitting at the dinner table, talking about that day's Sunday-school, Pa said, 'If I'm going to keep on going out among dressed-up folks I must get a pair of new boots. Look.'

He stretched out his foot. His mended boot was cracked clear across the toes.

They all looked at his red knitted sock showing through that gaping slit. The edges of leather were thin and curling back between little cracks. Pa said, 'It won't hold another patch.'

'Oh, I wanted you to get boots, Charles,' Ma said. 'And you brought home that calico for my dress.'

Pa made up his mind. 'I'll get me a new pair when I go

to town next Saturday. They will cost three dollars, but we'll make out somehow till I harvest the wheat.'

All that week Pa was making hay. He had helped put up Mr. Nelson's hay and earned the use of Mr. Nelson's fine, quick mowing-machine. He said it was wonderful weather for making hay. He had never known such a dry, sunny summer.

Laura hated to go to school. She wanted to be out in the hay-field with Pa, watching the marvellous machine with its long knives snickety-snicking behind the wheels, cutting through great swathes of grass.

Saturday morning she went to the field on the wagon, and helped Pa bring in the last load of hay. They looked at the wheat-field, standing up taller than Laura above the mown land. Its level top was rough with wheat-heads, bent with the weight of ripening wheat. They picked three long, fat ones and took them to the house to show Ma.

When that crop was harvested, Pa said, they'd be out of debt and have more money than they knew what to do with. He'd have a buggy, Ma would have a silk dress, they'd all have new shoes and eat beef every Sunday.

After dinner he put on a clean shirt and took three dollars out of the fiddle-box. He was going to town to get his new boots. He walked, because the horses had been working all that week and he left them at home to rest.

It was late that afternoon when Pa came walking home, Laura saw him on the knoll and she and Jack ran up from the old crab's home in the creek and into the house behind him.

Ma turned around from the stove, where she was taking the Saturday baking of bread out of the oven.

'Where are your boots, Charles?' she asked.

'Well, Caroline,' Pa said. 'I saw Brother Alden and he told me he couldn't raise money enough to put a bell in the belfry. The folks in town had all given every cent they could, and he lacked just three dollars. So I gave him the money.'

'Oh, Charles!' was all Ma said.

Pa looked down at his cracked boot. 'I'll patch it,' he said. 'I can make it hold together somehow. And do you know, we'll hear that church bell ringing clear out here.'

Ma turned quickly back to the stove, and Laura went quietly out and sat down on the step. Her throat hurt her. She did so want Pa to have good new boots.

'Never mind, Caroline,' she heard Pa saying. 'It's not long to wait till I harvest the wheat.'

25

The Glittering Cloud

NOW THE WHEAT was almost ready to cut. Every day Pa looked at it. Every night he talked about it, and showed Laura some long, stiff wheat-heads. The plump grains were getting harder in their little husks. Pa said the weather was perfect for ripening wheat.

'If this keeps up,' he said, 'We'll start harvesting next week.'

The weather was very hot. The thin, high sky was too hot to look at. Air rose up in waves from the whole prairie, as it does from a hot stove. In the schoolhouse the children panted like lizards, and the sticky pine-juice dripped down the board walls.

Saturday morning Laura went walking with Pa to look at the wheat. It was almost as tall as Pa. He lifted her on to his shoulder so that she could see over the heavy, bending tops. The field was greeny gold.

At the dinner table Pa told Ma about it. He had never seen such a crop. There were forty bushels to the acre, and wheat was a dollar a bushel. They were rich now. This was a wonderful country. Now they could have anything they wanted. Laura listened and thought, now Pa would get his new boots.

She sat facing the open door and the sunshine streaming through it. Something seemed to dim the sunshine. Laura rubbed her eyes and looked again. The sunshine really was dim. It grew dimmer until there was no sunshine.

'I do believe a storm is coming up,' said Ma. 'There must be a cloud over the sun.'

Pa got up quickly and went to the door. A storm might hurt the wheat. He looked out, then he went out.

The light was queer. It was not like the changed light before a storm. The air did not press down as it did before a storm. Laura was frightened, she did not know why.

She ran outdoors, where Pa stood looking up at the sky. Ma and Mary came out, too, and Pa asked, 'What do you make of that, Caroline?'

A cloud was over the sun. It was not like any cloud they had ever seen before. It was a cloud of something like snowflakes, but they were larger than snowflakes, and thin and glittering. Light shone through each flickering particle.

There was no wind. The grasses were still and the hot air did not stir, but the edge of the cloud came on across the sky faster than wind. The hair stood up on Jack's neck. All at once he made a frightful sound up at that cloud, a growl and a whine.

Plunk! something hit Laura's head and fell to the ground. She looked down and saw the largest grasshopper she had ever seen. Then huge brown grasshoppers were hitting the ground all around her, hitting her head and her face and her arms. They came thudding down like hail.

The cloud was hailing grasshoppers. The cloud *was* grasshoppers. Their bodies hid the sun and made darkness. Their thin, large wings gleamed and glittered. The rasping whirring of their wings filled the whole air and they hit the ground and the house with the noise of a hailstorm.

Laura tried to beat them off. Their claws clung to her skin and her dress. They looked at her with bulging eyes, turning their heads this way and that. Mary ran screaming into the house. Grasshoppers covered the ground, there was not one bare bit to step on. Laura had to step on grasshoppers and they smashed squirming and slimy under her feet.

Ma was slamming the windows shut, all around the house. Pa came and stood just inside the front door, looking out. Laura and Jack stood close beside him. Grasshoppers beat down from the sky and swarmed thick over the ground. Their long wings were folded and their strong legs took them hopping everywhere. The air whirred and the roof went on sounding like a roof in a hailstorm.

Then Laura heard another sound, one big sound made of tiny nips and snips and gnawings.

'The wheat!' Pa shouted. He dashed out the back door and ran towards the wheat-field.

The grasshoppers were eating. You could not hear one grasshopper eat, unless you listened very carefully while you held him and fed him grass. Millions and millions of grasshoppers were eating now. You could hear the millions of jaws biting and chewing.

Pa came running back to the stable. Through the window Laura saw him hitching Sam and David to the wagon. He began pitching old dirty hay from the manure-pile into the wagon, as fast as he could. Ma ran out, took the other pitchfork and helped him. Then he drove away to the wheat-field and Ma followed the wagon.

Pa drove around the field, throwing out little piles of stuff as he went. Ma stooped over one, then a thread of smoke rose from it and spread. Ma lighted pile after pile. Laura watched till a smudge of smoke hid the field and Ma and Pa and the wagon.

Grasshoppers were still falling from the sky. The light was still dim because grasshoppers covered the sun.

Ma came back to the house, and in the closed lean-to she took off her dress and her petticoats and killed the grasshoppers she shook out of them. She had lighted fires all around the wheat-field. Perhaps smoke would keep the grasshoppers from eating the wheat.

Ma and Mary and Laura were quiet in the shut, smothery house. Carrie was so little that she cried, even in Ma's arms. She cried herself to sleep. Through the walls came the sound of grasshoppers eating.

The darkness went away. The sun shone again. All over the ground was a crawling, hopping mass of grasshoppers. They were eating all the soft, short grass off the knoll. The tall prairie grasses swayed and bent and fell.

'Oh, look,' Laura said, low, at the window.

They were eating the willow tops. The willows' leaves

were thin and bare twigs stuck out. Then whole branches were bare, and knobby with masses of grasshoppers.

'I don't want to look any more,' Mary said, and she went away from the window. Laura did not want to look any more, either, but she could not stop looking.

The hens were funny. The two hens and their gawky pullets were eating grasshoppers with all their might. They were used to stretching their necks out low and running fast after grasshoppers and not catching them. Every time they stretched out now, they got a grasshopper right then. They were surprised. They kept stretching out their necks and trying to run in all directions at once.

'Well, we won't have to buy feed for the hens,' said Ma. 'There's no great loss without some gain.'

The green garden rows were wilting down. The

potatoes, the carrots, the beets and beans were being eaten away. The long leaves were eaten off the cornstalks, and the tassels, and the ears of young corn in their green husks fell covered with grasshoppers.

There was nothing anybody could do about it.

Smoke still hid the wheat-field. Sometimes Laura saw Pa moving dimly in it. He stirred up the smouldering fires and thick smoke hid him again.

When it was time to go for Spot, Laura put on stockings and shoes and a shawl. Spot was standing in the old ford of Plum Creek, shaking her skin and switching her tail. The herd went mournfully lowing beyond the old dug-out. Laura was sure that cattle could not eat grass so full of grasshoppers. If the grasshoppers ate all the grass, the cattle would starve.

Grasshoppers were thick under her petticoats and on her dress and shawl. She kept striking them off her face and hands. Her shoes and Spot's feet crunched grasshoppers.

Ma came out in a shawl to do the milking. Laura helped her. They could not keep grasshoppers out of the milk. Ma had brought a cloth to cover the pail but they could not keep it covered while they milked into it. Ma skimmed out the grasshoppers with a tin cup.

Grasshoppers went into the house with them. Their clothes were full of grasshoppers. Some jumped on to the hot stove where Mary was starting supper. Ma covered the food till they had chased and smashed every grasshopper. She swept them up and shovelled them into the stove.

Pa came into the house long enough to eat supper while Sam and David were eating theirs. Ma did not ask him what was happening to the wheat. She only smiled and said: 'Don't worry, Charles. We've always got along.'

Pa's throat rasped and Ma said: 'Have another cup

of tea, Charles. It will help get the smoke out of your throat.'

When Pa had drunk the tea, he went back to the wheat-field with another load of old hay and manure.

In bed, Laura and Mary could still hear the whirring and snipping and chewing. Laura felt claws crawling on her. There were no grasshoppers in bed, but she could not brush the feeling off her arms and cheeks. In the dark she saw grasshopper's bulging eyes and felt their claws crawling until she went to sleep.

Pa was not downstairs next morning. All night he had been working to keep the smoke over the wheat, and he did not come to breakfast. He was still working.

The whole prairie was changed. The grasses did not wave; they had fallen in ridges. The rising sun made all the prairie rough with shadows where the tall grasses had sunk against each other.

The willow trees were bare. In the plum thickets only a few plumpits hung to the leafless branches. The nipping, clicking, gnawing sound of the grasshoppers' eating was still going on.

At noon Pa came driving the wagon out of the smoke. He put Sam and David into the stable, and slowly came to the house. His face was black with smoke and his eye-balls were red. He hung his hat on the nail behind the door and sat down at the table.

'It's no use, Caroline,' he said. 'Smoke won't stop them. They keep dropping down through it and hopping in from all sides. The wheat is falling now. They're cutting it off like a scythe. And eating it, straw and all.'

He put his elbows on the table and hid his face with his hands. Laura and Mary sat still. Only Carrie on her high stool rattled her spoon and reached her little hand towards the bread. She was too young to understand.

'Never mind, Charles,' Ma said. 'We've been through hard times before.'

Laura looked down at Pa's patched boots under the table and her throat swelled and ached. Pa could not have new boots now.

Pa's hands came down from his face and he picked up his knife and fork. His beard smiled, but his eyes would not twinkle. They were dull and dim.

'Don't worry, Caroline,' he said. 'We did all we could, and we'll pull through somehow.'

Then Laura remembered that the new house was not paid for. Pa had said he would pay for it when he harvested the wheat.

It was a quiet meal, and when it was over Pa lay down on the floor and went to sleep. Ma slipped a pillow under his head and laid her finger on her lips to tell Laura and Mary to be still.

They took Carrie into the bedroom and kept her quiet with their paper dolls. The only sound was the sound of the grasshoppers' eating.

Day after day the grasshoppers kept on eating. They ate all the wheat and the oats. They ate every green thing—all the garden and all the prairie grass.

'Oh, Pa, what will the rabbits do?' Laura asked. 'And the poor birds?'

'Look around you, Laura,' Pa said.

The rabbits had all gone away. The little birds of the grass tops were gone. The birds that were left were eating grasshoppers. And prairie hens ran with outstretched necks, gobbling grasshoppers.

When Sunday came, Pa and Laura and Mary walked to Sunday-school. The sun shone so bright and hot that Ma said she would stay at home with Carrie, and Pa left Sam and David in the shady stable.

There had been no rain for so long that Laura walked across Plum Creek on dry stones. The whole prairie was bare and brown. Millions of brown grasshoppers whirred low over it. Not a green thing was in sight anywhere.

All the way, Laura and Mary brushed off grasshoppers. When they came to the church, brown grasshoppers were thick on their petticoats. They lifted their skirts and brushed them off before they went in. But careful as they were, the grasshoppers had spit tobacco-juice on their best Sunday dresses.

Nothing would take out the horrid stains. They would have to wear their best dresses with the brown spots on them.

Many people in town were going back East. Christy and Cassie had to go. Laura said good-bye to Christy and Mary said good-bye to Cassie, their best friends.

They did not go to school any more. They must save their shoes for winter and they could not bear to walk barefooted on grasshoppers. School would be ended soon, anyway, and Ma said she would teach them through the winter so they would not be behind their classes when school opened again next spring.

Pa worked for Mr. Nelson and earned the use of Mr. Nelson's plough. He began to plough the bare wheat-field, to make it ready for next year's wheat crop.

26

Grasshopper Eggs

ONE DAY LAURA and Jack wandered down to the creek. Mary liked to sit and read and work sums on the slate, but Laura grew tired of that. Outdoors was so miserable that she did not much like to play, either.

Plum Creek was almost dry. Only a little water seeped through the pebbly sand. The bare willow did not shade the footbridge now. Under the leafless plum thicket the water was scummy. The old crab had gone away.

The dry earth was hot, the sunshine was scorching and the sky was a brassy colour. The whirring of grasshoppers sounded like heat. There were no good smells any more.

Then Laura saw a queer thing. All over the knoll grasshoppers were sitting still with their tails down in the ground. They did not stir, even when Laura poked them.

She poked one away from the hole in which it was sitting, and with a stick she dug out of the hole a grey thing. It was like a fat worm, but it was not alive. She did not know what it was. Jack snuffed at it, and wondered, too.

Laura started towards the wheat-field to ask Pa about it. But Pa was not ploughing. Sam and David were standing still with the plough, and Pa was walking on the unploughed ground, looking at it. Then Laura saw him go to the plough and lift it out of the furrow. He went, driving Sam and David towards the stable with the idle plough.

Laura knew that only something dreadful would make Pa stop work in the middle of the morning. She went as fast as she could to the stable. Sam and David were in their stalls and Pa was hanging up their sweaty harness. He came out, and did not smile at Laura. She tagged slowly after him into the house.

Ma looked up at him and said, 'Charles! What is the matter now?'

'The grasshoppers are laying their eggs,' said Pa. 'The ground's honeycombed with them. Look at the dooryard, and you'll see the pits where the eggs are buried a couple of inches deep. All over the wheat-field. Everywhere. You can't put your finger down between them. Look here.'

He took one of those grey things from his pocket and held it out on his hand.

'That's one of 'em, a pod of grasshopper eggs. I've been cutting them open. There's thirty-five or forty eggs in every pod. There's a pod in every hole. There's eight or ten holes to the square foot. All over this whole country.'

Ma dropped down in a chair and let her hands fall helpless at her sides.

'We've got no more chance of making a crop next year than we have of flying,' said Pa. 'When those eggs hatch, there won't be a green thing left in this part of the world.'

'Oh, Charles!' Ma said. 'What will we do?'

Pa slumped down on a bench and said, 'I don't know.'

Mary's braids swung over the edge of the ladder hole and her face looked down between them. She looked anxiously at Laura and Laura looked up at her. Then Mary backed down the ladder without a sound. She stood close beside Laura, backed against the wall.

Pa straightened up. His dim eyes brightened with a fierce light, not like the twinkle Laura had always seen in them.

'But I do know this, Caroline,' he said. 'No pesky mess of grasshoppers can best us! We'll do something! You'll see! We'll get along somehow.'

10

'Yes, Charles,' said Ma.

'Why not?' said Pa. 'We're healthy, we've got a roof over our heads; we're better off than lots of folks. You get an early dinner, Caroline. I'm going to town. I'll find something to do. Don't you worry!'

While he was gone to town, Ma and Mary and Laura planned a fine supper for him. Ma scalded a pan of sour milk and made pretty white balls of cottage cheese. Mary and Laura sliced cold boiled potatoes and Ma made a sauce for them. There were bread and butter and milk besides.

Then they washed and combed their hair. They put on their best dresses and their hair ribbons. They put Carrie's white dress on her, and brushed her hair and tied the string of Indian beads around her neck. They were all waiting when Pa came up the grasshoppery knoll.

That was a merry supper. When they had eaten every bit of it, Pa pushed back his plate and said 'Well, Caroline.'

'Yes, Charles?' Ma said.

'Here's the way out,' said Pa. 'I'm going *east* tomorrow morning.'

'Oh, Charles! No!' Ma cried out.

'It's all right, Laura,' Pa said. He meant, 'Don't cry,' and Laura did not cry.

'It's harvest time back there,' Pa told them. 'The grasshoppers went only about a hundred miles east of here. Beyond that there's crops. It's the only chance to get a job, and all the men in the West are heading for those jobs. I've got to get there quick.'

'If you think it's for the best,' Ma said, 'the girls and I can get along. But, oh, Charles, it will be such a long walk for you!'

'Shucks! What's a couple of hundred miles?' said Pa. But he glanced at his old patched boots. Laura knew he was wondering if they would last to walk so far. 'A couple of hundred miles don't amount to anything!' he said.

Then he took his fiddle out of its box. He played for a long time in the twilight, while Laura and Mary sat close to him and Ma rocked Carrie near by.

He played 'Dixie Land,' and 'We'll Rally Round the Flag, Boys!' He played 'All the Blue Bonnets Are Over the Border,' and

> Oh, Susanna, don't you cry for me!
> I'm going to California
> With my washpan on my knee!

He played 'The Campbells Are Coming, Hurrah! Hurrah!' Then he played 'Life Let Us Cherish.' And he put away the fiddle. He must go to bed early, to get an early start in the morning.

'Take good care of the old fiddle, Caroline,' he said. 'It puts heart into a man.'

After breakfast, at dawn, Pa kissed them all and went away. His extra shirt and pair of socks were rolled in his jumper and slung on his shoulder. Just before he crossed Plum Creek he looked back and waved. Then he went on, all the way out of sight, without turning again. Jack stood pressed close against Laura.

They all stood still for a moment after Pa was gone. Then Ma said, cheerfully, 'We have to take care of everything now, girls. Mary and Laura, you hurry with the cow to meet the herd.'

She went briskly into the house with Carrie while Laura and Mary ran to let Spot out of the stable and drive her towards the creek. No prairie grass was left, and the hungry cattle could only wander along the creek banks, eating willow sprouts and plum brush and a little dead, dry grass left from last summer.

27

Rain

EVERYTHING WAS FLAT and dull when Pa was gone. Laura and Mary could not even count the days till he would come back. They could only think of him walking farther and farther away in his patched boots.

Jack was a sober dog now and his nose was turning grey. Often he looked at the empty road where Pa had gone, and sighed, and lay down to watch it. But he did not really hope that Pa could come.

The dead, eaten prairie was flat under the hot sky. Dust devils rose up and whirled across it. The far-away edge of it seemed to crawl like a snake. Ma said that was caused by the heat waves of the air.

The only shade was in the house. There were no leaves on willows or plum thickets. Plum Creek dried up. There was only a little water in its pools. The well was dry, and the old spring by the dugout was only a drip. Ma set a pail under it, to fill during the night. In the morning she brought it to the house and left another pail to fill during the day.

When the morning work was done, Ma and Mary and Laura and Carrie sat in the house. The scorching winds whizzed by and the hungry cattle never stopped lowing.

Spot was thin. Her hip joints stuck up sharp, all her ribs showed, and there were hollows around her eyes. All day she went mooing with the other cattle, looking for something to eat. They had eaten all the little bushes along the creek and gnawed the willow branches as high as they could reach. Spot's milk was bitter, and every day she gave less of it.

Sam and David stood in the stable. They could not have all the hay they wanted, because the hay-stacks must last till next spring. When Laura led them down the dry creek-bed to the old swimming-hole, they curled their noses at the warm, scummy water. But they had to drink it. Cows and horses had to bear things, too.

Saturday, Laura went to the Nelsons' to see if a letter had come from Pa. She went along the little path beyond the footbridge. It did not go wandering forever through pleasant places. It went to Mr. Nelson's.

Mr. Nelson's house was long and low and its board walls were whitewashed. His long, low sod stable had a thick roof made of hay. They did not look like Pa's house and Pa's stable. They cuddled to the ground, under a slope of the prairie, and they looked as if they spoke Norwegian.

The house was shining clean inside. The big bed was plumped high with feathers and the pillows were high and fat. On the wall hung a beautiful picture of a lady dressed in blue. Its frame was thick gold, and bright pink mosquito-netting covered the lady and the frame, to keep the flies off.

There was no letter from Pa. Mrs. Nelson said that Mr. Nelson would ask again at the post-office, next Saturday.

'Thank you, ma'am,' Laura said, and she hurried fast along the path. Then she walked slowly across the foot-bridge, and more and more slowly up the knoll.

Ma said, 'Never mind, girls. There will be a letter next Saturday.'

But next Saturday there was no letter.

They did not go to Sunday-school any more. Carrie

could not walk so far and she was too heavy for Ma to carry. Laura and Mary must save their shoes. They could not go to Sunday-school barefooted, and if they wore out their shoes they would have no shoes next winter.

So on Sundays they put on their best dresses, but not their shoes or ribbons. Mary and Laura said their Bible verses to Ma, and she read to them from the Bible.

One Sunday she read to them about the plague of locusts, long ago in Bible times. Locusts were grasshoppers. Ma read:

'And the locusts went up over the land of Egypt, and rested in all the coasts of Egypt; very grievous were they.

'For they covered the face of the whole earth, so that the land was darkened; and they did eat every herb of the land, and all the fruits of the trees which the hail had left; and there remained not any green thing on the trees, or in the herbs of the field, through all the land of Egypt.'

Laura knew how true that was. When she repeated those verses she thought, 'through all the land of Minnesota.'

Then Ma read the promise that God made to good people, 'to bring them out of that land to a good land and a large, unto a land flowing with milk and honey.'

'Oh, where is that, Ma?' Mary asked, and Laura asked, 'How could land flow with milk and honey?' She did not want to walk in milky, sticky honey.

Ma rested the big Bible on her knees and thought. Then she said, 'Well, your Pa thinks it will be right here in Minnesota.'

'How could it be?' Laura asked.

'Maybe it will be, if we stick it out,' said Ma. 'Well, Laura, if good milch cows were eating grass all over this land, they would give a great deal of milk, and then the land would be flowing with milk. Bees would get honey out of all the wild flowers that grow out of the land, and then the land would be flowing with honey.'

'Oh,' Laura said. 'I'm glad we wouldn't have to walk in it.'

Carrie beat the Bible with her little fists and cried: 'I'm hot! I'm pricky!' Ma picked her up but she pushed at Ma and whimpered, 'You're hot!'

Poor little Carrie's skin was red with heat rash. Laura and Mary were sweltering inside their underwaists and drawers, and petticoat-waists and petticoat, and long-sleeved, high-necked dresses with tight waistbands around their middles. The backs of their necks were smothering under their braids.

Carrie wanted a drink, but she pushed the cup away and made a face and said, 'Nasty!'

'You'd better drink it,' Mary told her. 'I want a cold drink, too, but there isn't any.'

'I wish I had a drink of well water,' said Laura.

'I wish I had an icicle,' said Mary.

Then Laura said, 'I wish I was an Indian and didn't have to wear clothes.'

'Laura!' said Ma. 'And on Sunday!'

Laura thought, 'Well, I do!' The wood smell of the house was a hot smell. On all the brown streaks in the boards the juice was dripping down sticky and drying in hard yellow beads. The hot wind never stopped whizzing by and the cattle never stopped mourning, 'Moo-oo, moo-oo.' Jack turned on his side and groaned a long sigh.

Ma sighed, too, and said. 'Seems to me I'd give almost anything for a breath of air.'

At that very minute a breath of air came into the house. Carrie stopped whimpering. Jack lifted up his head. Ma said, 'Girls, did you——' Then another cool breath came.

Ma went out through the lean-to, to the shady end of the house. Laura scampered after her, and Mary came leading Carrie. Outdoors was like a baking-oven. The hot air came scorching against Laura's face.

In the northwest sky there was a cloud. It was small in the enormous, brassy sky. But it was a cloud, and it made a streak of shade on the prairie. The shadow seemed to move, but perhaps that was only the heat waves. No, it really was coming nearer.

'Oh, please, please, please!' Laura kept saying, silently, with all her might. They all stood shading their eyes and looking at that cloud and its shadow.

The cloud kept coming nearer. It grew larger. It was a thick, dark streak in the air above the prairie. Its edge rolled and swelled in big puffs. Now gusts of cool air came, mixed with gusts hotter than ever.

All over the prairie, dust devils rose up wild and wicked, whirling their dust arms. The sun still burned on the house and the stable and the cracked, pitted earth. The shadow of the cloud was far away.

Suddenly a fire-white streak zigzagged, and a grey curtain fell from the cloud and hung there, hiding the sky beyond it. That was rain. Then a growl of thunder came.

'It's too far away, girls,' Ma said. 'I'm afraid it won't get to us. But, anyway, the air's cooler.'

A smell of rain came on streaks of coolness through the hot wind.

'Oh, maybe it will get to us, Ma! Maybe it will!' Laura said. Inside themselves they were all saying, 'Please, please, please!'

The wind blew cooler. Slowly, slowly, the cloud shadow grew larger. Now the cloud spread wide in the sky. Suddenly a shadow rushed across the flat land and up the knoll, and fast after it came the marching rain. It came up the knoll like millions of tiny trampling feet, and rain poured down on the house and on Ma and Mary and Laura and Carrie.

'Get in, quick!' Ma exclaimed.

The lean-to was noisy with rain on its roof. Cool air blew through it into the smothery house. Ma opened the front door. She fastened back the curtains and opened every window.

A sick smell steamed up from the ground, but the rain poured down and washed it away. Rain drummed on the roof, rain poured from the eaves. Rain washed the air and made it good to breathe. Sweet air rushed through the house. It lifted the heaviness out of Laura's head and made her skin feel good.

Streams of muddy water ran swiftly over the hard ground. They poured into its cracks and filled them up. They dimpled and swirled over the pits where the grasshoppers' eggs were and left smooth mud there. Overhead the lightning flickered sharp and thunder crashed.

Carrie clapped her hands and shouted; Mary and Laura danced and laughed. Jack wiggled and scampered like a puppy; he looked out at the rain from every window, and when the thunder banged and crashed he growled at it, 'Who's afraid of you!'

'I do believe it is going to last till sunset,' Ma said.

Just before sunset the rain went away. Down across Plum Creek and away across the prairie to the east it went, leaving only a few sparkling drops falling in the sunshine. Then the cloud turned purple and red and curled gold edges against the clear sky. The sun sank and the stars came out. The air was cool and the earth was damp and grateful.

The only thing that Laura wished was that Pa could be there.

Next day the sun rose burning hot. The sky was brassy and the winds were scorching. And before night tiny thin spears of grass were pricking up from the ground.

In a few days there was a green streak across the brown prairie. Grass came up where the rain had fallen, and the hungry cattle grazed there. Every morning Laura put Sam and David on picket lines so they could eat the good grass, too.

The cattle stopped bawling. Spot's bones did not show any more. She gave more milk, and it was sweet, good milk. The knoll was green again, and the willows and the plums were putting out tiny leaves.

28

The Letter

ALL DAY LONG Laura missed Pa, and at night when the wind blew lonesomely over the dark land, she felt hollow and aching.

At first she talked about him; she wondered how far he had walked that day; she hoped his old, patched boots were lasting; she wondered where he was camping that night. Later she did not speak about him to Ma. Ma was thinking about him all the time and she did not like to talk about it. She did not like even to count the days till Saturday.

'The time will go faster,' she said, 'if we think of other things.'

All day Saturday they hoped that Mr. Nelson was finding a letter from Pa at the post-office in town. Laura and Jack went far along the prairie road to wait for Mr. Nelson's wagon. The grasshoppers had eaten everything, and now they were going away, not in one big cloud as they had come but in little, short-flying clouds. Still, millions of grasshoppers were left.

There was no letter from Pa. 'Never mind,' Ma said. 'One will come.'

Once when Laura was slowly coming up the knoll without a letter, she thought, 'Suppose no letter ever comes?'

She tried not to think that again. But she did. One day she looked at Mary and knew that Mary was thinking it, too.

That night Laura could not bear it any longer. She asked Ma, 'Pa will come home, won't he?'

'Of course, Pa will come home!' Ma exclaimed. Then Laura and Mary knew that Ma, too, was afraid that something had happened to Pa.

Perhaps his boots had fallen to pieces and he was limping barefooted. Perhaps cattle had hurt him. Perhaps a train had hit him. He had not taken his gun; perhaps wolves had got him. Maybe in dark woods at night a panther had leaped on him from a tree.

The next Saturday afternoon, when Laura and Jack were starting to meet Mr. Nelson, she saw him coming across the footbridge. Something white was in his hand. Laura flew down the knoll. The white thing was a letter.

'Oh, thank you! Thank you!' Laura said. She ran to the house so fast that she could not breathe. Ma was washing Carrie's face. She took the letter in her shaking wet hands, and sat down.

'It's from Pa,' she said. Her hand shook so she could hardly take a hairpin from her hair. She slit the envelope and drew out the letter. She unfolded it, and there was a piece of paper money.

'Pa's all right,' Ma said. She snatched her apron up to her face and cried.

Her wet face came out of the apron shining with joy. She kept wiping her eyes while she read the letter to Mary and Laura.

Pa had had to walk three hundred miles before he found a job. Now he was working in the wheat-fields and getting a dollar a day. He sent Ma five dollars and kept three for new boots. Crops were good where he was, and if Ma and the girls were making out all right, he would stay there as long as the work lasted.

They missed him and wanted him to come home. But he was safe, and already he had new boots. They were very happy that day.

29

The Darkest Hour is just before Dawn

NOW THE WINDS blew cooler and the sun was not so hot at noon. Mornings were chilly, and the grasshoppers hopped feebly until the sunshine warmed them.

One morning a thick frost covered the ground. It coated every twig and chip with a white fuzz and it burned Laura's bare feet. She saw millions of grasshoppers sitting perfectly stiff.

In a few days there was not one grasshopper left anywhere.

Winter was near, and Pa had not come. The wind was sharp. It did not whiz any more; it shrieked and wailed. The sky was grey and a cold grey rain fell. The rain turned to snow, and still Pa did not come.

Laura had to wear shoes when she went outdoors. They hurt her feet. She did not know why. Those shoes had never hurt her feet before. Mary's shoes hurt Mary's feet, too.

All the wood that Pa had chopped was gone, and Mary and Laura picked up the scattered chips. The cold bit their noses and their fingers while they pried the last chips from the frozen ground. Wrapped in shawls, they went searching under the willows, picking up the little dead branches that made a poor fire.

Then one afternoon Mrs. Nelson came visiting. She brought her baby Anna with her.

Mrs. Nelson was plump and pretty. Her hair was as golden as Mary's, her eyes were blue, and when she laughed, as she often did, she showed rows of very white teeth. Laura liked Mrs. Nelson, but she was not glad to see Anna.

Anna was a little larger than Carrie but she could not understand a word that Laura or Mary said, and they could not understand her. She talked Norwegian. It was no fun to play with her, and in the summertime Mary and Laura ran down to the creek when Mrs. Nelson and Anna came. But it was cold. They must stay in the warm house and play with Anna. Ma said so.

'Now girls,' Ma said, 'go get your dolls and play nicely with Anna.'

Laura brought the box of paper dolls that Ma had cut out of wrapping-paper, and they sat down to play on the floor by the open oven door. Anna laughed when she saw the paper dolls. She grabbed into the box, took out a paper lady, and tore her in two.

Laura and Mary were horrified. Carrie stared with round eyes. Ma and Mrs. Nelson went on talking and did not see Anna waving the halves of the paper lady and laughing. Laura put the cover on the paper-doll box, but in a little while Anna was tired of the torn paper lady and wanted another. Laura did not know what to do, and neither did Mary.

If Anna did not get what she wanted she bawled. She was little and she was company and they must not make her cry. But if she got the paper dolls she would tear them all up. Then Mary whispered, 'Get Charlotte. She can't hurt Charlotte.'

Laura scurried up the ladder while Mary kept Anna quiet. Darling Charlotte lay in her box under the eaves, smiling with her red yarn mouth and her shoe-button eyes. Laura lifted her carefully and smoothed her wavy black-yarn hair and her skirts. Charlotte had no feet, and her hands were only stitched on the flat ends of her arms, because she was a rag doll. But Laura loved her dearly.

Charlotte had been Laura's very own since Christmas morning long ago in the Big Woods of Wisconsin.

Laura carried her down the ladder, and Anna shouted for her. Laura put Charlotte carefully in Anna's arms. Anna hugged her tight. But hugging could not hurt Charlotte. Laura watched anxiously while Anna tugged at Charlotte's shoe-button eyes and pulled her wavy yarn hair, and even banged her against the floor. But Anna could not really hurt Charlotte, and Laura meant to straighten her skirts and her hair when Anna went away.

At last that long visit was ended. Mrs. Nelson was going and taking Anna. Then a terrible thing happened. Anna would not give up Charlotte.

Perhaps she thought Charlotte was hers. Maybe she told her mother that Laura had given her Charlotte. Mrs. Nelson smiled. Laura tried to take Charlotte, and Anna howled.

'I want my doll!' Laura said. But Anna hung on to Charlotte and kicked and bawled.

'For shame, Laura,' Ma said, 'Anna's little and she's company. You are too big to play with dolls, anyway. Let Anna have her.'

Laura had to mind Ma. She stood at the window and saw Anna skipping down the knoll, swinging Charlotte by one arm.

'For shame, Laura,' Ma said again. 'A great girl like you, sulking about a rag doll. Stop it, this minute. You don't want that doll, you hardly ever played with it. You must not be so selfish.'

Laura quietly climbed the ladder and sat down on her box by the window. She did not cry, but she felt crying inside her because Charlotte was gone. Pa was not there, and Charlotte's box was empty. The wind went howling by the eaves. Everything was empty and cold.

'I'm sorry, Laura,' Ma said that night. 'I wouldn't have given your doll away if I'd known you care so much. But we must not think only of ourselves. Think how happy you've made Anna.'

Next morning Mr. Nelson came driving up with a load of Pa's wood that he had cut. He worked all day, chopping wood for Ma, and the woodpile was big again.

'You see how good Mr. Nelson is to us,' said Ma. 'The Nelsons are real good neighbours. Now aren't you glad you gave Anna your doll?'

'No, Ma,' said Laura. Her heart was crying all the time for Pa and for Charlotte.

Cold rains fell again, and froze. No more letters came from Pa. Ma thought he must have started to come home. In the night Laura listened to the wind and wondered where Pa was. Often in the mornings the woodpile was full of driven snow, and still Pa did not come. Every Saturday afternoon Laura put on her stockings and shoes, wrapped herself in Ma's big shawl, and went to the Nelsons'.

She knocked and asked if Mr. Nelson had got a letter for Ma. She would not go in, she did not want to see Charlotte there. Mrs. Nelson said that no letter had come, and Laura thanked her and went home.

One stormy day she caught sight of something in the Nelsons' barnyard. She stood still and looked. It was Charlotte, drowned and frozen in a puddle. Anna had thrown Charlotte away.

Laura could hardly go on to the door. She could hardly

speak to Mrs. Nelson. Mrs. Nelson said the weather was so bad that Mr. Nelson had not gone to town, but he would surely go next week. Laura said, 'Thank you, ma'am,' and turned away.

Sleety rain was beating down on Charlotte. Anna had

scalped her. Charlotte's beautiful wavy hair was ripped loose, and her smiling yarn mouth was torn and bleeding red on her cheek. One shoe-button eye was gone. But she was Charlotte.

Laura snatched her up and hid her under the shawl.

She ran panting against the angry wind and the sleet, all the way home. Ma started up, frightened, when she saw Laura.

'What is it! What is it? Tell me!' Ma said.

'Mr. Nelson didn't go to town,' Laura answered. 'But, oh, Ma—look.'

'What on earth?' said Ma.

'It's Charlotte,' Laura said. 'I—I stole her. I don't care, Ma, I don't care if I did!'

'There, there, don't be so excited,' said Ma. 'Come here and tell me all about it,' and she drew Laura down on her lap in the rocking chair.

They decided that it had not been wrong for Laura to take back Charlotte. It had been a terrible experience for Charlotte, but Laura had rescued her and Ma promised to make her as good as new.

Ma ripped off her torn hair and the bits of her mouth and her remaining eye and her face. They thawed Charlotte and wrung her out, and Ma washed her thoroughly clean and starched and ironed her while Laura chose from the scrap-bag a new, pale pink face for her and new button eyes.

That night when Laura went to bed she laid Charlotte in her box. Charlotte was clean and crisp, her red mouth smiled, her eyes shone black, and she had golden-brown yarn hair braided in two wee braids and tied with blue yarn bows.

Laura went to sleep cuddled against Mary under the patchwork comforters. The wind was howling and sleety rain beat on the roof. It was so cold that Laura and Mary pulled the comforters over their heads.

A terrific crash woke them. They were scared in the dark under the comforters. Then they heard a loud voice downstairs. It said,

'I declare! I dropped that armful of wood, didn't I?'

Ma was laughing, 'You did that on purpose, Charles, to wake up the girls.'

Laura flew screaming out of bed and screaming down the ladder. She jumped into Pa's arms, and so did Mary. Then what a racket of talking, laughing, jumping up and down!

Pa's blue eyes twinkled. His hair stood straight up. He was wearing new, whole boots. He had walked two hundred miles from eastern Minnesota. He had walked from town in the night, in the storm. Now he was here!

'For shame, girls, in your nightgowns!' said Ma. 'Go dress yourselves. Breakfast is almost ready.'

They dressed faster than ever before. They tumbled down the ladder and hugged Pa, and washed their hands and faces and hugged Pa, and smoothed their hair and hugged him. Jack waggled in circles and Carrie pounded the table with her spoon and sang, 'Pa's come home! Pa's come home!'

At last they were all at the table. Pa said he had been too busy, towards the last, to write. He said, 'They kept us humping on that thresher from before dawn till after dark. And when I could start home, I didn't stop to write. I didn't bring any presents, either, but I've got money to buy them.'

'The best present you could bring us, Charles, was coming home,' Ma told him.

After breakfast Pa went to see the stock. They all went with him and Jack stayed close at his heels. Pa was pleased that Sam and David and Spot looked so well. He said he couldn't have taken better care of everything, himself. Ma told him that Mary and Laura had been a great help to her.

'Gosh!' Pa said. 'It's good to be home.' Then he asked, 'What's the matter with your feet, Laura?'

She had forgotten her feet. She could walk without limping when she remembered to. She said, 'My shoes hurt, Pa.'

In the house, Pa sat down and took Carrie on his knee. Then he reached down and felt Laura's shoes.

'Ouch! My toes are tight!' Laura exclaimed.

'I should say they are!' said Pa. 'Your feet have grown since last winter. How are yours, Mary?'

Mary said her toes were tight, too.

'Take off your shoes, Mary,' said Pa. 'And Laura, you put them on.'

Mary's shoes did not pinch Laura's feet. They were good shoes, without one rip or hole in them.

'They will look almost like new when I have greased them well,' said Pa. 'Mary must have new shoes. Laura can wear Mary's, and Laura's shoes can wait for Carrie to grow to them. It won't take her long. Now what else is lacking, Caroline? Think what we need, and we'll get what we can of it. Just as soon as I can hitch up we're all going to town!'

30

Going to Town

H OW THEY HURRIED and scurried then! They
dressed in their winter best, bundled up in coats
and shawls, and climbed into the wagon. The sun
shone bright and the frosty air nipped their noses. Sleet
sparkled on the frozen-hard ground.

Pa was on the wagon seat, with Ma and Carrie snug
beside him. Laura and Mary wrapped their shawls
around each other and snuggled together on their blanket
in the bottom of the wagon. Jack sat on the doorstep and
watched them go; he knew they would come back soon.

Even Sam and David seemed to know that everything
was all right, now that Pa was home again. They trotted
gaily, till Pa said, 'Whoa!' and hitched them to the
hitching-posts in front of Mr. Fitch's store.

First, Pa paid Mr. Fitch part of the money he owed Mr.
Fitch for the boards that built the house. Then, he paid for
the flour and sugar that Mr. Nelson had brought to Ma
while Pa was gone. Next, Pa counted the money that was
left, and he and Ma bought Mary's shoes.

The shoes were so new and shining on Mary's feet that
Laura felt it was not fair that Mary was the oldest. Mary's
shoes would always fit Laura, and Laura would never
have new shoes. Then Ma said, 'Now, a dress for Laura.'

Laura hurried to Ma at the counter. Mr. Fitch was
taking down bolts of beautiful woollen cloth.

The winter before, Ma had let out every tuck and seam

in Laura's winter dress. This winter it was very short, and there were holes in the sleeves where Laura's elbows had gone through them because they were so tight. Ma had patched them neatly, and the patches did not show, but in that dress Laura felt skimpy and patched. Still, she had not dreamed of a whole new dress.

'What do you think of this golden-brown flannel, Laura?' Ma asked.

Laura could not speak. Mr. Fitch said, 'I guarantee it will wear well.'

Ma laid some narrow red braid across the golden-brown, saying, 'I think three rows of this braid, around the neckband and the cuffs and the waistband. What do you think, Laura? Would that be pretty?'

'Oh yes, Ma!' Laura said. She looked up, and her eyes and Pa's bright blue eyes danced together.

'Get it, Caroline,' said Pa. Mr. Fitch measured off the beautiful golden-brown flannel and the red braid.

Then Mary must have a new dress, but she did not like anything there. So they all crossed the street to Mr. Oleson's store. There they found dark blue flannel and narrow gilt braid, which was just what Mary wanted.

Mary and Laura were admiring it while Mr. Oleson measured, when Nellie Oleson came in. She was wearing a little fur shoulder cape.

'Hello!' she said, and she sniffed at the blue flannel. She said it was all right for country folks. Then she turned to show off her fur, and said, 'See what *I* got!'

They looked at it, and Nellie asked, 'Don't you wish you had a fur cape, Laura? But your Pa couldn't buy you one. Your Pa's not a storekeeper.'

Laura dared not slap Nellie. She was so angry that she could not speak. She did turn her back, and Nellie went away laughing.

Ma was buying warm cloth to make a cloak for Carrie. Pa was buying navy beans and flour and cornmeal and salt and sugar and tea. Then he must get the kerosene-can filled, and stop at the post-office. It was after noon, and growing colder, before they left town, so Pa hurried Sam and David and they trotted swiftly all the way home.

After the dinner dishes were washed and put away, Ma opened the bundles and they all enjoyed looking their fill at the pretty dressgoods.

'I'll make your dresses as quickly as I can, girls,' said Ma. 'Because now that Pa is home we'll all be going to Sunday-school again.'

'Where's that grey challis you got for yourself, Caroline?' Pa asked her. Ma flushed pink and her head bowed while Pa looked at her. 'You mean to say you didn't get it?' he said.

Ma flashed at him. 'What about that new overcoat for yourself, Charles?'

Pa looked uncomfortable. 'I know, Caroline,' he said. 'But there won't be any crops next year when those grass-hopper eggs hatch, and it's a long time till I can maybe get some work, next harvest. My old coat is good enough.'

'That's just what I thought,' said Ma, smiling at him.

After supper, when night and lamplight came, Pa took his fiddle out of the box and tuned it lovingly.

'I have missed this,' he said, looking around at them all. Then he began to play. He played 'When Johnnie Comes Marching Home.' He played 'The sweet little girl, the pretty little girl, the girl I left behind me!' He played and sang 'My Old Kentucky Home' and 'Swanee River.' Then he played and they all sang with him,

''Mid pleasures and palaces though we may roam,
    Be it ever so humble, there's no place like home.'

31

Surprise

THAT WAS ANOTHER mild winter without much snow. It was still grasshopper weather. But chill winds blew, the sky was grey, and the best place for little girls was in the cosy house.

Pa was gone outdoors all day. He hauled logs and chopped them into wood for the stove. He followed frozen Plum Creek far upstream where nobody lived, and set traps along the banks for muskrat and otter and mink.

Every morning Laura and Mary studied their books and worked sums on the slate. Every afternoon Ma heard their lessons. She said they were good little scholars, and she was sure that when they went to school again they would find they had kept up with their classes.

Every Sunday they went to Sunday-school. Laura saw Nellie Oleson showing off her fur cape. She remembered what Nellie had said about Pa, and she burned hot inside. She knew that hot feeling was wicked. She knew she must forgive Nellie, or she would never be an angel. She thought hard about the pictures of beautiful angels in the big paper-covered Bible at home. But they wore long white nightgowns. Not one of them wore a fur cape.

One happy Sunday was the Sunday when the Reverend Alden came from eastern Minnesota to preach in this Western church. He preached for a long time, while Laura looked at his soft blue eyes and watched his beard

160

wagging. She hoped he would speak to her after church. And he did.

'Here are my little country girls, Mary and Laura!' he said. He remembered their names.

Laura was wearing her new dress that day. The skirt was long enough, and the sleeves were long, too. They made her coat sleeves look shorter than ever, but the red braid on the cuffs was pretty.

'What a pretty new dress, Laura!' the Reverend Alden said.

Laura almost forgave Nellie Oleson that day. Then came Sundays when the Reverend Alden stayed at his own far church and in Sunday-school Nellie Oleson turned up her nose at Laura and flounced her shoulders under the fur cape. Hot wickedness boiled up in Laura again.

One afternoon Ma said there would be no lessons, because they must all get ready to go to town that night. Laura and Mary were astonished.

'But we never go to town at night!' Mary said.

'There must always be a first time,' said Ma.

'But why must there be, Ma?' Laura asked. 'Why are we going to town at night?'

'It's a surprise,' said Ma. 'Now, no more questions. We must all take baths, and be our very nicest.'

In the middle of the week, Ma brought in the washtub and heated water for Mary's bath. Then again for Laura's bath, and again for Carrie's. There had never been such scrubbing and scampering, such a changing to fresh drawers and petticoats, such brushing of shoes and braiding of hair and tying on of hair ribbons. There had never been such a wondering.

Supper was early. After supper, Pa bathed in the bedroom. Laura and Mary put on their new dresses. They knew better than to ask any more questions, but they wondered and whispered together.

The wagon box was full of clean hay. Pa put Mary and Laura in it and wrapped blankets around them. He climbed to the seat beside Ma and drove away towards town.

The stars were small and frosty in the dark sky. The horses' feet clippety-clopped and the wagon rattled over the hard ground.

Pa heard something else. 'Whoa!' he said, pulling up the reins. Sam and David stopped. There was nothing but vast, dark coldness and stillness pricked by the stars. Then the stillness blossomed into the loveliest sound.

Two clear notes sounded, and sounded again and again.

No one moved. Only Sam and David tinkled their bits together and breathed. Those two notes went on, full and loud, soft and low. They seemed to be the stars singing.

Too soon Ma murmured, 'We'd better be getting on, Charles,' and the wagon rattled on. Still through its rattling Laura could hear those swaying notes.

'Oh, Pa, what is it?' she asked, and Pa said, 'It's the new church bell, Laura.'

It was for this that Pa had worn his old patched boots.

The town seemed asleep. The stores were dark as Pa drove past them. Then Laura exclaimed, 'Oh, look at the church! How pretty the church is!'

The church was full of light. Light spilled out of all its windows and ran out into the darkness from the door when it opened to let someone in. Laura almost jumped out from under the blankets before she remembered that she must never stand up in the wagon when the horses were going.

Pa drove to the church steps and helped them all out. He told them to go in, but they waited in the cold until

he had covered Sam and David with their blankets. Then he came, and they all went into the church together.

Laura's mouth fell open and her eyes stretched to look at what she saw. She held Mary's hand tightly and they followed Ma and Pa. They sat down. Then Laura could look with all her might.

Standing in front of the crowded benches was a tree. Laura decided it must be a tree. She could see its trunk and branches. But she had never before seen such a tree.

Where leaves would be in summer, there were clusters and streamers of thin green paper. Thick among them hung little sacks made of pink mosquito-bar. Laura was almost sure that she could see candy in them. From the branches hung packages wrapped in coloured paper, red packages and pink packages and yellow packages, all tied with coloured string. Silk scarves were draped among them. Red mittens hung by the cord that would go around your neck and keep them from being lost if you were wearing them. A pair of new shoes hung by their heels from a branch. Lavish strings of white popcorn were looped over all this.

Under the tree and leaning against it were all kinds of things. Laura saw a crinkly-bright washboard, a wooden tub, a churn and dasher, a sled made of new boards, a shovel, a long-handled pitchfork.

Laura was too excited to speak. She squeezed Mary's hand tighter and tighter, and she looked up at Ma, wanting so much to know what that was. Ma smiled down at her and answered. 'That is a Christmas tree, girls. Do you think it is pretty?'

They could not answer. They nodded while they kept on looking at the wonderful tree. They were hardly even surprised to know that this was Christmas, though they had not expected Christmas yet because there was not enough snow. Just then Laura saw the most wonderful thing of all. From a far branch of that tree hung a little fur cape, and a muff to match!

The Reverend Alden was there. He preached about Christmas, but Laura was looking at that tree and she could not hear what he said. Everyone stood up to sing and Laura stood up, but she could not sing. Not a sound would come out of her throat. In the whole world, there couldn't be a store so wonderful to look at as that tree.

After the singing, Mr. Tower and Mr. Beadle began taking things off it, and reading out names. Mrs. Tower and Miss Beadle brought those things down past the benches, and gave them to the person whose name was on them.

Everything on that tree was a Christmas present for somebody!

When Laura knew that, the lamps and people and voices and even the tree began to whirl. They whirled faster, noisier, and more excited. Someone gave her a pink mosquito-bar bag. It did have candy in it, and a big popcorn ball. Mary had one, too. So did Carrie. Every girl and boy had one. Then Mary had a pair of blue mittens. Then Laura had a red pair.

Ma opened a big package, and there was a warm, big, brown-and-red plaid shawl for her. Pa got a woolly muffler. Then Carrie had a rag doll with a china head. She screamed for joy. Through the laughing and talking and rustling of papers Mr. Beadle and Mr. Tower went on shouting names.

The little fur cape and muff still hung on the tree, and Laura wanted them. She wanted to look at them as long as she could. She wanted to know who got them. They could not be for Nellie Oleson who already had a fur cape.

Laura did not expect anything more. But to Mary came

a pretty little booklet with Bible pictures in it, from Mrs. Tower.

Mr. Tower was taking the little fur cape and the muff from the tree. He read a name, but Laura could not hear it through all the joyful noise. She lost sight of the cape and muff among all the people. They were gone now.

Then to Carrie came a cunning little brown-spotted white china dog. But Carrie's arms and her eyes were full of her doll. So Laura held and stroked and laughed over the sleek little dog.

'Merry Christmas, Laura!' Miss Beadle said, and in Laura's hand she put a beautiful little box. It was made of snow-white, gleaming china. On its top stood a wee, gold-coloured tea pot and a gold-coloured tiny cup in a gold-coloured saucer.

The top of the box lifted off. Inside was a nice place to keep a breast-pin, if some day Laura had a breast-pin. Ma said it was a jewel-box.

There had never been such a Christmas as this. It was such a large, rich Christmas, the whole church full of Christmas. There were so many lamps, so many people, so much noise and laughter, and so many happinesses in it. Laura felt full and bursting, as if that whole big rich Christmas were inside her, and her mittens and her beautiful jewel-box with the wee gold cup-and-saucer and tea-pot, and her candy and her popcorn ball. And suddenly someone said, 'These are for you, Laura.'

Mrs. Tower stood smiling, holding out the little fur cape and muff.

'For me?' Laura said. 'For me?' Then everything else vanished while with both arms she hugged the soft furs.

She hugged them tighter and tighter, trying to believe they were really hers, that silky-soft little brown fur cape and the muff.

All around her Christmas went on, but Laura knew only the softness of those furs. People were going home. Carrie was standing on the bench while Ma fastened her coat and tied her hood more snugly. Ma was saying, 'Thank you so much for the shawl, Brother Alden. It is just what I needed.'

Pa said, 'And I thank you for the muffler. It will feel good when I come to town in the cold.'

The Reverend Alden sat down on the bench and asked, 'And does Mary's coat fit?'

Laura had not noticed Mary's coat until then. Mary had on a new dark-blue coat. It was long, and its sleeves came to Mary's wrists. Mary buttoned it up, and it fitted.

'And how does this little girl like her furs?' the Reverend Alden smiled. He drew Laura between his knees. He laid the fur cape around her shoulders and fastened it at the throat. He put the cord of the muff around her neck, and her hands went inside the silky muff.

'There!' the Reverend Alden said. 'Now my little country girls will be warm when they come to Sunday-school.'

'What do you say, Laura?' Ma asked, but the Reverend Alden said, 'There is no need. The way her eyes are shining is enough.'

Laura could not speak. The golden-brown fur cuddled her neck and softly hugged her shoulders. Down her front it hid the threadbare fastenings of her coat. The muff came far up her wrists and hid the shortness of her coat sleeves.

'She's a little brown bird with red trimmings,' the Reverend Alden said.

Then Laura laughed. It was true. Her hair and her coat, her dress and the wonderful furs, were brown. Her hood and mittens and the braid on her dress were red.

'I'll tell my church people back East about our little brown bird,' said the Reverend Alden. 'You see, when I told them about our church out here, they said they must send a box for the Christmas tree. They all gave things they had. The little girls who sent your furs and Mary's coat needed larger ones.'

'Thank you, sir,' said Laura. 'And please, sir, tell them thank you, too.' For when she could speak, her manners were as nice as Mary's.

Then they all said good night and Merry Christmas to the Reverend Alden. Mary was so beautiful in her Christmas coat. Carrie was so pretty on Pa's arm. Pa and Ma were smiling so happily, and Laura was all gladness.

Mr. and Mrs. Oleson were going home, too. Mr. Oleson's arms were full of things, and so were Nellie's and Willie's. No wickedness boiled up in Laura now; she only felt a little bit of mean gladness.

'Merry Christmas, Nellie,' Laura said. Nellie stared, while Laura walked quietly on, with her hands snuggled deep in the soft muff. Her cape was prettier than Nellie's, and Nellie had no muff.

32

Grasshoppers Walking

AFTER CHRISTMAS THERE were a few snowy Sundays but Pa made a bobsled of split willows and they all went to Sunday-school, snug in the new coat and the furs, the shawl and muffler.

One morning Pa said the chinook was blowing. The chinook was a warm wind from the north-west. In a day it melted the snow away, and Plum Creek was running full. Then came rains, pouring day and night. Plum Creek roared humping down its middle and swirled far beyond its low banks.

Then the air was mild, and the creek was tame again. Suddenly the plums and the willows blossomed and their new leaves uncurled. The prairies were green with grass, and Mary and Laura and Carrie ran barefooted over the fresh softness.

Every day was warmer than the day before, till hot summer came. It was time for Laura and Mary to go to school, but they did not go that year, because Pa must go away again and Ma wanted them at home with her. The summer was very hot. Dry, hot winds blew and there was no rain.

One day when Pa came in to dinner he said, 'The grasshoppers are hatching. This hot sun is bringing them out of the eggs and up through the ground like corn popping.'

Laura ran out to see. The grass on the knoll was hopping full of tiny green things. Laura caught one in her

hands and looked at it. Its wee, small wings and its tiny
legs and its little head and even its eyes were the colour
of the grass. It was so very tiny and so perfect. Laura
could hardly believe it would ever be a big, brown, ugly
grasshopper.

'They'll be big, fast enough,' said Pa. 'Eating every
growing thing.'

Day by day more and more grasshoppers hatched out
of the ground. Green grasshoppers of all sizes were swarming everywhere and eating. The wind could not blow loud
enough to hide the sound of their jaws, nipping, gnawing,
chewing.

They ate all the green garden rows. They ate the green
potato tops. They ate the grass, and the willow leaves, and
the green plum thickets and the small green plums. They
ate the whole prairie bare and brown. And they grew.

They grew large and brown and ugly. Their big eyes
bulged and their horny legs took them hopping everywhere. Thick over all the ground they were hopping, and
Laura and Mary stayed in the house.

There was no rain, and the days went by hotter and
hotter, uglier and uglier and filled with the sound of grasshoppers until it seemed more than could be borne.

'Oh, Charles,' Ma said one morning, 'seems to me I just
can't bear one more day of this.'

Ma was sick. Her face was white and thin, and she sat
down tired as she spoke.

Pa did not answer. For days he had been going out and
coming in with a still, tight face. He did not sing or
whistle any more. It was worst of all when he did not
answer Ma. He walked to the door and stood looking
out.

Even Carrie was still. They could feel the heat of the
day beginning, and hear the grasshoppers. But the grass-

hoppers were making a new sound. Laura ran to look out
at them, excited, and Pa was excited, too.

'Caroline!' he said. 'Here's a strange thing. Come look!'

All across the dooryard the grasshoppers were walking
shoulder to shoulder and end to end, so crowded that the
ground seemed to be moving. Not a single one hopped.
Not one turned its head. As fast as they could go, they
were all walking west.

Ma stood beside Pa, looking. Mary asked, 'Oh, Pa,
what does it mean?' and Pa said, 'I don't know.'

He shaded his eyes and looked far to west and east. 'It's
the same, as far as the eye can see. The whole ground is
crawling, crawling west.'

Ma whispered, 'Oh, if they would all go away!'

They all stood looking at the strange sight. Only Carrie
climbed on to her high chair and beat the table with her
spoon.

'In a minute, Carrie,' Ma said. She kept on watching
the grasshoppers walking by. There was no space between
them and no end to them.

'I want my breakfast!' Carrie shouted. No one else
moved. Finally Carrie shouted, almost crying, 'Ma! Ma!'

'There, you shall have your breakfast,' Ma said, turning
around. Then she cried out, 'My goodness!'

Grasshoppers were walking over Carrie. They came
pouring in the eastern window, side by side and end to
end, across the window sill and down the wall and over
the floor. They went up the legs of the table and the
benches and Carrie's high stool. Under the table and
benches, and over the table and benches and Carrie, they
were walking west.

'Shut the window!' said Ma.

Laura ran on the grasshoppers to shut it. Pa went outdoors and around the house. He came in and said,

'Better shut the upstairs windows. Grasshoppers are as thick walking up the east side of the house as they are on the ground, and they are not going around the attic window. They are going right in.'

All up the wall and across the roof went the sound of their raspy claws crawling. The house seemed full of them. Ma and Laura swept them up and threw them out the western window. None came in from the west, though the whole western side of the house was covered with grasshoppers that had walked over the roof and were walking down to the ground and going on west with the others.

That whole day long the grasshoppers walked west. All the next day they went on walking west. And all the third day they walked without stopping.

No grasshopper turned out of its way for anything.

They walked steadily over the house. They walked over the stable. They walked over Spot until Pa shut her in the stable. They walked into Plum Creek and drowned, and those behind kept on walking in and drowning until dead grasshoppers choked the creek and filled the water and live grasshoppers walked across on them.

All day the sun beat hot on the house. All day it was full of the crawling sound that went up the wall and over the roof and down. All day grasshoppers' heads with bulging eyes, and grasshoppers' legs clutching, were thick along the bottom edge of the shut windows; all day they tried to walk up the sleek glass and fell back, while thousands more pushed up and tried and fell.

Ma was pale and tight. Pa did not talk and his eyes could not twinkle. Laura could not shake the crawling sound out of her ears nor brush it off her skin.

The fourth day came and the grasshoppers went on walking. The sun shone hotter than ever, with a terribly bright light.

It was nearly noon when Pa came from the stable shouting: 'Caroline! Caroline! Look outdoors! The grasshoppers are flying!'

Laura and Mary ran to the door. Everywhere grasshoppers were spreading their wings and rising from the ground. More and more of them filled the air, flying higher and higher, till the sunshine dimmed and darkened and went out as it had done when the grasshoppers came.

Laura ran outdoors. She looked straight up at the sun through a cloud that seemed almost like snowflakes. It was a dark cloud, gleaming, glittering, shimmering bright and whiter as she looked higher and farther into it. And it was rising instead of falling.

The cloud passed over the sun and went on west until it could be seen no longer.

There was not a grasshopper left in the air or on the ground, except here and there a crippled one that could not fly but still hobbled westward.

The stillness was like the stillness after a storm.

Ma went into the house and threw herself down in the rocking-chair. 'My Lord!' she said. 'My Lord!' The words were praying, but they sounded like, 'Thank you!'

Laura and Mary sat on the doorstep. They could sit on the doorstep now; there were no grasshoppers.

'How still it is!' Mary said.

Pa leaned in the doorway and said, earnestly, 'I would like some one to tell me how they all knew at once that it was time to go, and how they knew which way was west and their ancestral home.'

But no one could tell him.

33

Wheels of Fire

ALL THE DAYS were peaceful after that July day when the grasshoppers flew away.

Rain fell and grass grew again over all the land that they had eaten bare and left brown and ugly. Ragweeds grew faster, and careless weeds, and the big, spreading tumbleweeds like bushes.

Willows and cottonwoods and plum thickets put out leaves again. There would be no fruit, for blossom-time was past. There would be no wheat. But wild hay was growing coarse in low places by the creek. Potatoes lived, and there were fish in the fish-trap.

Pa hitched Sam and David to Mr. Nelson's plough, and ploughed part of the weedy wheat-field. He ploughed a wide fire-break west of the house, from the creek to the creek again. On the field he sowed turnip seeds.

'It's late,' he said. 'The old folks say to sow turnips the twenty-fifth of July, wet or dry. But I guess the old folks didn't figure on grasshoppers. And likely there will be as many turnips as you and the girls can handle, Caroline. I won't be here to do it.'

He must go away to the East again, to work where there were harvests, for the house was not yet paid for and he must buy salt and cornmeal and sugar. He could not stay to cut the hay that Sam and David and Spot must have to eat next winter. But Mr. Nelson agreed to cut and stack Pa's wild hay for a share of it.

Then one early morning Pa went walking away. He went whistling out of sight, with his jumper-roll on his shoulder. But there was not one hole in his boots. He would not mind the walk, and some day he would come walking back again.

In the mornings after the chores and the housework were done, Laura and Mary studied their books. In the afternoons Ma heard their lessons. Then they might play or sew their seams, till time to meet the herd and bring Spot and her calf home. Then came chores again and supper and the supper dishes and bedtime.

After Mr. Nelson stacked Pa's hay by the stable, the days were warm on the sunny side of the stacks, but their shady sides were cool. The wind blew chill and the mornings were frosty.

One morning when Laura drove Spot and her calf to meet the herd, Johnny was having trouble with the cattle. He was trying to drive them out on the prairie to the west, where the frostbitten, brown grass was tall. The cattle did not want to go. They kept turning and dodging back.

Laura and Jack helped him drive them. The sun was coming up then and the sky was clear. But before Laura got back to the house, she saw a low cloud in the west. She wrinkled her nose and sniffed long and deep, and she remembered Indian Territory.

'Ma!' she called. Ma came outdoors and looked at the cloud.

'It's far away, Laura,' Ma said. 'Likely it won't come so far.'

All morning the wind blew out of the west. At noon it was blowing more strongly, and Ma and Mary and Laura stood in the dooryard and watched the dark cloud coming nearer.

'I wonder where the herd is,' Ma worried.

At last they could see a flickering brightness under the cloud.

'If the cows are safe across the creek we needn't worry,' said Ma. 'Fire can't cross that fire-break. Better come in the house, girls, and eat your dinner.'

She took Carrie into the house, but Laura and Mary looked just once more at the smoke rolling nearer. Then Mary pointed and opened her mouth but could not speak. Laura screamed, 'Ma! Ma! A wheel of fire!'

In front of the red-flickering smoke a wheel of fire came rolling swiftly, setting fire to the grass as it came. Another and another, another, came rolling fast before the wind. The first one was whirling across the fire-break.

With water-pail and mop Ma ran to meet it. She struck it with the wet mop and beat it out black on the ground. She ran to meet the next one, but more and more were coming.

'Stay back, Laura!' she said.

Laura stayed backed flat against the house, holding Mary's hand tight, and watching. In the house Carrie was crying because Ma had shut her in.

The wheels of fire came on, faster and faster. They were the big tumbleweeds, that had ripened round and dry and pulled up their small roots so that the wind would blow them far and scatter their seeds. Now they were burning, but still they rolled before the roaring wind and the roaring big fire that followed them.

Smoke swirled now around Ma where she ran, beating with her mop at those fiery swift wheels. Jack shivered against Laura's legs and tears ran out of her smarting eyes.

Mr. Nelson's grey colt came galloping and Mr. Nelson jumped off it at the stable. He grabbed a pitchfork and shouted: 'Run quick! Bring wet rags!' He went running to help Ma.

Laura and Mary ran to the creek with gunny sacks. They ran back with them sopping wet and Mr. Nelson put one on the pitchfork tines. Ma's pail was empty; they ran and filled it.

The wheels of fire were running up the knoll. Streaks of fire followed through the dry grass. Ma and Mr. Nelson fought them with the mop and the wet sacks.

'The hay-stacks! The hay-stacks!' Laura screamed. One wheel of fire had got to the hay-stacks. Mr. Nelson and Ma went running through the smoke. Another wheel came rolling over the black-burned ground to the house. Laura was so frightened that she did not know what she was doing. Carrie was in the house. Laura beat that burning wheel to death with a wet gunny sack.

Then there were no more wheels. Ma and Mr. Nelson had stopped the fire at the hay-stack. Bits of sooty hay and grass swirled in the air, while the big fire rushed to the fire-break.

It could not get across. It ran fast to the south, to the creek. It ran north and came to the creek there. It could not go any farther, so it dwindled down and died where it was.

The clouds of smoke were blowing away and the prairie fire was over. Mr. Nelson said he had gone on his grey colt after the cattle; they were safe on the other side of the creek.

'We are grateful to you, Mr. Nelson,' said Ma. 'You saved our place. The girls and I could never have done it alone.'

When he had gone away she said, 'There is nothing in the world so good as good neighbours. Come now, girls, and wash, and eat your dinner.'

34

Marks on the Slate

AFTER THE PRAIRIE fire the weather was so cold
that Ma said they must hurry to dig the potatoes
and pull the turnips before they froze.

She dug the potatoes while Mary and Laura picked
them up and carried them down to the cellar in pails. The
wind blew hard and sharp. They wore their shawls, but of
course not their mittens. Mary's nose was red and Laura's
was icy cold, and their hands were stiff and their feet were
numb. But they were glad they had so many potatoes.

It was good to thaw by the stove when the chores were
done, and to smell the warm smells of potatoes boiling and
fish frying. It was good to eat and to go to bed.

Then in dark, gloomy weather they pulled the turnips.
That was harder than picking up potatoes. The turnips
were big and stubborn, and often Laura pulled till she
sat down hard when the turnip came up.

All the juicy green tops must be cut off with the butcher
knife. The juice wet their hands and the wind chapped
them till they cracked and bled, and Ma made a salve
of lard and bees-wax melted together, to rub on their
hands at night.

But Spot and her calf ate the juicy turnip tops and
saved them. And it was good to know that there were
turnips enough in the cellar to last all winter long. There
would be boiled turnips, and mashed turnips and creamed
turnips. And in the winter evenings a plate of raw turnips

would be on the table by the lamp; they would peel off the thick rinds and eat the raw turnips in crisp, juicy slices.

One day they put the last turnip in the cellar, and Ma said, 'Well, it can freeze now.'

Sure enough, that night the ground froze, and in the morning snow was falling thick outside the windows.

Now Mary thought of a way to count the days until Pa would come home. His last letter had said that two more weeks would finish the threshing where he was. Mary brought out the slate, and on it she made a mark for each day of one week, seven marks. Under them she made another mark for each day of the next week, seven more marks.

The last mark was for the day he would come. But when they showed the slate to Ma, she said, 'Better make marks for another week, for Pa to walk home on.'

So Mary slowly made seven marks more. Laura did not like to see so many marks between now and the time that Pa would come home. But every night before they went to bed, Mary rubbed out one mark. That was one day gone.

Every morning Laura thought, 'This whole day must go by before Mary can rub out another mark.'

Outdoors smelled good in the chilly mornings. The sun had melted away the snow, but the ground was hard and frosty. Plum Creek was still awake. Brown leaves were floating away on the water under the wintry blue sky.

At night it was cosy to be in the lamplit house by the warm stove. Laura played with Carrie and Jack on the clean, smooth floor. Ma sat comfortably mending, and Mary's book was spread under the lamp.

'It's bedtime, girls,' Ma said, taking off her thimble. Then Mary rubbed out one more mark, and put the slate away.

One night she rubbed out the first day of the last week. They all watched her do it, and Mary said, as she put the slate away, 'Pa is walking home now! Those are the marks he will walk on.'

In the corner Jack suddenly made a glad sound, as if he understood her. He ran to the door. He stood up against the door, scratching and whining and waggling. Then Laura heard, faintly whistling through the wind, 'When Johnny Comes Marching Home.'

'It's Pa! Pa!' she shrieked and tore the door open and ran pell-mell down through the windy dark with Jack bounding ahead.

'Hullo, half-pint!' Pa said, hugging her tight. 'Good dog, Jack!' Lamplight streamed from the door and Mary was coming, and Ma and Carrie. 'How's my little one?' Pa said, giving Carrie a toss. 'Here's my big girl,' and he pulled Mary's braid. 'Give me a kiss, Caroline, if you can reach me through these wild Indians.'

Then there was supper to get for Pa, and no one thought of going to bed. Laura and Mary told him everything at once, about the wheels of fire and potatoes and turnips and how big Spot's calf was and how far they had studied in their books, and Mary said: 'But, Pa, you can't be here. You didn't walk off the marks on the slate.'

She showed him the marks still there, the marks he was to walk on.

'I see!' said Pa. 'But you did not rub out the marks for the days it took my letter to come so far. I hurried fast all the way, too, for they say it's already a hard winter in the north. What do we need to get in town, Caroline?'

Ma said they did not need anything. They had eaten so many fish and potatoes that the flour was still holding out, and the sugar, and even the tea. Only the salt was low, and it would last several days.

'Then I'd better get the wood up before we go to town,' said Pa. 'I don't like the sound of that wind, and they tell me that Minnesota blizzards come up fast and sudden. I heard of some folks that went to town and a blizzard came up so quickly they couldn't get back. Their children at home burned all the furniture, but they froze stark stiff before the blizzard cleared up enough so the folks could get home.'

35

Keeping House

Now in the daytimes Pa was driving the wagon up and down Plum Creek, and bringing load after load of logs to the pile by the door. He cut down old plum trees and old willows and cotton-woods, leaving the little ones to grow. He hauled them and stacked them, and chopped and split them into stove wood, till he had a big woodpile.

With his short-handled axe in his belt, his traps on his arm, and his gun against his shoulder, he walked far up Plum Creek, setting traps for muskrat and mink and otter and fox.

One evening at supper Pa said he had found a beaver meadow. But he did not set traps there because so few beavers were left. He had seen a fox and shot at it, but missed.

'I am all out of practice hunting,' he said. 'It's a fine place we have here, but there isn't much game. Makes a fellow think of places out West where——'

'Where there are no schools for the children, Charles,' said Ma.

'You're right, Caroline. You usually are,' Pa said. 'Listen to that wind. We'll have a storm tomorrow.'

But the next day was mild as spring. The air was soft and warm and the sun shone brightly. In the middle of the morning Pa came to the house.

'Let's have an early dinner and take a walk to town this afternoon,' he said to Ma. 'This is too nice a day for you to stay indoors. Time enough for that when winter really comes.'

'But the children,' said Ma. 'We can't take Carrie and walk so far.'

'Shucks!' Pa laughed at her. 'Mary and Laura are great girls now. They can take care of Carrie for one afternoon.'

'Of course we can, Ma,' said Mary; and Laura said, 'Of course we can!'

They watched Pa and Ma starting gaily away. Ma was so pretty, in her brown-and-red Christmas shawl, with her brown knit hood tied under her chin, and she stepped so quickly and looked up at Pa so merrily that Laura thought she was like a bird.

Then Laura swept the floor while Mary cleared the table. Mary washed the dishes and Laura wiped them and put them in the cupboard. They put the red-checked cloth on the table. Now the whole long afternoon was before them and they could do as they pleased.

First, they decided to play school. Mary said she must be Teacher, because she was older and besides she knew more. Laura knew that was true. So Mary was Teacher and she liked it, but Laura was soon tired of that play.

'I know,' Laura said. 'Let's both teach Carrie her letters.'

They sat Carrie on a bench and held the book before her, and both did their best. But Carrie did not like it. She would not learn the letters, so they had to stop that.

'Well,' said Laura, 'let's play keeping house.'

'We *are* keeping house,' said Mary. 'What is the use of playing it?'

The house was empty and still, with Ma gone. Ma was so quiet and gentle that she never made any noise, but now the whole house was listening for her.

Laura went outdoors for a while by herself, but she came back. The afternoon grew longer and longer. There was nothing at all to do. Even Jack walked up and down restlessly.

He asked to go out, but when Laura opened the door he would not go. He lay down and got up, and walked around and around the room. He came to Laura and looked at her earnestly.

'What is it, Jack?' Laura asked him. He stared hard at her, but she could not understand, and he almost howled.

'Don't, Jack!' Laura told him, quickly. 'You scare me.'

'Is it something outdoors?' Mary wondered. Laura ran out, but on the doorstep Jack took hold of her dress and pulled her back. Outdoors was bitter cold. Laura shut the door.

'Look,' she said. 'The sunshine's dark. Are the grass-hoppers coming back?'

'Not in the winter-time, goosie,' said Mary. 'Maybe it's rain.'

'Goosie yourself!' Laura said back. 'It doesn't rain in the winter-time.'

'Well, snow, then! What's the difference?' Mary was angry and so was Laura. They would have gone on quarrelling, but suddenly there was no sunshine. They ran to look through the bedroom window.

A dark cloud with a fleecy white underside was rolling fast from the north-west.

Mary and Laura looked out of the front window. Surely it was time for Pa and Ma to come, but they were nowhere in sight.

'Maybe it's a blizzard,' said Mary.

'Like Pa told us about,' said Laura.

They looked at each other through the grey air. They were thinking of those children who froze stark stiff.

13

'The woodbox is empty,' said Laura.

Mary grabbed her. 'You can't!' said Mary. 'Ma told us to stay in the house if it stormed.' Laura jerked away and Mary said, 'Besides, Jack won't let you.'

'We've got to bring in wood before the storm gets here,' Laura told her. 'Hurry!'

They could hear a strange sound in the wind, like a far-away screaming. They put on their shawls and pinned them under their chins with their large shawl-pins. They put on their mittens.

Laura was ready first. She told Jack, 'We've got to bring in wood, Jack.' He seemed to understand. He went out with her and stayed close at her heels. The wind was colder than icicles. Laura ran to the woodpile, piled up a big armful of wood, and ran back, with Jack behind her. She could not open the door while she held the wood. Mary opened it for her.

Then they did not know what to do. The cloud was coming swiftly, and they must both bring in wood before the storm got there. They could not open the door when their arms were full of wood. They could not leave the door open and let the cold come in.

'I tan open the door,' said Carrie.

'You can't,' Mary said.

'I tan, too!' said Carrie, and she reached up both hands and turned the door knob. She could do it! Carrie was big enough to open the door.

Laura and Mary hurried fast, bringing in wood. Carrie opened the door when they came to it, and shut it behind them. Mary could carry larger armfuls, but Laura was quicker.

They filled the woodbox before it began to snow. The snow came suddenly with a whirling blast, and it was small hard grains like sand. It stung Laura's face where it struck. When Carrie opened the door, it swirled into the house in a white cloud.

Laura and Mary forgot that Ma had told them to stay in the house when it stormed. They forgot everything but bringing in wood. They ran frantically back and forth, bringing each time all the wood they could stagger under.

They piled wood around the woodbox and around the

stove. They piled it against the wall. They made the piles higher, and bigger.

Bang! they banged the door. They ran to the woodpile. Clop-clop-clop they stacked the wood on their arms. They ran to the door. Bump! it went open, and bang! they back-bumped it shut, and thumpity-thud-thump! they flung down the wood and ran back, outdoors, to the wood-pile, and panting back again.

They could hardly see the woodpile in the swirling whiteness. Snow was driven all in among the wood. They could hardly see the house, and Jack was a dark blob hurrying beside them. The hard snow scoured their faces. Laura's arms ached and her chest panted and all the time she thought, 'Oh, where is Pa? Where is Ma?' and she felt 'Hurry! Hurry!' and she heard the wind screeching.

The woodpile was gone. Mary took a few sticks and Laura took a few sticks and there were no more. They ran to the door together, and Laura opened it and Jack bounded in. Carrie was at the front window, clapping her hands and squealing. Laura dropped her sticks of wood and turned just in time to see Pa and Ma burst, running, out of the whirling whiteness of snow.

Pa was holding Ma's hand and pulling to help her run. They burst into the house and slammed the door and stood panting, covered with snow. No one said anything while Pa and Ma looked at Laura and Mary, who stood all snowy in shawls and mittens.

At last Mary said in a small voice, 'We did go out in the storm, Ma. We forgot.'

Laura's head bowed down and she said, 'We didn't want to burn up the furniture, Pa, and freeze stark stiff.'

'Well, I'll be darned!' said Pa. 'If they didn't move the whole woodpile in. All the wood I cut to last a couple of weeks.'

There, piled up in the house, was the whole woodpile. Melted snow was leaking out of it and spreading in puddles. A wet path went to the door, where snow lay unmelted.

Then Pa's great laugh rang out, and Ma's gentle smile shone warm on Mary and Laura. They knew they were forgiven for disobeying, because they had been wise to bring in wood, though perhaps not quite so much wood.

Sometime soon they would be old enough not to make any mistakes, and then they could always decide what to do. They would not have to obey Pa and Ma any more.

They bustled to take off Ma's shawl and hood and brush the snow from them and hang them up to dry. Pa hurried to the stable to do the chores before the storm grew worse. Then while Ma rested, they stacked the wood neatly as she told them, and they swept and mopped the floor.

The house was neat and cosy again. The tea-kettle hummed, the fire shone brightly from the draughts above the stove hearth. Snow swished against the windows.

Pa came in. 'Here is the little milk I could get here with. The wind blew it up out of the pail. Caroline, this is a terrible storm. I couldn't see an inch, and the wind comes from all directions at once. I thought I was on the path, but I couldn't see the house, and—well, I just barely bumped against the corner. Another foot to the left and I never would have got in.'

'*Charles!*' Ma said.

'Nothing to be scared about now,' said Pa. 'But if we hadn't run all the way from town and beat this storm here—' Then his eyes twinkled, he rumpled Mary's hair and pulled Laura's ear. 'I'm glad all this wood is in the house, too,' he said.

36
Prairie Winter

NEXT DAY THE storm was even worse. It could not be seen through the windows, for snow swished so thickly against them that the glass was like white glass. All around the house the wind was howling.

When Pa started to the stable, snow whirled thick into the lean-to, and outdoors was a wall of whiteness. He took down a coil of rope from a nail in the lean-to.

'I'm afraid to try it without something to guide me back,' he said. 'With this rope tied to the far end of the clothes-line I ought to reach the stable.'

They waited, frightened, till Pa came back. The wind had taken almost all the milk out of the pail, and Pa had to thaw by the stove before he could talk. He had felt his way along the clothes-line fastened to the lean-to, till he came to the clothes-line post. Then he tied an end of his rope to the post and went on, unwinding the rope from his arm as he went.

He could not see anything but the whirling snow. Suddenly something hit him, and it was the stable wall. He felt along it till he came to the door, and there he fastened the end of the rope.

So he did the chores and came back, holding on to the rope.

All day the storm lasted. The windows were white and the wind never stopped howling and screaming. It was pleasant in the warm house. Laura and Mary did their lessons, then Pa played the fiddle while Ma rocked and knitted, and bean soup simmered on the stove.

All night the storm lasted, and all the next day. Firelight danced out of the stove's draught, and Pa told stories and played the fiddle.

Next morning the wind was only whizzing, and the sun shone. Through the window Laura saw snow scudding before the wind in fast white swirls over the ground. The whole world looked like Plum Creek foaming in flood, only the flood was snow. Even the sunshine was bitter cold.

'Well, I guess the storm is over,' said Pa. 'If I can get to town tomorrow, I am going to lay in a supply of food.'

Next day the snow was in drifts on the ground. The wind blew only a smoke of snow up the sides and off the tops of the drifts. Pa drove to town and brought back big sacks of cornmeal, flour, sugar, and beans. It was enough food to last a long time.

'Seems strange to have to figure where meat is coming from,' Pa said. 'In Wisconsin we always had plenty of bear meat and venison, and in Indian Territory there were deer and antelope, jackrabbits, turkeys, and geese, all the meat a man could want. Here there are only little cotton-tail rabbits.'

'We will have to plan ahead and raise meat,' said Ma. 'Think how easy it will be to fatten our own meat, where we can raise such fields of grain for feed.'

'Yes,' Pa said. 'Next year we will raise a wheat crop, surely.'

Next day another blizzard came. Again that low, dark cloud rolled swiftly up from the north-west till it blotted out the sun and covered the whole sky and the wind went, howling and shrieking, whirling snow until nothing could be seen but a blur of whiteness.

Pa followed the rope to the stable and back. Ma cooked

and cleaned and mended and helped Mary and Laura with their lessons. They did the dishes, made their bed, and swept the floors, kept their hands and faces clean and neatly braided their hair. They studied their books and played with Carrie and Jack. They drew pictures on their slate, and taught Carrie to make her A B C's.

Mary was still sewing nine-patch blocks. Now Laura started a bear's-track quilt. It was harder than a nine-patch, because there were bias seams, very hard to make smooth. Every seam must be exactly right before Ma would let her make another, and often Laura worked several days on one short seam.

So they were busy all day long. And all the days ran together, with blizzard after blizzard. No sooner did one blizzard end with a day of cold sunshine, than another began. On the sunny day Pa worked quickly, chopping more wood, visiting his traps, pitching hay from the snowy stacks into the stable. Even though the sunny day was not Monday, Ma washed the clothes and hung them on the clothes-line to freeze dry. That day there were no lessons. Laura and Mary and Carrie, bundled stiff in thick wraps, could play outdoors in the sunshine.

Next day another blizzard came, but Pa and Ma had everything ready for it.

If the sunny day were Sunday, they could hear the church bell. Clear and sweet it rang through the cold, and they all stood outdoors and listened.

They could not go to Sunday-school; a blizzard might come before they could reach home. But every Sunday they had a little Sunday-school of their own.

Laura and Mary repeated their Bible verses. Ma read a Bible story and a psalm. Then Pa played hymns on the fiddle, and they all sang. They sang:

'When gloomy clouds across the sky
  Cast shadows o'er the land,
Bright rays of hope illume my path,
  For Jesus holds my hand.'

Every Sunday Pa played and they sang:

'Sweet Sabbath school more dear to me
  Than fairest palace dome,
My heart e'er turns with joy to thee,
  My own dear Sabbath home.'

37

The Long Blizzard

A storm was dying down at supper-time one day, and Pa said: 'Tomorrow I'm going to town. I need some tobacco for my pipe and I want to hear the news. Do you need anything, Caroline?'

'No, Charles,' said Ma. 'Don't go. These blizzards come up so fast.'

'There'll be no danger tomorrow,' said Pa. 'We've just had a three-days' blizzard. There's plenty of wood chopped to last through the next one, and I can take time to go to town now.'

'Well, if you think best,' Ma said. 'At least, Charles, promise me that you will stay in town if a storm comes up.'

'I wouldn't try to stir a step without safe hold of a rope, in one of these storms,' said Pa. 'But it is not like you, Caroline, to be afraid to have me go anywhere.'

'I can't help it,' Ma answered. 'I don't feel right about your going. I have a feeling—it's just foolishness, I guess.'

Pa laughed. 'I'll bring in the woodpile, just in case I do have to stay in town.'

He filled the woodbox and piled wood high around it. Ma urged him to put on an extra pair of socks, to keep his feet from being frost-bitten. So Laura brought the boot-jack and Pa pulled off his boots and drew another pair of socks over those he already wore. Ma gave him a new pair which she had just finished knitting of thick, warm wool.

'I do wish you had a buffalo overcoat,' said Ma. 'That old coat is worn so thin.'

'And I wish you had some diamonds,' said Pa. 'Don't you worry, Caroline. It won't be long till spring.'

Pa smiled at them while he buckled the belt of his old, threadbare overcoat and put on his warm felt cap.

'That wind is so bitter cold, Charles,' Ma worried. 'Do pull down the earflaps.'

'Not this morning!' said Pa. 'Let the wind whistle! Now you girls be good, all of you, till I come back.' And his eyes twinkled at Laura as he shut the door behind him.

After Laura and Mary had washed and wiped the dishes, swept the floor, made their bed, and dusted, they settled down with their books. But the house was so cosy and pretty that Laura kept looking up at it.

The black stove was polished till it gleamed. A kettle of beans was bubbling on its top and bread was baking in the oven. Sunshine slanted through the shining windows between the pink-edged curtains. The red-checked cloth was on the table. Beside the clock on its shelf stood Carrie's little brown-and-white dog, and Laura's sweet jewel-box. And the little pink-and-white shepherdess stood smiling on the wood-brown bracket.

Ma had brought her mending-basket to her rocking-chair by the window, and Carrie sat on the footstool by her knee. While Ma rocked and mended, she heard Carrie say her letters in the primer. Carrie told big A and little a, big B and little b, then she laughed and talked and looked at the pictures. She was still so little that she did not have to keep quiet and study.

The clock struck twelve. Laura watched its pendulum wagging, and the black hands moving on the round white face. It was time for Pa to come home. The beans were cooked, the bread was baked. Everything was ready for Pa's dinner.

Laura's eyes strayed to the window. She stared a moment before she knew that something was wrong with the sunshine.

'Ma!' she cried, 'the sun is a funny colour.'

Ma looked up from her mending, startled. She went quickly into the bedroom, where she could see the north-west, and she came quietly back.

'You may put away your books, girls,' she said. 'Bundle up and bring in more wood. If Pa hasn't started home he will stay in town and we will need more wood in the house.'

From the woodpile Laura and Mary saw the dark cloud coming. They hurried, they ran, but there was time only to get into the house with their armloads of wood before the storm came howling. It seemed angry that they had got the two loads of wood. Snow whirled so thickly that they could not see the doorstep, and Ma said:

'That will do for now. The storm can't get much worse, and Pa may come in a few minutes.'

Mary and Laura took off their wraps and warmed their cold-stiff hands. Then they waited for Pa.

The wind shrieked and howled and jeered around the house. Snow swished against the blank windows. The long black hand of the clock moved slowly around its face, the short hand moved to one, and then to two.

Ma dished up three bowls of the hot beans. She broke into pieces a small loaf of the fresh warm bread.

'Here, girls,' she said. 'You might as well eat your dinner. Pa must have stayed in town.'

She had forgotten to fill a bowl for herself. Then she forgot to eat until Mary reminded her. Even then she did not really eat; she said she was not hungry.

The storm was growing worse. The house trembled in the wind. Cold crept over the floor, and powdery snow was driven in around the windows and the doors that Pa had made so tight.

'Pa has surely stayed in town,' Ma said. 'He will stay there all night, and I'd better do the chores now.'

She drew on Pa's old, tall stable-boots. Her little feet were lost in them, but they would keep out the snow. She fastened Pa's jumper snug at her throat and belted it around her waist. She tied her hood and put on her mittens.

'May I go with you, Ma?' Laura asked.

'No,' said Ma. 'Now listen to me. Be careful of fire. Nobody but Mary is to touch the stove, no matter how long I am gone. Nobody is to go outdoors, or even open a door, till I come back.'

She hung the milk-pail on her arm, and reached through the whirling snow till she got hold of the clothes-line. She shut the back door behind her.

Laura ran to the darkened window, but she could not see Ma. She could see nothing but the whirling whiteness swishing against the glass. The wind screamed and howled and gibbered. There seemed to be voices in it.

Ma would go step by step, holding tight to the clothes-line. She would come to the post and go on, blind in the hard snow whirling and scratching her cheeks. Laura tried to think slowly, one step at a time, till now, surely, Ma bumped against the stable door.

Ma opened the door and blew in with the snow. She turned and pushed the door shut quickly, and dropped the latch into its notch. The stable would be warm from the heat of the animals, and steamy with their breath. It was quiet there; the storm was outside, and the sod walls were thick. Now Sam and David turned their heads and whickered to Ma. The cow coaxed, 'Moo-oo,' and the big calf cried, 'Baw!' The pullets were scratching here and there, and one of the hens was saying to herself, 'Crai-ai-kree-eek.'

Ma would clean all the stalls with the pitchfork. Forkful by forkful she threw the old bedding on the manure-pile. Then she took the hay they had left in their mangers, and spread it to make them clean beds.

From the hay-pile she pitched fresh hay into manger

after manger, till all four mangers were full. Sam and David and Spot and her calf munched the rustling good hay. They were not very thirsty, because Pa had watered them all before he went to town.

With the old knife that Pa kept by the turnip-pile Ma cut up turnips. She put some in each feedbox, and now the horses and cattle crunched the crisp turnips. Ma looked at the hens' water-dish to make sure they had water. She scattered a little corn for them, and gave them a turnip to peck.

Now she must be milking Spot.

Laura waited until she was sure that Ma was hanging up the milking-stool. Carefully fastening the stable door behind her, Ma came back towards the house, holding tight to the rope.

But she did not come. Laura waited a long time. She made up her mind to wait longer, and she did. The wind was shaking the house now. Snow as fine and grainy as sugar covered the window sill and sifted off to the floor and did not melt.

Laura shivered in her shawl. She kept on staring at the blank window-panes, hearing the swishing snow and the howling, jeering winds. She was thinking of the children whose Pa and Ma never came. They burned all the furniture and froze stark stiff.

Then Laura could be still no longer. The fire was burning well, but only that end of the room was really warm. Laura pulled the rocking-chair near the open oven and set Carrie in it and straightened her dress. Carrie rocked the chair gaily, while Laura and Mary went on waiting.

At last the back door burst open. Laura flew to Ma. Mary took the milk-pail while Laura untied Ma's hood. Ma was too cold and breathless to speak. They helped her out of the jumper.

The first thing she said was, 'Is there any milk left?'

There was a little milk in the bottom of the pail, and some was frozen to the pail's inside.

'The wind is terrible,' Ma said. She warmed her hands, and then she lighted the lamp and set it on the window sill.

'Why are you doing that, Ma?' Mary asked her, and Ma said, 'Don't you think the lamplight's pretty, shining against the snow outside?'

When she was rested, they ate their supper of bread and milk. Then they all sat still by the stove and listened. They heard the voices howling and shrieking in the wind, and the house creaking, and the snow swishing.

'This will never do!' said Ma. 'Let's play bean-porridge hot! Mary, you and Laura play it together, and, Carrie, you hold up your hands. We'll do it faster than Mary and Laura can!'

So they all played bean-porridge hot, faster and faster until they could not say the rhymes, for laughing. Then Mary and Laura washed the supper cups, while Ma settled down to her knitting.

Carrie wanted more bean-porridge hot, so Mary and Laura took turns playing it with her. Every time they stopped she shouted, 'More! More!'

The voices in the storm howled and giggled and shrieked, and the house trembled. Laura was patting on Carrie's hands,

> 'Some like it hot, some like it cold,
> Some like it in the pot, nine days——'

The stovepipe sharply rattled. Laura looked up and screamed, 'Ma! The house is on fire!'

A ball of fire was rolling down the stovepipe. It was bigger than Ma's big ball of yarn. It rolled across the stove and dropped to the floor as Ma sprang up. She snatched up her skirts and stamped on it. But it seemed to jump through her foot, and it rolled to the knitting she had dropped.

Ma tried to brush it into the ashpan. It ran in front of her knitting needles, but it followed the needles back. Another ball of fire had rolled down the stovepipe, and another. They rolled across the floor after the knitting needles and did not burn the floor.

'My goodness!' Ma said.

While they watched those balls of fire rolling, suddenly there were only two. Then there were none. No one had seen where they went.

'That is the strangest thing I ever saw,' said Ma. She was afraid.

All the hair on Jack's back was standing up. He walked to the door, lifted up his nose, and howled.

Mary cowered in her chair and Ma put her hands over her ears. 'For pity's sake, Jack, hush,' she begged him.

Laura ran to Jack, but he did not want to be hugged. He went back to his corner and lay with his nose on his paws, his hair bristling and his eyes shining in the shadow.

Ma held Carrie, and Laura and Mary crowded into the rocking-chair, too. They heard the wild voices of the storm and felt Jack's eyes shining, till Ma said:

'Better run along to bed, girls. The sooner you're asleep, the sooner it will be morning.'

She kissed them good night, and Mary climbed the attic ladder. But Laura stopped half-way up. Ma was warming Carrie's nightgown by the oven. Laura asked her, low, 'Pa did stay in town, didn't he?'

Ma did not look up. She said cheerfully, 'Why, surely, Laura. No doubt he and Mr. Fitch are sitting by the stove now, telling stories and cracking jokes.'

Laura went on to bed. Deep in the night she woke and

saw lamplight shining up through the ladder-hole. She crept out of bed into the cold, and kneeling on the floor she looked down.

Ma sat alone in her chair. Her head was bowed and she was very still, but her eyes were open, looking at her hands clasped in her lap. The lamp was shining in the window.

For a long time Laura looked down. Ma did not move. The lamp went on shining. The storm howled and hooted after things that fled shrieking through the enormous dark around the frightened house. At last Laura crept silently back to bed and lay shivering.

38

The Day of Games

IT WAS LATE next morning when Ma called Laura to breakfast. The storm was fiercer and wilder. Furry-white frost covered the windows, and inside that good tight house the sugary snow was over the floor and the bedcovers. Upstairs was so cold that Laura snatched up her clothes and hurried down to dress by the stove.

Mary was already dressed and buttoning Carrie up. Hot cornmeal mush, and milk, with the new white bread and butter, were on the table. The daylight was dim white. Frost was thick on every window pane.

Ma shivered over the stove. 'Well,' she said, 'the stock must be fed.'

She put on Pa's boots and jumper, and wrapped herself in the big shawl. She told Mary and Laura that she would be gone longer this time, because she must water the horses and the cattle.

When she was gone, Mary was scared and still. But Laura could not bear to be still. 'Come on,' she told Mary. 'We've got the work to do.'

They washed and wiped the dishes. They shook the snow off their bedcovers and made their bed. They warmed again by the stove, then they polished it, and Mary cleaned the woodbox while Laura swept the floors.

Ma had not come back. So Laura took the dust-cloth and wiped the window sills and the benches and every curve of Ma's willow rocking-chair. She climbed on a bench and very carefully wiped the clock-shelf and the clock, and the little brown-spotted dog and her own jewel-box with the gold tea pot and cup-and-saucer on top. But she did not touch the pretty china shepherdess standing on the bracket that Pa had carved for Ma. Ma allowed no one else to touch the shepherdess.

While Laura was dusting, Mary combed Carrie's hair and put the red-checked cloth on the table, and got out the school-books and the slate.

At last the wind howled into the lean-to with a cloud of snow and Ma.

Her skirt and her shawl were frozen stiff with ice. She had had to draw water from the well for the horses and Spot and the calf. The wind had flung the water on her and the cold had frozen her soaked clothes. She had not been able to get to the barn with enough water. But under the icy shawl she had saved almost all the milk.

She rested a little, and said she must bring in wood. Mary and Laura begged her to let them bring it, but Ma said:

'No. You girls are not big enough and you'd be lost. You do not know what this storm is like. I'll get the wood. You open the door for me.'

She piled wood high on the woodbox and around it, while they opened and shut the door for her. Then she rested, and they mopped up the puddles of snow melting from the wood.

'You are good girls,' Ma said. She looked around at the house, and praised them for doing the work so nicely while she was gone. 'Now,' she said, 'you may study your lessons.'

Laura and Mary sat down to their books. Laura looked steadily at the page, but she could not study. She heard the storm howling and she heard things in the air moaning

and shrieking. Snow swish-swished against the windows.
She tried not to think of Pa. Suddenly the words on the
page smeared together and a drop of water splashed on
them.

She was ashamed. It would be shameful even for Carrie
to cry, and Laura was eight years old. She looked sidewise to make sure that Mary had not seen that tear fall.
Mary's eyes were shut so tight that her whole face was
crinkled, and Mary's mouth was wobbling.

'I don't believe we want lessons, girls!' Ma said.
'Suppose we don't do anything today but play. Think what
we'll play first. Pussy-in-the-corner! Would you like that?'

'Oh yes!' they said.

Laura stood in one corner. Mary in another, and Carrie
in the third. There were only three corners, because the
stove was in one. Ma stood in the middle of the floor and
cried, 'Poor pussy wants a corner!'

Then all at once they ran out of their corners and each
tried to get into another corner. Jack was excited. Ma
dodged into Mary's corner, and that left Mary out to
be poor pussy. Then Laura fell over Jack, and that left
Laura out. Carrie ran laughing into the wrong corners at
first, but she soon learned.

They all ran till they were gasping from running and
shouting and laughing. They had to rest, and Ma said,
'Bring me the slate and I'll tell you a story.'

'Why do you need a slate to tell a story?' Laura asked
as she laid the slate in Ma's lap.

'You'll see,' said Ma, and she told this story:

Far in the woods there was a pond, like

this:

The pond was full of fishes, like this:

Down below the pond lived two home-
steaders, each in a little tent, because
they had not built their houses yet:
They went often to the pond to fish, and
they made crooked paths: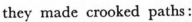
A little way from the pond lived an old
man and an old woman in a little house
with a window:
One day the old woman went to the pond
to get a pail of water:
And she saw the fishes all flying out of the
pond, like this:
The old woman ran back as fast as she
could go, to tell the old man, 'All the
fishes are flying out of the pond!' The old
man stuck his long nose out of the house
to have a good look
And he said: 'Pshaw! It's nothing but tadpoles!'

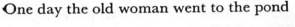

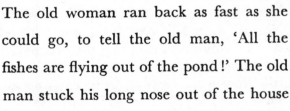

'It's a bird!' Carrie yelled, and she clapped her hands
and laughed till she rolled off the footstool. Laura and
Mary laughed too and coaxed, 'Tell us another, Ma!
Please!'

'Well, if I must,' said Ma, and she began, 'This is the
house that Jack built for two pieces of money.'

She covered both sides of the slate with the pictures of that story. Ma let Mary and Laura read it and look at the pictures as long as they liked. Then she asked, 'Mary, can you tell that story?'

'Yes!' Mary answered.

Ma wiped the slate clean and gave it to Mary. 'Write it on the slate, then,' she said. 'And Laura and Carrie, I have new playthings for you.'

She gave her thimble to Laura, and Mary's thimble to Carrie, and she showed them that pressing the thimbles into the frost on the windows made perfect circles. They could make pictures on the windows.

With thimble-circles Laura made a Christmas tree. She made birds flying. She made a log house with smoke coming out of the chimney. She even made a roly-poly man and a roly-poly woman. Carrie made just circles.

When Laura finished her window and Mary looked up from the slate, the room was dusky. Ma smiled at them.

'We have been so busy we forgot all about dinner,' she said. 'Come eat your suppers now.'

'Don't you have to do the chores first?' Laura asked.

'Not tonight,' said Ma. 'It was so late when I fed the stock this morning that I gave them enough to last till tomorrow. Maybe the storm will not be so bad then.'

All at once Laura felt miserable. So did Mary. And Carrie whimpered, 'I want Pa!'

'Hush, Carrie!' Ma said, and Carrie hushed.

'We must not worry about Pa,' Ma said, firmly. She lighted the lamp, but she did not set it in the window. 'Come eat your suppers now,' she said again, 'and then we'll all go to bed.'

39

The Third Day

ALL NIGHT THE house shook and jarred in the wind. Next day the storm was worse than ever. The noises of the wind were more terrible and snow struck the windows with an icy rattle.

Ma made ready to go to the stable. 'Eat your breakfast, girls, and be careful with the fire,' she said. Then she was gone into the storm.

After a long time she came back and another day began.

It was a dark, long day. They huddled close to the stove and the cold pressed against their backs. Carrie was fretful, and Ma's smile was tired. Laura and Mary studied hard, but they did not know their lessons very well. The hands of the clock moved so slowly that they seemed not to move at all.

At last the grey light faded away and night was there again. The lamplight shone on the board walls and the white-frosted windows. If Pa had been there he would have played the fiddle and they would all have been cosy and happy.

'Come, come!' Ma said. 'We mustn't sit like this. Would you like to play cat's cradle?'

Jack had left his supper untouched. He sighed mournfully in his corner. Mary and Laura looked at each other, and then Laura said: 'No, thank you, Ma. We want to go to bed.'

She cuddled her back tight against Mary's back in the icy-cold bed. The storm was shaking the house; it recaked and shuddered all over. Rattling snow scoured the roof. Laura's head was tucked well under the covers, but the sounds in the storm were worse then wolves. Cold tears ran down her cheeks.

40

The Fourth Day

IN THE MORNING those sounds were gone from the wind. It was blowing with a steady wailing scream and the house stood still. But the roaring fire in the stove gave hardly any heat.

'The cold is worse,' Ma said. 'Don't try to do the housework properly. Wrap up in your shawls and keep Carrie with you close to the stove.'

Soon after Ma came back from the stable, the frost on the eastern window glowed faintly yellow. Laura ran to breathe on it and scratched away the ice until she made a peep-hole. Outdoors the sun was shining!

Ma looked out, then Mary and Laura took turns looking out at the snow blowing in waves over the ground. The sky looked like ice. Even the air looked cold above that fast-blowing flood of snow, and the sunshine that came through the peep-hole was no warmer than a shadow.

Sidewise from the peep-hole, Laura glimpsed something dark. A furry big animal was wading deep in the blowing snow. A bear, she thought. It shambled behind the corner of the house and darkened the front window.

'Ma!' she cried. The door opened, the snowy, furry animal came in. Pa's eyes looked out of its face. Pa's voice said, 'Have you been good girls while I was gone?'

Ma ran to him. Laura and Mary and Carrie ran, crying and laughing. Ma helped him out of his coat. The fur was full of snow that showered on the floor. Pa let the coat drop, too.

'Charles! You're frozen!' Ma said.

'Just about,' said Pa. 'And I'm hungry as a wolf. Let me sit down by the fire, Caroline, and feed me.'

His face was thin and his eyes large. He sat shivering, close to the oven, and said he was only cold, not frost-bitten. Ma quickly warmed some of the bean broth and gave it to him.

'That's good,' he said. 'That warms a fellow.'

Ma pulled off his boots and he put his feet up to the heat from the oven.

'Charles,' Ma asked, 'did you—Were you——' She stood smiling with her mouth trembling.

'Now, Caroline, don't you ever worry about me,' said Pa. 'I'm bound to come home to take care of you and the girls.' He lifted Carrie to his knee, and put an arm around Laura, and the other around Mary. 'What did you think, Mary?'

'I thought you would come,' Mary answered.

'That's the girl! And you, Laura?'

'I didn't think you were with Mr. Fitch telling stories,' said Laura. 'I—I kept wishing hard.'

'There you are, Caroline! How could a fellow fail to get home?' Pa asked Ma. 'Give me some more of that broth, and I'll tell you all about it.'

They waited while he rested, and ate bean broth with bread, and drank hot tea. His hair and his beard were wet with snow melting in them. Ma dried them with a towel. He took her hand and drew her down beside him and asked:

'Caroline, do you know what this weather means? It means we'll have a bumper crop of wheat next year!'

'Does it, Charles?' said Ma.

'We won't have any grasshoppers next summer. They say in town that grasshoppers come only when the summers are hot and dry and the winters are mild. We are getting so much snow now that we're bound to have fine crops next year.'

'That's good, Charles,' Ma said, quietly.

'Well, they were talking about all this in the store, but I knew I ought to start home. Just as I was leaving, Fitch showed me the buffalo coat. He got it cheap from a man who went east on the last train running, and had to have money to buy his ticket. Fitch said I could have the coat for ten dollars. Ten dollars is a lot of money, but——'

'I'm glad you got the coat, Charles,' said Ma.

'As it turned out, it's lucky I did, though I didn't know it then. But going to town, the wind went right through me. It was cold enough to freeze the nose off a brass monkey. And seemed like my old coat didn't even strain that wind. So when Fitch told me to pay him when I sell my trapped furs next spring, I put that buffalo coat on over my old one.

'As soon as I was out on the prairie I saw the cloud in the north-west, but it was so small and far away that I thought I could beat it home. Pretty soon I began to run, but I was no more than half-way when the storm struck me. I couldn't see my hand before my face.

'It would be all right if these blizzard winds didn't come from all directions at once. I don't know how they do it. When a storm comes from the north-west, a man ought to be able to go straight north by keeping the wind on his left cheek. But a fellow can't do anything like that in a blizzard.

'Still, it seemed I ought to be able to walk straight ahead, even if I couldn't see or tell directions. So I kept on walking, straight ahead, I thought. Till I knew I was lost.

I had come a good two miles without getting to the creek, and I had no idea which way to turn. The only thing to do was to keep on going. I had to walk till the storm quit. If I stopped I'd freeze.

'So I set myself to outwalk the storm. I walked and walked. I could not see any more than if I had been stone blind. I could hear nothing but the wind. I kept on walking in that white blur. I don't know if you noticed, there seem to be voices howling and things screaming overhead, in a blizzard?'

'Yes, Pa, I heard them!' Laura said.

'So did I,' said Mary. And Ma nodded.

'And balls of fire,' said Laura.

'Balls of fire?' Pa asked.

'That will keep, Laura,' said Ma. 'Go on, Charles. What did you do?'

'I kept on walking,' Pa answered. 'I walked till the white blur turned grey and then black, and I knew it was night. I figured I had been walking four hours, and these blizzards last three days and nights. But I kept on walking.

Pa stopped, and Ma said, 'I had the lamp burning in the window for you.'

'I didn't see it,' said Pa. 'I kept straining my eyes to see something, but all I saw was the dark. Then of a sudden, everything gave way under me and I went straight down, must have been ten feet. It seemed farther.

'I had no idea what had happened or where I was. But I was out of the wind. The blizzard was yelling and shrieking overhead, but the air was fairly still where I was. I felt around me. There was snow banked up as high as I could reach on three sides of me, and the other side was a kind of wall of bare ground, sloping back at the bottom.

'It didn't take me long to figure that I'd walked off the bank of some gully, somewhere on the prairie. I crawled back under the bank, and there I was with solid ground at my back and overhead, snug as a bear in a den. I didn't believe I would freeze there, out of the wind and with the buffalo coat to keep warmth in my body. So I curled up in it and went to sleep, being pretty tired.

'My, I was glad I had that coat, and a good warm cap with earflaps, and that extra pair of thick socks, Caroline.

'When I woke up I could hear the blizzard, but faintly. There was solid snow in front of me, coated over with ice where my breath had melted it. The blizzard had filled up the hole I had made when I fell. There must have been six feet of snow over me, but the air was good. I moved my arms and legs and fingers and toes, and felt my nose and ears to make sure I was not freezing. I could still hear the storm, so I went to sleep again.

'How long has it been, Caroline?'

'Three days and nights,' said Ma. 'This is the fourth day.'

Then Pa asked Mary and Laura, 'Do you know what day this is?'

'Is it Sunday?' Mary guessed.

'It's the day before Christmas,' said Ma.

Laura and Mary had forgotten all about Christmas. Laura asked, 'Did you sleep all that time, Pa?'

'No,' said Pa. 'I kept on sleeping and waking up hungry, and sleeping some more, till I woke up just about starved. I was bringing home some oyster crackers for Christmas. They were in a pocket of the buffalo coat. I took a handful of those crackers out of the paper bag and ate them. I felt out in the snow and took a handful, and I ate that for a drink. Then all I could do was lie there and wait for the storm to stop.

'I tell you, Caroline, it was mighty hard to do that, thinking of you and the girls and knowing you would go out in the blizzard to do the chores. But I knew I could not get home till the blizzard stopped.

'So I waited a long time, till I was so hungry again that I ate all the rest of the oyster crackers. They were no bigger than the end of my thumb. One of them wasn't

half a mouthful, and the whole half-pound of them wasn't very filling.

'Then I went on waiting, sleeping some. I guessed it was night again. Whenever I woke I listened closely, and I could hear the dim sound of the blizzard. I could tell by that sound that the snow was getting thicker over me, but the air was still good in my den. The heat of my blood was keeping me from freezing.

'I tried to sleep all I could, but I was so hungry that I kept waking up. Finally I was too hungry to sleep at all. Girls, I was bound and determined I would not do it, but after some time I did. I took the paper bag out of the inside pocket of my old overcoat, and I ate every bit of the Christmas candy. I'm sorry.'

Laura hugged him from one side and Mary hugged him from the other. They hugged him hard and Laura said, 'Oh Pa, I am so glad you did!'

'So am I, Pa! So am I!' said Mary. They were truly glad.

'Well,' Pa said, 'we'll have a big wheat crop next year, and you girls won't have to wait till next Christmas for candy.'

'Was it good, Pa?' Laura asked. 'Did you feel better after you ate it?'

'It was very good, and I felt much better,' said Pa. 'I went right to sleep and I must have slept most of yesterday and last night. Suddenly I sat up wide awake. I could not hear a sound.

'Now, was I buried so deep in snow that I couldn't hear the blizzard, or had it stopped? I listened hard. It was so still that I could hear the silence.

'Girls, I began digging on that snow like a badger. I wasn't slow in digging up out of that den. I came scrabbling through the top of that snow bank, and where do you suppose I was?

'I was on the bank of Plum Creek, just above the place where we set the fish-trap, Laura.'

'Why, I can see that place from the window,' said Laura.

'Yes. And I could see this house,' said Pa. All that long, terrible time he had been so near. The lamp in the window had not been able to shine into the blizzard at all, or he would have seen its light.

'My legs were so stiff and cramped that I could hardly stand on them,' said Pa. 'But I saw this house and I started for home just as fast as I could go. And here I am!' he finished, hugging Laura and Mary.

Then he went to the big buffalo coat and he took out of one of its pockets a flat, square-edge can of bright tin. He asked, 'What do you think I have brought you for Christmas dinner?'

They could not guess.

'Oysters!' said Pa. 'Nice, fresh oysters! They were frozen solid when I got them, and they are frozen solid yet. Better put them in the lean-to, Caroline, so they will stay that way till tomorrow.'

Laura touched the can. It was cold as ice.

'I ate up the oyster crackers, and I ate up the Christmas candy, but by jinks,' said Pa, 'I brought the oysters home!'

41

Christmas Eve

P A WENT EARLY to do the chores that evening, and
Jack went with him, staying close to his heels. Jack
did not intend to lose sight of Pa again.

They came in, cold and snowy. Pa stamped the snow
from his feet and hung his old coat with his cap on the nail
by the lean-to door. 'The wind is rising again,' he said.
'We will have another blizzard before morning.'

'Just so you are here, Charles, I don't care how much it
storms,' said Ma.

Jack lay down contentedly and Pa sat warming his
hands by the stove.

'Laura,' he said, 'if you'll bring me the fiddle-box I'll
play you a tune.'

Laura brought the fiddle-box to him. Pa tuned the
fiddle and rosined the bow, and then while Ma cooked
supper he filled the house with music.

'Oh, Charley he's a fine young man,
        Oh, Charley he's a dandy!
Charley likes to kiss the girls
        And he can do it handy!

'I don't want none of your weevily wheat,
        I don't want none of your barley,
I want fine flour in half an hour,
        To bake a cake for Charley!'

Pa's voice rollicked with the rollicking tune, and Carrie laughed and clapped her hands, and Laura's feet were dancing.

Then the fiddle changed the tune and Pa began to sing about Lily Dale.

> ' 'Twas a calm, still night,
> And the moon's pale light
> Shone soft o'er hill and dale. . . .'

Pa glanced at Ma, busy at the stove, while Mary and Laura sat listening, and the fiddle slipped into frolicking up and down with his voice.

> 'Mary put the dishes on,
> The dishes on, the dishes on,
> Mary put the dishes on,
> We'll all take tea!'

'And what shall I do, Pa?' Laura cried, while Mary ran to get the plates and cups from the cupboard. The fiddle and Pa kept singing, down all the steps they had just gone up.

> 'Laura take them off again,
> Off again, off again,
> Laura clear the table when
> We've all gone away!'

So Laura knew that Mary was to set the table for supper and she was to clear away afterwards.

The wind was screaming fiercer and louder outside. Snow whirled swish-swishing against the windows. But Pa's fiddle sang in the warm, lamplighted house. The dishes made small clinking sounds as Mary set the table. Carrie rocked herself in the rocking-chair and Ma went gently between the table and the stove. In the middle of the table she set a milk-pan full of beautiful brown baked beans, and now from the oven she took the square baking-pan full of golden corn-bread. The rich brown smell and the sweet golden smell curled deliciously together in the air.

Pa's fiddle laughed and sang,

> 'I'm Captain Jinks of the Horse Marines,
> I feed my horse on corn and beans
> Although 'tis far beyond my means, for
> I'm Captain Jinks of the Horse Marines!
> I'm Captain of the army!'

Laura patted Jack's furry smooth forehead and scratched his ears for him, and then with both hands she gave his head a quick, happy squeeze. Everything was so good. Grasshoppers were gone, and next year Pa could harvest the wheat. Tomorrow was Christmas, with oyster stew for dinner. There would be no presents and no candy, but Laura could not think of anything she wanted and she was so glad that the Christmas candy had helped to bring Pa safe home again.

'Supper is ready,' Ma said in her gentle voice.

Pa laid the fiddle in its box. He stood up and looked around at them all. His blue eyes shone at them.

'Look, Caroline,' he said, 'how Laura's eyes are shining.'